D1706467

WHISPERS

IN THE

STORM

RUTH FREY

To Donna
Each day is a new adventure,
Live it well.

Ruth Frey
10.5.14

Whispers In The Storm is a work of fiction. The characters are from the imagination of the author. Any resemblance to real people, alive or dead, is coincidental. The account of the wagon train was taken from an unpublished diary, so some of the places are real, but the people are not.

This novel is dedicated to the people I love who live in my home:
my daughter Lorinda
my grandsons, Lucas and Jared
and my granddaughter, Baylie.

And to the people who live in my heart:
my parents Walter and Millie Niewohner,
my son Johnny,
and my husband Bob.

CONTENTS

**Part Three: California Secrets
Revealed**

ACKNOWLEDGMENTS

THE WORDS THANK YOU ARE SO EASY TO SAY, BUT THEY HOLD SO MUCH GRATITUDE. THANK YOU:

To Linda Gilland for saying "I have a diary, do you want to have it?"

To my writing group for all their support and words of wisdom: Mavis Chitwood, LaVern Winegardner, Gladys Bryson, Ruth Buttler and Carol McClintock.

To my Bible study group for encouragement and prayers: Cheryl Ellertson, Shirley Christiansen, Marion Hekkala, Jean DuBois, Joyce Smith, Lori Sebern, Karen Silveira, Ora June Hubert, Susie Hubert, Pam Hubble, Judy Mertes, and Jetta Ollek.

To my dear friend Karen Silveira for all her help.

To Manuel Silveira.for the help with the computer and processing the cover art. Even though, he doesn't read romance novels.

To Marianne White for editing the book.

To Darrel and Charlene White for sponsoring one day at the Corban Writers Conference.

To David Stanford who suggested I publish through Amazon and for helping me spread the word to readers through his network on Facebook.

To Ed Brandt and Pam Bridgehouse for helping with the Spanish.

To William Lindberg for assisting me with typesetting the cover art and with the formatting and uploading of this book.

And to you Dear Reader for taking the time to read my book. I hope you enjoyed it.

PROLOGUE

A man on the run doesn't think clearly. He acts on impulse. So it was with William O'Shea. He knew his decision to travel to the next town was wrong when the fingers of lightning flashed across the night sky and thunder crashed over the land. But all he could think about was keeping Sarah and her unborn child out of the hands of the Hollinger family.

When the narrow covered bridge seemingly sprang out of the darkness with the streaking light, the wild-eyed, frightened horses bolted over the embankment and raced toward the fast moving river. Unable to control the animals, William felt the carriage tipping. The lynch pin snapped and the horses broke free. End over end the carriage tumbled, until it finally came to rest on the eroding bank of the swollen river.

"Sarah! Sarah! Where are you?" William called, struggling to free himself from the wreckage.

A shaft of light from the vehicle's lantern illuminated the small figure of his young sister lying in the river mud, trapped beneath the carriage wheel. Blood, oozing from the deep gash above her right eye, ran through Sarah's sun yellow hair. Muck covered the blue silk dress and her black velvet traveling cloak.

"Do not be try'n to move. I'll be lift'n the wreckage off you," William said, in his thick Irish brogue, as he pulled frantically at the wheel, while at the same time trying to lift the conveyance with his shoulder. The muddy rim slipped and the carriage fell back onto Sarah. An agonized scream escaped her lips.

William dropped to his knees by Sarah's side. He placed his handkerchief over the wound. "Hold onto this." He gently lifted her hand to the cloth. Tucking a lap blanket beneath her head, he said softly, "I'll be goin' for help. There's a house just across the field. Be back as soon as I can." He stretched the canvas from the carriage's top to shield her from the downpour that had accompanied the last clap of thunder. Then he ran through the soggy field toward the lights of the large hall.

Inside the manor, John Brighton nervously paced the parlor floor. Elizabeth, having been uncomfortable all day, had retired to her room early. As night gathered, her discomfort turned into full labor. A slave had been dispatched to fetch Dr. Bardlow from the nearby town of Mill Creek.

About nine o'clock, a heavy knock sounded on the front door. John sprang to open it. "Dr. Bardlow, I thought you would never get here. . . ."

Instead of the good doctor standing on the threshold a stranger dressed in black and covered with mud greeted John. "My sister is trapped 'neath the carriage wheel. 'Twas a terrible accident. I can't be free'n her. I'm needin' some help!" He grabbed John's arm and pulled him out the door.

"Yes, yes, my dear man. Where is she?"

"She is just off the road, beyond the pasture by the river."

Turning to the darkie who ran the house, John said,

"Seth, tell Timothy to get some ropes, lanterns, blankets, four field hands and meet us at the lower pasture. Hurry!" John snapped up a lantern from the verandah and followed the stranger into the night.

"Sarah, it's William. I have brought help." He knelt beside his sister and took the blood-soaked cloth from her head.

She winced. "Oh, that sorry I am, William, for all the hurt I've been causing you."

"Don't be thinkin' that way. You aren't causing me any hurt a'tall, a'tall." He leaned closer to whisper, "Just be rememberin' I love you and the wee babe you're carryin'." He pushed the blood splattered curls away from her pale cheek.

Sarah's lips curved into a bittersweet smile as she tried not to show the terror that surged through her body with each piercing breath.

"On the count of three, lift together," John ordered. "One, two, three, lift." The four slaves each took a wheel and eased the carriage away from the young woman.

"Can you move?" John asked, holding the lantern high to see how badly she was hurt.

Blood stained the dress just above her round, protruding belly. John's face turned ashen, "My God, man, you did not tell me she was expecting."

"William, I cannot feel my legs," Sarah clasped his lapel, trying to pull herself up. Her blue eyes screamed the pain she felt as her hands slipped and she slumped back into the mud.

"We will use the blanket as a stretcher. Be careful when you lift her," John directed. "Hurry! The river is rising fast."

Once the slaves had secured Sarah on the blanket, each slave took a corner and ran through the rain to the house. Carrying her frail body was tantamount to carrying a child for these four strong field workers. In truth, Sarah was still a child, barely seventeen. But her time was upon her and she began to contract with hard labor.

Upstairs in the manor, Elizabeth tried not to yell when the sharp pains pulled her apart. After Cole was born, she had vowed never to get pregnant again, but the joy of having a baby girl overshadowed the birthing ordeal. "This one has to be a girl. I will never go through this misery again," she said through clenched teeth.

"Pain is the trade for the joy. Make you love the baby all the more," Rahab, Elizabeth's handmaid, said.

"It better be a girl. I want a girl more than life itself."

"Now, don't you be talk'n that way. The good Lord gives what he wills. And we just praise Him for a healthy youngin'."

The sounds of the men coming upstairs startled Elizabeth. "John, John, what is happening?" she called.

John appeared in the doorway. "There has been an accident on the road. A young woman is hurt. I have had her put into the room across the hall. How are you doing?"

"Do you really want to know?" Elizabeth gritted her teeth as another contraction washed over her.

"Hold on Ellie. Dr. Bardlow should be here soon." John stepped to the large canopy bed and took his wife's hand. "I love you."

"I know, dear, but right now I would prefer you did not see me like this."

"You look beautiful. I wish I could take this pain away from you."

"So do I." Ellie's familiar teasing smile brightened her sweaty face but her large, green eyes revealed the anguish she could not conceal.

"Daddy, who are these people?" ten year old Cole asked, coming into his parent's room.

"They had an accident on our property. The woman is badly hurt. Now, son, you should not be in here. Go back to your room. When the baby is born, we will call you. Rahab, take Master Cole."

"Come along, Massa Cole do as your daddy say. You don't needs to be in the way." The slave guided the boy down the hall.

"Dr. Bardlow," Seth said, opening the door. "Hurry! There is a lady hurt bad upstairs, and Miss Elizabeth gonna have that baby any minute now."

The doctor bounded up the stairs. First he entered Elizabeth's room to see her progress.

"You still have a little longer to go," Dr. Bardlow said, after examining Elizabeth.

"Do not tell me that, doctor. I have been suffering for hours."

"Yes, and you still have a little longer to go."

"In that case, step across the hall and tend to the woman who was hurt in the carriage accident. I do not need you watching over me."

As he entered Sarah's room, Doctor Bardlow was still musing over a woman's plight. His expression sobered. "No one told me she was expecting too." He moved over to the bedside. "How far along are you?" Reaching into his bag, he pulled out the hearing horn and placed it on Sarah's stomach.

"She's havin' contractions already but the babe is early," William said. He was seated on a chair by the bed wrapped in a blanket. The fire in the hearth was not warm enough to keep him from shivering.

"Are you the husband?"

"No. Her brother."

"Where is her husband? He should be here."

"The man is dead. Killed in a huntin' accident."

"Oh, I'm sorry." Speaking with authority, the doctor continued, "I want everyone to leave except you." He pointed to the black woman standing by the bed holding a pan of hot water. "I will need your help. And you, my good man," Dr. Bardlow surveyed William over the top of his wire rimmed glasses, "Get some dry clothes on before you come down with something."

A short time later, the doctor emerged from the room. Taking William aside, he spoke softly. "I do not believe there is much any of us can do for your sister except pray. She is all broken up inside. I have tended to her wounds and have given her some medication to let her rest easier. I am not sure about the baby."

"Can I see her?"

"Yes, stay with her. I will check on Mrs. Brighton and be back as soon as I can."

A hush fell over the house as the clock on the mantel in the parlor ticked away the next hour. Servants spoke in whispers. Only the moaning of the two women broke the stillness. At last, the sound of a slap resounded down the hall, followed by a sharp baby's cry.

"It's a boy," Dr. Bardlow told John, as he crossed from one room to the other.

"And Ellie, how is she?"

"She is fine, a bit tired, but doing fine. You can go in."

John rushed to his wife's bed where she held a small bundle wrapped in a white cotton blanket.

"Look, John, another boy." Ellie tried not to show her sorrow.

"Ellie, I know you had your heart set on a girl. I hope you are not too disappointed."

"No. No. It is the will of God. Just look at him. He is perfect in every way. I thought we would call him Daniel, after my grandfather, if that is alright with you."

"Daniel is a fine name for such a perfect little boy." John could scarcely hold back his enthusiasm and delight over having another son.

Elizabeth's joy of a healthy child exceeded the disappointment of not having a daughter. She began to hum softly to her little Danny.

From across the hall another slap was heard and the cry of another baby. "It is a girl," Dr. Bardlow said, placing the child in her mother's arms.

"Hello, sweetheart. I have been waiting for you." Sarah's words came slow and labored. Her shallow breathing and the blood in her mouth told a story Dr. Bardlow knew very well.

"You can come in now but her time is…," the doctor whispered to William, shaking his head.

"Is she not beautiful?" Sarah's words could hardly be heard.

"Just like you."

"I want to call her Sarah. Let her live the. . . life I will never have."

"Don't you be talkin' that way. You'll be gettin' better. Just rest now."

"Promise me Charles' brother will never get his hands on her." Tears glistened in her blue eyes. "My Sarah has to be loved. If Edward finds her, he will kill her."

"There, there, now. Don't be upsettin' yourself so. I will see that she doesn't fall into Edward's hands."

Turning to the small bundle in her arms, Sarah thought, *I wish I could see you grow up, little Sarah. I love you with all my heart, but you will never know that. I pray God will keep you in His loving care all the days of your life. I have so much I want to tell you, but my time is comin' to an end.* She stroked the baby's head and touched her tiny hands. "She is so beautiful, my little Sar. . . ." A rattle of air left her throat as all color faded from Sarah's face, draining it to porcelain white.

"No! Sarah, don't die!" William clutched his sister's limp body to his breast, almost crushing the baby in his grief. Tears flooded down his round face as mournful sobs escaped from deep within him. "Don't be leavin' me. Don't be leavin' me."

Jilla, the servant, gently pried the baby loose and cradled her in her arms. "Poor baby. Your mammy is gone home to be with Jesus. What will become of you now?"

Through his tear soaked thoughts the slave's words penetrated William's mind. *What will I do with a baby?* "Sarah, don't leave. What are we to be doin' without you? I have no home, no place to live. I cannot be carin' for a wee babe."

"The missus can," Jilla said, half to herself but loud enough to be heard.

"What?"

"I says, the missus can. The doctor say she just give birth to another boy and she had her heart set on a girl. She would be a good mammy for this little lost lamb. Massa John and the missus is good Christian people. Treats us good. No one will ever know she weren't born to Miss Lizabeth."

"That's out of the question. I cannot be givin' away my own flesh and blood. She is all I have left of my family." His brow knotted into dark worry lines. *What kind of a future could I give a wee lass? I'm on the run from the Hollinger family. If they find me, they find her. We will live the rest of our lives lookin' over our shoulder. Is this what Sarah had in mind when she said to take care of the child? What am I to do?* Turning to the slave, William asked, "The child would be safe here?"

"Safe as in the arms of her mammy."

"Will they be good to her? Will they love her?"

"Like she was their own. It's better livin' in a fine house like this, than on the road with you."

William took the baby from Jilla's arms. "Surely, God wants you to have a better life than I can give you." He looked up at the slave. "Not that I'm not a good person. I just haven't made my fortune yet." Turning to his sister, he said, "Goodbye sweet Sarah. I will be seein' you in the great hereafter. Sleep well." He turned and slowly left the room as Jilla pulled the sheet over Sarah's face.

William stood in the hall, cradling the baby, rocking her back and forth, when he heard the sounds of soft humming coming from the room across the way. He looked in and saw Elizabeth and John with their new son. "I don't want to be intrudin' in on you, but my sister has passed on, leavin' me with this wee babe. I don't know what I am to be doin' with her. The Negress said. . . well. . . uh. . . ." William stammered trying to find suitable words. *Who in his right mind would give a white child away*, he thought. *These people will think me mad.*

"Come in. This is my wife, Mrs. Brighton, and our new son, Daniel. My name is John." He held out his hand to William. "We are sorry about your sister. Dr. Bardlow told us she could not live much longer."

"I am William O'Shea, good to meet you. Aye. Sarah was hurt worse than I thought, and the ordeal of giving birth was more than she could bear. 'Tis all my fault. I should have stayed in the last town instead of tryin' to . . ."

"Blaming yourself is not the answer. You did not know this would happen. It is no one's fault." John tried to give words of comfort.

"What is the baby?" Elizabeth asked.

"A girl. My sister named her Sarah before she. . . died." William ground the toe of his boot into the carpet like a schoolboy about to be scolded. "I have not the wherewithal to be carin' for a babe. I have no wife, yet. I have been too busy tryin' to get my fortune made to settle down with a wife and family. I was wonderin' if the two of you might consider takin' the wee babe in? Just until I get situated someplace."

"Do not be hasty," John said. "You have just had a tragic loss. You need time. Stay with us for a few days and see if you might think differently in a little while.

"Yes. It is much too important a decision to make on the impulse of a tragic moment. Please, may I hold the little darling?" Elizabeth gave Daniel to John and held out her arms for William to place Sarah into them.

"Mama, may I see the baby?" Cole asked, coming into the room. "Daddy said I could see it when it was born."

"Yes, dear. Look there are two babies. One is a boy named Daniel, and the other is a girl, Sarah. Sarah is. . . ."

"Twins! We have twins. Oh, Mama I am so happy." Cole's face wore a toothy grin, and his gray eyes twinkled like his father's. "This is the best present I have ever had, a brother and a sister."

"Now, wait a minute," John started to explain.

"That's right, young man. You have a brother and a sister," William interrupted. "Every lad needs a wee sister to be carin' for."

"Can I, Daddy? Can I help with the babies?"

"We will see. Now I think you need some sleep. The babies will be here in the morning, so off to bed with you."

When Cole left the room, John turned to William. "You should not have done that. Now Cole thinks the girl is ours. I do not lie to my son. It will take some doing to explain she is not his sister."

"Then do not say that. If you will love her, then raise her as your own."

"If we take this child and raise her as our own, there will be no turning back. We will not have you coming to claim her in five or ten years when it is convenient for you. She will be a Brighton. The outside world will never know the truth. I will not have whisperings and gossip about her."

William thought for a long while. He was torn between his desire to keep what remained of his family and what would be best for Sarah. He wanted her to be raised in a stable, peaceful home. He believed that is what she would have living with the Brighton's. With a sigh, he answered, "Then so be it. The child is yours. All I ask is that from time to time you send me word as to how she is."

John looked at Ellie. Her face answered his question before he spoke the words. "Then let it be written that on September 9, 1845, Elizabeth Brighton gave birth to twins, a son Daniel and a daughter Sarah."

The next morning William's sister was buried on the

hill in the Brighton family cemetery.

"I will not be havin' a last name put on the headstone. She is no longer an O'Shea and to put Hollinger on the stone would be givin' notice to Edward Hollinger where to find her.

I do not ever want that evil man to find her."

"Edward Hollinger?" John questioned.

"Aye. He is the brother of Sarah's husband. Edward has employed a man by the name of Molack to bring Sarah and the babe back. Molack has three sons and they have a reputation of never giving up. If they should find Sarah's grave, they may find the wee babe. Watch out for them."

"Why does this Edward Hollinger want Sarah and the baby?"

"Greed! Charles, Sarah's husband, was the oldest and favored by his father. The family fortune was his. Edward killed Charles to get his hands on the money. Sarah could never prove Charles was murdered. Now, we fear Edward would kill the babe too."

"Do not worry," John assured William. "We will keep the baby safe. No one knows that Ellie had only a son except for the doctor. He is an old friend and will not tell anyone. Nor will the two slave women. I have signed their manumission papers for their silence. Since they are free, they will have to leave the state." Pausing for a moment and looking into William's blue eyes, John continued, "Let us know where you settle and we will send reports of the child's progress. Good luck to you, William O'Shea."

"Aye, and to all of you.

PART ONE

ROSEWOOD PLANTATION

CHAPTER 1

I never desired a life filled with adventure. Change and uncertainty frightened me. My fear of the outside world consumed me after the death of my twin brother, Danny. He came down with the fever while visiting friends away from the safety of Rosewood Plantation, and died within days. Since that time, I rarely ventured past our estate markers. The world beyond the stone pillars that marked the boundaries of our plantation could fall into ruin, but I believed I would be safe at Rosewood. Cole, my older brother, lived the adventures which beckoned to him from beyond the mountains and across the many great rivers. Daddy often said Cole had itchy feet that carried him along a risky road. I wanted none of that. My dream was to marry a man who loved me for who I was, not for what I had, and to live at Rosewood forever.

*   *   *

"Cole will be home again for Christmas," Mama said, after reading the letter he sent from Independence. "I cannot wait to see him. It has been too long since he has been home. My arms are empty without my children close to me."

"I am here, Mama," I said, getting up from my chair in front of the hearth and latching my arms around Mama's neck. "I am always going to be here."

"Yes, my dear." She patted my hand.

"We all miss Cole, Ellie," Daddy said, knocking the ashes out of his pipe. "I wish he would get this restless nonsense out of his head and come home to help run the plantation."

"If Cole was here, we would not need Mr. Lutz as our overseer," I mused aloud, my arms still fastened around Mama.

Daddy cleared his throat. "Mr. Lutz is getting on in years. He has been feeling poorly lately."

"You did not tell me he was ill," Mama said.

"No? I thought I had."

"No, John. I would have remembered."

"Well, I might have to look around for someone to take his place."

"Tell Cole he is needed at home to help run Rosewood. After all, this will all belong to him someday," I said.

"Sarah, what an excellent idea," Mama agreed.

"I will have a talk with him when he comes home." Daddy refilled his pipe and lit it. The aroma of sweet tobacco encompassed him.

A cold draft came slipping under the parlor door. "What did Cole write in his letter?" I asked, returning to my place beside the fire.

Mama read aloud:

My dear family,

I miss all of you and am looking forward to being with you again for Christmas. December of 1860 shall long live in my memory as the coldest weather of my twenty-five years. Snow is higher than a horse's belly out here on the plains. I shall be happy to be some place warm again. I should be there on the twenty-third of December. Looking forward to eating some good Southern cooking. See you soon.

All my love,

Cole

"He does write a good letter, short but to the point." Daddy's gray eyes twinkled with pride.

"He is probably as thin as a stick. We will make all his favorite foods," Mama mused, holding the letter in both hands as if it were scripture. Her green eyes moved across the words for the third time, but not the last. Each word would be engraved in her memory before she would slip it into the keepsake box with the rest of Cole's letters.

I giggled. "If the truth be known, Cole likes anything set on a plate in front of him. He would probably eat an old harness if Leah cooked it in her special wine sauce."

Daddy laughed, "Leah is good at many things, but I do not think even her special sauces could do much for an old harness. But knowing Cole, he would probably eat it and tell her it was delicious."

"You two stop it. Cole does not like to hurt people's feelings. So he goes out of his way to be polite. Is not that the way of a Southern gentleman?" Mama's eyes flashed scorn in our direction.

"Yes dear, you are absolutely right. Cole is the perfect Southern gentleman. I have often wondered how he gets along out there on the frontier with all those hostiles."

"Quite well, I would imagine." Mama's tone indicated she had had enough of our teasing.

I covered my mouth with my hand and hid behind the book I was reading so Mama could not see the difficulty I was having controlling my giggles.

Daddy hid behind his newspaper.

My heart fluttered with joy at the thought that Cole was coming home. As Daddy said, we all missed him. But my feelings went beyond just missing him, and I did not understand why. Of course, I loved him. He was my brother. However, I scarcely knew him because he had been on one great adventure after another for most of my life. But that other feeling of uneasiness, of being tongue-tied and awkward whenever he came near, that feeling unsettled me. He usually embarrassed me with the slightest of looks. His casual words, that meant nothing when spoken by someone else, would cause me to blush. Yet, I adored him. I listened to his every word, and tried to imagine myself living his kind of life.

Cole, true to his word, arrived at Rosewood on the morning of the twenty-third. Old Seth flung the door open to greet the 'prodigal son' home from his quests. Mama ran into his arms and Daddy waited his turn to embrace his oldest son and heir.

I watched from the balcony. There he stood, tall, handsome, with thick black hair falling to his collar. He held his hat and satchel in one hand and received Mama in the other. I wanted to make my entrance when I could catch his gray eyes watching me. Not often venturing off our property, I had few opportunities to practice my woman's wiles, and after all, I was fifteen.

Slowly I descended the curved, oak staircase, gracefully fanning myself with a blue lace fan that matched my dress. My hoop skirt gently glided over each step as I executed a perfect entrance. My heart raced as I accomplished my goal.

Cole's eyes fixed on me and a smile brightened his face. "Sarah, my you have become quite the young lady." He released Mama and stepped forward.

"Cole, I am so happy you are home." Suddenly, I forgot that I wanted to impress him with how womanly I had become and ran into his open arms. "We have missed you. Are you going to stay home this time?"

"That is the question I have wanted to ask," Mama said, directing the way into the parlor with a sweep of her hand.

"I cannot say for sure, but I have been thinking about it."

Daddy's face broke into a wide smile. "Best news I have heard in a long time."

"With all the rumors of war I have been hearing out beyond the Missouri, thought I might be needed here at home."

"War? What war?" Mama asked.

"It is nothing, dear," Daddy reassured her. "People have been talking about going to war for the past thirty years. Georgia first started to talk about secession when Andrew Jackson was president. That was because of the Cherokee Indians. Now there is talk of war over slavery. I cannot believe those men we elected are such fools as to go to war over something as trivial as slavery."

"Trivial?" I echoed.

"Yes. Slavery has just about seen its day. In the future, machines will do the work of ten field slaves in less time and expense. Look at the cotton gin. Slave women worked days to comb out the seeds that the gin can do in hours."

"But, Daddy, since the gin was invented, we need more slaves to plant and harvest because it takes less time to produce more finished cotton. And without the plantation owners, how will the darkies survive? Who will take care of them?"

"You mean, how will we survive without the darkies taking care of us?" Cole corrected. "I guess many a fine lady will have to learn to do her own cooking and cleaning."

I could tell Cole was teasing me to get my temper flying, just as he had when we were children. Though I could feel heat rising in my cheeks, I refused to give way to his taunting. But Mama took exception to his statement.

"Cole Brighton, saying such things, even in jest, is uncalled for. I do not know about the rest of the country, but Rosewood will continue the same as always. Now, I do not want to hear another word about war or unpleasantness. This is Christmas and the family is all here. We will have a grand celebration."

By midday, Uncle Chad, Aunt Maggie and Cousin Amy Ann arrived from Richmond. Uncle Chad was Mama's older brother and the only close relative we had on either side of the family. We always invited them down for the Christmas holidays, and they usually stayed for a month. I loved Cousin Amy Ann. She was three years my senior and enjoyed talking about her fascinating life in Virginia's state capitol. She had been introduced into society last season, but was taking her time choosing a husband.

"That is the most beautiful Christmas tree I have ever seen," Amy Ann said, entering the hall. "It must be twelve feet tall." She held her brown silk spoon bonnet on her head as she leaned backwards to see the top.

The aroma of pine mingled with bayberry to fill the entry hall with Christmas fragrances. Garlands of holly twisted around the banister of the curved staircase and across the balcony. The doors to the parlor and to Daddy's office, on opposite sides of the entry, were framed in large red ribbons with mistletoe and evergreens intertwined.

Mama escorted Aunt Maggie into the parlor for

afternoon tea, while Uncle Chad, Cole and Daddy went into the office for brandy and cigars.

"Come upstairs, Amy Ann. You have your usual rooms." I started to run up the staircase.

"Sarah, walk, do not run," came the sharp admonishment from Mr. Jolette, my tutor, as he arrived in the hall. "Ladies never run. They glide gracefully over the floor." He set down his valise and demonstrated the way a lady should walk. "Is this not correct, Miss Kensington?"

Amy Ann controlled her desire to laugh. "You are quite right, Mr. Jolette. We shall refrain from running in the future."

"Are you leaving now?" I asked.

"Yes, I will be on my way to visit family for the holidays. You keep up with your studies, and I will see you in January. I have already said my well wishes to your parents."

"Have you seen Cole?" I asked, knowing that Mr. Jolette favored him.

"Indeed I have, thank you. He is looking fit for being in such an adverse environment. Wouldn't you say?"

"I would. Now, you have a safe journey and a Merry Christmas."

"Thank you and a Merry Christmas to you, too and to you, Miss Kensington."

"Thank you." Amy Ann curtsied.

Mr. Jolette picked up his bag, bowed slightly, turned sharply and hurried out the door.

Amy Ann leaned close to me, "He is certainly a strange man," she whispered.

"He is. But he is really very nice. However, I do resent being treated like a child by him and everyone else. I do not think I need to continue my schooling. I would love to be married and have a home of my own."

"You would actually leave Rosewood?"

"Well, no. Daddy said I could have the land on the

other side of Meadow Ridge."

Amy Ann smiled. We resumed our way up the stairs, walking slowly, to the second floor where the servants had readied the guest rooms.

"You must be exhausted. I know you want to rest and freshen up before dinner, but I am just dying to hear all about the men who have been courting you," I said, with the curiosity of a school girl.

"Not much to tell. Oh, going to the theater, or out to dine in the most elegant restaurants is very exciting. I was invited to the Governor's Ball and the Grand Cotillion. However, when I think of actually marrying any of the suitors, I turn cold. I do not believe any of these men would love me for myself, but rather, for what I have. It will be quite a feather in anyone's cap to marry into the Kensington fortune."

"Amy Ann, you are so beautiful. Any man would be proud to have you for his wife. You have the autumn hair and meadow green eyes like all the Kensington women. Just like Mama and her mama before her. I should think you would be attracting men like drunks to whiskey."

"Sarah Elizabeth, where did you pick up such language?" Shock and a touch of laughter laced Amy Ann's soft voice.

"That is the way the horse buyers talk when they think there are no ladies about. But do not change the subject. Just look at yourself in the mirror." We stood side by side in front of the cheval glass. "Look at me. I have this yellow, straw colored hair and water blue eyes, and I will not be growing much taller. I stand at an even five feet. You, on the other hand, have vibrant coloring, and you are tall and willowy."

"That is the trouble. I am too tall. No man wants a wife towering over him. But it really does not matter. If I do not pick someone soon, Mother and Father will. I will have no choice. Love is not a consideration. The family name or the bloodlines are what is important. Does the man have his own place in society and his own fortune? The Kensington's have a position to maintain, and I am just a commodity on the market. It is almost like breeding horses. I am so unhappy. All I want to do this Christmas is rest, and I do not want to meet any prospective suitors."

"Oh, dear, Mama has taken liberty to invite some young men and their families from the nearby plantations to our Christmas party. It is a kind of celebration for Cole's homecoming. But we thought it would be grand if you could meet someone from North Carolina and come down here to live. We could be like sisters."

"That is a pleasant thought, but I could never live on a plantation. It is all too rural for me. I love the city, the commotion, and the noise of people moving along the streets." She stretched out her arms and twirled around the room. The skirt of her brown taffeta traveling dress swished as it moved. "Cabs pick me up at my door and take me to the theater, or to shop, or out to dine. No, Sarah, I could never live like you do here in the country. Not even for love."

"What? There is nothing wrong. . . ." I drew in a deep breath before my anger blurted out hateful words.

Amy Ann's eyes widened. "We can talk again later. I think I should rest now."

"Yes. You rest." I left her room and went down the hall to my room at the head of the stairs. "There is nothing wrong with living on a plantation." I said aloud. "I am every bit as educated and well-mannered as she. And she talks about love as if it is a choice. The mind cannot dominate the desires of the heart. Can it?" I looked out of my window across the fruit orchards and beyond to the cotton fields. From the house to the horizon, the land belonged to us; cotton, orchards, horses, and slaves - - all ours.

CHAPTER 2

Our family Christmas took place on Christmas Eve. I wore my white satin gown with green ribbons laced around the off-shoulder neckline that tied in a large bow in front. Lily, my maid, wove the same colored green ribbon through my cascading curls. As Lilly hooked the last button on my white kid house shoes, a knock sounded on the door.

"Sarah, are you ready to go downstairs?" came Cole's voice.

"Hurry, Lily."

"Last one. There. You done." Lily gave the hem of my dress a quick tug, pulling it over my petticoats.

I smoothed the dress with my hands and stood as tall as my short stature would allow, shoulders back, chin up. "Come in."

My heart leaped when I saw Cole's expression. His lips curled in what seemed an involuntary smile. "You're beautiful." He held me in his gaze longer than comfort dictated before he cleared his throat and released me. "Everyone is waiting. I was dispatched to fetch you."

"In that case, we will not tarry." I held out my hand and

Cole escorted me down the stairs and into the parlor.

We entered amidst talk of horses and fashion, depending on which side of the room one happened to be standing. Amy Ann dominated the women's conversation. She was breathtaking. Her autumn colored hair set off the milky complexion that favored the women of the Kensington family. A stunning blue-black velvet dress hugged her thin body before billowing into a full skirt that seemed to float with each graceful step.

"Now our family is complete," Uncle Chad said, stepping forward to take my hand. "My, Sarah, I think you get more beautiful with each passing year. We must be in the presence of the most beautiful women in the entire South. Rather I should say, the entire country."

"Well spoken, brother-in-law, the entire country indeed." Daddy smiled at Mama as he stepped to her side.

"Sarah, you will have to save a dance for me tomorrow night at the Christmas Ball," Uncle Chad said.

"No, Chad," Mama said. "Sarah has not yet had her coming out. She will dine with us, but then she will go to her room. She cannot attend a social function until she is presented and that will be next spring."

"Oh, Mama. Please. Just this once, let me stay for the party," I begged.

"Yes, dear. No one knows what will happen this next year," Daddy said. "Sarah will have this Christmas to remember. It is here in our home with our friends, no one will say a word. We will act as if it is natural and expected. She will dance with all the fathers of the young men we have invited to dance with Amy Ann." Mama started to protest again, but Daddy put his finger to her lips and whispered, "Trust me."

Seth appeared in the doorway to announce dinner was served in the family dining room.

Christmas Eve dinner was a simple affair. The small family dining room was more intimate for conversation. The meal started with pumpkin soup accompanied by roasted vegetables. The conversation ebbed and flowed as each course came and went. My thoughts were lost in the fact that I was going to be able to participate in the dance tomorrow night. Yes, this was going to be the best Christmas ever.

As Seth served the coffee during our last course, Daddy told him to have our people gather out front. Soon the big bell at the kitchen door could be heard calling the slaves to the house. It was time for Daddy to give out the gifts.

By the time Daddy, Mama, Cole and I came out onto the verandah, all the slaves had gathered. Three wagons filled with new work clothes and shoes for everyone, bright colored material for the women to make dresses and head bandannas, warm winter coats for the men, and peppermint sticks for all the children. Oranges, apples, and nuts were special treats for everyone. Daddy always gave Seth, Toby, and Joseph bottles of Christmas cheer to be passed out among the men. Tomorrow would be a day of rest for the field workers, so tonight promised to be a time of dancing and singing.

Waiting until last to give Mr. Lutz his gift, Daddy wanted the slaves to see that he approved of Mr. Lutz's authority. The man seemed thinner than usual. His face had lost the robust color of health. Daddy was right, Mr. Lutz looked very ill. Daddy always gave him a large sum of money as a Christmas bonus and a bottle of fine brandy.

After the workers had received their gifts and Daddy had told them how pleased he was with their work, the slaves went away singing. Our family Christmas continued with the opening of our gifts. Chairs had been placed around the tree and all the gifts lay under the beautifully decorated boughs. The tree candles sparkled like diamonds in sunlight. I searched the array of items to discover which one was mine. A jewelry box encrusted with gold and rubies for Mama, a silver laden saddle for Daddy, a blue velvet dress with a matching cloak for me along with a star sapphire pendant necklace. Amy Ann received an emerald necklace with diamonds to go with her new green ball gown. Aunt Maggie delighted with joy and a tear in her eye when she saw the set of silver and diamond combs to set off her dark hair, along with a matching diamond necklace. Uncle Chad received a complete set of medical books bound in fine red leather. But with all these wonderful gifts, Cole's was the best, a foal to be born in our stable within the next few days. This horse promised to be the finest Rosewood had ever produced, sired by Remembrance out of Fire Wind. The offspring of these two prize winners embraced the hopes and dreams Daddy and I had for the future of the Rosewood Stables, and he gave it to Cole - - Cole, who did not seem to care if he ever lived on the plantation again. He would take our dreams away from us.

Heat rose in my face as I contemplated whether to remain seated or to go to my room in protest.

Seemingly embarrassed by the generous gift, Cole stammered, "I. . . I do not know what to say. It is too much. I know what this horse means to the stables. To say thank you for such a magnificent gift does not express how I feel. But I could never take the foal to the frontier."

"Then stay home," Mama said. A ray of hope danced in her eyes.

Cole did not answer. He looked from her to me and then to the tree. A faraway longing coated his eyes, mingled with the frightened expression of a fox being chased.

I realized Cole had become a prisoner in his world as much as I had in mine, and each of us was powerless to change it. My jealousy subsided.

After the gifts were exchanged and statements of delight and thank you expressed, everyone adjourned to the parlor to sing carols around the spinet. Cole and I ended the evening by singing a duet of *Silent Night*. The fire in the hearth crackled and sparked while candles shimmered their light around the room.

"I am going for a walk. Come with me," Cole whispered, pulling me aside as everyone else mounted the stairs to go to their rooms when the evening ended.

"Are you coming, Sarah?" Mama called.

"Yes, I will be there in a minute. I am putting my music away." I gathered a handful of sheet music and tucked it away in a book. Turning to Cole, I whispered, "I have to go up."

Servants waited for us to leave before they could extinguish the candles and bank the fire.

"I will wait for you on the back stairs. Hurry," Cole said, taking my arm and directing me up the stairs. "And do not tell Amy Ann. I have had enough of her chatter for one evening."

I thought it was a little odd to be going for a walk at such a late hour, but I agreed to meet him in a few minutes.

Lily, who had fallen asleep in the chair, woke and quickly started laying out my nightdress when I entered the room.

"I am not going to go to bed just yet. Cole and I are going for a walk. Get my black boots, and help me take off my house shoes."

"You goin' out now? It ain't fitin'."

"None of that talk. Do as I say and be quick about it."

Lily did as she was told, and minutes later I grabbed my wool cape and met Cole at the back stairs. He stood in the shadows, leaning against the wall with his arms folded across his chest. He presented such a dashing appearance dressed in his long, black coat, tight-fitting breeches, white shirt and black vest. He had removed his bow tie and unbuttoned the tight collar.

With his gloved hand he took my arm and we descended the stairs together to the main floor, down the hall and out through the glass doors onto the verandah. The night air felt crisp with a touch of frost kissing the ground. A silver ring encircled the full moon. With only moonlight to guide us, Cole led the way down the steps into the rose garden, through the white latticed gate, onto the path that led beyond the carriage house and into the wooded ravine. I knew the path well.

"This trail seems to draw me to it each time I come home." Cole tightened his grip on my arm as we entered the shadows beneath the trees.

"I know what you mean. It is a lovely walk. Especially in spring when the daffodils and iris push their way through last autumn's leaves and make the woods come alive with color and the fragrance of dogwoods and azaleas linger in the air."

At the bottom of the ravine, a narrow foot bridge spanned a brook. Wild ferns lined the water's edge. Cole put his arm around my back and guided me onto the wooden planks.

"Watch your step, would not want you to fall in."

"Do not be silly. I am not going to fall."

Emerging from the woods on the other side of the ravine, we saw the small rise of our family cemetery. A high wrought-iron fence, to keep animals away, surrounded the hill. The fence had two openings, one a double gate, large enough for the hearse to enter, faced the road on the other side. A pedestrian gate faced the manor. Two long leaf pine trees guarded the opening. We entered through the small gate.

"Do you come here often?" Cole asked.

"Yes, quite often. I miss Danny so. I feel a sense of closeness with him here. I know it has been five years, but sometimes it seems as if it just happened. I am lonely without him. People say to put it behind me and get on with my life. They do not know how it is when a part of you dies. It is as if my spirit were thirsty, and I do not have the power to quench it."

"What about friends? Do you have someone you can talk with?"

"No. I do not need anyone. I have my horse, Misty

Morn. Together we explore the plantation."

"But you never leave it."

"Why should I? I have everything I need right here at Rosewood."

"Everything except friends. Oh, Sarah, dear sweet little sister, you are missing so much of life. Someone as beautiful as you was never meant to be hidden away behind the stone boundary markers of a plantation." His eyes narrowed and sorrow veiled his face as he put his arm around me. The faint aroma of musk mingled with the outdoor fragrances of pine and oak.

"If Danny had not been away from home, he would never have gotten the fever."

"You don't know that. He might have gotten it right here. Many people come down with swamp fever even living on grand plantations."

"I do not want to argue with you. I cannot help the way I feel." I slipped out from under his arm and walked up the hill to a grave under an old oak tree. The name on the headstone simply read SARAH – no last name, no dates, no words of eulogy – just Sarah.

"I have often wondered who she was," I said, tracing the letters with my fingers. "I asked Mama, but she did not know, just someone who was killed in an accident on our property. It seems strange to me she should be buried here in our family cemetery.

"When I was quite young, I made up stories about her. She and Daddy had a love affair before he married Mama. She was the young, beautiful woman from a mysterious, far away land. Oh, my dreams were so grand." I laughed softly to cover my embarrassment of actually telling someone my fanciful stories. "You must think I am silly."

"No, not at all. I find it fascinating that you actually have an imagination. You have always seemed so straightforward, not given to dreams or fantasy. Somewhat on the boring side."

"What! Boring! Just because I do not flitter around like

some of those women you know, does not mean I am boring. I am sensible, mature, reserved. . . that's it reserved, certainly not boring." I squared my shoulders and stomped down the hill. "I believe I would like to return to the house now."

Cole laughed.

The sound grated on me like gravel in my shoe. "You did it to me again, didn't you?"

"Come on, Stormy, you make it so easy for me to pick on you. You fly into a rage over the smallest things. I had some concern yesterday when you did not follow suit when I talked about the war, and I got caught in Mama's crossfire. But tonight you did not disappoint me."

"You are a strange person, Cole Brighton. I would think you would have better things to do than tease your little sister."

"I would if you did not make teasing you so pleasurable. Now, come along, I will tell you what I know about this dead woman." We climbed to the top of the hill again and sat on a stone bench beneath the oak tree. "It happened the night you and Danny were born. The worst summer storm I can remember had just split the sky." I sat quietly as Cole related the story of the dreadful night. He finished with, "You have to remember that I was only ten and they kept sending me to my room. But as I recall the woman was badly crushed by her carriage. She died that night. After the funeral, the woman's brother left. I do not remember ever seeing him again. I did hear talk from time to time amongst the slaves that the woman was expecting a child. I guess it died too."

"That is such a sad story. I like mine better."

After a brief silence, Cole blew warm air into his gloved hands and stood up. "We should be going. Getting a little cold out here, and it is already Christmas morning. Just think, on a night like this, shepherds heard the angels sing."

"My, you have the heart of a poet."

"Actually, that of a gypsy."

"Yes, you always were a rover, and if the truth be known, I suppose a bit of a scoundrel too."

He laughed and leaned close to my ear as if to whisper a deep, mysterious secret. "Some people may agree with you. I have such a shadowy background coming from the noble, Southern family of Brighton."

"Get on with you." I pushed him away. "I thought you were going to tell me something about your life in the wilderness."

"It would not interest you."

He took my hands and lifted me from the bench. Without another word, he directed me down the path returning to the hall. We walked in silence, feeling no need to fill the space between us with words. At my bedroom door his lips brushed my cheek as he whispered, "Sweet dreams. Remember to save a dance for me tomorrow night."

CHAPTER 3

Morning arrived quickly. Lily's knock on my door, and coming in to lay out my clothes, woke me out of a wonderful sleep. A dream that seemed so real had held me captive, and I loathed to let it go.

"Merry Christmas, Miss Sarah. Get up, it's mornin'. Everybody is up 'ceptin you. I brung some hot water." She poured the water into a basin, stoked the log in the hearth to bring it back to life, flung open the heavy drapes on the window to let in the light, laid out my clothes, and left the room with a backward call, "Get up now, you hear? Be back in a minute to help you dress."

"And a Merry Christmas to you too, Lily," I said, as she closed the door behind her. Reluctantly, I sat on the edge of the bed hugging my pillow. That man, was he real or was he just a dream? He was tall with dark hair and sparkling eyes. He took me in his arms, and we danced out onto the verandah in the moonlight. In my mind I could hear the music again. I closed my eyes and I felt him close to me, holding me. His body pressed brazenly against mine. The aroma of his cologne intoxicated my senses as champagne would my body. Lightheadedness flooded over me. He lifted my chin to his face. His warm breath caressed my lips, gently, lovingly he . . .he. . .the knock came loud on the door.

"Sarah, are you awake?" Cole called.

"I am now. Come in." I pulled the bedclothes around me.

"Just wanted to see how you were. You did not get much sleep."

"Neither did you."

"I never need much." After a brief pause, he continued. "Say nothing about last night."

"Why?"

"No reason. It would just be better if you did not say anything. Not even to Mama. Promise?"

"If you do not want me to, I will not." I had no intention of telling anyone. Last night was so magical I could not bring myself to give any part of it away. Secrets are always fun, and this one created a special bond with Cole.

He smiled. "That's a good girl. Now hurry and dress. See you downstairs."

By mid-afternoon guests started arriving. I felt elegant in my blue Christmas gown, with my hair pinned in curls on top of my head. For the first time, Mama allowed me to wear my hair up, a sign of becoming a woman. Daddy, Mama, Cole and I greeted our guests as they entered. Daddy, being the perfect host, remembered to comment on each woman's newest ailment, and each man's prized horse. He remembered everyone's special topic of interest and brought it into the conversation.

Mama was in her element. She directed the servants as a great general would direct an army. Guests, who were staying the night, or longer, were taken to their rooms to freshen up. Other people were ushered into the ballroom. Trays of spiced or toasted nuts were circulated around the rooms along with glasses of Christmas punch. Cole amazed everyone with his memory for names. It was as if he had never been away. He was indeed his father's son. His charm spread over our guests like a blanket of pixie dust. He mesmerized them by talking of places he had been, painting vivid pictures of high, snow-capped mountains and half naked, savage Indians.

I stood at the end of the receiving line. As the women passed me, I could see the surprised expression on their faces, but not a word was spoken aloud. If anyone had an objection to my hair pinned up, or that I wore a ball gown, not a person displayed enough bravery to speak up. I beamed and joyously greeted each guest. The evening was mine.

At eight o'clock sharp, Seth rang the chime for dinner. The double doors to the grand dining room were opened to display a lavishly set table. Gold chargers held a garden of hand painted, rose encircled, white china plates bordered with a wide, gold rim. Engraved roses adorned the gold flatware that stretched out on either side of the place setting. A "B" monogrammed the flatware and the gold chalice placed at the head of each service. Other crystal goblets were placed on either side of the chalice. Candelabras graced the center of the table, and crystal bowls with piles of gold balls spilled over onto the white Damask tablecloth. Green and red garlands ran the length of the table, draped the doors, windows, and across the marble fireplace. A small fire took the chill from the room.

All morning I had wanted to sneak a peek into the dining room, but the servants shooed me away. Now, standing at the entrance, my breath caught in my throat. Everyone entering proclaimed their delight.

I sat between Mr. Sharply, the banker, and Dr. Bardlow. Cole was seated across the table from me. After everyone had their place and the room quieted, Daddy said the blessing. I was too excited to hear what he said. I just echoed with an "Amen" when the prayer was over. The first course of oysters in the shell was accompanied by a French wine poured into the gold chalice.

Daddy stood and offered a toast, "To good friends, a warm hearth, and a peaceful 1861." Everyone's voice chimed in agreement.

I drank the wine with zest. The warm, fruity liquid tickled my nose, and lingered on my lips.

As each course was brought in, the servants whistled old Christmas carols to assure Daddy, and our guests, that none of the food had been sampled in route from the kitchen to the table. Seth oversaw the servants as they held the beautiful rose patterned tureens and ladled the lobster bisque into the soup plates. Kickshaws of radishes and olives and crystal saltcellars with tiny gold spoons had been placed at each setting. Lamb broth with vegetables was served after the bisque soup plates were removed. Lamb was not my favorite, but I took a small sampling.

I listened to the conversations at my end of the table. Mr. Sharply was trying to talk Mama into exerting her influence over Daddy to give some of our river pasture to make a road on our side of the river. "It would be good for the entire community if we had a road that ran from Mill Creek to Wilmington."

"I am sure it would. But I have no desire to run my husband's business. You need to talk with him." Mama's gentle manner offset her dismissal of the subject. Mr. Sharply turned to his lamb broth and commented on the delicious food. He did not approach the subject of land again that evening.

Cole fascinated Mrs. Chambers with his picturesque descriptions of the West.

"Lovely. Just lovely," she exclaimed. But as the Amontillado was being poured, she came to her real purpose for being so taken with Cole. "You must be ready to settle down with a wife by now. My Nora Jane is such a lovely girl. Would you not say? She would make a splendid wife for the right man."

Cole grabbed for his sherry and downed it in one gulp. He tugged at his collar as if it had suddenly become tight around his throat. He looked down the table at Nora Jane where she was enjoying the conversation with Daddy.

"Yes, I have always thought that Nora Jane was well turned out. You and Mr. Chambers have done a splendid job raising her. She is quite the fine lady. Do you think she would be happy living on the frontier? Nights do get lonely and a wife would help me considerable. She would never lack for something to do. The Indian women could teach her how to make clothes out of Buffalo hides."

"No. No, Cole. You miss my point. I thought you should come home to settle down on the plantation. Nora Jane could never live on the frontier."

"What a pity," Cole mused.

Silence fell between them as the shrimp timbales and German wine were served.

At the other end of the table, I could see Amy Ann enjoying herself talking to both of the young men on either side of her. I could not hear what was being said, but she seemed to laugh at everything.

I took only a small portion of bass served with Leah's special sauce and none of the herb potatoes. When the red wine was poured to accompany the beef fillet, Seth had my glass filled only half. He came forward and whispered in my ear, "Your mama say to go slow on da wine."

Conversations were becoming muddled in my head and I had difficulty focusing on individual words. When the platter of beef was served to me, I slipped the serving fork under a large portion. I looked up into the waiter's face as he furrowed his brow and gave a slight shake of his head. A smaller piece was suggested. I complied. The saddle of mutton was served with mint jelly, but I let it pass by. Sweet breads, terrapin and another red wine were followed by cauliflower with cheese sauce, celery and baked apples stuffed with yams.

Doctor Bardlow talked with Aunt Maggie. Like a paddle wheeler on the river, Aunt Maggie rolled onto her favorite subject, her childhood home in Boston. How she missed Boston. I listened halfheartedly as I watched the flicker of the centerpiece candles and the light dancing off the gold balls in the crystal bowls. The room seemed quite warm. When the cherry punch was served, I gulped it down quickly.

"The punch is to be sipped. It cleans the palate so you can enjoy the Canvas Back duck and the delicious fruit sauce." Dr. Bardlow lowered his chin to look at me over the rim of his spectacles. A smile lit up his round face as he glanced at Mama.

I was still savoring the fruit sauce on my fork when the salads were carried into the room. Orange soufflé, glace fruits, pineapples as a symbol of hospitality, coffee, and cheeses finished off the meal. One by one, the plates and glasses had been removed as each course progressed through the evening. Now nothing remained except for the golden chargers and coffee cups and saucers. My coffee contained more cream and sugar than coffee, and I cherished each drop. I felt warm and satisfied.

At the appropriate time, Mama rose from her chair indicating the meal was over. Daddy escorted her into the ballroom for the second half of the evening. Everyone followed. Dr. Bardlow took my hand to help me up.

"Oh my, I feel a little strange. I do not think I can stand."

"I should not wonder. You need some fresh air." Dr. Bardlow motioned to Cole. "I think Sarah needs to have a turn in the garden."

"I will take her. You join the others." Cole took my arm and pulled me out of the chair. "Come, little sister, a walk will do you good."

The north side of the manor hosted a wonderful English Knot garden, filled with herbs and fragrant shrubs. We walked along the stone path toward the magnolia grove that separated our house from the overseers place. The star filled sky of last night had been replaced by a cloud cover that threatened rain, or perhaps a dusting of snow. The sharp edges of a cold wind blew against us, and I moved closer to Cole.

"Are you feeling better?" Cole asked, opening his coat to receive me against his warm body.

"A little." I could hear the music and the laughter of our guests floating on the night wind. "Dance with me. I like being with you. Last night was so wonderful."

Cole's arm tightened around me, "Yes it was. But I think if we stayed out here we would be missed. Better be getting back now."

"You are right. You are always right."

"Not always, but I am this time."

We retraced our steps quicker than I wanted. When we entered the manor, Daddy waited for us by the side door. "Dr. Bardlow said you needed some fresh air. Are you able to dance now?" His delight could not be concealed. Daddy found humor in almost every situation.

"Being grown up comes with a price, I suppose." I could feel the beginnings of a headache coming on.

"No. It comes with responsibility." Daddy took my arm and we entered the ballroom.

Candlelight sparkled off the three massive crystal chandeliers that lined the center of the hand-tooled copper ceiling. The orchestra sat on a raised platform against the semicircle backdrop of seven marble, Doric columns that resembled a Greek theater.

Daddy's name appeared first on my dance card. He was my prince, and I was his "golden treasure" as he fondly called me. Next, Mr. Chambers took my hand and we glided around the oak floor inlaid with mahogany roses. Dr. Bardlow would not be outdone. And Mr. Sharply danced elegantly. But all the while I looked for Cole. He had asked me to save a dance for him, but his name was not on my card. He always seemed to be engaged when I was free. The evening slipped away in a whirl.

I wished I had not had quite so much wine at dinner, or that I had not stayed out so late last night, because as the evening wore on, I could scarcely keep my eyes open.

I sat on a chair by the fireplace and watched everyone dance. Cousin Amy Ann captured the hearts of at least two of our guests. What a pity she could never fall in love with a man from North Carolina. We are all too rural for her, she had said just yesterday. Nora Jane danced with Cole more than once, to the delight of her mother. Everything seemed well and good. I could no longer wait for Cole to claim his dance. I yawned and stretched. It was time for me to go to my room and see if my mysterious lover from last night waited for me in my dreams.

As I left, I overheard Mr. Sharply and Daddy talking. "John, did you hear South Carolina voted for secession? President Buchanan said that the states have no right to secede, but the federal government can do nothing to prevent such actions. As I see it, we have no choice but to set up our own government, and if that means war, then so be it."

"We have known that we have been sitting on a powder keg since November. During Breckinridge's campaign, Southerners made it quite clear that they will secede if Lincoln is elected. Now comes the time to fish or cut bait, and men like Senator Davis are not about to cut and run. I do not like it." Daddy's voice held a hard edge. "I do not like it one bit."

My thoughts reeled. *War! Was Cole right, are we going to go to war?*

CHAPTER 4

Events spiraled toward war faster than anyone dreamed possible. By February, seven states had seceded from the Union. Representatives from those states met in Alabama to organize the Confederate States of America and to elect Jefferson Davis president. Davis had served as secretary of war under President Pierce and was a senator from Mississippi.

*   *   *

"It looks like the hard times are upon us," Daddy said, putting down the letter he had received from his friend in South Carolina. "Those fools are actually going to secede from the union. Too many lives were lost fighting to gain freedom from England. Now we are going to war again, this time with our own people."

"John, is it really coming to that?" Mama asked, spreading her breakfast bun with honey. "At Christmas you said it was just all rumors."

"Rumors have a way of coming true," Cole

commented matter-of-factly.

"I'm not going to worry. As I have said before, life at Rosewood will continue the same as always. Whatever those politicians want to do, they have no control over us." Mama seemed her usual collected self. "Now, we will not get ourselves so worked up about nothing. Sarah, you are dawdling. Eat your breakfast. Mr. Jolette is almost ready to begin your studies."

I looked across the table at Mr. Jolette, who was surveying his empty plate, probably contemplating filling it again. But when he heard Mama say that he was almost ready to begin my studies, he just smiled. His was an unusual circumstance. He was not a member of the family, but he had the full run of the manor, and he took his meals with the family. He lived in a set of rooms on the third floor where most of the guest rooms were. Other than the times I spent in the classroom, or at meals, I rarely saw him.

Cole finished his breakfast and turned to Daddy. "I plan to work with the horses today unless you need me for something else. Did I tell you that I decided to name my Christmas colt Shadow Run?"

"That's a good name. You go ahead and do what you need to do. I'll be in my office most of the day. I have some papers to go over." Daddy's cheery face had faded into lines of worry as he got up and slowly left the breakfast room.

"I am going into town today to buy a new bonnet. Would you care to come along, Sarah?" Mama extended the invitation.

"No. I will stay here."

Cole turned his head to hold me in his gaze. "Why not go with her? It will be a nice drive. The weather is clear, and you should be home long before candle lighting time."

"No. I have classes and after that, well, I. . . I just have things to do."

"Cole, let it be. Do not push the child. If she wishes

not to go, she does not have to." Mama's voice sounded strong and determined. With her tone she said let the subject drop.

"That's the problem. She never has to do what she wishes not to do. Believe me, the day will come when she will not have a choice. She cannot hide here at Rosewood forever. The South is changing. And we must change with it or die." Cole stood up. "Excuse me, ladies, Mr. Jolette." He tossed his napkin on the table and abruptly quit the room.

Stunned, Mama, Mr. Jolette, and I sat in the comfort of the sunlit room. The aroma of breakfast still lingered in the air. The sounds of the servants bustling about, softly humming as they worked, filled the manor with the beginning of a new day. But Cole's words echoed in my ears. 'The South is changing. . . change with it or die.'

During the next two months, Daddy went on several business trips. After each trip he sequestered himself in his office. I overheard him tell Cole that he had cashed in some stocks for gold. "Gold will always be a stable commodity. Investing in paper is risky. The Confederate currency that is coming out could be a disaster for the South. We need to hope for the best, but prepare for the worst."

While Daddy was away on his business trips, Cole took over running Rosewood. Mr. Lutz had taken to his bed during the first week of February and never regained his strength. He died on March twenty-second and was buried in the cemetery in Mill Creek next to his wife and son, who were killed in a carriage accident years ago. Cole set about finding a new overseer. In case of war, we needed someone to run the plantation.

Whether we were prepared or not, war was upon us. On April 12, 1861, General Pierre Beauregard commanded the harbor batteries to open fire on Fort Sumter, which housed a U.S. Army garrison in the harbor of Charleston, South Carolina. By June, North Carolina seceded along with Virginia, Arkansas, and Tennessee.

Three hundred and fourteen regular army personnel, all of them officers, made up the entire Confederate army. The Confederate Congress asked for volunteers. Young and old alike left their farms and businesses to fight for a cause, a way of life. Despite their objections to war, Daddy and Cole believed in the South. They enlisted.

Pride enveloped Mama and me the morning Daddy and Cole prepared to ride out to join the Confederate army. "Now, you be careful and do not take any chances, you hear," Mama admonished, as Daddy took her in his arms and kissed her.

"Ellie, do not let such a beautiful face be filled with worry. I will be careful. I love you more than life itself. I have never thought of another woman since the day I first met you. You must know I have always been faithful to you alone."

"Yes, John, and I belong to you completely. I would not want to live without you. Please come home to me."

They held each other, not wanting to let go. Finally, Daddy broke the embrace. "It's time."

Daddy took me into his arms. "You take care of your mama. I love you my golden treasure." His fingers twisted one of my curls. "We will be home before you know it. Do not cry. I don't want to remember you crying."

I dried my tears and tried to smile. "I will do my best," I said, walking with him to his horse.

He mounted.

Cole kissed Mama goodbye. He turned to me, placed his arm around my shoulders and we walked to his horse. "For the first time in my life I do not want to leave." His embraced tightened. "Take care of Shadow Run."

"Is it the horse you do not want to leave or is it Rosewood?"

A sadness crossed his face. "It's you, and of course Mama too, and the horse and Rosewood, all of this." He swept his hand toward the house. "I just have an empty feeling. You know I have hired an overseer to help with the work. He should be here the first of the week. He seems to be a good man. His name is Frank Molack."

Most of the darkies had gathered around the front of the manor to watch the Master ride off to war. How strange. Daddy and Cole were going to fight to keep them slaves and yet they came to wish them well.

Cole mounted his horse. "This war will not take long. We shall give those Yankees a good beating and be home before harvest."

"Watch that it is not you that gets the beating, brother dear. I hear those Yankees breathe fire like dragons."

"Worry not, little sister, even if I have to travel through hell fire, I shall return home. You just make sure to brush my colt every day."

"Me? Take care of a horse? Do not be silly."

Cole laughed. "You might be surprised at what you can accomplish if you put your mind to it."

They rode out together, father and son, wearing beautiful Confederate gray uniforms and taking along some of our finest horses. Seth was too old to go to war, so Bowe went in his place to take care of Daddy's and Cole's needs and to tend to the horses. Darkies ran along with them shouting cheers.

"Keep the home fires burning. Be home before harvest," Daddy reaffirmed, calling back over his shoulder.

Cole added, "Put a lamp in the window for us."

At the end of the drive, they stopped to take one more lingering look as if to engrave the image of the manor, Mama and me into their memories. More men from our valley joined them on the road and they rode away together.

I ran upstairs to watch from the balcony off Mama's room. I believed I could see them long after they had crossed the bridge and had turned onto the road heading north.

Seth let Mr. Molack into Daddy's office. "Miz Lizabath,

Mr. Molack is here to see you."

"Do come in. We have been expecting you," Mama said, standing up from behind Daddy's desk. "This is my daughter, Sarah." Mama gestured in my direction. "Please have a seat."

"I'll stand." His dark eyes took hold of me and refused to move. They were hooded by heavy eyelids and bushy brows that gave the impression of evil lurking in the shadows.

"Cole tells me that you have experience overseeing a plantation," Mama continued, ignoring his rudeness.

"Ya. Done this before. Your son said that I would have my own house and get paid fifty a month." He walked around the office, picking things up and looking at them, as if estimating their price.

"Yes, that is right. Now I have a few things I want to go over with you." Mama sat down behind the big desk and started to look through some papers where she had jotted some notes.

"All you need to know is that I can do the job. I'll keep this plantation going as if it were my own, Mrs. Brighton. I am not one who takes orders. I give them. Now if someone will show me where I can put my belongings, I can get busy."

Mama was taken aback. All she could do was stammer, "Se. . .Seth will show you to the house."

"Then I'll see you at dinner." He turned and left.

"Why, I never," I said. "Cole said he was a good man. He sure had Cole fooled. Get rid of him. We do not need him."

"It might not be as easy as all that. We need to wait and see."

CHAPTER 5

The battle of Manassas Junction took place on July 21. Colonel Stuart kept General Patterson at bay in the Shenandoah Valley while General Beauregard moved against General McDowell at the junction some twenty-five miles away. That day the Confederate army achieved a great victory. McDowell and the Union army were routed. We let ourselves believe that Daddy was right. They would be home before harvest.

*   *   *

Mr. Frank Molack took charge of managing Rosewood. His medium height and stocky build proved to be the bane of his life. Often times he could be seen stretching when standing next to someone taller than he. His dark features cast an ominous shadow over his face. A black beard covered his weak chin.

At first the plantation ran smoothly, as if Daddy had been taken away on another business trip, and he would be home shortly. But as the war gained momentum, Mr.

Molack became a tyrannical taskmaster. The sound of the whip echoed across the fields as the workers' backs became his prey. He wanted to keep the slaves in line. His strategy backfired. Slave after slave left Rosewood to find freedom on the underground railroad. The field hollers, songs sung by the Negroes as they worked in the fields, became silent. Harvest time came and went.

Daddy's enlistment ended just before Christmas and he came home. The war had taken its toll on him. His face held the deep lines of seeing too much death, too many young lives lost. The gaiety of the holiday season was subdued by the horrors of war. We spent the day quietly, just the three of us. Cole was somewhere in Virginia, and Uncle Chad was tending to the wounded in a field hospital. Our hearts were lonely for them. Mama tried to make Christmas wonderful by having a delicious meal served in the family dining room. A small tree decorated the entry hall with a few gifts under its branches. Mama and I had a new pair of boots made for Daddy which he desperately needed. Daddy gave Mama a set of combs for her autumn colored hair, and I received a silver mirror and brush.

"Oh, Daddy, these are wonderful." I threw my arms around his neck and covered his face with kisses. "I am never going to let you go again."

Daddy laughed, but his heart was not in the sound. "Come now, Treasure, you know that cannot be."

Fingering the crest of her mother-of-pearl combs, Mama said, "Taylor's still have some items worth buying. But the prices are climbing higher than a cat's back." A tear slid down her face. This was the first Christmas her family was not together. "Did you happen to see Chad when you were in Virginia?"

"Yes. He is working in a field hospital. He said that he wants to send Maggie and Amy Ann to Boston to be with her family until the war is over."

"I suppose they will be safer there," Mama mused.

"Aunt Maggie was never a Southerner. She tried, but she never really fit in," I said, trying not to sound bitter over her good fortune of getting out of harm's way. "Sarah, this is family you are speaking ill of," Mama chided. "If your Uncle Chad thinks it best for his wife and child to be sent North, then that is his business. We shall be safe right here in North Carolina."

"I have something to tell you," Daddy said. His voice turned cold, and his eyes diverted their gaze to the Christmas tree. "I have signed up again. I shall be leaving shortly after the first of the year."

"John, no! You have served your time. Let the others fight this nasty war. You are needed here at Rosewood. Mr. Molack is not the man Cole thought he was. He is beating the slaves, and many of them have run off. I am afraid of that man." Her eyes turned towards me. "We do not want him in charge of running the plantation. You need to be here to see to it he does not put us into ruin."

"Ellie, I am needed at the war. Our way of life is being threatened. There will be no plantation to put into ruin if the North wins. I will talk to Mr. Molack. If he does not change his ways, then I will send him packing. But I have sought for another overseer, there are none to be had. It is my duty to fight for our cause, and if we do not have Mr. Molack, who will run things while I am away?"

"I will."

"Oh, Ellie, you are a very capable woman hosting social events, but being in charge of a plantation is another matter altogether." I could hear the condescending tone in Daddy's voice.

Mama's temper rose as she pulled herself erect in her chair. "John, I do not think we can trust that man." Mama's jaw tightened.

"Sometimes things start out simple, but they get out of hand. I have little control over the matter at the moment. If I had known that it was Molack Cole had hired, I would have stopped it immediately. But now it is too late."

"Did you know of Mr. Molack before?" Mama questioned.

"I had heard of him a long time ago from William O'Shea."

Mama's hand flew to her mouth as she gasped and looked at me. "That was such a long time ago. Surely he cannot be the same man."

"Who is he?" I asked.

"Nothing for you to worry about, dear," Daddy said, "I do not know if he is the same man or not. Just stay out of his way. We need a white man on the property to keep the darkies in their place. If they should revolt, you ladies would not be safe in your beds."

"Our slaves would never hurt us," Mama protested.

"We still have Mr. Jolette. He is very capable of protecting us," I interjected.

Daddy dismissed my suggestion. "I will make sure Mr. Molack knows his bounds." At that, Daddy ended the conversation. His decision had already been made, and nothing Mama nor I could say would change his mind.

Daddy did talk with Mr. Molack, and for a while after Daddy returned to the war, the beatings stopped. The threat of dismissal kept the sinister man from overstepping his bounds. However, his manner belied his true nature, and he kept a wary eye on Mama. He did not want Mama sending poor reports to Daddy about the management of Rosewood.

Daddy had received a field commission to colonel under the direct command of General A. S. Johnston. By April, both Daddy and Cole found themselves in the Shiloh campaign. The setting for the Shiloh slaughter was a picturesque peach orchard and a meadow with a Methodist meeting house in the middle of the field. The conflict took its name from the meeting house, Shiloh. After the battle, peach blossoms covered the valiant soldiers who had fallen. Eleven thousand Confederate soldiers died those two days at Shiloh. Along with them were General A. S. Johnston and Colonel John Brighton, Daddy.

The cadence beat slowly as the procession moved up the hill toward the cemetery. Mama and I walked behind the hearse as friends followed. Toby, our stable slave, had been sent to Goldsboro with a wagon to meet the train that brought Bowe, and Daddy's coffin home. Uncle Chad had come down from Virginia to accompany Daddy's body to be laid to rest beside his father.

Standing far off, the darkies sang lamenting songs while Reverend Tadwell delivered the graveside service.

"In my Father's house are many mansions . . . ," he began, citing the text out of Matthew. His words became a drone in my ears as my thoughts drifted to happier days.

'Do not hold his head too tight. Give him some rein. That is it. Show him you are the boss. Take command, or he will go his own way. That's it, Sarah. You will make a fine horsewoman someday.' Daddy's deep melodious laughter, that made others laugh with him, rang in my ears once again. When I dismounted, he hugged me in his tight bear-like grip. Swinging me around, he said, 'That's my girl. You are my golden treasure. The treasure of my life'. . . Standing on the hill of our family cemetery, tears washed my face. "This is my Daddy!" I wanted to scream. "Do not put him into the ground. Stop covering him with dirt." But I just stood there like stone.

". . .the Lord gives, and the Lord takes away. Blessed be the name of the Lord. Now we commit the body of our dear departed husband, father, and friend into the hands of Almighty God, and may he rest in peace," Reverend Tadwell concluded.

After the service, the guests gathered at the house for refreshments.

"I am so very sorry. John was a good friend," said Mr. Sharply. "If there is anything my Hester or I can do, please do not hesitate to let us know."

"Thank you. You are too kind," Mama said, holding her handkerchief to dry her eyes.

Having Uncle Chad with us in our time of sorrow was a great comfort. He stayed at Mama's side, watching that the strain would not take its toll. "You need to rest," came his words filled with the wisdom of a doctor. "Please sit down. Stay in one place and let everyone come to you."

"We have not seen Cole," Mrs. Chambers commented, looking around the room.

"We were unable to locate him," Uncle Chad said, as Mama started to cry anew. "He was the one who found John's body and carried him off the field. But the last time anyone has seen Cole was on the second day at Shiloh. No one has heard from him since."

"He will come home. He is not dead," Mama sobbed.

Mr. Jolette took it upon himself to direct the servants and to keep the trays of food circulating, which was more help than he would ever know.

I sat by the window where the lamp burned for Cole. My heart ached with loneliness. Disbelief and anger sojourned within my soul. How could God let this happen to my Daddy? He was a good man. No one came to me with words of comfort. As if words could ease the pain. My thoughts flew back to the time seven years ago when Danny died. The darkies had waited outside for three days singing lamentations and raising prayers to God, but Danny died anyway. Mama's screams careened down the stairwell. Then, as now, everyone went to her with comfort. Only Cole came to find me. I hid in the shadows beneath the stairs. He held me close to him and told me that he would always be there for me. That night in the shadows seemed so long ago. But my need for Cole is deeper now than it was then. I felt lonely for Cole, and I wondered where he was. Did his heart ache for me and home? Is he cold and alone lying in the mud somewhere? Is he hurt? He knows Daddy is dead, why didn't he come home with the body? I cried as if tears could wash away all the pain. Where is Cole? Is he dead too?

After the guests left, our house felt empty and cold. It was as if a black shroud covered the manor.

CHAPTER 6

As time passed, Mr. Molack became the dominant authority at Rosewood. He moved from the overseer's house into the main house and took up residency down the hall in the large bedroom at the opposite corner from Mama's room. Daddy's office became his office. Mama protested, to no avail. Mama's words seemed to fall on stone. Mr. Molack ruled with the whip, and even Mama and I feared him. The slaves would never assault a white man, and Mr. Jolette proved to be spineless. We were captives in our own home.

One night, in the dead of night, came a soft tap at my bedroom door. "Sarah, Sarah, it's Mama. Let me in." We had taken to locking our doors months ago. I got up and opened the door. There she stood, fully dressed in her widow's black, high collar, long sleeves, buttons from throat to hem. "Get dressed quickly and come with me. Not a sound now, or we may wake the devil." I knew she referred to Mr. Molack.

I too, dressed in black, which had become our uniform of the war. When I stepped into the hall, I noticed that Lily was not on her mat outside my door. Mama placed her finger to her lips and motioned me to follow her. We went down the front stairs, out through the doors leading to the rose garden, and onto the path that led beyond the carriage house. The almost full moon climbed into the sky, and by its light we picked our way to the old sycamore tree about one hundred feet to the east of the carriage house. There sat a large chest filled with family heirlooms that Mama had removed from the manor night after night without Molack noticing they were missing.

"While I gathered all these things, I hid the chest in the underbrush of the ravine. But now I need your help to bury it," Mama said, in a low, soft voice. "We have been safe here at Rosewood so far, but I fear Mr. Molack will take our valuables to sell them. They have no meaning for him, only what price he can get for them. Or, God forbid, should the Yankees come this way, they will loot anything they can get their filthy hands on. We need to save everything we can. Look inside here." Mama lifted the lid of the chest to show me the things she had salvaged from the house.

All the jewelry the Brighton women had worn and handed down for generations lay in a box. "Even my sapphire pendant necklace," I said. "I have not missed it. I had asked Seth about these golden candlesticks from the parlor, but he just smiled and gave me a wink. So I asked no more questions." I touched the ornate sockets. "I have no idea how you managed to remove all these things without Mr. Molack wondering where they were."

"He is too busy playing master of the manor to notice the little things."

My fingers ran over other items in the chest: most of the gold flatware, all the gold goblets, some of the fine brandy that Daddy had loved so dearly and Mr. Molack partook of freely, more silver and gold treasures that would bring a tidy sum should they be sold, and a pair of double-barrel dueling pistols which belonged to Mama's grandfather.

Mama picked up one of the old pistols, "I remember

when Grandfather tried to teach me to shoot these pistols. My mama became livid. 'Ladies do not shoot pistols,' she scolded. But Grandfather did not listen to her. Every day we went into the woods behind the slaves' quarters and he would show me how to load and shoot. I became quite good at it. He gave these to me when John and I married. He said it was a warning to John to treat me lovingly and with respect." Her voice broke as she took a deep breath and said in a whisper more to herself than to me, "He always did." She took the gun from my hand and put it back into the case. "Quickly, now, we must get this buried tonight." She handed me a shovel and heavy gloves.

Not sure how to use the shovel, I did the best I could. The ground was rock hard and laced with tree roots. Despite the heavy gloves, blisters soon formed. Just when I thought it to be a hopeless cause, Seth, Joseph, Toby, and Toby's son, Michael, came from the stable with a pick, more shovels, and Old Danger, the mule.

"This is no work for you, ladies. Stand back. We do it," Toby said, removing his coat.

They worked feverishly all night, digging a deep hole and using old Danger to lower the chest into the ground by ropes. Two more slaves brought planks to place over the hole and burlap to cover the planks. Dirt and leaves covered the burlap disguising the ground to look undisturbed. I placed a large rock in the center of the leaves to mark the spot. Michael dumped the remainder of the dirt in the garden beyond the chicken yard.

By the time we finished, the sky was turning pink. I remembered another night when I had taken the path through the rose garden, past the carriage house and stayed out until morning. That was a wonderful, almost magical night. Tonight was quite different. This night was filled with fear, the uncertainty of a dark future. Mama and I returned to the house as we had come, climbed the stairs, and went to our bedrooms.

*　　*　　*

Days drifted in and out of each other while tension in the house mounted. One morning while Mama, Mr. Jolette and I were having breakfast, Mr. Molack entered the room and announced, "I have invited some people over for dinner tonight. They are, shall we say, business associates. They are expecting to be received by the ladies of Rosewood. You will act as hostesses."

"I believe this is not the proper time for us to be entertaining with the war and my husband's death," Mama said.

"Did I ask for your opinion? I said I expect you to be the sweet, charming ladies of Rosewood and receive my guests. You will do this, or I can make things difficult for you."

"What can you do to me that has not been done by this war?"

"My dear lady, I know where the secrets of the plantation are hidden. Your husband thought I could not see what stands in front of me. If I deem it necessary to destroy what is yours to get what I want, I will do it."

"You would not dare!"

"Try me." His black eyes glared across the table at Mama and then at me and back again to Mama. A smile curled his lips as he leaned forward placing the palms of his hands on the table. In a low voice, he said, "I am sure you do not want me to let certain people up North know what I have found."

Mama's face turned ashen. I could feel the air charged with contempt like electricity before a storm.

Mr. Jolette jumped to his feet. "Now, Mr. Molack, see here, my good man. You have no authority to . . . ."

"Sit down! This does not concern you. You are only an employee at Rosewood."

Mr. Molack's dark eyes burned a hole through Mr.

Jolette's courage. He sank back into his chair. "I will not have you poking your nose into my business. If you want to continue to take your meals with the family, I will thank you to keep your thoughts to yourself." He turned again toward Mama. His voice softened. "As I was saying, my guests expect to be greeted by the lady of the manor. You will not disappoint them."

"Very well, just this once."

I had no understanding of everything about their conversation, but I could see that Mama's composure had changed from defiance to intense fear.

That night I stood on the balcony overlooking the foyer as Mr. Molack's guests arrived. A shiver ran up my spine. "I cannot believe the unsavory caliber of men he calls business associates," I said, entering Mama's room. "I saw them as Seth opened the door. They look more like riverboat gamblers and dandies than businessmen. Mama, what are we going to do?"

"Not much we can do at this moment. We will be polite, gracious, and excuse ourselves as soon as possible. Now, come along. Chin up and smile."

"Ah, there you are. Gentlemen, may I present the charming hostesses of Rosewood, Mrs. Brighton and her lovely daughter, Sarah." The five men turned to look at us as we entered the parlor. Mr. Molack came close to Mama to escort her to a chair. "Why are you wearing that wretched black dress? This is a party."

"We are in mourning for the master of this house. I will never wear anything but black in honor of my husband." Mama ignored his growl of malcontent.

The evening went surprisingly well. To my delight, the men talked of faraway places and towns with romantic names such as New Orleans, Natchez, and Memphis. They told of life on the river before the war. Even Mr. Molack's countenance seemed less menacing. For a few hours, the horrors of the times disappeared, and I could pretend Rosewood was once again the jewel of the coastal plantations, glittering with light and gaiety. But when dinner was over, Mama and I retired to our rooms while the gentlemen went into Daddy's office to discuss business and to drink Daddy's brandy.

The next morning, Mama and I stayed in our rooms until after Mr. Molack's guests left. By the time we came down to breakfast, Mr. Jolette had already eaten and left the house for a brisk walk before classes. As we were finishing our meal, Mr. Molack came into the breakfast room.

"Good morning, ladies. Such a grand morning." He walked over to the sideboard and poured a cup of coffee. "Mind if I join you?" Not waiting for an answer, he pulled out a chair from the table and sat across from Mama.

"You want 'nother breakfast, sir?" Seth asked with a surprised look on his face.

"No, just coffee. You servants can go. Clean up later." He waved the back of his hand at them as a dismissal.

Mama drew in her breath. "How rude!"

"I never liked them hovering, listening to every word."

"Since we are on the subject of listening," Mama started, "You did not listen when my husband warned you about whipping the field workers. I have heard reports of vicious beatings. I want it to stop. And I did not like the way you talked to Mr. Jolette yesterday morning. He is more than an employee. He is a friend of the family."

"Your husband, the good man that he was, is dead. I am the one who has to keep this plantation working. If I let these slaves run off, who will work the fields? You or perhaps Miss Sarah? No, I think not. The only respect the slaves have is for the whip. I do what I have to. As for Mr. Jolette, he's like a pimple on my rump, annoying but harmless. If you want him here, tell him to stay out of my business." He pounded his fist on the table.

Mama gasped at such vulgar language and his display of temper.

He paused for a moment. His anger subsided, and in

a cold voice he continued, "You know, Ellie." He reached across the table and touched Mama's hand. "After last night, you don't mind if I call you Ellie?"

Mama quickly pulled back her hand. "I most certainly do! How dare you take such liberties with me!" She got up and quit the room, taking me by the hand and pulling me along with her. "The nerve of that man calling me by my first name. Not even Elizabeth, but Ellie. The name your daddy called me. It's bad enough that we have to live in the same house with such a vulgar creature, but for him to assume he is my equal is going too far. When Cole comes home, he will get rid of that horrid man."

The slaves were not in the room, but they overheard Mama putting Mr. Molack in his place. By noon the plantation was buzzing with the gossip. The darkies talked behind Molack's back and laughed at him.

After my morning lessons, I usually took Misty Morn for a ride. I felt free from the stress that brewed at the house. Misty and I were gone for hours just riding around the plantation. I loved to listen to the slaves sing while they worked in the fields. Lately the songs were sad, very sad, or there were no songs at all. But today the songs had a different tempo. The songs told of the mistress of the house gaining her rightful place. When I returned to the stable I heard Mr. Molack yelling at Toby.

"That bitch! I'll show her who's boss."

"Yes, sir, you's the boss," Toby agreed. "But Miss Lizabeth is the . . . ."

"Shut up! Don't tell me she is the owner. She's not. I am. Do you hear? I am! When I'm good and ready, she'll pay."

I dashed into the house and up to Mama's bedroom to tell her what I had heard. But all she could say was, "Sarah, ladies do not run. We need to work on some of our social etiquette. This wretched war will end someday, soon I hope, and we need to behave as the ladies of Rosewood. Your daddy would want us to never forget who we are."

She sat calmly doing her needlepoint. I admired Mama's strength. She grieved for Daddy, but she never allowed herself to crumble. And she never believed for one minute that Cole would not come home. She knew in her heart, the heart of a mother, that her son still lived. She received an inner strength and peace from her faith. A faith I was beginning to doubt.

Meal times became intolerable after Mr. Molack decided to take his meals with the family. He picked on Mr. Jolette mercilessly until Mr. Jolette relented and started taking his meals in his room. After that, Mama and I ate in silence and left the table as quickly as possible. Mr. Molack brooded about his lack of control over Mama.

One morning as we were leaving, Mr. Molack shouted, "Sit down! I haven't finished yet."

Mama returned. "I do believe Mr. Jolette is in the library. It is time for Sarah's lessons. She mustn't keep him waiting."

"I said sit down," Mr. Molack repeated.

"Run along dear. I will stay here and keep Mr. Molack company." She resumed her place at the table.

I loathed leaving Mama alone with him, but I was happy to get away from under his piercing gaze.

Lily, my maid, waited for me outside the heavy oak door of the library. She always chaperoned me while I was with Mr. Jolette. I had no doubt that she could read and do her numbers the same as I. She learned right along with me. Often times I would watch her lips forming the words as she said them to herself, or she would count on her fingers to cipher her sums. I waited for her to finish before I said the correct answer. If she had the same answer, she nodded her head. Our little game made the boredom of the classroom less tedious.

Dressed in black with a white pinafore apron and a bandanna covering her kinky black hair, she smiled warmly when she saw me coming down the hall. "Hurry,

Miss Sarah. Mr. Jolette be waitin' on you."

"Coming. It was difficult getting away from the breakfast room with Mr. Molack there."

I loved the library with all its books lining the walls. It was a round room nestled on the south side of Mama's sewing room and across the hall from the large dining room, at the front of the manor. Hidden within the walls behind movable bookshelves were large storage spaces. Danny and I used to hide in them when we were told to do something we had no desire to do. Large windows overlooked the rose garden, beyond to the carriage house, and to the green pastures filled with fine American Saddle horses and a few Arabians.

"Miss Sarah, we are late," Mr. Jolette scolded, looking at his pocket watch. "Time is one commodity we can never afford to waste. Everyone is given the same amount each day, and what one does with it determines if one is successful or not."

I had no answer for him. This speech rang old in my ears for I had heard it more times than I cared to count. I tried to be on time, but other things always seemed to distract me. I bristled at being treated as a child.

Mr. Jolette had a way of pronouncing each word as if it tasted sweet in his mouth. He must have been in his late thirties, not married. A woman would have had to be quite desperate to become his wife. He was so precise in everything he did; it would have driven me mad to be with him all the time. Tall and thin, immaculately dressed, he metered each of his movements like a dance. Since he had come to Rosewood highly recommended almost twelve years ago, he was the only tutor I ever had. Accomplished in both academic and social instruction, Daddy believed him to be a Godsend. Three hours in the morning and two hours in the late afternoon were devoted to the classroom.

"Are we ready to begin?" he asked.

"Yes, sir," I took my seat behind the desk by the

windows. Lily sat in the forest green chair at the door. Mr. Jolette towered over me, looking to see if I had the correct page in the textbook. The scent of lye soap mingled with lavender strongly accosted my nose.

"Page 163. That's it." The pointer stabbed into the book, preventing me from turning another page. He paced back and forth, or should I say glided, tapping his hand with the pointer.

Today, we will start the French and Indian War. The year . . . ."

The door flung open and in strutted Mr. Molack in his dark menacing fashion. He took a seat in the green winged-back chair on the opposite side of the door from Lily. "Continue the lesson. I'll not interrupt."

Mr. Jolette cleared his throat. "We were just about to begin with the French and Indian War."

"Tell me, Mr. Jolette, how is our Sarah doing? Is she a good student?"

I chafed to think that Mr. Molack took it upon himself to oversee my education. And to refer to me as 'our Sarah' was going too far. "What gives you the right to come in here and disrupt my schooling?"

He ignored me and waited for Mr. Jolette's answer.

"She is a fine student. Sarah learns very quickly and retains almost everything she reads. She has a remarkable memory. When she wants to, that is." He gave a slight smile in my direction.

"How is she in the social graces, such as dancing, or entertaining and the like? Will she make a good wife?"

"I never! How dare you!" I jumped to my feet.

"Sit down, Sarah," Mr. Molack's cold voice slapped back at me. "This does not concern you. I am simply trying to determine if the money we pay Mr. Jolette is a good investment."

"Teaching the social graces, as you call them, at this stage of Sarah's life is more a refinement than teaching. I was also employed to teach reading, writing, ciphering, history, and French."

"You tell me that she knows all of that. She can read and do her numbers. What more does she need to know? How much more can you teach her?"

"History. She does not have a good grasp of history."

"Neither do I."

"Mrs. Brighton wants her to learn French," Mr. Jolette continued.

"Whatever for? We live in a country that speaks English. That is all she needs. No, Mr. Jolette, I believe we must terminate your employment. What Sarah needs to know now, you cannot teach her."

"No!" I shouted, staring in horror at the dark figure still seated by the door. "You cannot do this."

"It's done." Mr. Molack slowly stood and left the room.

Lily sat quietly in the chair with her mouth open and eyes as large as walnuts. I could tell she could hardly wait to get into the kitchen to tell the others.

Mr. Jolette showed no sign of great dismay. He just stared at the closed door.

"Mr. Jolette, I am so sorry. Mama will surely have something to say about this."

"That is quite all right, Miss Sarah. I have wanted to join the army anyway. This gives me the freedom to do so. Life here at Rosewood has gotten unbearable. I had been planning to leave. I just did not know how to tell you."

"You cannot leave. Rosewood has been your home for almost twelve years. You came here when I was just a child. You were Cole's teacher, and mine. You are family."

"You are growing up. Soon my work would have been finished anyway. I think this is for the best." He took a deep breath to choke back the quiver in his voice.

My eyes began to sting as a tear escaped and ran down my cheek. "Where will you go?"

"I will make do. I still have family in New Bern. I will go

to them for a while, and then we shall see."

"I shall miss you."

"Thank you. I will say goodbye to Mrs. Brighton and be gone before evening. I wish you the very best of everything." He took me in his arms for the first time and gave me a hug. "I will miss you, too."

That night found Mr. Molack in Daddy's office, drinking. Mama and I dined alone, still furious over the day's events. We retired early. My mysterious lover came calling, as was his habit on nights when I had been overcome by stress. With him I felt safe and free from the troubles of the real world. We strolled in the moonlight. He whispered the words I wanted to hear and touched my cheek with a warm hand. I heard the sound of wood cracking and a muffled scream coming from far away. Why did this invade my dream? People were struggling. I had no desire to wake up. I tried to hold on to my lover, but he faded. I realized in horror that the struggle came from Mama's room. I bounded out of bed and threw open the door. The door of Mama's room hung half from the jam and lay half splintered on the floor. By the light of the fireplace, I could see a dark figure on top of Mama on the bed. I rushed in and grabbed a vase off the vanity to smash it over his head. He released his grip on Mama, swung around and hit me. I flew across the room. A pain stabbed at my head. Everything went black.

CHAPTER 7

Morning's light found me in Mama's bed with a wet towel across my forehead. Already dressed, Mama stood by the window with her back toward me.

"What happened?" I moaned.

In a cold, lifeless voice, she said, "Molack hit you and your head struck the table."

"I remember now, I must have been unconscious for hours if it's daylight already."

"Yes."

Painfully, I sat up. My head throbbed and the room spun. Slowly the image of last night came into focus. "Mama, are you all right? What did he do to you?"

She turned around to show me the bruises that covered the left side of her face from temple to chin. Her left eye was swollen shut and her lip split. Dried blood still clung to the corners of her mouth.

"That devil. I wish he was dead." Ignoring my own pain, I bounded to her side to hold her in my arms. I suspected the worst, but I could not bring myself to ask. Words could not pass between us, only silence.

We did not go down for breakfast nor at noon. Our meals were brought up to Mama's room where we intended to spend the rest of the day. Toward evening Mr. Molack sent orders that he insisted we dine with him. Mama declined.

Downstairs we could hear the shattering of glass as he flew into a rage at the slave's report. After he finished smashing the china, he stormed out of the house and rode off in the direction of the slave quarters. Mama slept in my room that night.

The next morning, Mr. Molack had the carpenter fix the door of Mama's bedroom, and he had all the locks removed from the bedroom doors. He ordered the servants out of the house at night. Even our maids were told to stay in the slave quarters at night. He said that he did not want any slaves in the house while we slept for fear of a slave uprising and they might kill us in our beds.

Time does not heal all wounds. Sometimes, it only makes them fester and poisons the soul. Weeks passed. We planned our days to avoid seeing the devil that lived in our house and held our lives in his hands.

One afternoon, Mr. Molack confronted Mama and me as we came down the hall. Mama moved to one side and he moved in front of her, not allowing her to pass. He leaned his arm against the wall blocking me from going around him. Mama trembled with fear at the mere sight of him, and she rarely lifted her eyes to meet his. But today Mama's rage boiled to the surface. Her soft southern voice gave way to screaming. "You are not the master of this plantation. Cole is! You cannot hold us prisoner in our own home. Get out! I will have the authorities on you."

His voice came cold through clenched teeth. "Cole is dead. Get it through your pretty head that I am running things around here now. Your life depends on me." A wicked smile spread across his dark features.

"We will see about that. I will speak to Mr. Sharply at the bank and. . . ."

"And you will what?" The smile quickly faded. "There is nothing you can do. So get used to it. I'm tired of you defying me at every turn. You'll find I can hurt you more than you think."

"What more can you do to me?"

"Have you forgotten? Look at your daughter. She is such a lovely child, or should I say woman. A family up north would be most interested to see her."

"You monster!" Mama raised her hand to strike his face.

He caught her wrist and pulled her close to him. "Your eyes flash with fire when you're angry. God, you're beautiful." His free hand moved to Mama's throat as he twisted her arm behind her back and held her tight against his body. "I think, if you were truthful with yourself, Ellie, you would admit you rather enjoyed. . . ."

"Let her go!" I screamed, pounding my fists into his back.

"I don't have time right now, but I'll have to teach the two of you some respect one of these days." He shoved Mama away from him. The venom of his words hung on the air long after he went down the hall and out through the glass doors.

"What did he mean by a family up north would be interested to see me?" I asked. "He said that before."

"Who knows what an evil man like that means by anything he says. I am too upset to talk about it anymore. I am going to my room."

The lustful appetites of greed, power and sex consumed Frank Molack. He revived the tradition held by many plantation owners that the master of the house had the first rights to the virgin slave girls. Mama and I were powerless to stop him. Young girls were taken to the overseer's house where he took his pleasure. When he was finished, they were dismissed.

No one questioned what was happening at Rosewood. To the outside world everything seemed to be normal. Molack accompanied Mama and me to church on Sundays. And he allowed us to go into town each Tuesday to volunteer at the church to roll bandages and to pack food to be sent to our soldiers. Mama believed she was helping Cole.

Willingly, I left Rosewood. For the first time in years, I felt safer away from the plantation than I did within our property markers. However, when the carriage came to the end of the drive, I thought my heart would burst within me. I looked back at the manor, contemplating jumping out of the carriage and returning to the safety of my room. My hands shook and beads of perspiration formed on my upper lip. I became short of breath. I reconsidered my decision to go into town. *It's just like going to church on Sunday,* I told myself. *Mama is with me. Everything will be fine.* Mama's smile reassured me as she placed her hand over mine to keep them still. She nodded to Toby to drive on. Each Tuesday the trip became easier.

One Tuesday, Mama approached Reverend Tadwell. "I was wondering if I might have a word with you, privately?"

"Why certainly, Mrs. Brighton." He took her arm and escorted her into his office.

I waited outside, knowing how difficult it must be to tell the reverend our impossible situation at the plantation. Presently they emerged from the study.

"I am not sure what I can do, but I will look into what you have told me. If you are afraid of him, you and Sarah are welcome to stay with Mrs. Tadwell and me here in town."

"Thank you, Pastor, but if we leave the plantation he will destroy it."

Driving back to Rosewood, I asked, "Did you tell Reverend Tadwell about the night you were attacked?"

"No, dear. That is something I cannot bring myself to tell anyone. Not even the pastor of my church."

Reverend Tadwell did come out to talk with Mr. Molack a few days later. But Frank Molack had a way with words that convinced Reverend Tadwell things were not as desperate as Mama had described. Thomas Tadwell left the plantation thinking that everything was fine at Rosewood.

Molack watched him drive away. A smile and a friendly wave accompanied the reverend on his way. But Molack's countenance changed once he turned to us. "Did you really think that simpleton would believe you?"

"What did you tell him?" Mama demanded.

"I said you were distraught over the death of your husband. From time to time your mind wanders. I told him I would see to it that you and our dear Sarah were well cared for. He even thanked me for being so kind."

"How dare you say such a thing!" I yelled, stomping my foot.

"Now, Sarah, we will live here as one happy family, and we won't go talking to the reverend, or anyone else about what is happening here on our plantation." Mr. Molack stepped close to me, touching a curl and bringing it over my shoulder. "You are such a lovely child." His eyes moved up and down my body and rested on my bosom. He licked his lips in lustful anticipation.

"You leave her alone!" Mama shouted, grabbing me out of harms reach.

Sometime during the next few days, Mama made a trip to the old sycamore tree to retrieve the pair of silver, double-barreled, pearl handled dueling pistols.

I spent my days trying to avoid Mr. Molack, but he always seemed to be near me. As I saddled my horse to ride away from the house, he forbade me to leave.

"It's too dangerous in times like these. You need to stay close to the house."

"The only danger I can see is you," I said, running out of the stable.

The cemetery happened to be the only place I felt

safe. Molack never ventured up the hill. I guess he feared the dead, he himself being more dead than alive, driven by insatiable desires. At the cemetery, I spent hours talking to Daddy, or Danny, or God. "Oh, God, please let them hear me. Let them know that we miss them. Bring Cole home soon. God! Do YOU hear me? I cannot bear this life anymore. You have to do something!" *It's no use praying,* I thought. *My prayers are like whispers in the storm. No one hears them.*

That night I heard footsteps in the hall. They stopped at my door. The door opened. Mr. Molack came in.

I sat up in bed, pulling the quilt up around me. "Get out!" I screamed.

He came over to the bed and pulled back the mosquito netting. "Don't scream. I won't hurt you." His hand reached out to touch my hair. "Such lovely hair, like golden threads in sunlight. You are so soft, so beautiful. You have no idea how much I want you." The smell of whisky spewed out of his mouth.

"Don't fight me. You can't win. I'm too strong for you. You're so young, so desirable. I've watched you. It doesn't matter how much I could get paid for you, I want you for myself. I knew if I waited long enough, I would find you. Now you're mine."

"Never!"

"Yes, my dear, I. . . I. . . . "

A loud sound crashed through the air. Then another. I screamed and held my ears. The look of surprise flashed across Mr. Molack's face as he grabbed the right side of his chest. Blood gushed through his white shirt. Mama stood in the doorway with both pistols in her hands, one of them smoking. She cocked the hammers of the other gun as Mr. Molack lunged toward her. She sidestepped. He staggered past her, stumbling down the stairs, falling most of the way. From the top of the stairs, Mama fired again. Missed. Mr. Molack staggered across the entry hall to the front door. All of the slaves were awake and came running to see what was happening.

"Open the door for him," Mama called to Seth, who stood next to Daddy's office. I grabbed my robe and followed her down the stairs.

Mr. Molack careened down the twelve steps to the red bricks in front of the house. "Get me a horse! Somebody get me a horse!" he commanded, holding onto the hitching post. Blood ran down his arm and dripped onto the bricks. Lanterns held by the slaves gave more than enough light for Mama to see him clearly.

Through labored breathing, he howled, "You think you have the upper hand, don't you? You made the worst mistake of your life. I'll be back. When I do, I'll have my two brothers with me, and you'll curse the day you were born. I'll make slaves out of you, both of you. Do you hear me! Slaves! And when I'm finished with her, I'll turn her over to the Hollingers."

"No, you will not," Mama said, coldly. "The shame of what you have done to me, tearing my spirit from me and linking it with yours, I will have to endure that pain for the rest of my life, but I cannot allow you to spread your evil over my daughter. I will not live in fear of you or your kind anymore."

At that moment the horror in Frank Molack's eyes indicated that he knew the foolishness of his words. He had misjudged the Christian woman standing before him. He thought he had broken her as one would break a spirited horse. In his mind, he had the victory. He was wrong, dead wrong.

Standing on the verandah, Mama took careful aim and shot him one last time. "Threaten me will you. Bury him in the woods," she said, showing no emotion.

The slaves standing around wanted to cheer, but the shock of seeing Mama with smoking pistols and actually killing Mr. Molack gave way to mere whispers. At that moment a large owl came screeching down out of the trees. Only its white underbelly could be seen.

"It's a ghost," one slave whispered.

"An evil omen," said another.

"A curse has been put on the Misses." The superstitions of the past gave voice to the slaves' fears.

"Leah, get some women to scrub the blood from the bricks. Seth, Toby, and Joseph come into the parlor," Mama said, turning to go into the house.

Inside, Mama sat in the chair by the window next to the table that always had a lamp burning for Cole. It gave the only light in the room. She sat with her hands folded in her lap. Seth, Toby and Joseph stood with their backs to the door, facing her. I was on the settee by the fireplace, shaking from head to toe. Mama calmly and with a determined tone in her voice, said, "I am running Rosewood now until Master Cole returns home. I have little experience, but that will not matter. This is my proposal. For all the slaves who stay and work the land when the harvest is in and the crop is sold, they will get paid for their labor out of the profits."

"Mama! What are you saying? You cannot pay slaves." I could not believe my ears.

She waved my words aside with her hand and continued, "Well, what do you say? I know you will be free if the North wins this dreadful war. However, should the South win, you will remain slaves. I have no power to keep you on the land if you want to leave. The question is whether you value freedom more than money.

"Toby, I would like you to take charge of the stables and all the animals. Seth, you will continue to be in charge of the manor, but let Leah run the kitchen. And Joseph, you will work the field hands. For all those who want to leave, I will not stop them. Remember, here at Rosewood we still have food. Life up north is not as sweet as one might think. Talk it over in the quarters tonight and let me know in the morning." Turning to me she said, "Come along, Sarah. We can still get a few hours of sleep. Tomorrow will be a busy day."

For the remainder of the night, sleep came in bits and pieces. I was tormented by horrifying images of blood and Mr. Molack's dead body on the bricks. I lay awake staring into the blackness of my room, afraid to close my eyes, wishing morning would come quickly and afraid of what would happen when it did. Relief washed over me when at last morning arrived and Lily came in to lay out my clothes.

Lily came to us when she was in her teens, abused by a cruel master and with child. She was a spunky girl and a hard worker. After she learned to trust us and feel the safety of Rosewood, she always had a smile on her face and a song on her lips. That was until Mr. Molack took over. This morning we had our cheery Lily back.

"Mornin', Miss Sarah. The sun is just a shinin' as bright as can be. Your mama says she and you is goin' to town this mornin'. So you needs to get up and gets yourself ready." She bustled about the room, filling the basin with hot water, laying out my black dress and undergarments, and throwing open the heavy, blue velvet drapes to let the morning sun come pouring into my room. All the while, she chattered on about what a wonderful day this was going to be.

I smiled. *Someone's happy,* I thought. I took a deep breath to push back the night's lingering images. "Tell me, Lily, how is that son of yours these days? I have not seen much of Jacob lately. He must be about ten by now." I remember stories Daddy told about when he had won Lily from Mr. Lasiter in a horse race. Daddy suspected Lily's son was actually Mr. Lasiter's offspring. The boy had very light skin and hazel eyes. The resemblance to the Lasiter family was quite unmistakable. Daddy loved to torment Mr. Lasiter by taking the boy into town every time he thought Mr. Lasiter might be there. Daddy never said a word, but Mr. Lasiter knew that Daddy had guessed his wanton deed. I was sure that if Mr. Lasiter knew Lily was with child, he would never have lost her to Daddy. He would have sold her down river to hide his indiscretions. Daddy frowned on such practices as the master taking a black mistress and fathering black children. No matter how white the child appeared, it would always be considered black, and in North Carolina, the child would always be a slave. Daddy wondered how a man could allow his child to become a slave. Daddy often said, 'What a man does in darkness will be revealed in the light, and the callousness of a man's actions will reflect in his life.'

"Jacob is gettin' tall. I keeps him busy so he's not under foot. When Mr. Mol . . . when . . . I keeps him out of sight. No needs to give that man any more devilment to think 'bout than he already did. I feared he would sell Jacob for meanness sake."

I shuddered. "No need to worry anymore. His hurting days are over. He cannot reach back from the grave to hurt you nor Jacob."

Coming downstairs, I saw Mama in Daddy's office going over some papers, but I let her be. Instead, I looked out the front door to see if Molack's body had been taken away. Two servant girls hard at work scrubbing the bricks gave the only indication of last night's events. In the side garden, an old man gently pruned Mama's rose bushes and pulled weeds. Sounds of creaking wagons rumbling along the field roads floated on the warm sunlit air. The soft humming as the servants went about their work in the house, and the aroma of breakfast wafting from the breakfast room gave no hint that anything out of the ordinary had happened. It was as if Mr. Molack never existed.

After breakfast, Mama ordered the carriage to be brought around so she and I could travel into town and talk with Mr. Sharply at the bank.

I still dreaded leaving Rosewood. My breath came in gasps as we neared the end of the drive. I closed my eyes and pretended I was with my mysterious lover. But when the sound of the horse's hooves changed from the clatter on the brick drive to the muffled sound of the dirt road, a pain pierced my heart and fear took over.

Mama held my shaking hands. "That's all right, dear." Her voice gave the assurance I needed.

I forced myself to think of something, anything else. "What are you going to tell Mr. Sharply about Mr. Molack not being with us?"

"I will have to think on that. When the time comes, I am sure I will say something suitable." She sat poised and seemingly calm. Her autumn hair escaping from beneath her black silk bonnet framed her face in a refreshing glow that made her look younger than she had looked in many months.

Toby stayed with the carriage under the shade of an old elm tree, while Mama and I went into the bank. The large brownstone building recently had bars added on the windows, as if bars could keep out marauders. Inside, a teller's counter ran along the north wall. To the rear of the room, a half wall with a gate in the center designated Mr. Sharply's office.

As we approached, Mr. Sharply quickly cleared the papers from his desk. He rolled down his sleeves and put on his suit coat before he opened the gate. "Come in, come in. What brings you two ladies into town on such a sultry day? Not that I have a complaint. It's always a pleasure to see you, especially you, Miss Sarah. I have heard that you are venturing off the property lately. And how are things out at Rosewood? The wife and I have wanted to come out to visit, but you know how busy I have been. Please have a seat." He motioned to two leather covered chairs that were in front of the massive dark walnut desk. The smell of cigars and brandy lingered on the stagnant air. Mr. Sharply, a tall, thin, slightly round shouldered man sported white hair parted in the middle and a clipped beard and mustache. His worried brown eyes made him look much older than his forty-six years.

Mama leisurely fanned herself. "You need not apologize. We can see how busy you are by all the papers you cleared from your desk, and we know the difficult times in which we live. That is precisely why we have come to see you. We are in dire straits. It seems that Mr. Molack has left us. He is gone without a word as to when, or if he will return. We are at a total loss." Mama lied, without even a hint of a nervous smile touching her lips or the slightest color change in her complexion.

I fanned my face vigorously to keep from blushing and drawing attention to her lie.

"Gone!" Mr. Sharply snapped. "I just saw him the other day over at the Mercantile. As a matter of fact, he said something about getting married. Yes. He was talking that since both John and Cole are dead, Sarah would inherit Rosewood. Or at least her husband would."

"And he planned to be her husband?" Mama gasped.

"I believe that was his intention. He followed me to the bank and we drew up loan papers for two thousand dollars. See, I have them right here." Mr. Sharply fumbled through some papers he had in the side drawer of the desk. "Yes, here they are. See. Everything is in order." He handed the papers to Mama.

"He put Rosewood up as collateral? How could you let him do that?"

Mr. Sharply looked surprised. "He had full power to handle the account of Rosewood. Since he took all the money out of the accounts we handled for you, I assumed he needed some cash to pay for immediate transactions."

"He did what? You mean to tell me I have no money in this bank."

"That's right. Mr. Molack drew everything out soon after John was killed. He said you wanted to keep the money close to home where you could get your hands on it. Of course, John cashed in his bonds before the war, and Mr. Molack withdrew the balance of the money and closed out the account."

Mama jumped to her feet. Her soft voice strained as she tried not to yell. "How could you let Molack do that?"

"As I said, he had full power to handle the account. Cole set it up that way. I should have contacted you about the matter, but . . . ."

"You thought I would not know anything about our finances. So why bother a woman with such matters." Mama's anger boiled to the surface. "You let that man rob us blind and you did nothing to stop it. I will have no further business with this bank."

"The note still has to be paid. I can hold off for a while, but . . . ."

"Take the matter up with Mr. Molack. He signed for the money and he is the one who owes it. Not me." Mama grabbed my hand and we quickly left the bank.

"Rosewood is still the collateral," Mr. Sharply called after us. "But if I can be of any assistance to you in any way, please let me know."

Mama and I left the bank without another word.

"We need a few things at the Emporium," Mama said as we crossed the dusty street from the bank to the wood framed store on the corner.

I mimicked Mr. Sharply in a singsong voice. "'If I can be of any assistance to you in any way, please let me know.' What further assistance could he possibly be? We have no money. It's the land he wants. He has wanted our land for years. Remember that Christmas when he asked you to talk to Daddy about selling the river pasture?"

"Yes, dear, I remember. You need to remember that you are a lady. It is not becoming to behave as someone below your station. I believe Molack was true to his word, probably for the first time in his miserable life. He did leave us penniless. Now we need to find a way to reverse our finances."

Mr. Taylor stood at the rear of the long, narrow shop sweeping up a spill of dry beans. In times past, he would have thrown all of them away, but not today. They came too dear. He scooped them up into a wooden bin to be sold for an outrageous price.

The quiet shop smelled of peaches, dill, fresh ground

coffee, soap, yard goods, and the musty odors of the old store which mingled into many happy childhood memories. Mr. Taylor always gave Danny and me a butterscotch candy when we came into the store with Daddy. I thought kindly of Mr. Taylor whenever I smelled butterscotch.

"Good morning, Mrs. Brighton, Miss Sarah. How are you today? What can I do for you?" Mr. Taylor said in his cheeriest voice, as he put the broom aside and wiped his massive hands on the crisp, white, butcher's apron that covered his dark gray trousers and multicolored vest. His sleeves were rolled up and his coat was nowhere to be seen. He mopped his flushed, round face and the back of his neck with his handkerchief as he waited for Mama's reply.

"We are doing quite nicely, thank you. But financially, we are totally at your mercy. We have just come from the bank, and Mr. Sharply told us that Mr. Molack has closed out our account. And now Mr. Molack has left us to manage for ourselves." Mama looked directly into Mr. Taylor's eyes, took a deep breath, and continued. "We need to do some good old fashioned bartering. Rosewood can use some supplies from your store, and I have a house full of furniture to pay for them. Would you be interested?"

"I most certainly would, if you are talking about your large dining room set, or John's office desk and bookcase. Yes, I think we can do business." He seemed pleased with himself for making such a shrewd business transaction. As he figured the cost, he asked, "Who will be running Rosewood now?"

"I will. That is, until Master Cole returns home."

"Mr. Cole? I thought he was killed at Shiloh with your husband. Mr. Molack said. . . ."

"I could not care less what Mr. Molack said," Mama interrupted. "Why does everyone keep telling me Cole is dead? He is not dead. I do not want to hear another word about it. Now, here is my list of things we need." Mama fished the list out of her handbag and handed it to Mr. Taylor.

The ticking of the clock on the back wall resonated through the quiet store. Glass counters displayed dry goods such as: books, lamps, soaps, candles, needles and thread, combs and brushes, bolts of material in various colors, lace, yarn, dishes, and flatware all much too costly for anyone to buy. Half empty shelves from floor to ceiling lined the narrow shop from front to back. Baskets of freshly picked fruit stood against the back counter. Bins marked flour, sugar, rice, and beans lined the wall behind the glass case.

From the haberdashery shop, which one entered through an arch and stepped down two steps, wafted into the main part of the store the aroma of sweet tobacco, leather, dyes from woolen suits, and mustache soap. The scent brought back wonderful memories of Daddy, masculine and strong, gentle and loving, a man of laughter and of sorrows, a man whom I dearly missed.

The millinery shop, hidden in the alcove to the right of the main store, enticed me with ribbons, lace, feathers of all colors and black bonnets displayed in the window. I wandered around the store running my fingers over the bolts of material, the lace, ribbons and other merchandise offered at unbelievably high prices. Sitting down at the vanity with the triple mirrors, I tried on a black, taffeta bonnet. Wide ribbons tied on the right side just under my ear.

"You look lovely, my dear. Although, black isn't your color. It should be blue, to match your eyes," Mrs. Tadwell said, poking her head through the open doorway. "I saw you in here and thought I would stop to see how things were going. Are you and your mama getting along better with Mr. Molack?"

I swallowed hard. Not turning around to look at her, but seeing her reflection in the mirror, I said, "Oh, have you not heard? Mr. Molack has left us. He is gone without a word as to where, or if he will return." I repeated Mama's lie almost word for word. Lying was difficult. I had always been taught to tell the truth. Daddy often said, 'If a person does not have the truth on his side, he has nothing.'

"That seems odd, but I am glad things have worked out for you. Remember me to your mama. I must be getting back to the parsonage. See you on Sunday." She waved her hankie goodbye as she continued on her way home.

I replaced the bonnet on the stand and returned to the main part of the store where I heard Mr. Taylor complaining about the empty shelves.

"It's this war. We cannot get anything past the blockades. Nothing is coming into the South, not even mail. As you know, Europe was ready to recognize the Confederacy, but after Antietam, and Lincoln issuing that preliminary warning proclamation of emancipation for all slaves in the seceding states, well, after that, the much needed support Europe could give us went up in smoke like most of the South. What little goods I do get cost me dearly. So I need to raise my prices or take too much of a loss. But with higher prices no one can buy my goods because no one has the money, or they are afraid to let go of it. It's a vicious circle."

"Is your son working today?" I asked, looking around for Andrew.

"No." Mr. Taylor took a deep breath. "That's another thing. Old men and politicians make the wars, but young boys are the ones who have to fight and maybe die in them. Andrew has joined the Confederate army, much to the grief of his mother."

I had no words to comfort Mr. Taylor. I believed it was Andrew's duty to fight, but his father's pain mingled with mine, and I felt his sorrow. Mama came to my rescue.

"I wonder if we might work out a business arrangement? I have eggs and butter that I could sell to you for goods. Also cheese if you would like it."

"Oh, my dear lady, that would be a Godsend.

Anything. Fruit, eggs, butter, cheese, maybe some chickens. I will take anything. Some of my other suppliers have abandoned me. They can get better prices elsewhere. If you just want goods, I can do that for you. I'm having a difficult time keeping my shop going. Your goods will truly help me. If the war lasts much longer, we will all be in ruin."

"Yes, Mr. Taylor, I agree with you," Mama said. "We would love to stay and chat, but we do need to be going. So we can expect your wagon out in the morning to pick up the furniture and bring the supplies I ordered. I will set up a schedule for delivery of the eggs and butter, and I will see about the rest."

"I'll be there early, before I open the store."

"We will be waiting. Come along Sarah." As we left the store, Mama continued evaluating Mr. Taylor. "That man can talk your ear off and all he wants to do is complain about the war. We have our own problems. I do not have the time to spend all day listening to him."

I followed Mama out of the store, across the street and into the carriage. "Take us home, Toby." Mama turned to me. "I need time to think. Our finances are much worse than I imagined. When we get home we will search Mr. Molack's room and the overseer's house. He has to have put the money somewhere. And I will find it."

The drive home was as lovely as always. Sunlight shimmered across the green grass of the meadows that flanked the near side of Mill Creek. Mockingbirds and catbirds called out from the branches of the buckthorns and the sourwoods that lined the road. The fragrance of the basswood embraced us as we silently rode home. Everything seemed the same as always, the old road, Spanish moss hanging from trees, the peace and beauty of the land I called home. But the undercurrents of the war were slowly pulling us down, and we were helpless to stop it.

CHAPTER 8

Names such as Chancellorsville, Vicksburg, Brandy Station, and Gettysburg were burned into our memories, like the fires that burned across our beloved land. The death toll mounted. Summer and autumn of 1863 proved to be a turning point for the war, as well as for our lives at Rosewood.

Mama and I had searched Mr. Molack's room and the overseer's house for the money he had taken from the bank. But it was nowhere to be found. Knowing Mr. Molack, he had probably spent it or gambled it away. Mama turned to her own resolve. She took to running the plantation like a general in a campaign. Sitting at the writing desk, she carefully worked out her schedules for the next few months: egg and butter deliveries, what percentage of the fruit would be sold, and the cotton harvest. She had decided to store the cotton in our barns instead of sending it to Wilmington to rot on the docks waiting for a blockade runner. When the war was over, England would be desperate for cotton, and we would have one of the first shipments out. In the meantime, we would sustain ourselves by selling butter and eggs, fruit, and furniture to Mr. Taylor.

I could no longer justify my pampered life filled with idleness. I needed to contribute to the welfare of Rosewood. I knew what Mama would say, 'Ladies do not do that sort of thing.' I couldn't have cared less. Doing needlepoint and making samples seemed a waste of my time. Mr. Jolette had taught me to read and write, and all the things a fine Southern lady should know to maintain her position, but I knew deep down in the depths of my soul that was not enough. I remembered what Cole had said that Christmas so long ago about taking care of ourselves if the slaves gained their freedom. Mama thought he was teasing, but as the war continued and the South seemed to be losing ground, his words held a sharp sting to them. As Daddy had prepared for the war, I knew I had to plan for life after the war.

The summer crops of cherries, plums, and peaches ripened. Pickers brought our share of each crop into the kitchen to be put up into jars, or cooked for jams or compote. The aroma of hot fruit, sorghum and spices filled the cook room and drifted up the stairwell to entice me down into the kitchen.

"May I help?" I asked Leah. All the laughing and chattering I had heard coming from the kitchen stopped as soon as the slave women saw me. A silent pall fell over the room.

Lily beamed at the thought of my learning how to preserve fruit. She wiped her hands on her white, plum-stained apron and sauntered over to me holding a clean apron. "My, my, my, would you ever believe you see the day that Miss Sarah be down here in the kitchen puttin' up fruit?" She handed the apron to me. "You best be puttin' this on, or you gets your dress splashed with juice."

"This is certainly messy." I looked at the seven women sitting at the table peeling and cutting plums, and at the big black kettles on the wood stove and the kettle in the hearth.

Leah stood by the stove, holding a large wooden paddle, stirring the bubbling fruit. "No need for you to be down here, Miss Sarah. We doin' just fine." Her graying hair was tied up in a white bandanna, and a white apron covered her black dress. Leah stood taller than the other women, thin and willowy, and in her youth she was a beauty beyond compare among her people. Through the years, I had heard the slave women tell stories of how all the young men of the plantation wanted Leah for a wife, but she had given her heart to a man who belonged to River Hall. It was a love that was never meant to be, because Daddy would never sell her to River Hall, nor would Mr. James sell his slave to Rosewood. I remembered Daddy's answer when I asked him about Leah.

"She is much too valuable not to have an offspring. I gave her to a man from our holdings. Her happiness was never an issue. I believed that she would learn to love him, and if she could not, such is the way of life."

I thought of Amy Ann and how her parents would arrange a marriage for her if she did not pick a suitor within a proper time. I wondered how she was doing in Boston and if she married for love or for another fortune. The man that Leah married was good to her, the stories say, but they never told if she was happy with him. He was killed in a carriage accident after only ten years of marriage. Leah remained childless. I felt sad for Leah.

I want to marry for love, I thought. *What would life be worth if I did not have someone to love me?*

As the years passed, Leah took to running our kitchen and virtually the entire house. She seemed content. What Leah said, the other servants took as gospel, except for Seth.

Seth believed he ran the house. I cannot remember a day when he did not answer the front door for guests, or serve the meals in the dining rooms, or tend to Daddy's needs. He walked slightly stooped now because of his advanced age. His tight, curly hair was almost white. But the sparkle still danced in his black eyes when he remembered the old days when he and his wife, Rose, now buried in the cemetery out behind the slave quarters, ran the house together.

One of the women dropped a knife and the clatter woke me from my daydreams. "Leah, I know you have no need for my help, but I want to learn how to do this." I took the apron from Lily, tied it over my black dress, and rolled up my sleeves.

Leah looked at me through disbelieving eyes and shook her head. "You be more in the way than a help, but if you wants to learn, sit yourself down at the table and gets a knife and start cuttin'."

Working in the kitchen brought a rewarding sense of accomplishment. As the jars were filled with hot fruit and stored on the pantry shelves, I could count my progress. I felt the satisfaction of a job well done. I liked that feeling.

In the days to come, I remembered that Cole had asked me to tend to his horse. I could never do the labor myself, I had to draw the line somewhere, but I could direct the work. Since Mama had given Toby charge of running the stables, I decided to be his overseer.

I saw Shadow Run romping through the pasture with some fillies. He had grown into a beautiful stallion, taller than most Arabians, standing at about fifteen hands, with powerful hindquarters and a broad chest. The black mane, tail and four black stockings accentuated his silver gray coat. Not a prettier horse had ever been born to the Rosewood stables, nor one as mischievous.

At the age of fifteen, Michael, Toby's son, stood almost as tall as his father. His grin and happy nature made him a very likable young man. Daddy always said, 'Some people have a special calling from the Lord to work with animals, Michael has such a calling.' All the animals seemed to love him, except Shadow Run.

My long, low whistle brought Misty Morn and Shadow Run to the fence to receive the carrots I brought. "Here you are. No pushing. I have one for each of you." I patted Misty Morn on the neck, and rubbed her soft, chestnut muzzle. But when I reached up to pet Shadow Run, he shied away. "One of these days you will let me pet you."

"That horse's a devil," Michael said, coming up behind me. "Master Cole gonna have a hard time ridin' him. He's three years old and never been rode. Can't even get close to him. I puts him in the barn, and he undoes the gate and gets out all by himself."

"We will have to fix the latch so he cannot open the gate. I would not want him getting out and running away," I said.

"He won't run away. He likes the good oats I feeds him."

"All the same, get the latch fixed."

My eighteenth birthday passed unnoticed, Mama had too much on her mind, and I didn't really care about birthdays anymore. By September, Rosewood was at risk. The egg, butter, and fruit money was hardly enough. We emptied room after room, bartering the furniture for goods we could not grow on the plantation. Our home became smaller and smaller as the door to each emptied room was locked. The house servants were moved from the third floor down into the workrooms off the kitchen. Those rooms were warmer in the winter and cooler in the summer. To save heating wood, I sealed off the top floors, slaves quarters and guest rooms.

"The misses is cursed. The night she shot Mr. Molack his spirit swooped down on her and cursed her good," Pearl said to Leah in the kitchen one morning. "I is gonna leave one of these nights. Don't wants to stay in a cursed house."

"You are a silly girl," I said, overhearing her as I entered. "Rosewood is not cursed. We still have food to eat and beds to sleep in. The war will not last forever. When Master Cole comes home we will buy new furniture. Things will be the way they were before the war. Rosewood will be filled with music and laughter again. You will see. Life beyond the stone pillars of our property is not as good as you might think. You are safe here. Out there, the evil Yankees will get you. We are doing just fine here." I turned and walked out of the room. Tears started to sting my eyes. How long could I go on believing Cole was coming home, and that everything would be just fine? My steps echoed up the stairs and through the empty hall. Reality told me that everything was not just fine, but I refused to believe it.

My warning did not stop Pearl from leaving. Sometime during the next few days, she slipped away. We had no power to keep a frightened slave girl on the plantation.

We welcomed October with its cool days and cold nights. The air took on a new freshness, a fragrance of cut hay, of ripe apples, of leaves turning red and gold in the hazy sun. Autumn had always been my favorite season and October my favorite month. The feeling of a renewed hope emerged from the cool, hazy days which enveloped me and cradled my senses.

The apple and pear harvests were adequate enough to provide for the purchase of oats and feed for the animals to see them through the winter. Our barns and pantries were full. The pigs, milk cows, and chickens promised a full larder for the winter.

"Bring them horses into the stable. It's gonna storm. It's a bad one," Toby shouted to make himself heard above the wind as he ran down the road behind the house leading to the river pasture. "Get them cows and pigs in the barn and bar the door."

Standing on the side verandah, Mama and I watched the storm approach. "Sarah, go out there and get Shadow Run into the stable. He's out again, and he will not let Michael catch him. I will help with the other horses in the pasture down by the river."

"You, Mama?"

"Yes. If you can do it, Sarah, so can I. Now hurry."

Pulling my shawl over my hair, I headed toward the

pasture beyond the carriage house. Mama went the other direction to the river. Lightning flashed. The sky blazed. Thunder rolled like cannon fire. Shadow Run spooked, running away from me faster than I had ever seen him run before. I called and whistled to no avail. He cleared the fence and was gone into the storm.

Another flash of lightning, a crack of thunder and the sky opened, releasing torrents of rain. I hurried to the stable. Inside, the other Arabian horses were in their stalls nervously pawing the ground. They moved about in an unsettling fashion, eyes wild with fear.

"Horses knows this gonna be a storm to reckon with." Michael tied a rope onto each halter, securing it to the stall gate. "We gots to keep them from kickin' the stall to pieces."

"Shadow jumped the fence and ran into the ravine. I have to go after him."

"You can't. This storm's too bad. You mama be mad if'n she know you out there."

"Yes, I can. Mama's down at the river trying to get the saddle horses in. I will ride just a little ways. He couldn't have gotten far."

"You mama's down in the river meadow?"

"Yes. She's helping with the. . . ."

"That's bad. River's risin' fast. The pasture soon be under water. I goes down to help. You stay here with the horses."

"No! I'm coming, too."

"You jest be in the way. Stay here." Michael turned on his heel and ran out of the barn.

"I am sick of people telling me I am in the way. I am going." I yelled as I followed him into the rain. Black clouds darkened the sky. Evening was fading quickly into night.

In the lower pasture, several men were already hard at work trying to get the frightened horses to high ground. Mama was nowhere to be seen. Running as fast as he could, Michael approached Joseph who had a rope around the neck of a horse caught in a bog.

"Grab his tail and help pull'um free," Joseph yelled. The wind howled in protest.

Michael did as he was told. I grabbed the other end of the rope behind Joseph. Straining with all our might against the line, we pulled frantically. Finally the bog gave way, and the horse lunged forward. Joseph stumbled backwards. I went down into the mud with the weight of this giant of a man on top of me.

"Miss Sarah, ya all right?" Joseph scrambled to his feet.

I wiped splattered mud off my face with the back of my hand, nodding. "Yes."

"Ya looks funny covered with mud. Ya sure nothin' broke?" He extended his hand to help me to my feet, all the while trying to suppress a laugh.

"Yes. I am fine. But, Joseph, Mama came down here to help get the horses in before the rain started. I have not seen her anywhere."

Joseph looked around then called to Toby, "Ya sees Miss Lizabeth?"

"No. She come down here in this storm?"

"Miss Sarah say she come to help get the horses in 'fore the rain start. Get a lantern and go up river. I'll go down river. Michael, get back to the house and see if'n she went home. Miss Sarah, take two men and gets the horses off'n this meadow. The rest of you men," Joseph cupped his hands around his mouth and yelled to be heard above the moan of the wind, "Spread out and find Miss Lizabeth."

All eleven American Saddle Horses were gathered at the east end of the meadow. Jake and Aaron helped me prod the animals to higher ground. We had just cleared the crest of the hill when lightning struck a cottonwood tree and set it ablaze. The horses bolted.

"Let them go," I called. "They are out of danger up

here on the high ground. We can gather them in the morning, or when the storm's over. I want to get back to the meadow and look for Mama."

Aaron put his hand on my shoulder to stop me from going over the edge of the bluff. "Ya stay up here, Miss Sarah. Ya sees everythin' that's goin' on from here. Best ya don't go down there."

The trees served as windbreaks for us while we watched from the brow of the bluff the progress being made in the pasture below. The lanterns designated the position of each man as he made his way methodically across the open meadow. Suddenly, a lantern down river started to circle high above the carrier's head.

"Look, Miss Sarah," Jake said pointing to the circling lantern. "They found somethin'."

"Please, God, let her be all right," I whispered, offering a quick prayer. "Can you see? Is it Mama?" I wiped the rain out of my eyes, straining to see into the darkness.

"Yes'um, it's her. They found her."

"I am going to run to tell Leah at the house. Jake, you fetch Mrs. Olson. She knows about these things," I ordered, running down the hill to the road that led to the back of the manor.

"They are coming! They found her. Quick, get some hot water and blankets. Bring them up to Mama's room," I shouted as I ran through the kitchen door and up the back stairs to the second floor. "Lily, help me get out of these wet clothes." I rushed into my room with Lily close on my heels to help me out of the muddy dress and shoes.

"You is soaked to the skin. What you doin' out there in the storm?"

"Why do you ask foolish questions? Just help me." The thought crossed my mind that I could work in the kitchen and oversee the work in the stable, but I could not dress myself. Buttons and laces were up the back, and corsets held me in so tightly that I could not bend over to remove my own shoes. I washed the mud off my face and arms. Lily unlaced my undergarments, and I put on a robe. We waited for the men to bring Mama up stairs. Time has no mercy when one waits.

Finally, I heard the men coming up the back stairs. Joseph carried Mama's limp body. Her ashen face and autumn hair were caked with mud.

"Bring her in here and lay her on the bed." Holding the lamp high, I led the way down the hall. "Is she. . . is she. . . ?" My eyes begged Joseph for an answer to the question I could not find words to ask.

"She's alive." He gently laid her on the green canopy bed. His shirt had been ripped to shreds, revealing a muscular chest and arms with the scars from Molack's whip. I winced when I saw them.

"Thank God she's alive. I sent Jake for Mrs. Olson. I hope the bridge does not wash out." I took a deep breath when remembering the story of the woman named Sarah, who was buried in our family cemetery, and the accident of the overturned carriage the night I was born.

As Joseph turned to leave, I touched one of the scars on his back. "I am so sorry."

"Weren't your fault. Some men are jest bad. They takes pleasure in hurtin' others."

"I hope that kind of evil will never touch Rosewood again."

The men left the room and went down into the kitchen to wait. With the help of Leah, I took Mama's dress and shoes off and washed the mud from her body. A strange feeling came over me. I was no longer the child but the caregiver. For the first time in my life, Mama needed my help. I remembered Mama taking care of Grandma Brighton. Grandmother became the child and Mama the adult. *"Is this the way of life one generation taking over for the other?"* I thought. We wrapped Mama in a warm blanket and pulled the bed covers over her. Her breathing came slow and shallow, like someone in a deep sleep.

"What is keeping Mrs. Olson?" I paced the floor, gesturing wildly with my hands. "She should be here by now."

"She be here soon. Ain't been an hour yet." Leah's reassuring words fell to the floor. I found no comfort in them.

I stood at the glass door, which led onto the balcony, watching for the buggy to turn from the road onto the drive. At last, I saw the side lanterns of the carriage. "She's here. Mrs. Olson is here. Open the door for her and bring her upstairs," I shouted from the top of the stairs.

I did not need to tell Seth to open the door, because he waited beside the gaping opening, an umbrella in his hand, ready to help the elderly lady from the carriage onto the verandah and to bring her up to the bedroom. Mrs. Olson had been helping Dr. Bardlow for the last six years, ever since she and her husband moved into Mill Creek. Mrs. Olson was a herbalist for a long time, and she was right handy as a midwife.

"Dr. Bardlow," Seth said. "Why you come? Where's Mrs. Olson?"

"She's out to the Feller's place. Jake came to get me when he couldn't get anyone else. When I heard what happened and that it was Ellie, ah, Mrs. Brighton, I insisted I come. Is she in her room?"

"This way." Seth motioned toward the stairs and started to lead the way.

"Don't bother. I know this house better than my own." He took the stairs two at a time, like a man in his youth instead of one in his mid-sixties. The man had put on weight in his senior years, as evidenced by buttons straining too close over his burly chest. He looked up at me over the wire rims of his spectacles as he neared the second floor. In his day, Dr. Robert Bardlow knew the insides and outsides of almost every planter's family in this region of the coastal plain. And his handprint was on the backside of every planter's child, including mine.

"Thank God you have come," I said. "Did Jake tell you what happened?"

"Just that she was found in the river."

"There is not much more to tell. She must have slipped and fallen into the water. She's alive, but just barely." I left the room while Dr. Bardlow examined Mama. Leah stayed to help.

When he came out of Mama's room, he had a worried look on his face. "There doesn't seem to be any broken bones. I'll have to wait until she wakes up to be sure. Her lungs don't sound good. I want to keep her propped up with pillows to help her breathe easier. I'll stay the night to keep an eye on her. You get some sleep. There's nothing you can do. She is in the hands of God. If there's a change, I'll call you." His arms closed around me in a comforting hug. "Don't cry. We have to be strong in times like these." The aroma of pipe tobacco mingled with apple surrounded this gentle man.

Tears ran down my face as I stood in the darkness of my room looking out of the window at the lightning illuminating the sky. The sound of the wind whistling around the corners of the house and the rain splashing against the window blended with my desperate prayer. "Dear God, let Mama be all right. What will I do if she dies? I cannot live without her. Was Pearl right? Is there a curse on Rosewood? God, I cannot go on. I need Cole to come home. Where is he? You have to keep him alive and bring him home. Do You hear me? I cannot pretend to be strong anymore. Give me a sign that everything will be all right. Let Shadow come home. I cannot have lost him, too." I said the words, but I could not believe the action would take place. I threw myself onto the bed as uncontrollable sobs shook my body. I repeated over and over again, "Cole, Cole, Cole."

CHAPTER 9

For a brief moment I had forgotten the pain of the night before. For that short time, I lay comfortable and warm, dreading having to get up and face the cold room. I waited for Lily to come in with hot water and stoke the fire back to life. Then the wave of reality flooded over me as I vaguely remembered Dr. Bardlow coming in to cover me with the eiderdown comforter.

"She's sleeping peacefully now," he had said. "She will be fine in a few days. Have no worries."

I could not wake up enough to respond to his words, but the fear that had gripped my soul gave way in a wash of peace.

"Last night!" I said aloud, bolting to a sitting position. "Mama, the storm, Shadow Run." I sprang from the bed, ignoring the chilly room with the cold floors, and ran down the hall to Mama's room. Opening the door slowly, I looked in. Sitting in the chair by the window slept the doctor. Mama was awake. She motioned for me to enter.

"What happened?" she whispered.

"You tell me. Joseph found you on the bank of the river. I thought you were going to die. Dr. Bardlow stayed the night to keep watch over you."

"Yes, I see he kept a vigilant watch on me." She smiled as she nodded her head toward the sleeping man. "I really have no idea what happened. One minute I was chasing horses and the next I was in the water being swept down river."

"How awful. You must have been frightened."

"Yes. Indeed I was. The oddest thing, though, I remember feeling as if I were pushed. Thank God that Joseph found me."

"Pushed? That is indeed very odd, since you were out there alone." A shiver ran up my spine. "Well, I am glad to see you are doing much better this morning. Do you feel like having breakfast? What do you say to hot porridge, apple compote, some sausage, fresh muffins, and coffee?"

"Sounds delicious."

"Good morning. You seem chipper this fine morning," Dr. Bardlow said, stretching and yawning. "I must have fallen asleep. That breakfast you just described sounds good to me, too."

"Then breakfast for two, served in madam's private dining room, coming right up."

Lily was waiting to help me dress when I returned to my room. My usual black dress served me well. I rolled up the long sleeves and let the skirt hang limp from lack of petticoats to make working easier. However, without the petticoats, the hem was too long, so I tied a sash around my waist and pulled the dress up so I would not trip over the long skirt. Because I did not take time to have Lily adorn my hair properly, I grabbed my straw hat on the way out of the room. I would simply push my hair under the hat when I left the house. I headed downstairs with Lily close on my heels.

Leah and Jacob, Lily's son, were in the kitchen when we entered. "Mornin', Miss Sarah, how is your mama doin' this mornin'? The doctor stayin' for breakfast?" Leah asked.

"Yes. They want porr. . . oh, you have the trays already made for them."

Lily stepped in front of me. "You sit yourself down and Leah gets you breakfast. I takes the trays up to your mama and the good doctor. Jacob can help me."

"I am not very hungry this morning." I picked a bite out of a muffin. "My, Jacob is getting to be a big boy." I stuffed the muffin morsel into my mouth as I watched the boy sitting at the table with his hands folded as if he was waiting for his own breakfast. He wore a handed down white shirt which had turned dingy over the years. The sleeves were rolled up and pinned so his hands were free to do his work. A rope cinched up his waist, and the shirt hung to his knees. I had never noticed before how poorly slave children were dressed. His long, light chocolate colored legs stuck out from beneath the shirt in an almost embarrassing fashion. "Why are you not out with the men helping in the fields?"

"He's not gonna to be a field hand. He is gonna be in the house. Don't wants him to work like a mule all his life," Lily said, taking one of the trays. "Jacob, you takes this tray. Now, be careful you don't spill nothin'."

I smiled, wondering what his life would be like if the South loses the war. But today my mind focused on other things besides a little slave boy. My concerns turned to the horses, particular Shadow Run.

The men were already clearing away the rubble left in the wake of the storm's onslaught by the time I had finished the breakfast Leah insisted I eat, and got out to see the damage. Debris and pieces of the roof lay on the ground. Huge limbs had broken off trees hundreds of years old. I stepped over or around boards, branches and shingles on my way to the stable to see if the horses were safe.

Toby met me on the way with his disturbing news. "Oh, Miss Sarah, the south orchard is gone. Burnt by lightnin'. The rain put it out before it could burn the woods, but the trees is all gone. One of the barns blowed down flat. Killed some cows and pigs. Chickens is scattered all over the place. I put men to workin' to save what's left."

"What about the horses?"

"That's only good news. All them is safe. 'Cepten' Mr. Cole's horse. He ain't come back." Toby looked at the ground, not wanting to make eye contact for fear I would be angry with him. He stood twisting his hat in his hands. "But soon as I gets this mess picked up, I goes lookin' for him."

"I will take Misty and hunt for Shadow on the backside of the property. You look over against Garland Hills."

"You be careful. Them woods turns into swamp before you knows it."

"Toby, you are such a worrier. I have been riding through the woods all my life."

"All the same. You be careful."

Michael had already saddled Misty Morn before I got to the stable. Much to the dismay of Mama, I used Daddy's old saddle. If I was going to work like a man, I would ride like a man. I found riding astride was easier than riding side-saddle. I reached between my legs and grabbed the hem of my dress and tucked it into the sash, then I mounted the horse.

I guided Misty down the wagon road toward the south field. I gasped when I saw the destruction from the fire. Only charred twigs reached up from the ashes that covered the ground. Heat still rose from smoldering wood, making breathing difficult. The thought crossed my mind that Shadow Run might have been caught in the fire, but I dismissed the idea almost as quickly as it came. Blackened acres upon acres stretched before me. Not a sound could be heard, not a bird, not an animal, nothing. At first I held Misty to a slow walk as I could not seem to comprehend the destruction, but then all I wanted to do was run, get away. I urged Misty forward, faster and faster. We reached the wooded edge of the field, and still I prodded her on.

Last night's storm had uprooted huge trees. Familiar trails were blocked. I detoured around the debris. All morning Misty and I searched, but had no success. The sun hit its zenith and started to descend when I realized I was lost. I had never gone this far before. Absorbed in my quest, I had not paid much attention to where I was going. The realization of my circumstances closed in upon me and fear took over.

"Come on, Misty. We need to turn around and backtrack. Try to get out of these woods to an open meadow where I can get some sense of the direction to Rosewood." I patted Misty on the neck trying to sound brave.

The marshy ground oozed beneath the horse's hooves. Small animals scurried unseen beneath the underbrush, while crows jeered at me from their perches high above in the trees. Nothing looked familiar. The trees grew denser. A thicket blocked my way. Even though the air held the coolness of autumn, I perspired. Each way I turned seemed wrong.

The growling in my stomach told me I had missed the noon meal. "I am glad Leah insisted I eat breakfast. I am sure Toby will be out looking for us before long. He knows the direction we came. He will find us, have no fear." I leaned forward and patted Misty's neck. She tossed her head as if to agree with me.

Through the trees I saw smoke, not the smoke of a forest fire, but that of a chimney. Joy and relief rushed to bring tears to my eyes. "Thank God. I can get help at that house." I turned Misty toward the direction of the smoke. The ground became dryer. Flatness gave way to a gradual incline and the trees thinned out.

"Hello," I called. "Is someone home?" No answer. The log cabin had a door and one window in front. By the looks of the moss covered logs and rotten wood, it had been there for a hundred years, falling into disrepair. Trees towered over the small building. Surely someone was home because smoke billowed from the stone chimney and a dim light shone through the small window. "Hello, is anyone here? I need some help." I dismounted and quickly walked to the door. I knocked. No answer. Lifting the latch, I opened the door. Foolishly, I entered. A draft slammed the door shut behind me.

The fire in the hearth and the fading light coming through the dirty window dimly lit the small room. A black kettle, hanging on a brace over the fire, bubbled the hearty aroma of stew that made my stomach growl even louder. Freshly baked, uncut bread sat on the rude table. One tin plate and a cup were placed on the table in front of the only chair. In the corner, an unmade bed completed the simple furnishings of the dirty cabin. I had never been in a place of such meager means. Not even our slaves' quarters were in such a low estate. The underlying stench of body odor was evident even with the wonderful aroma of stew and bread.

I was about to take a piece of bread when the door flew open and in walked a burly man with a shock of red hair and a thick, curly, red beard. He carried a wooden bucket filled with water in one hand and a rifle in the other. He wore unwashed trousers and suspenders pulled over a dirty red union suit.

"What the hell ya doin' in my house?" he roared.

I cowered away. "I. . . I am lost," I stammered. "I saw the smoke from your chimney and came for help. I did not mean any harm."

"Ya didn't mean no harm, but ya sure enough caused it. Can't ya leave a man be? Ya're trespassin'. Get out!"

"Please, just tell me where the road is so I can return home and I will be happy to be on my way."

He took a step forward and slammed the bucket and the rifle on the table. "Just who the hell are ya?"

"Please, do not swear at me." I almost started to cry. "My name is Sarah Brighton from Rosewood Plantation over by Mill Creek off the River Road."

"I jest asked who ya was. I didn't ask for a damn geography lesson. I know where Rosewood Plantation is. Come over here into the light. Let me get a good look at ya."

I stepped closer to the fire.

His almost colorless blue eyes narrowed as they surveyed me. He reached up and swept my hat from my head releasing my yellow curls to fall freely to my shoulders and down my back. His eyes sparkled. "What's it worth to ya?"

I stooped to retrieve my hat, but I never took my eyes away from him. I stood up quickly. "I do not understand what you mean. One does not ask for payment to do a charitable act."

"I'm not in a charitable mood. A pretty little thing like ya alone in the woods. It's startin' to get dark. What'll ya give me to show ya the way to the plantation?" He licked his lips like a dog about to devour a bone.

I slowly backed up. "I do not have anything."

"That's a mighty fine lookin' horse out there."

"No! She's not for sale." I rounded the end of the table and started for the door.

"Ya don't wanta get home very bad. What ya gonna give me?" He stepped between me and the door, blocking my way.

"I have some Hard Times Tokens good to be redeemed at Mr. Taylor's store. You tell me how to get home, and I will give them to you." I was quite proud of my deal. I moved back to the end of the table to keep out of his reach.

"Hard Times Tokens ain't worth my time."

"I assure you that they are quite valuable. You can buy anything with them."

"Quiet! Tokens ain't no good to me." He banged his fist on the table.

I ducked away. Fearing his wrath would find me as his next target I yelled, "What do you want?"

He rubbed his beard as his eyes glinted with mischief. "I'll take no less than five dollars, Yankee."

"That's robbery! I do not have that much money."

"Maybe we can work out a deal. Ya can stay here as my house guest and work off the payment. Kinda indentured servant, ya might say. I've always fancied to have myself a house girl."

I gasped. "All right! I will give you the money. Just tell me how to get home." My heartbeat sounded in my ears like a drum and the palms of my hands became sweaty. "I have a five dollar gold piece I will give you. But it is back at the plantation." It was then that I realized fear fathers lies. For someone who was taught never to tell a falsehood, lies dripped off my lips like water.

"Gold? Ya have gold that ya good Southern people didn't give to the war effort? Can I believe ya?" He studied my face for a moment. "I'll tell ya what I'm gonna do. I'll take ya home myself. Ya can pay me for my troubles when I deliver ya to ya door." He moved away from the door and back to the fireplace to stir the kettle and swing the brace out of the heat.

"Then we should get started. It will be dark soon." I hurried past him on the other side of the table and out the door. The fresh afternoon air filled my lungs. "I have really done it this time," I whispered to Misty. "I thought he would just tell me how to get to the road, not take me home. What am I going to do? I have to keep up the falsehood until I see the stone pillars. Then what?"

"I'll get my horse," he said, coming up behind me. "Now, don't think you'll trick old Bayard and ride away from me."

"I would not dream of it." I pulled my skirt between my legs and tucked the hem into the sash. I mounted Misty. "Get ready to run when I tell you," I whispered to her. "I have no knowledge of how I get myself into situations like this."

"Bayard, is that you name?" I asked, as we rode away from the cabin.

"Don't ask questions. All I want is the twenty dollar gold piece. So jest shut up and we'll get along fine."

"Twenty! I said five. Five dollar gold piece."

"Don't ya go tricking me, now."

I said not another word as we rode on a winding, often blocked, trail. It didn't matter if he thought I had twenty or only five dollars. I had neither. We crossed a stream that had been partially dammed by a fallen tree. I wondered where he was taking me. The sun was sinking fast. Soon it would be dark. Then suddenly we came out of the forest at the crossroads where I recognized the old mill. We were on the back road into town, Old Mill Creek Road.

"I know where I am now. You need not trouble yourself any further. Thank you for your kindness."

"Kindness! I didn't do it for kindness. Ya said gold, and gold is what ya're goin' to give me. Unless ya want to satisfy my needs another way."

I shuddered. "Then we should hurry. Everyone will be worried about me by now." I nudged Misty forward. She responded to my command without hesitation. Quickly she was at a full out run. To my surprise, Bayard's horse stayed with her stride for stride. We rounded the turn by the two tall pine trees and I saw the stone pillar that marked the corner of our property. I made it home. These were my fields, my pastures. A feeling of relief gave flight to the fear that had been with me most of the day. "Thank you God," I whispered, under my breath.

As we entered the drive, the man grabbed Misty's rein, pulling her to a stop. Two army officers were in the front yard. "Who are those men?"

"I have no idea. Part of our army, I suppose. They are wearing the beautiful gray Confederate uniforms."

"What do they want?"

"I do not have the slightest idea. Why not go and ask them?"

"I don't want to go up there with those men standin' 'round. I'll be back later for the gold." He turned to me, yanked a handful of hair at the back of my head, knocking my hat into my lap and pulling my face close to his. His lips curled to reveal yellow, tobacco stained teeth. "Don't try to cheat me, or ya'll be sorry. Ya don't want to know what I'll do if I have to come back and teach ya a lesson." His colorless eyes groped my face. Without warning his mouth covered mine. The taste of stale tobacco and whisky drenched my tongue. My stomach churned. His tongue descended deep into my mouth. His rough, calloused hand moved down to my throat, squeezing until he was choking me.

Fear quickened my heartbeat. I clamped my teeth down hard. My fist found its mark on the side of his face. He pulled away, releasing his grip on my throat. Blood trickled out of the side of his mouth. He wiped it on his sleeve. "Don't try to cheat me out of my money. If ya don't pay, I'll be back to finish what I've started."

I wiped my lips, spitting the vile taste out of my mouth.

He pushed me forward, letting go of Misty's bridle. "I'm goin' to be watchin' ya."

I kicked Misty harder than I had ever kicked her before. She obeyed in an instant, racing up the drive to the house and safety.

Before the Army men could see me, Mama invited them into the house for coffee. Toby signaled to me from behind the carriage house. I had no idea what was going on, but I turned Misty aside and rode to the carriage house.

"Quick, Miss Sarah, bring Misty in here. Them Army men gonna take all the horses."

"What? They cannot take our horses."

"Yes'um. They is. They says the horses is needed to fight the war. We hids most of the Arabians, but the

112

Saddle horses is all goin'. Somebody told the Army that we has the horses and they comes to carry them away. And there ain't nothin' we's can do 'bout it."

"Mama almost lost her life saving those horses, and now the Army is taking them. We should have sold them instead of bartering off our furniture. What about Shadow? Did he come home?"

"Yes'um. We hid him in the swamp with the other horses."

"Good. You keep the horses, and the rest of the animals out of sight, and I will have a talk with those army officers."

I entered the house through the kitchen and went up the backstairs to my room. Lily brought hot water and a fresh dress for me to change into. I needed to make a good impression on this cavalry officer.

"Captain Ward, I would like to introduce my daughter, Sarah, this is Captain Ward and Sergeant Miller. They are here to steal our horses." Mama was serving the last of our coffee in the parlor as I entered the room.

"Now, Mrs. Brighton, you should not put it that way. I am here to enlist your horses in the war effort. We need every animal we can get our hands on." The tall cavalry officer stood at the fireplace with his elbow on the mantel. The other man, who was seated on the settee opposite Mama, stood as I entered.

I smiled. "I thought we only needed to fear the Yankees. I did not realize our own army would put our lives at risk."

"We have our orders. We will leave one carriage horse, but all the others have to be taken. When the war is over you can appeal to Richmond for the return of your property." Captain Ward seemed to be in an awkward position, but not one that he would shirk for a smile from a Southern lady.

I realized our horses were lost to us, forever.

Chapter 10

On my way from the stable to the house, I gazed
down the lane, longing to see Cole, hoping not to
encounter Bayard lurking behind one of the trees. I had
caught glimpses of him from time to time, but he never
ventured onto our property. Once again, Rosewood
became my sanctuary. Today, the lane was empty.

Since Mama's accident, almost three months ago, Dr.
Bardlow came often to see her. His concern showed on
his face as Mama seemed to be getting worse instead of
better. Her cough hung on like an unwanted house guest.
Laudanum was the only drug that gave any relief to her
coughing spasms when they took hold of her. Winter drug
on from cold to bitter cold and spring was a long way off.

As I approached Dr. Bardlow, he said, "Sarah, I
wanted to talk to you before I left. I am quite concerned
about your mama. She does not appear to have the desire
to get well."

"I know. Daddy's death was more than she can
endure. The only hope that is keeping her alive is that
Cole will come home soon." I did not tell him about the
guilt that had been eating at her since the night she shot

Mr. Molack. In her mind's eye she could still see Molack's blood stains on the bricks at the foot of the front steps, even though she had slave girls scrubbing the bricks daily.

"A broken spirit is difficult to overcome. She needs something to get her mind active again. Give her a new direction in her life." The doctor put his black bag into his carriage, as he looked around to see if anyone was near enough to overhear his words before he continued. "Sarah, you know how poorly the war is going for our side. Our supply lines are cut, and our men are dying from lack of food and medical attention. Rosewood is in a very strategic location between Wilmington, our only open sea port, and the interior of the South. This is a good place for a hospital of sorts. We could set one up in your barn, and the farm can supply enough food to feed an army. Blockade runners have gotten good at getting in and out of the harbor. Their supplies could be brought by the river and distributed from here. It might be the trick that brings your mama around and you would be helping the South."

"How will the soldiers know we have a hospital here?"

"Actually, the request comes from General Lee. He asked me to find a suitable place." Dr. Bardlow searched my face for some reaction. His cloudy blue eyes, hidden behind wire frame spectacles, urged me to say yes.

Almost without thought, I agreed. "Yes. I think this will be just what Mama needs to get back into living again. We will do it."

"That's what I had hoped you would say. Now, you must remember, no one can be trusted. This has to remain a secret. The safety of our troops depends on it. Even Union spies dwell in fine mansions of the South."

"I cannot believe any of our friends would be a Yankee spy. But I will not say a word to anyone."

Barely a week later, Dr. Bardlow had turned our largest barn into a hospital. He came out daily under the guise of treating Mama. So it was that Rosewood became known as Safe Harbor. By day we worked a struggling plantation, but by night we became a haven for wounded, starving soldiers. Shrouded in a cloak of darkness, soldiers slipped in and out of our barn while slaves kept watch for Yankees.

Time drifted from winter, into spring, through a hot summer, a beautiful autumn and turned toward winter again. The news of the war became as dismal as the weather. Cold, bleak days covered the land. General Sherman marched five columns of Union troops across Georgia, cutting a fifty mile wide swath to the sea, destroying crops, railroads, bridges, and plantations. After the fall of Savannah on December 21, Sherman turned his troops north toward the Carolinas.

General Lee detached a division to defend Wilmington. Sounds of distant cannon fire rolled across our land. Mingling with peals of thunder came the rumbling of heavy wagons along River Road. Troops moved into position. Finally, the war was knocking on our door.

Frost crunched beneath my shoes as I walked from the house to the barn. I held my coat close around me to prevent the wind from snatching it, and holding me in its icy grip. The pewter-colored sky had threatened rain all day.

Inside the barn, men lay on hay and cotton bales which served as makeshift beds. Dr. Bardlow worked over a man lying on a plank table in the center of the barn. Two lanterns, hung from rafters, gave light to the operating area.

Dr. Bardlow did not look up as I approached. He continued bandaging the arm and chest of the young man on the table. "General Johnston has been ordered to lead a remnant of the able-bodied survivors from Hood's army against Sherman."

"General Johnston?" I asked. "Wasn't he killed at Shiloh the same day as Daddy?"

"No. This is a different General Johnston. As I was saying, he has a hit-and-run tactic that's tantamount to a gnat in a horse's ear, annoying but not lethal. So we can expect to get more casualties just like this young man. Somewhere, someway, I have to get my hands on more morphine. Your daddy's brandy just does not kill the pain enough if I should have to amputate. Look at this poor man. He will have a hangover when he wakes up and a headache to go along with the pain in his chest."

My stomach churned. The stench of blood, together with decaying flesh, assailed my nostrils. *"I will never get used to this,"* I thought, as I took my place beside the doctor to help hold the bandages. The young corporal, despite his drunken stupor, writhed in pain. My heart ached as tears filled my eyes. I thought about Cole far away, maybe hurt. My hand touched the corporal's face. His cheek felt smooth and soft. *He does not even shave yet,* I thought. *His mother must be worried about him.* "Will he live?" I whispered.

"Yes. He will live to fight another day." Dr. Bardlow wiped his hands on a towel. "Joseph, carry him over to that blanket. Be careful. I do not want to start him bleeding again. Sarah, have one of the women get me some hot water," Dr. Bardlow said, turning to me. "We do not know what causes all the infection, but I think it's best to wash everything in boiling water before I start on someone else. One can never be too clean. We wash the dishes when we eat off them, so I wash my cutting instruments after I use them. You remember that."

"I never planned to be a doctor. I came to fetch Joseph because the meal is ready to be carried out." I folded the bloody sheet and picked up bandages. "We cannot leave these things lying around, in case the Yankees come."

Dr. Bardlow took the linens out of my hands. "I will do this. By the way, I hear that Major Ward and his men will be calling on you shortly. He's a fine man. You might give him one of your warm smiles and flutter those long dark eyelashes at him. He's not married."

"Go on with you, Doctor." My face felt the heat of a

blush rising. "Where do you get such ideas? You will give this young man the wrong impression of me." Dr. Bardlow and I walked over to the wounded man. I covered him with a blanket.

"Oh, no, miss. We all know who you are. An angel sent from God to help us poor soldiers." The wounded soldier tried to smile through his pain. His sandy blond hair was matted with sweat, even though the coldness of winter penetrated the barn.

"That's the brandy talking. I am not an angel, just a Southerner like you. Rest now and get yourself strong, so you can go home to your mama."

The corporal closed his eyes, quickly falling into a restless sleep. Dr. Bardlow motioned for me to follow him away from the wounded man.

"You have done a wonderful job here. I could not have helped all these men if it was not for you and your mama. The South owes you a debt of gratitude."

"In that case, tell Major Ward to give us back our horses. I remember him. He was the one who came last year and took our horses for the Confederate cause. He did not seem to notice me then, and I do not think fluttering my eyelashes will make him notice me now."

Safe Harbor had been empty for a few days. I busied myself by doing stable chores, waiting for the next wave of wounded men. Major Ward and his men had been spotted some miles away. We made the barn ready for them.

The knock sounded loudly at the door. I answered it. "Major Ward, do come in and warm yourself by the fire. We have been expecting you. Some of our people reported seeing you coming up the lane. Supper will be served shortly in the dining room. Cots are being made ready for you and your officers in the guest rooms. We have set plank tables in the barn for your men. I know the barn is not a very pleasant place, but it is dry."

A smile of recognition flashed across his face, but he did not acknowledge that he remembered me. "Do not apologize. What you and Mrs. Brighton are doing is a kindness we will never forget. My men are worn out, cold, and hungry. You have given us a place to rest for a while. What more can we ask?"

"We are proud to be able to help our boys who are so bravely fighting against those blue devils."

"As for my officers and I, we must decline your gracious offer. We will take our meal with the men and sleep in the barn as well. I have never asked more of my men than I am willing to give. I won't start now. However, your kind offer is tempting. If we could have met at another time, under different circumstances, I would have loved to come calling on you."

I smiled and could feel my face grow hot. "I am sure I would have been delighted. But for the matters of today, we have had word that Yankees are moving through the swamp, heading this way. They should be here before noon tomorrow."

"We will be gone by then. We have no time to waste. General Johnston is moving onto Goldsboro, and we will be meeting up with him. The Yankee troops will undoubtedly be slowed by the swamp. I know we were. But if they are coming this way, they know about Goldsboro." He tipped his hat and bowed as he took his leave.

A big, black kettle of hearty Southern stew filled with plenty of beef, carrots, potatoes, and green beans was carried out to the barn. I carried a basket of hot biscuits, butter and jam, while Lily and Toby carried a bucket of milk and a bucket of water. I watched Major Ward talk with his men, showing concern for their welfare. I wondered if Cole showed such an interest in the people of his command. Dr. Bardlow was correct in one thing, Major Ward was a fine looking man. His hazel eyes danced as the light from the lantern illuminated his well-defined features. His thin, Greek nose and square jaw softened with his warm smile. *Yes,* I thought. *If this was another time I would let you come calling on me.*

Darkness was still hanging in the sky when Lily woke me. "Toby say Yankees is comin' up Mill Creek road."

"Already? Quick, get my dress." I sprang out of bed and dressed faster than I had ever dressed before. "Run and tell Toby to put the horses in the corral in the thicket and to put feed bags on the horses to keep them quiet."

When I got to the barn, Major Ward and his men had already left. Last night's rain made it easy to follow their tracks in the mud. I ordered some of our men to run the milk cows over the tracks to obliterate them. I had several women clean the barn of any traces of bandages, blankets, or anything that would indicate that men had stayed there. I burnt candles to rid the barn of the stench of blood. I felt certain that everything was in order when I saw Major Ward running from the ravine.

"We are trapped. The bridge is blocked by a Yankee guard and a patrol is coming up the road. You and your mother stay in the house. We may have to make a fight of it."

"No. We will be caught in the middle. Quick, get all your men into the house. The attic is a safe place." I turned to Jacob, Lily's son, "Run and keep an eye out. Let me know when the Yankees turn onto the lane. Hurry!"

The last man got into the house. Once again, the cows were herded up the road behind the house to erase the soldier's tracks. Inside, the men removed their muddy boots before Leah hustled them upstairs to the attic. Women washed the kitchen floor and the stairs. Thick blankets were hung over the windows. The soldiers sat quietly on the floor. All was ready. We waited. My insides quivered with the heightened sense of fear. All these years of war, the fighting was always someplace else. Now, it was coming up the road. I had no idea what to do. *Act normal*, I thought. *Do not do anything to draw suspicion or give those devils an excuse to search the house.*

Mama and I were about to take bread, cheese, apples, and water to the attic when a knock came at the door. My heart beat like a hammer on an anvil in my chest. We left the food on the back stairs as we rushed to the entry hall. Seth's fearful expression turned to surprise as he opened the door. Reverend Tadwell and his wife, Martha, stood at the threshold.

When Mrs. Tadwell saw Mama, she announced in her cheeriest voice, "We have missed you in church, lately. Tom and I thought it would be nice to come to visit. But we did not expect to see so many Yankees on the road."

"Yankees! Are they close?" Mama asked.

"At the old mill."

Mama turned to me, "Sarah, did you hear that? Yankees are at the old mill."

"Do you think they are coming this way?" I asked.

"Yes," Pastor Tadwell answered. "And soon."

"Do come into the parlor," Mama invited. "Sarah, have Seth bring some tea and cakes. Then, dear, you need to tend to things upstairs." Turning to Mrs. Tadwell, Mama continued, "Sarah is the one who is running the plantation these days, since Mr. Molack left us without help. My health is so delicate, I can do very little." Mama seated herself stately on the settee. She looked pale in the gray morning light. Dark circles had formed under her green eyes and her autumn hair was giving way to silver strands. "I cannot seem to rid myself of this dreadful cough. It makes sitting in church impossible. I never know when a spasm will come upon me. It is so embarrassing if I should have to leave during the sermon." Mama continued to talk as if we did not have an attic full of Confederate soldiers or as if the Yankees were not about to descend upon us.

I took my leave as quickly as possible without being rude. Once outside the parlor I lifted my skirts, and ran as fast as I could down the hall to the back stairs and down into the kitchen, thinking all the while what Mr. Jolette would have said if he saw me running through the house. Breathlessly, I entered the cooking room. "Mama wants tea served in the parlor. Pastor and Mrs. Tadwell are here."

"We knows. Seth told us. What we gonna do if'n they sees the soldiers?" Lily asked, wringing her hands in her apron.

"I am not worried if the Tadwells see the soldiers. It is the Yankees that I am worried about. They are at the crossroads already. Mama and I did not have time to carry the food up to the attic. Lily, you take it up and tell everyone to sit very still."

Toby knocked at the kitchen door. "Miss Sarah, them horses all in the safe corral. Michael stayin' in the thicket makin' sure no one sees 'em."

"Good. Now everyone stay calm. The Yankees will not hurt you."

"What 'bout you, Miss Sarah? You gonna be safe?" Leah asked.

"Yes, Leah. Mama and I will be fine."

Jacob bolted into the kitchen. "Dr. Bardlow's here. Coimin' up the drive."

"What next? Jacob run and tell him that we have the soldiers in the attic. Leah, I guess we are going to have three more for breakfast."

"Yes'um. I wants to tell you most of the food's been put into the rounds in the walls of the library so the Yankees don't get it."

"Good. It looks like you have everything well in hand. I will rejoin our guests in the parlor and wait for the enemy."

Our guests engaged in polite conversation as we waited for the Yankees to arrive. Mama kept looking out the window. I could tell she grew more and more agitated as the clock ticked off the minutes. Seth brought in a tray with bowls of porridge topped with applesauce for everyone. The rest of the breakfast consisted of muffins with butter and peach jam and hot tea. This delightful meal was served in the parlor.

Reverend Tadwell gave the blessing. "Lord thank you

for this day, the food that is here before us and the friends gathered here in the house. Keep everyone gathered in this house safe from our enemies. Your will be done in all things. In Jesus name we pray. Amen."

Everyone agreed with a whispered, "Amen."

Mama served the tea with trembling hands. "I do not know what is the matter with me, I cannot stop shaking. Sarah, have Seth bring in some wood for a fire. It is cold in here. Martha, do you feel the cold air?" Mama held the tea cup with both hands to keep them warm.

"Well, a little. A fire would be nice." Martha Tadwell settled back onto the sofa with her bowl of porridge. "Breakfast with friends, such a lovely idea. We left the house so early this morning that we didn't have time to make our own breakfast."

Mama walked to the window again. "Sarah," she motioned for me to come closer to her as she whispered. "Why are the women not scrubbing the bricks?"

"The rain, Mama. We cannot have women scrubbing in the rain."

"That does not matter. If the Yankees see all that blood, they will know what I have done. Get those girls out there, now."

Before I could answer, Mama started coughing. The spell shook her violently, until blood spittle soaked her handkerchief. She was gasping for breath. With the help of Reverend Tadwell, Dr. Bardlow took Mama upstairs to her room. I ran ahead of them to prop up the pillows. When the men laid her on the bed, I covered her with a quilt. Dr. Bardlow gave her a large dose of laudanum.

"She will rest now. The laudanum will calm the coughing." Dr. Bardlow ushered us to the door, closing it behind him.

Martha stood at the window when we returned to the parlor. "They are turning onto the drive," she said in a stone cold voice.

An instant surge of heat raced through my body and I

seemed to feel the blood banging against the ends of my fingertips. "I guess I will go out to meet them. See if Yankees really breathe fire like all the stories say."

"We will go with you," Dr. Bardlow offered, taking my hand.

We stood on the gallery as the soldiers marched up to the house. These men were war torn, ragged, and weary, but they were not as depressed and emaciated looking as our troops. The Yankees still marched in rank and file, heads held high. They were the conquerors coming to loot the spoils of the vanquished land. My mouth turned to cotton as the young captain halted his horse in front of the steps, the very spot where Mama killed Mr. Molack.

"We have orders to burn every plantation. You have fifteen minutes to get your things and clear the manor before we set the torch to it."

"Are the mighty Yankees warring against women these days?" I asked, stepping forward. "This land belongs to me and my mother."

"Who are you?" The officer pointed to Dr. Bardlow.

"This is Dr. Bardlow and Reverend and Mrs. Tadwell. They have come to visit. They do not live here. My mama is upstairs in bed. She is very ill."

"What's wrong with her?" asked the Yankee.

"She has cholera," Dr. Bardlow lied.

Reverend Tadwell gave him a sideways glance, but said nothing.

Dr. Bardlow continued, "She is too ill to be moved. If you set fire to the house, you will be killing an innocent woman."

The look on the captain's face was that of surprise and doubt.

I invited, "If you doubt his word, you may go up to her room and see for yourself."

Mama coughed several times.

"No. No. I believe you." The young officer slowly

backed his horse away. His men started backing away on impulse. The Captain gave orders to his men. "Let the manor stand, but burn the barns and the stable. Torch the fields. Round up all the animals. Take all the food you can find."

"How are we supposed to live if you take everything?" I shouted.

"I have my orders. I can't leave anything behind to be used by the Rebels. Oh, sergeant, make sure you destroy the gardens."

"Yes, sir," the sergeant responded.

"That horse and carriage belongs to the Reverend and Mrs. Tadwell, and that one is the doctor's. They need them to call on the sick and dying. Surely even a Yankee would not deny the comfort of God's word to the dying or medical treatment to the sick," I said.

The captain smiled at me. "You are as bold as brass. Not one Rebel has spoken up to me the way you have. I will give you the horses and buggies to help the sick and dying. And I will give the doctor and reverend a written pass for safe passage through our lines to tend to their people. However, in return, you must have supper with me tonight."

"I would sooner dine with Satan."

"Ah, ah, ah, I have done a favor for you. That is no way to repay a kindness. I will be here at eight."

"If you want to be fed, you better leave something for my cook to fix."

The captain laughed as he rode away in the direction of the fields.

White smoke billowed from the outbuildings as one by one they were set aflame. The old wood burned with intense heat, barely giving heed to the fact it was wet. However, since the rain had soaked the orchards and fields, they were impossible to burn. Last of all, smoke spilled out of the carriage house. Their work completed, the Yankees bivouacked for the night in our front yard.

I shouted in frustration, "I will not dine with that Yankee! He has destroyed Rosewood."

"Hush, child. You must have dinner with the captain," Martha Tadwell urged. "While you are entertaining the Yankees, Dr. Bardlow and Tom will clean out the attic."

"What?"

"You heard me. Now scoot along and make yourself pretty for your guest."

A table and two chairs were set on the verandah outside the glass doors leading into the hall next to the ballroom. This gallery overlooked the knot garden, which had been thoroughly trampled under the hooves of the Yankee's horses. It was on the opposite side of the manor from the back stairs leading into the attic.

My work worn black dress had been hemmed to make working easier. Now, having on layers of petticoats, the white lace showed from beneath the dress. I wrapped a white batiste collar shawl around my shoulders, pinned my hair up in curls atop my head, and forced myself to smile.

Surprisingly, the Yankee captain's demeanor was charming. His New England accent reminded me of Aunt Maggie's and I could not resist smiling.

"You seem to find me amusing," he commented.

"No. Not you, but rather how you say your sentences, the sound of your words. You remind me of my Aunt. She came from Boston."

"Oh. What's her name? Perhaps I know the family."

"No. You would not. They are quite wealthy."

"And I, being a Yankee captain, am not. My, you are a bit of a snob."

"Well, are you? Wealthy that is?"

"No."

"Then I am not a snob. I am just telling the truth."

He smiled. "I guess I deserved that."

At each sound I tensed. Was that the back door? Are those the footsteps of Yankee soldiers walking around the house? Or are they Confederate soldiers leaving the safety of the attic? I picked at my food, too nervous to eat.

"You seem to be on edge," the captain noticed.

"I believe this is called giving aid to the enemy. When the South wins, I may be arrested for having dinner with a Yankee."

He laughed. "You do have a sense of humor. Do you not understand the war is all but over? The North has routed the Confederate army. Lee is on the run. It's only a matter of time before Lee surrenders."

Because we have given everything to the war, I did not want to hear of our losing. Our entire way of life is at stake. Daddy, and perhaps Cole, gave their lives to preserve the South. We cannot lose now. I turned to the captain, "Sir, I may be compelled to dine with you, but I will not be forced to hear about the war. Let us speak of more pleasant things."

As the clouds cleared, I saw shadows moving along the edge of the hedge row. I dropped my fork with a clatter. "Oh, how clumsy of me," I said.

The captain reached to retrieve it.

Seth served the next course of roast pork with potatoes in herb sauce. "Dr. Bardlow is done." He rolled his black eyes.

"What does that mean?" The captain asked.

"That means that my mother is sleeping for the evening and that the Reverend and Mrs. Tadwell will probably be leaving shortly. It has been a long day. Seth, see if the Tadwells would like to stay the night. It is too dark and stormy for them to be going back into town at this late hour."

"Yes'um." Seth left the captain and me alone.

I felt pleased with myself that I had deceived the Yankees. I could have been a spy for the Confederate army. I could have played the cloak and dagger game with the best of them. I could have. . . .

"Sir, sorry to interrupt," a corporal announced, as he raced up the steps. "A Rebel unit has been seen crossing the river."

"Miss Brighton, thank you for a most pleasant evening." The captain rose to leave.

"I must say, Yankee manners are quite rude. A Southern gentleman would never allow a lady to dine alone. After all, it was at your request that the servants went to all this trouble." My mind reeled. Grasping at any argument to keep him from leaving, I licked my lips and fluttered my eyelashes at him.

"Well now, Miss Brighton, I do not believe you are offering what I think. So as enticing as your suggestion is, I am still an officer in the Union Army, and we are still at war." Turning to the corporal, he said, "Tell the sergeant to break camp. We will catch the Johnny Rebs on the other side of the river. Be quick about it." He turned back to me. "It is difficult to think of you as the enemy. I would like to think you enjoyed my company. Maybe we will see each other again." He lifted my hand to his lips and kissed it. Then he followed the corporal into the night.

In the early light of the next morning, Dr. Bardlow and I surveyed the devastation of my land. The enemy carried away everything they could get their hands on. Only the manor remained untouched because the Blue Devils feared catching cholera more than their greed dictated. My own wagons had been loaded with my goods and driven away. Cows, chickens, pigs, and goats were all herded down the road. The Union Army had moved over us like Moses leading the children of Israel out of Egypt, taking the spoils of the nation with them. The land looked as if an onslaught of locust had descended upon it, devouring everything. In the Yankee wake came the black horde of freed slaves looting the rest of the slim pickings. Rosewood lay in ruin.

Tears stung my eyes as we walked along the muddy road toward the burned out stable. The smell of smoke and charred wood lingered on the damp air.

Dr. Bardlow broke the silence. "We will have to close Safe Harbor."

"No. The Yankees have done their worst. They will not be back this way. Our troops are safer now than before. We will keep the hospital. With the war so close at hand, we may be busier than ever."

Reverend Tadwell came walking up the road from the other direction. "I could not sleep, so I thought I would have a closer look at the damage. The carriage house can be fixed with a little work. The exterior structure is sound. The Yankees did not get all the chickens. I heard some roosting in the ravine. You still have the Arabians that you hid in the thicket. So you see, all is not lost."

Dr. Bardlow rubbed his chin. "I believe that's two stallions and three mares. Good breeding stock."

"Well, then, I guess I start over. But first, Reverend Tadwell, explain to me why you and Mrs. Tadwell came out here yesterday. How did you know about the soldiers in the attic?"

The tall, thin man smiled. "Sarah, I have known about Safe Harbor since the very beginning. Martha and I thought you might need some help. It's as simple as that. As far as knowing the soldiers were in the attic, Martha guessed. Her woman's intuition I suppose. Now, we can stand here and talk about what needs to be done, or we can get started."

CHAPTER 11

"It's over! It's over!" Shouts and gun shots came from a lone rider charging up the lane. In the distance, the chiming of church bells rang from Mill Creek and from Gray Hill beyond the river. Across the land peals echoed. The hooves of the lone horse clattered on the bricks as the rider rode up the drive. Breathlessly, he shouted, "The war's over! Lee surrendered to General Grant in Virginia. General Johnston surrendered to Sherman at Raleigh. Yahoo! The war is over!"

"Can we believe him?" a young soldier asked as he stepped out of the rebuilt carriage house and stood beside me.

"Listen to the bells. I have never heard them ring other than on Sunday. It has to be true. You can go home and be with your family." I felt joy as if I could dance on air. The killing and bloodshed had ended. We did not have to live in fear anymore. But at the same time, an emptiness beyond words crept into the pit of my stomach. This war was all for nothing. Daddy died for nothing!

Stunned, the soldier's face took on the shadow of death. He said the words that no Southerner wanted to hear. "Lee surrendered. That means we lost." Hopelessness clung to his voice.

"But we are still alive. Go home. Go home to the people who love you."

Dr. Bardlow came out of the carriage house wiping his hands on a towel. "Thank God. Did not know how much longer we could go on. Sarah, run up and tell your mama. She has been waiting to hear this news for a long time."

"Is it true, Miss Sarah? Is what that man says true? Did them Yankees win?" Seth asked, as I entered the house through the front door.

"Yes, Seth, it is true. I guess you are free. All of you are free," I said, as the house slaves gathered in the entry hall. At first, silence. Then a resounding hallelujah swept through the slaves as they realized what I had said.

"Freedom, sweet Jesus, freedom," Lily started to sing. Soon the others joined in, clapping their hands and dancing around the hall.

"I never thought I'd see the day I'd be free," Seth said to me.

"Neither did I." I patted his arm and slowly climbed the stairs. "Neither did I."

"Mama, are you sleeping?" I opened her bedroom door slowly.

"No, dear, just resting. I can hear the church bells from across the river and I saw the rider. Is it over? Is it really over?"

"Yes. Lee surrendered to Grant in Virginia, and Johnston surrendered to Sherman at Raleigh."

"Now, Cole will come home."

"Do not get your hopes up, Mama. It has been years since anyone has heard from him. So many men were killed at Shiloh. We do not know if Cole was one of them."

"No. He will be coming home." She turned her face to the window. "I will see my first born before I die."

"Do not talk that way. You will get better when we

have a warm summer. Not all this rain to chill the bones. Everyone gets depressed when the rain does not let up for days at a time. But when you are outside in your garden this summer and when the air is fresh and warm, you will feel much better."

"Yes, dear, you are right. Summer will bring new life into these weary bones." She closed her eyes. I quietly left the room.

The song of the slaves woke me the next morning, as they came to say goodbye. Freedom overshadowed the insecurity of not having a home or possessions. Freedom became a commodity more precious than life itself. The words of their song, a song I had heard many times before, took on a new meaning.

When Israel was in Egypt's land,
Let my people go!
Oppressed so hard they could not stand,
Let my people go!

Go down, Moses,
Way down in Egypt land;
Tell ol' Pharaoh,
Let my people go!

Thus spoke the Lord, bold Moses said,
Let my people go!
If not, I'll smite your first-born dead,
Let my people go!

Go down, Moses,
Way down in Egypt land;
Tell ol' Pharaoh,
Let my people go!

No more shall they in bondage toil,
Let my people go!
Let them come out with Egypt's spoil,
Let my people go!

Go down, Moses,
Way down in Egypt land;
Tell ol' Pharaoh,
Let my people go!

I stood on the verandah as the people of the plantation came and stood on the bricks in front of the manor. Their song slowly became silent. I knew that this was the end of the way of life as I had known it. Seth broke the silence.

"I gots nowhere to go. I was born on this land, and I is gonna die on this land. Please, Miss Sarah, tell ol' Seth he can stay." Tears glistened in his black eyes. "My Rose is buried behind the slave quarters. I wants to be there too."

"Of course, you can stay. Anyone who wants can stay. Lily, you and Jacob have a home here for as long as you like."

"No. We is gonna have a good life. Joseph and us is gonna gets a place of our own. Them Yankees say the government is givin' forty acres and a mule to every freed black man." In one hand Lily held a cloth bundle holding everything she and Jacob owned. Her other hand closed in a tight grip on Jacob's wrist.

Sadness stole into my heart. "I wish you well." I walked down the steps and gave Jacob a hug. "You be a good boy, you hear."

"I'll stay," Leah said. "But just 'til your mama is feelin' better and till Master Cole comes home. And one more thin' I wants from you. I wants to learn to read."

I sucked in my breath. "You know it's against the law to teach a slave to read."

"I ain't a slave no more."

I winced at her words. "I guess you are right." Cole's teasing words about the fine plantation ladies doing their own work tugged at my memory. "And you can teach me how to cook, since I will have to be doing that for myself from now on."

That was the harshest reality of the war. I would have to do the work of slaves if I wanted to survive. It was not if I wanted to work, it was now that I had to work. I retreated to the manor before my emotions reduced me to begging the slaves to stay. My footsteps echoed as I walked through the empty house, which only emphasized an inner emptiness that I did not know how to fill.

As the months passed with hard work, little to eat, and still no word from Cole, I became determined more than ever to bring the plantation back to its former elegance. I sold off everything of value, except for the horses. Most of the jewelry that Mama and I had hidden under the sycamores tree became payment for men to clear the fields and prune orchards. Gold goblets paid for the repairs on the stables and barns and feed for the animals. However, cotton or tobacco plants cost more than I had. I still needed to pay the loan from the bank. Men with carpetbags of money came into our town giving loans to start new crops. Sometimes the devil comes dressed like a friend. Mr. Sharply encouraged Mama to sign for a loan. She could pay him back and have seed money for the new crops. At harvest we could pay back the carpetbaggers. I tried to talk Mama out of putting her name onto the paper, but failed. Little did anyone know that this was the death knell for Rosewood.

One September day, when the sun beat down so hot I thought hell might be cooler, young Tom Wells, the postmaster's son, came racing up on his black horse to the manor. "Miss Sarah, Miss Sarah, you have a letter. It's from Missouri!"

My heart lunged into my throat as I ran to meet the breathless young man. "Is it from Cole?"

"Not sure. Looks like his hand."

I grabbed the letter. "It is! It's Cole's writing." I tore the envelope open with trembling hands.

"What does he say? Is he coming home?"

"Yes! Yes! He is alive and coming home. Cole's alive! ,I have to tell Mama." I lifted my skirt and sprinted toward the house, calling over my shoulder, "Thank you, Tom. Thank you for bringing us such good news."

CHAPTER 12

Wednesday afternoons brought the arrival of Reverend and Mrs. Tadwell bearing their cheery news from the ladies sewing circle. Pastor Tadwell gave excerpts from his Sunday sermons. He led a short Bible study, offered prayers and accompanied Mrs. Tadwell in rousing hymns. Martha Tadwell had a voice that could fill a concert hall. Most Wednesdays I stayed just long enough to be sociable before excusing myself to continue my work.

This afternoon, as I left the room, I heard Mrs. Tadwell comment, "She is such a dear child."

"She is not a child anymore," Mama corrected. "She is twenty."

"She does not look that old. I suppose it is because she is so small and her womanly figure is hidden beneath that loose, black dress and apron. Such a shame, she is a pretty girl. Where will she find a husband? So many young men were lost." Martha clicked her tongue. "Sarah's almost past marrying age. She may have to settle for what she can get."

I had heard enough. I headed out to the stables. The

horses loved me and the attention I gave them. "I will never settle for just anyone. I want to marry for love," I said aloud. I remembered what Cousin Amy Ann had said the Christmas before the war. Men loved her for what she had, not for herself. "Will that be true?" I asked Misty, as I brushed her coat. "Men won't love me because I do not have a large dowry? I cannot stay here at Rosewood all my life. What will happen when Cole marries and brings his bride to be mistress of Rosewood Hall? That will never do. I will have to leave. I could not bear to be called the spinster sister or the maiden aunt. Where will I go? What will I do?" I thought of the freed slaves leaving the plantation with only what they could carry, and some had only the clothes on their backs. Tears filled my eyes as I started to rake the stalls, shoveling the old straw and manure into the wheelbarrow and dumping it in the garden behind the old hen house.

The Yankees had tried to destroy the gardens by trampling the young plants. But seeds have a will to live. With water and care the gardens sprouted again. Of course, the plants were not in nice rows, but they were growing.

With dirty, calloused hands, I wiped my face when I heard Mrs. Tadwell call my name. "Sarah, we are leaving."

I pushed the empty wheelbarrow back to the carriage house, dipped the corner of my apron into a water bucket to wash my tear stained face before I emerged through the double doors.

"Father wants to be home before this storm breaks," Martha said, looking at the thick black clouds hanging heavy in the sky. As I approached, she turned toward me. "Oh, you have been crying."

"No. It is the dust from the horses that got into my eyes."

"You will not have to work so hard when Cole gets home. He can do all the heavy chores. Then you won't need to dress like a darkie anymore."

"Come along, Mother," Reverend Tadwell called. "This storm is not waiting for you to stand around talking."

"I have to go, dear." Martha took my hands in hers. "Your mama is resting. Leah said she would take supper up to her so you do not have to rush. We will see you next Wednesday. Take heart, it will not be much longer."

The carriage tilted to one side as Mrs. Tadwell got in. I watched them go down the brick drive and out onto the dirt road. As always, my eyes scanned the lane for anyone walking or on horseback. The lane was empty.

Darkness had crept across the charred fields before my work was finished. I returned to the manor in an eerie twilight caused by the approaching storm. Leah, putting away the last of the cooking pots, turned as I entered the kitchen. "I heated some water for you in the bath house. Clean clothes and towels is on the table. You gets yourself washed up 'fore you comes to eat. Seth's gone to his room. Your mama's been fed. Biscuits and gravy and a slab of ham is on the stove. I'm goin' to bed. See you in the mornin'." She hung her apron on a hook by the back door and left.

"Goodnight, Leah." I took the towels, threadbare robe and night dress, and drug myself down the whistle walk to the brick building outside the back door. The bath house used to be the old kitchen when the hall was first built. Daddy had moved the kitchen into the house and turned the old one into a laundry and bath. Daddy, Cole, and even Mr. Molack would bathe in the copper tub after a day of hard labor. Now that I did all the work, I loved to soak in the hot water. Using the bath house was much easier than carrying the hot water buckets up to my room, filling the tub, and after my bath emptying it by carrying the water outside again.

Water boiled in copper kettles hanging in the open hearth over a crackling fire. The huge tub stood in the middle of the windowless room on the brick floor waiting for me to fill it with half hot water from the kettles and half cold water from the buckets that sat beside the tub. Large drying racks, two chairs, a small round table beside the tub holding a candle and yellow soap, and a water pump were the only other furnishings in the room. I hung the towels and clothes over the front rack near the fire and poured the hot water into the tub. Sitting on a chair, I unbuttoned my shoes and pulled them off. The rough, uneven floor felt warm. Slowly I unbuttoned my dress. When I stood up, the dress draped over the chair. I couldn't remember when I had been so tired. Each day there seemed to be more work to be done than the day before.

I climbed into the tub and immersed slowly into the deliciously hot, soothing water. I let it massage deep into my aching bones and muscles. Steam rose in circular swirls to the soot covered ceiling. The only light came from the glowing flames of the fire. My body melted into serenity.

Drip, drip, drip came the disturbing sound. I opened my eyes to see water dripping from the sooty beam into my bath. Ripples of soot undulated their way to the sides of the tub. I did not know how long I had been asleep, but it must have been quite some time because the bath water had already turned cold. Quickly I jumped up, stepped out of the tub onto the chilly bricks, and poured the bucket of cold water over my shoulders to rinse off the soot. My teeth chattered. Dim embers in the hearth, a mere remembrance of the fire, jealously guarded what little light they gave. I made my way to the rack where the towels and my clothes hung.

"No. I cannot believe this. They are soaked." Fumbling with the Lucifer, I finally lit the candle and looked up to see where the water came from as I felt a sooty drip splash on my forehead. "Oh, no, the roof is leaking. One more thing to add to my list of things to do. Fix the roof." Another drip splashed on my shoulder as I moved closer to the fire. I threw a few small pieces of wood into the hearth, hoping to bring the fire back to life while I evaluated my choices. *One, I could put on the wet, soot streaked robe and night dress. Two, I could put on the dirty work dress again. Or three, I could make a dash for the house naked, hoping no one sees me.* The third option did not appeal to me at all. Actually, none of the suggestions did. But I had to do something. I could not stay in the bath house all night. At last I opted to put on only the thin robe and run for the manor.

Slowly opening the door and leaving the warmth of the bath house behind, I stepped out into the cold night rain and ran toward the light shining through the half opened kitchen door. Suddenly, from the shadows emerged a tall figure wearing a hat pulled down to his eyes and a rain slicker. He carried saddlebags slung over his shoulder and a rifle in his right hand. I gasped and turned to run back to the security of the bath house.

"Sarah," came the unmistakable voice.

"Cole!" I turned around and ran into his arms. He opened his coat to receive me and closed it around me as we let the rain wash over us. "Is it really you? We have been waiting for so long. I did not think you would ever come home."

"I sent a letter telling you I was alive and I would be home as soon as possible."

"Yes. But the war has been over for months." I looked into his face lit by the shaft of light coming through the kitchen door. His black hair fell to his shoulders. A full beard and mustache covered the lower portion of his face but those gray eyes were still the same. My fingers touched his face and traced the contour of his cheek. "I cannot believe it is really you."

"I can tell you weren't expecting me tonight."

"What?"

"Your clothes or should I say lack of them."

"Oh, no!" In my joy of seeing Cole, I had forgotten that I had on only a wet, threadbare robe. "Do not look! Turn you back. I can explain but let me get into the house first." As I ran to the door, I could hear Cole's melodious laughter. *I will never live this down*, I thought. I mounted the back stairs and ran down the hall to my room. I quickly put on a black dress with a white shawl wrapped over my shoulders.

When I returned to the kitchen, Cole had rekindled the fire in the fireplace. His slicker and hat hung on a chair to dry. He stood in front of the fire with his back toward me. His shirt was made of tan leather with fringe along the arms, and the trousers were his heavy Confederate gray uniform, a bit worse for wear. His muddy boots were by the fire with wet socks draped over them. Cole stood barefoot.

"Don't just stand there, come in," he said.

"How did you know I was here?"

"I can hear you."

"But I was quiet."

"Only to someone who lives in the comforts of a house. On the frontier you would have been shot by an Indian five minutes ago."

I looked at him in wide-eyed disbelief. "Then I shall be glad I am not on the frontier." I walked to the hearth to warm myself by the fire. "Cole, Mama has waited for such a long time. It is not fair to make her wait another minute. We must go up to her room straight away." I put my hand on his arm. "But I need caution you. She is not well. So do not be taken aback when you see her."

"I need to put on some clean clothes and shave first. I hoped to be rid of all this before I saw her." He put his hand on his chin and rubbed his beard.

"She will not care what you look like. All she will see is her son."

"The master of the house looking like a beggar, but you're right. I want to see her as much as she wants to see me. I've missed both of you more than words can ever say. You were never far from my thoughts."

I lit a lamp and led the way up the back stairs.

"Mama, are you asleep?" I asked, as I opened the door to her room. "I have brought someone to see you."

"Mama," Cole said, stepping out from behind me.

"Cole, my boy! Is it really you or am I still dreaming?"

"Yes, Mama, it's really me."

"Praise God, you are home." Tears immediately glistened in her green eyes. "Now I can die in peace. God has brought you home to me."

"Do not talk about dying." He rushed to her bed. Taking her frail hand in his, he kissed it. "I have come home to take care of you and Sarah. Everything is going to be as it once was. You are going to get well again."

"Your daddy is dead," she whispered.

"I know. I held him in my arms. He asked me to tell you that he loved you and Sarah." Cole's voice broke. He sat on the edge of the bed, took a deep breath, and continued. "He told me to take care of you. I cannot do that if you die. I promised Daddy and I never go back on my word."

She smiled slightly. "I am so glad you are home, but I cannot stay awake. Dr. Bardlow gave me some sleeping powders to take when I get a coughing spell at night so I can rest. I have taken some and now I cannot stay awake. We can talk in the morning. I will sleep better tonight than I have in a long time."

"I will sit with you until you fall asleep," Cole said, caressing her hand.

"I will leave the lamp here on the table for you and go down to the kitchen to fix something to eat," I whispered. "You might find some dry clothes in your closet. Mama could not bring herself to give them away. Surely something still fits."

"She's sleeping," Cole said, entering the kitchen, wearing a pair of black, wool trousers and a white, ruffled, long-sleeved shirt. The top buttons were undone and sleeves rolled up. "It seems that I lost a little weight." He laughed. "I never liked my clothes too snug, anyway."

I stood warming myself by the fire. I had divided the biscuits and gravy and ham, and I scrambled three eggs and put the food on two plates. "Sit down, supper is ready. Do you want milk or water? There is no coffee or tea."

"Water is fine. How sick is she? What does Dr. Bardlow say?"

"He says it is consumption. He thought that the warm weather would make her feel better, but it has not."

Cole looked at the food on his plate. "Where did you learn to cook?"

"I had to. There are a lot of things I had to learn, like taking care of the horses."

He reached across the table, took my hands and turning them over to look at the callouses on my palms. "I never thought I would see these hands with callouses. I'm here now. I'll take care of all the heavy work."

"Good. The roof on the bath house needs fixing." I took my hands out of his and started to eat. "Do you remember the last meal we had together in this house?"

"It was June 21, 1861, just before Daddy and I rode out to join the army in the Shenandoah Valley. A long time ago."

"How foolish I was to think the war would not affect us here at Rosewood. Everything has changed. I heard you tell Mama that you were with Daddy when he died."

Cole did not look up but continued to stare at his food, moving his eggs around with his fork. "I held him in my arms."

"I am glad you were there. I thought he died alone. I could not bear the thought of my Daddy lying in the mud alone. Tell me about it, if you can."

At first Cole sat quiet. The memory of that dreadful day was obviously running through his mind. Slowly he began to speak. "You should have seen the meadow, peaceful, beautiful, and bordered by a grove of peach trees in bloom. Then all hell broke out. We had misjudged how many Yankee troops there were. By the end of the first day, the meadow was covered with bodies, both theirs and ours.

"I looked for Daddy in our ranks, and when I couldn't find him, one of the soldiers said that he saw him over by the Methodist meeting house early in the afternoon. I crawled over bodies to the meeting house and found Daddy leaning against the side of the building, his hands bloody from holding his stomach. I knew immediately that all hope . . . ." Cole's voice faded into a whisper. After a moment, he continued.

"Daddy said he knew I would find him. He waited for me. He held out his bloody hands and shoved his ring and pocket watch into my hand, closing my fingers around them. 'You are the master of Rosewood now,' he said. 'Do what you think is right. Take care of your mama and our beloved Sarah. Tell them both that I love them dearly, and that my last thoughts were of them and home.' Then he said something about some gold. 'Sarah has the gold.' He started coughing. He whispered, 'Love you,' and he died."

I sat quietly for a long time. Finally, I said, "Gold? We do not have any gold. Goodness knows if we had gold, we would not have had to sell everything of value just to stay alive. And if we had gold, we certainly would not have taken out that dreadful loan to rebuild Rosewood."

"That's what he said. He pulled me close to him and said, 'Sarah has the gold.' Those were his last words before he died in my arms. I carried him back behind our lines to the hospital tent where Uncle Chad served as a field doctor."

"I remember the day we buried Daddy. Some plantation owner supplied ice for our soldiers at Shiloh. Uncle Chad packed Daddy's body in ice to bring him home. He's buried on the hill in the family cemetery. Uncle Chad was killed too, you know?"

"No. I didn't."

"At Cemetery Ridge. Fitting name, don't you think? He got hit when he went onto the field to get the wounded.

Aunt Maggie took Amy Ann back to Boston years ago. Uncle Chad believed they would be safer there than in Richmond. We received a letter from Aunt Maggie just the other week telling us that she and Amy Ann are recovering from the ravages of war, and she is trying to put her life back together. She encouraged Mama to do the same."

"I suppose it's easier to forget the war in Boston than it is here in the South where you live with it every day," Cole commented.

I folded my hands, placed my elbows on the table and cradled my chin on my hands. "Tell me about what happened to you. Why did you not write?"

"I couldn't. Shortly after Shiloh, I was captured and sent to a prison in the North. I thought surely I would die there. But since I was an officer, and had been on the frontier before the war, the Yankees let me escort wagon trains instead of rotting in a cell. I had to give my word as a Southern gentlemen, I wouldn't try to escape. I was assigned to General Pope, whose war record was found lacking, and he was banished, so to speak, to the Northwest. He hated Southerners and made my life a living hell. I wasn't permitted to write or get in touch with anyone in the South for fear that someone might come to rescue me. The man had nightmares of Rebs coming over the hills to attack his fort. He was more afraid of the Confederate army than the Indians."

"Why didn't you try to escape? You must have known we needed you here, especially since you knew Daddy had been killed?"

"Didn't you hear me? I gave my word. If a man doesn't have his word to stand for truth, then he has nothing. Don't you think I lived in agony knowing the fighting could come through the plantation? I thought about you every day. And I prayed to God to keep you safe."

"We did not fare too badly until the last few months. Food became scarce. The Yankees came through the land looting, killing and burning. And what they did not destroy, the black horde of runaway slaves following the troops did. Most of the plantations were put to the torch. If it was not for Dr. Bardlow, the manor would have been burned too. He stood on the verandah and lied to the Yankee captain. He said Mama had cholera. You should have seen those brave soldiers back away from the house. The lie worked. The Yankees were too afraid to come into the hall, and they did not want Mama to be moved outside. So they let the house stand, which was good, because we had an attic full of soldiers. The few animals we have left, we hid in a thicket corral beyond the south field. When the war ended, all the slaves left except Seth and Leah."

"What about Mr. Molack? He's still here, isn't he?"

"Seth is too old to do any work, so he is teaching me how to do things. Leah's a Godsend. I do not know what I would have done if she had not stayed."

Cole realized I avoided his question. He asked again, "What about Mr. Molack?"

"He's gone. He left without a word one night. Mama and I have been running things ever since."

He leaned across the table. "Now, try the truth. What really happened?"

"It is unimportant. What matters is that he is not here anymore." I got up and started clearing away the plates, when Cole grabbed my wrist.

"Sarah, tell me what went on here."

"If you must know, Mama shot him!" I blurted out, pointing to the ceiling in the direction of the master bedroom. "Now, you know. You have no idea how awful that man became. He ruled the plantation with a whip and a hand of iron. He made Mr. Jolette leave. I do not know why Mama did not just kick Molack out, but he seemed to have some power over her. Mama talked to Reverend Tadwell, and he did come to talk to Mr. Molack. But by the time the Reverend left, Molack had him convinced that Mama's emotional state was in question because of her grief over Daddy's death and you missing. She never told the Reverend that Molack had ravished her."

"Ravished her!" Cole bolted up, knocking the chair to the floor.

"It's too awful to talk about. We were prisoners in our own home. We needed his permission to leave the property, which he withheld more and more. He tried to become familiar with Mama, calling her Ellie and holding her hand. Her rejections infuriated him. I think she decided to kill him when he turned his attentions to me. She could endure anything for herself, but not when it threatened me. One night she shot him. Now she's up there dying of consumption, but more than that, of guilt. Until the slave women left, she had someone scrubbing the bricks out front every day, where Molack died and his blood ran onto the bricks. When she looks out there, even today, she can still see red stains. The slaves said she has a curse on her because a big white owl flew over the house when Molack died. They said it was his spirit. Some of the slaves left directly after that. We did not have the power to keep them, but most stayed until after the war."

"You said something about soldiers in the attic. Who were they?"

"I think you better sit down again."

"Is it that bad?" Cole picked up his chair and straddled it, leaning his arms across the back.

I continued. "I am not sure of the date when it all began, but one afternoon Dr. Bardlow came to me and asked if our barn could be used as a hospital." I told Cole about 'Safe Harbor' and how Mama and I worked to help our troops. As he listened, he kept shaking his head in disbelief. "When the Yankees came, I had no choice but to hide the soldiers in the attic. The Yankees would have caught our men if they had made a run for it."

"What would have happened if the Yankees burnt the manor?"

"Well, they did not. But that is not the end of our troubles."

"Go on, I'm listening."

"As I said, if I had the gold, Mama would not have taken out the loan the bank offered. But we did not know if you were alive or dead. Mama is . . . well you know how Mama is. And she believed the loan would give us what we needed to buy seed for planting and hire men to work the fields. I fought to keep the five Arabian horses, a carriage horse, and the old mule. I was not going to sell them if I did not have to. With the loan, I replanted the fields. Now the loan is coming due, and the cotton crop has been ruined by the early rains. The weather gets hot and then it rains. I do not know what I am going to do. Mr. Sharply, at the bank, will not extend the loan. He says that he got the money from the Northern Carpetbaggers and they need to be paid. But we know he has always had his eye on the lower pasture, and now it seems that his greed has extended to the entire plantation."

"How much is the loan?"

"Eight hundred dollars."

"That much. Well, I'll see what I can do. I'll have a talk with Mr. Sharply in the morning. Anything else I should know about?"

I did not look into Cole's eyes when I quickly blurted, "No."

"Oh, yes, I believe that. Come on, let me hear it. Might as well get it all out in the open at once, than bit by bit."

"There is this man, a terrible man, who said he would show me the way home for a price. That was when I got lost looking for your horse. I told him, the man, I would give him a gold piece if he brought me home. But when we arrived at the plantation, he saw Dr. Bardlow's carriage and the Confederate officers who came to take our horses and he did not come in for his reward, which was good because I did not have anything to give him. He said he would be back."

"Has he?"

"Not yet, but I see him watching the place from across

the road or following me when I go into town. He's always there. I try never to be alone."

"Since when do you go into town?"

"Since it was safer to be in town than here with Mr. Molack."

Cole shook his head. "I never thought things would be so bad here at home. I always had the vision of the lamp in the window and everything staying as I had left it. When a person is away from the ones he loves, he remembers them as he last saw them. They never age or get sick or die. In my mind, you were still the little girl with your unruly curls trying to escape from beneath your bonnet or out of your braids. But you've grown up. I can't believe you're running the plantation, actually taking care of the horses. You're amazing."

"You once told me that I might be surprised at what I could do if I put my mind to it."

"I'm the one who's surprised." Cole yawned and stretched. "No matter how dark things look, there's always a tomorrow. Don't worry. We'll work things out, you and I together. It's getting late and we have a busy day tomorrow. Do you mind if we continue this conversation in the morning?" Getting up, he helped me out of my chair. "Come on, you've done enough work for today. It'll be good to sleep in a soft bed."

We climbed the stairs to the main floor. He took my hand, leading me down the hall to the parlor. "We don't need this lamp in the window anymore," he said, as he walked to the table, turned down the wick, and blew out the flame. "Just the thought of this lamp shining for me in the window brought me through some mighty difficult times." With his hand on the small of my back, he directed me up the circular oak staircase. At my door, he kissed me on the cheek and said, "Goodnight. See you in the morning."

The clock on the mantel struck eleven. I sank into my bed feeling the safety and security I had missed for a long time. Cole was home.

CHAPTER 13

The next morning, I woke with a stuffy head, a sore throat and an ache-all-over feeling. Ignoring the sluggish malaise, I dressed as quickly as I could and hurried down to the kitchen to tell Leah and Seth that Cole had returned home. I was too late. Cole had already made his appearance and I had missed the joyful homecoming. Leah busied herself at the stove while Seth brought in firewood. Cole was sitting at the table drinking coffee. The kitchen smelled of freshly brewed coffee, biscuits baking, bacon frying, and porridge bubbling in the kettle.

My stomach growled as I entered. "Good morning everyone," I said with a scratchy voice. "Is that coffee I smell? Where did you get the coffee?"

"Master Cole brung it," Leah said. "You sits yourself down and I gets you a cup."

"Sarah, you sound awful," Cole commented.

"I think I am catching a cold."

"Shouldn't wonder, with you standing in the rain last night almost naked."

"Shush." I put my finger to my lips and looked to see if Seth or Leah had heard what Cole had said. They both continued with their work as if they did not hear a word spoken. But I knew better. The slaves were the silent listeners to every conversation and the unseen watchers of every action. If the truth be known, the slaves knew more about the goings on in the fine plantation houses than the owners. What is more, slaves knew what went on in the houses of the plantations for miles around. Gossip was a favorite pastime. I certainly did not want anyone gossiping about me.

Leaning across the table, I whispered, "I was not almost naked. And if you were a gentleman, you would forget what you saw and never mention it again."

"Well, little sister, that rain soaked, threadbare robe was tantamount to nothing. But you are right, I am a gentleman, so I will not speak of it again. However, I doubt if I will ever be able to erase that image from my memory. In my twilight years, if a smile crosses my lips and a twinkle dances in my eyes, you can bet I am remembering last night."

"Cole Brighton! I have always known you were a rounder."

"Now, now, do not go besmirching the good name of Brighton. After all, we come from the same bloodlines."

Leah came to the table with my coffee and a large bowl of porridge. "The eggs and biscuits will be done in a minute."

"What's on your schedule for today?" Cole asked.

"Today's Thursday. Dr. Bardlow will be out this afternoon and he will stay for supper. He comes out about three times a week to check on Mama. He does not do much for her as far as doctoring goes, but she likes his company, and he likes Leah's cooking. On Thursdays, I usually clean before he comes. Floors need mopping, furniture dusting, and Mama's room needs airing out. I also tend the gardens, and today I had planned on making soap. Leah's been saving tallow. We are getting low on soap. Of course, every day, I care for the animals.

Usually, I take one hour after dinner, during the heat of the day, to teach Leah to read. I am teaching her how to read and she is teaching me how to cook. If you want something to do, the bath house roof needs fixing, fences need mending, and I can give you a list of other things to do."

Cole smiled. "I think first I will spend the morning with Mama. After that, I will ride into town and talk with Mr. Sharply."

"Good luck. I have talked until I was out of breath. He says that his hands are tied. It is his backers from the North, those Yankees, that will not give an extension of the loan."

As I ate the cereal, I winced with each bite I swallowed.

By mid-afternoon, all the symptoms of a cold had developed. My body ached, I had a runny nose, and droplets of perspiration dampened my skin as I slowly mopped the entry hall floor. My thoughts drifted back to the wonderful days before the war. Days when all I had to do was to be the perfect student or to ride Misty Morn around the plantation, listening to the darkies sing in the fields. I missed riding Misty. Since the war, I did not have the time to ride or to do anything else that was fun. I sat back on my heels and wiped my face with the corner of my apron.

"I am going into town now. Want to come along?" Cole said, coming down the stairs.

I sucked in my breath. "Oh, Cole, you startled me." I put my hand over my pounding heart. "Do not sneak up on a body like that. Make some noise next time."

"You were so deep in thought a whole band of Indians could have come down the stairs and you would not have heard them. I finished with the animals and I am going to town. Want to come with me?"

"No. I have too much work to do. And if you think you are going to walk over my clean floor with those dirty boots, think again. Go down the back stairs."

Cole looked at his boots. "They aren't dirty . . . ."

"I am not going to argue the issue. Go out the back way."

"Give a girl a bit of authority and she goes for the throat. And speaking about throats, you should take something. You sound worse than this morning."

"I feel worse. My head hurts and I have a fever. What I need is . . . ." I looked up and my words seemed to echo through empty air. Cole was gone.

I backed out the front door right into Dr. Bardlow. "Dr. Bardlow! I did not see you." I wrung out the mopping rag and hung it over the bucket. Dr. Bardlow helped me to my feet.

"Was that Cole I saw riding toward town?"

"Yes. He came home last night."

"This will do your mama a world of good, put some life back into her weary body."

"Cole spent most of the morning with Mama. Now, he is on his way to speak with Mr. Sharply about our loan."

"I hope he can get an extension. The bank has called the loan on the Chamber's place."

"Chamberland? I do not believe it. What the war did not destroy, the money lenders will."

"These are desperate times for the landowners. Sarah, you look feverish." Dr. Bardlow reached out his hand and touched my forehead. "You are coming down with something. You should be in bed." He opened his black bag and fished out a little yellow packet. "This powder should bring your fever down. Take it with plenty of water and go to bed. Stay away from your mama. I do not want her catching whatever it is that you are getting. You should feel better in a few days."

"A few days! I do not have a few days to be sick in bed. Who will tend to Mama and do all the chores?"

"Cole is home. Let him take charge again. You just

rest."

On my way to my room later that day, I overheard Mama and Dr. Bardlow arguing.

"You have to tell her, Ellie."

"Robert, I cannot. I will not. Her love is all I have left and she will not love me if she knows the truth. It is too great of a risk. Promise me you will not tell her. Not now, not ever."

Reluctantly, Dr. Bardlow promised.

I wanted to confront the two of them with what secret they were keeping from me, but the powders were starting to make me drowsy. *Another time,* I thought.

"How did you ever get the saddle on Shadow?" I asked, coming into the paddock area and seeing Cole leading the horse around by a halter with the saddle securely tightened on Shadow's back.

"When he finally learned it would do no good to fight me, he let me put the saddle on him. All he needed was a little work and time. He's a smart horse."

"Have you ridden him yet?"

"That comes later. He needs to get used to the weight of the saddle first and he has to want me to ride him." Cole guided the horse gently around the enclosed space.

"Just how are you going to accomplish that?"

"Love and affection, two ingredients that works on almost everything. How are you feeling? It's good to see you up and outside."

"I am better, thank you. I have been feeling better for a few days but Leah would not let me get out of bed or come outside. She is like a mother hen watching over her chicks. I lost track of time. How many days have I been ill?"

"I have been home a week."

"A week! Dr. Bardlow's powders must have had some strong medicine. I do not remember much of the first few days."

"Your fever was pretty high, you were delirious at first. You talked about Yankees coming to get the horses. I am surprised you are up and dressed this morning. Maybe you should take a few more days to get your strength back."

"No. I cannot be in bed another day. I have work to do. I have to get back to the business of living. You went to town and talked with Mr. Sharply?"

"Yes, for all the good it did me. He still won't budge. The note is due the first of the year. We'll work out something.

"Zephyr, Shadow and I are going for a ride this afternoon. Would you care to come along? I am sure Misty Morn would like a good ride in the woods."

"Zephyr?" I asked.

"The Appaloosa I brought back from the frontier."

"I would love to go for a ride, but I have too much work to do. I am on my way to the chicken yard to get a hen for supper."

"I will do that for you."

"No. You will kill my good egg layers. I cannot make any money selling eggs if you kill off the good hens and leave the lazy ones."

"How do you know the difference?"

"Come along. I will show you."

He tied Shadow to the snubbing post and followed me through the stable, across the path leading to the ravine, through the salvaged apple orchard and into the barnyard.

"Here chick, chick, chick," I called, throwing corn on the ground. The chickens came running in a flurry of feathers, cackles, and clucks. "Now, while they are eating you swing this broomstick just above their heads." I picked up the old broomstick that was leaning against the chicken house. "The good layers are usually busy eating, so the stick misses them. The bad layers do not eat as much.

They have their heads up, looking around. The broom catches them in the neck." I clicked my tongue making a chopping motion with the side of my hand against Cole's throat. "Voila, we have supper."

"Where did you learn that?"

"From Leah, of course, certainly not from Mr. Jolette. The things he taught me seem to be worthless at the moment. I need to know how to make bread, how to kill a chicken or how to cook a meal, not the history of France or England. Surely not how to dance the latest steps or which fork one uses to eat a certain course at a meal. The way my life is turning out, I am so unprepared. The social graces do not matter anymore."

"I think you are doing just fine. Everything you need to know will come to you sooner or later. Life is a journey of trial and error. No one is always right the first time. Everyone makes mistakes."

"Even you?"

"Especially me. I just try harder the next time. Now, let me get the hen for supper. I will kill and clean it. You get the other chores done so that you can ride with me this afternoon when the Tadwells come to visit Mama."

"Did you have a nice ride?" Mrs. Tadwell asked, as I entered the parlor. She sat by herself on the settee by the fireplace. Her somber brown dress with a cream colored lace collar did not match her jolly nature. The Tadwells, being in the ministry, were quite poor, living mostly on donations from their parishioners. However, meager finances never diminished Martha Tadwell's smile.

"Yes, I did, thank you. It has been quite some time since I have ridden Misty. She loves to get out and stretch her legs. Cole is trying to show Shadow how much fun it is to have a rider on his back. So far, the horse is having none of it." I walked to Mrs. Tadwell's side, but I did not sit down on the settee because my dress was too dusty for Mama's nice furniture.

"Why are you down here by yourself? Where is the Reverend?" I asked, looking around the room.

"Elizabeth wanted to speak to Thomas alone. Sometimes it is difficult to talk when others are in the room. We are such good friends but he is still her pastor. If she has a spiritual need, it is best I am not there when they talk. If you know what I mean?" She leaned over to whisper the last statement as if telling some great secret.

"I suppose at times you might feel you are in the way, but I assure you Mama loves your visits. She looks forward to Wednesday afternoons. Would you care for some tea while we wait?"

"No, dear, I am fine. It is just that I am so saddened to see Elizabeth going down the way she is. Hardly any more life left in her. What can we do to help her?" Martha's smile faded as a look of concern filled her sienna eyes.

"I hope Reverend Tadwell is talking some sense into her. She wants to die. Her fear that she will not be buried next to Daddy is all consuming. If we lose the land, like the Chambers have, I do not know what she will do." My voice broke as tears flooded my eyes.

Martha stood up and put her chubby arms around my shoulders and enfolded me into her bosom. "There, there, dear we mustn't cry. We must believe that God is in control of all things. Even when the situation seems impossible, God can still change things for the very best for everyone. You need to have faith."

What did I expect a reverend's wife to say? How could she know that God does not listen to me anymore? He does not hear my prayers. Why should I have faith in a God who is silent?

Cole entered the parlor carrying his muddy boots. The big toe of his left foot stuck out through the hole in his gray stocking. "Good afternoon, ladies. I do not want you to think that I am ignoring you, but my clothes are rather dusty and I need to go and change."

Mrs. Tadwell held her gloved hand over her mouth to

suppress a giggle. "What are you doing carrying your boots?"

"Sarah won't let me walk on her floors with muddy boots. She gets quite hostile, you know." He winked at Mrs. Tadwell to let her know he was teasing.

"That is when I have just washed the floors," I said, slightly irritated that he should be mocking me.

"I believe you are right, Sarah. A man needs to take care not to cause more work than necessary," Mrs. Tadwell agreed.

Reverend Tadwell entered the parlor. "There you are, my dear." He gave Cole a sideways glance.

"The boots are muddy," Cole replied, holding them up for inspection.

"And Sarah won't let you walk across her clean floor," Reverend Tadwell surmised.

"Right, Thomas. Women are so protective of their things," Cole said, looking at me.

Surprise flooded my face. Cole had actually called the Reverend by his given name, Thomas. Calling people by their first name took on a familiarity bordering on rudeness. Adults could do such things but never children. I realized Cole put himself on an equal footing with the Reverend. With this simple gesture, Cole announced to the world he was the master of Rosewood. With that title came the authority and respect deserving of any landowner. I held my breath and waited to see what Reverend Tadwell would do.

"Women are the nesters. They want a home that is solid and secure, a place where they belong. That is why possessions are so important to them," Reverend Tadwell continued, seeming not to have noticed that Cole had called him by his Christian name.

I looked at Mrs. Tadwell beaming her usual sunny smile. *Would she mind if I called her Martha?* I mused.

"Well, my dear, we must be going," Thomas said. He

extended his hand to his wife.

"We will be by next Wednesday, as always. However, we hope to see you in church on Sunday," Mrs. Tadwell said.

"It all depends on how Mama is feeling. We do not want to leave her alone for too long at a time," Cole said, walking with Mrs. Tadwell to the door. "Leah and Seth usually attend Sunday services with their own gathering down at the old mill."

"Certainly, but now that you are home, people will want to see you."

"They know where I live. If they want to see me, they can come out anytime."

"Do what you can. Goodbye, dear. See you soon." She hugged me and took Cole's arm before he had a chance to put on his boots. "Do help me to the carriage. This damp air gets into my bones and makes me creak like an old barn."

The Reverend held me back for just a moment to let them get down the steps. "Elizabeth told me what happened to Mr. Molack. She gave me permission to reveal her confession to you and Cole. If you need to talk with someone, my door is always open."

"Thank you, but I think I have forgotten the entire incident. I am glad that he is dead. Mama has not forgotten nor has she been able to forgive herself. She is the one being eaten up with guilt."

"I reassured her that our loving God forgives all sins."

He held my hands in his long, thin, fingers and looked into my eyes. Was he wanting me to acknowledge my sin? A sin that was so detestable that I could not bring myself to put it into thoughts, much less words. A sin that gnawed on my soul in the dead of night. My feelings for Cole were eating me alive, but I could not tell anyone. What would he think of me? I became uneasy under the pastor's searching blue eyes. "If I need to talk, I will remember what you said." I slipped my hands out of his grasp.

Cole and I watched the carriage bounce down the brick drive and turn onto the road, barely missing two riders. The riders did not stop but kept coming up the lane and onto our drive. Reverend Tadwell turned the buggy around.

Cole sat on the steps to pull on his boots. "This looks like trouble."

I ran into the house to get Cole's gun and peek out from behind the double doors.

"Hello, there," Cole called. "Are you lost?"

"We're looking for the Brighton place. It's called Rosewood," the older of the two said. Both men wore tattered Yankee uniforms. Their unkempt appearance indicated they had been on the road for some time. A thick graying beard covered the lower part of the man's face who did the talking. Both men looked at Cole through the same hooded eyes that I remembered so well. Mr. Molack's eyes, black, dead pits.

"You have found it. How can I help you?" Cole asked, standing his full six feet, shoulders back, head high. He looked like a man ready for any situation.

"My name is George Molack and this here is Elias. We're lookin' for our brother, Frank. Ever heard of him?"

"Sure have. He was our overseer for a short time."

Holding Cole's gun, my hands shook and my knees banged together. *Do they know?* I thought. *Why now? After all these years, why today when Mama confessed to Reverend Tadwell that she had shot him. Is God dealing out justice?*

"We've been wonderin' what happened to him. Haven't heard from him in some time," George Molack said.

"I have been away at the war. Do not rightly know when he left. Sometime a few years back. He left my mother and sister to fend for themselves. If you find him, I sure want to talk to him. I have a score to settle."

"Last word we got was from here. He said he had a

good thing goin' for himself. Why would he leave?"

"I am sure I have no idea. Even good things sometimes turn sour. Hear tell he gambled more than he could pay. Maybe someone he owed money didn't take kindly to being hoodwinked. You might look in Wilmington on the waterfront. Some of the gambling establishments might know of him."

"We'll do that. But if we don't find him, we'll be back." They rode off as fast as their two lathered horses could carry them.

I came outside, still holding the gun and still shaking.

"Give me that," Cole said, taking the gun out of my hand. "You will shoot your foot off." He checked to see if the gun was loaded and put it into the band of his trousers.

"I thought you might need help," Reverend Tadwell said, getting out of the buggy and coming over to Cole.

"No. Not now. Maybe when they do not find Frank. They said they would be back."

"Perhaps you should have told the truth." Reverend Tadwell lowered his voice so that his wife could not hear him. "They would not kill a woman. She shot in self-defense."

Surprise washed over Cole's expression. "So you know. I do not think they would see it as self-defense. They are out for blood. An eye for an eye, so to speak. I have seen their kind before. We will just have to keep them on a wild goose chase until they tire of it."

"I am sure they will be back," I said, looking down the road at the dust settling.

Cole's forehead knotted in a frown. His gray eyes grew even grayer. In a voice scarcely above a whisper, he said, "Yes, I know they will."

CHAPTER 14

An early frost brought out Autumn's vibrant hues of red, orange, gold, rust, and yellow. This heralded the advent of a cold winter. Icy November winds moaned through the trees making the warmth of the fire in the hearth even more comfortable.

"I would like to celebrate Thanksgiving this year," Cole said one evening as we dined in Mama's room. "The last Thursday of November has been set aside to thank God for all the blessings He has given to us. We still have plenty to be thankful for."

Mama set her fork down. "It is a Yankee holiday. President Lincoln made the law. I cannot celebrate a Yankee holiday." She shook her head.

The thought of a party made my heart leap with excitement. "Oh, yes, a party. We do not have to call it Thanksgiving. We will have a homecoming party for Cole. It has been such a long time since we have had a party. The war is over. We need to get things back to the way they were before the war."

"No, Sarah," Cole said. "To observe Thanksgiving, and the meaning of the holiday, is the only reason I would want a celebration. If old friends would like to see me, they know where I am. Surely they would have come calling by now. I have not been a stranger in town. This holiday will be for the family which, as far as I am concerned, includes Dr. Bardlow and Reverend and Mrs. Tadwell, no one else."

"Look around you, Sarah," Mama said. "The hall is empty. Where would we put guests? We have no beds, no large dining room furniture, no chairs for people to sit. All we have left is a half-empty hall with shadows resting where our finery used to be. Do you really want our friends to see the meager state in which we live?"

I wanted the past five years to be erased. To see the lights and to hear the laughter again at Rosewood, a plantation known for its parties, would surely be a sign to everyone that we were not afraid of the Yankee land grabbers. I believed Mama would come out of her doldrums if, for one more time, she could be the elegant hostess of Rosewood. Both she and Cole were being unfair.

"I suppose you are right," I admitted, hanging my head, realizing that our plantation might never again ring with the sound of music and the gaiety of laughter. The Jewel of the Coastal Plantations had lost its sparkle.

"I heard some wild turkeys down by the river the other day," Cole said. "They should be fattened up, eating the wild rice that grows down there."

"And we have yams and butter beans and corn. Morels are growing in the burn of the apple orchard. I can gather some. Leah could bake pies, apple or pumpkin or maybe a buttermilk pie for you, Cole."

Cole grinned. "My mouth is watering just thinking about it."

Mama rolled her eyes toward heaven. "What did I do to raise you two so headstrong? I can see that no matter what I say, you already have your minds made up. Very well, but just a small family gathering."

Our guests arrived about mid-afternoon on the cold, blustery Thanksgiving Day. Seth greeted them at the door, took their coats and escorted them into the parlor where they could warm themselves by the roaring fire in the hearth. Cole served sherry to our guests as the aroma of roasted turkey and freshly baked apple and pumpkin pies drifted up the stairwell.

All morning, Leah and I busied ourselves in the kitchen preparing the luscious meal. I had lost track of time and now I had to dress quickly and also help Mama dress.

"Sarah do hurry. Our guests are already here. If I have told you once, I have told you a thousand times, you must pay more attention to time. It is rude to keep others waiting while you dilly-dally the day away."

"I was not dilly-dallying. I was working in the kitchen and setting the table. Mama wait until you see the table." I touched Mama's frail hand as she gave me the pearl combs for her hair. "We have just enough place settings for all of us. The table looks grand. I retrieved the last of the silver from the chest we buried. The chest is empty now. I will tell Cole to lift it out of the ground. It is still too heavy for me to lift alone. Remember that night we buried it?"

She looked at me in the mirror. Her green eyes darkened with sadness. "Such a long time ago."

"You look lovely, Mama. Do not cloud your face by thinking sad memories. Today is a joyous occasion. Our guests are waiting for us."

Mama and I descended the circular staircase leading into the entry hall. Slowly she took each step. I held her left arm as she steadied herself against the banister with her right hand.

"John," she gasped, when she saw Cole standing at the foot of the stairs, holding out his hand to receive her. She looked at me. Joy beyond words danced in her eyes.

"No Mama, that is Cole." I, too, could see Daddy in the

figure of Cole hidden in the half shadow of the entry hall.

"Yes, of course. For a moment he looked like John when we first met. He looks so much like his father."

Cole met us halfway up the stairs. The Southern gentleman, that he never aspired to be, became visible in his loving gestures. "Take my hand. I will not let you fall." He gently guided his mama down the stairs. "You are beautiful."

Mama had insisted on wearing her black dress. Her days for mourning would probably never come to an end. However, her silver streaked, red hair cascading in curls around her face and the ever so slight blush in her cheeks gave her a radiance we had missed for some time.

As we entered the parlor, Seth announced, "Master Cole, dinner is served." In his black suit, white shirt, and white gloves, Seth rolled back the years to a happier time. Memories of countless times he had announced dinner pulled at my heart.

"Thank you, Seth." Cole extended his arm to Mama to escort her into the dining room. Reverend Tadwell helped Martha, and I took the arm of the good doctor.

"Tell me, Dr. Bardlow, two months ago when I got so ill, that very day, I heard you and Mama arguing about something. Could you explain to me what the argument was all about?"

He stared into my eyes for a minute. I could tell he was searching for the right words to say. "No, my dear, I cannot say I remember having an argument with your mama. You might want to ask her about it."

"She made you promise not to tell someone something. Do you recall, now?"

"Not to tell someone something. You will have to be a little more specific than that." We turned into the dining room. "Look how beautiful everything is. Does this remind you of the times before the war?" He led me to my chair and pulled it out for me. In his opinion, the subject was closed.

Cole took his place at the head of the table. Mama sat at the other end. I was between Cole and Dr. Bardlow, and the Tadwells sat across the table.

Reverend Tadwell offered grace. "Let us hold hands and bow our heads. Almighty Father, we are truly thankful for what you have given to us. You watched over Cole, kept him safe and returned him to his family...."

I felt Cole's hand close around mine. His firm grip caused my blood to rush. I could feel it banging into the ends of my fingertips. Could Cole feel it too? Could Dr. Bardlow? I opened my eyes to see if my chest moved with my heartbeats. Shock took my breath away as I noticed for the first time how much cleavage the square cut neckline of my dress revealed. This was the green Christmas dress that was given to me so many years ago when I was but a child. Now I had become a woman. The loose fitting bodice had become snug. I felt my face growing warm.

". . . In the name of Jesus we pray. Amen," Reverend Tadwell concluded.

Cole gave my hand a slight squeeze as he winked at me.

I blushed even more. "My, it is warm in here." I fanned myself with my napkin.

Cole stood to carve the turkey. "Who wants white meat?"

The afternoon slipped away in a swirl of conversation, food, and laughter. Old memories were discussed as if the events had taken place yesterday.

"Do you remember when John fell asleep in church?" Mrs. Tadwell asked. "We did not know at the time he had been awake all night, birthing a foal. He started to snore when Elizabeth nudged him. He stood up and said 'Amen.' He could have crawled into his boots, that embarrassed he was." Everyone laughed at her story.

"The good memories are still there. It is truly a joy to share them with friends," Mama said, taking hold of

Reverend Tadwell's and Dr. Bardlow's hands. "Friends that are treasured as much as family."

"Shall we adjourn to the parlor where we can sit more comfortably?" I asked. "Coffee and pie will be served in there." The gentlemen stood and helped the ladies with their chairs. This time Dr. Bardlow escorted Mama. Cole stood behind me.

"You are positively radiant, little sister," Cole whispered in my ear, as he slid the chair out from beneath me.

"I refuse to give way to your teasing, dear brother. My mirror tells me what I look like and radiant is not in its vocabulary."

"Then your mirror lies."

The mantel clock chimed nine as our guests drove away. "You must be exhausted," Cole said to Mama, as he lifted her into his arms. "I will carry you up the stairs."

"No, Cole. Let me down. I can walk."

"I would not hear of it. You have had a long day. I do not want you to tax yourself too much and be sick all next week. Put your arms around my neck."

She did as she was told. "Sarah, please come and help me into bed."

"I will be right there. I want to take the coffee and dessert tray into the kitchen and see how the cleanup is coming."

"We is doin' it, Miss Sarah," Leah said, taking the tray from my hands. "You go and tend to your mama."

"Thank you, Leah."

I could see Mama's energy was spent. Her fingers fumbled to untie the strings of her corset. "Let me do that for you," I said, taking her hands aside. "We had a good time today, didn't we?" I slipped her nightgown over her head and helped her into bed.

"Yes. It was nice. Would you please call Cole. I want to talk to both of you."

I pulled the blankets tight around her, as if tucking in a child, before I went down the hall to fetch Cole.

"Cole, are you still dressed? Mama wants to talk with you."

He answered the door wearing only his trousers, no shirt, no shoes, no stockings. "What is it? Is she all right?"

"She's fine. Tired, but fine. She just wants to talk with both of us."

"Give me a minute to put on my shirt." He slipped his shirt over his masculine torso, buttoned it and tucked it into his trousers.

I stood in the doorway watching. I could not pull my eyes away from his tanned body. In the golden light of the lamp he looked bronze. Thick veins in his arms ran over his biceps and his abdominal muscles rippled over his ribs and stomach like a washboard.

"Shall we go?" He motioned me towards Mama's room.

"Oh, yes. Of course."

Mama lay in the light of the lamp looking like an angel. Sweet serenity veiled her face.

"Mama, we are here," I said softly.

She opened her eyes. "Sarah, would you please get my sewing basket from John's dresser."

The small, round, reddish-black basket had a tight fitting lid that was pulled open by a green glass ring. Mama pulled but could not open the lid. "Cole, open this for me. A letter is inside. Would you please read it, aloud?"

My dearest Elizabeth,

I grieve with you over the death of your beloved John. And I am saddened to hear of your illness. I wish you would consider coming to California. In the warm California

sun you will regain your strength.
Bring our dear Sarah with you. I
would so love to see her again. Come
before winter. Please, do not think
me forward, but if you need money, I
will send all you need. I am
anxiously awaiting your answer.

Love to all,

William

Cole and I looked at each other and then at Mama. She broke the silence.

"Martha told me tonight that the bank was foreclosing on our land. I am so very sorry that I signed my name to that loan. Mr. Sharply talked me into borrowing money by telling me it was the very best for Rosewood. I never thought we could lose the plantation. Do forgive me."

"There is nothing to forgive," Cole said. "I would have done the same thing if I had been here. No one can look into the future and see the disasters that lurk in the shadows. We will pray that God sends a miracle. Now, what is this about California and this William?" Cole held the letter at arm's length towards her.

"God has sent a miracle. Cole, I want you to promise me you will take Sarah to California."

"No! I will not go. I cannot leave you." I moved around the bed and took hold of Mama's hand. "This is my home." I knelt on the bed pulling Mama's hand to my cheek.

"I want to tell you of my heart's desire. Cole, please pull the chair over to the bed and sit. Sarah, sit here beside me." Mama slid over to make room beside her. "Today, when I came down the stairs, I thought I saw John standing there waiting for me but I realized soon enough it was Cole. I knew at that moment I did not want to get well. My world has passed. Everything is gone."

"No, Mama. You. . . ."

"Please, Sarah, let me finish. The two of you have your own lives to live. You need to get out there and find it. Sarah, you are becoming braver every day. You do things I could never do. You have conquered your fear of leaving the safety of Rosewood. Now you must face the future. I am asking Cole to go with you to California. He will keep you safe. Once you are at William's ranch, he will protect you."

"Who's this William?" Cole asked. "We have never even heard you mention his name before."

"William O'Shea, he is an uncle of sorts. Actually, an old friend of the family we just called uncle. You will like him Cole. The two of you are quite a bit alike. He has always been an adventurer, never wanting to stay in one place for too long."

"And you are sending Sarah to him for protection? How long has he been in California? No, better yet, the question is, will he still be there when we get there?" Cole stood and paced the floor.

Mama continued, "He will be there. He has a big ranch on the hills by the ocean. I know this is all strange to you now. You just have to trust me. Cole, I want your word you will take Sarah to William."

"I am not sure I can do that. I am not sure you are thinking rationally, asking me to take Sarah three thousand miles to give her over to some stranger."

"You can stay there, too. William will be happy to have you. Please, Cole, think about it. I do not need your answer tonight. Just think it over before you make a decision."

She turned her face away from the lamp and closed her eyes. "I am so very tired now. We will talk again in the morning. Please leave the lamp burning just a little. Good night." We were dismissed.

Cole and I stood outside my room not believing what we had just heard.

"I am not going to California," I said. "This is my home, I will not leave."

"Do not worry about it tonight. Get some sleep. We will talk in the morning."

"Cole, you and Mama do not have the right to make decisions for me anymore. I am an adult. I have the final word about what will happen to me. Not you. Not her. I know how you are. If you give your word, it is as if it is written on two tablets of stone. I will tell you right now, I do not care what you say. I am not going!"

The Christmas snow did not stay on the ground long after a soft rain began to fall. Slate gray clouds hung above the treetops day after day. I felt as dreary as the weather because I knew death was coming to visit Rosewood.

Mama grew weaker with each passing day, sleeping most of the time. Dr. Bardlow took up residence in the room across the hall. He became Mama's constant companion.

One morning in early January, when I entered Mama's room, Dr. Bardlow did not turn to look at me but continued looking out the window. He was crying.

"It's hard watching old friends die." He said softly, almost to himself.

I went to him and put my arms around his waist, burying my face into his black coat. His arms enfolded me. The old wool suit emitted the faint fragrance of sweet apples that laced his pipe tobacco and of comfrey root and melilot used in making an ointment for Mama to prevent dry skin and bedsores.

"Sarah, are you there?" Mama asked in a parched whisper.

"Yes, Mama, I am right here."

"Could I have some water?"

I handed her the glass of water that sat on the bed stand and lifted her head to help her drink.

"Is Cole coming to see me soon?" She asked.

"He will be up in a little while. He is tending to the horses and cutting some fire wood. He said he wants to spend all afternoon with you."

"Good, we have so much to talk about." A soft smile touched her lips as she closed her eyes again.

I knew what she wanted to talk to him about and I vowed not to let them be alone. Cole had a strong will but Mama's ways caused Cole's determination to turn to mush. He was just like Daddy and could not deny Mama anything. I knew once Cole promised, it would be as if it were carved in stone and I would be going to California, like it or not.

The afternoon came upon me sooner than I had expected. After dinner I helped Leah clean the kitchen and then we took time to do her lessons. I still found the idea of teaching a slave to read and write unsettling. I knew Lilly learned to read along with me as I did my letters and sounded out the words. But this was different. I was actually teaching Leah. However, Leah worked steadily to improve her skills and in just a short time she could read the Bible quite well, except for many Hebrew names that even I could not pronounce. Soon she would not need my help. Then she would be leaving. I did not want to think about that day. I had not the faintest idea how I would manage without her.

By the time I had finished with Leah's lesson, Cole was already upstairs sitting in the chair beside Mama's bed, holding her frail hands in his. Dr. Bardlow sat at the table taking his usual afternoon nap.

"Dr. Bardlow," I said, touching his shoulder. "Would you like to lie down for a while?"

He got up and stretched. "I do not want to sleep too long. Call me in an hour or so."

"I will," I said, turning to look at Cole and Mama. "And what have the two of you been talking about?"

"Just old times," Cole said, his eyes dancing with the

joy of remembrance.

"Do you remember the time when we went on the picnic down by Blue Lake and the Chambers met us there?" I asked, climbing onto the foot of the bed and leaning against a large pillow. I was determined to keep the conversation off California.

"Do I," Cole said, his white teeth shining through his grin. "Nora Jane and I wanted to be alone so we slipped away while everyone else was still eating. Little did I know what trouble that would cause me."

"Serves you right," I teased, shaking my finger in his face and laughing.

"Just how did you get. . . those hornets so angry?" Mama asked through gasping breaths.

"To this day I do not know," Cole said. "We were just sitting under the tree and all of a sudden they started to swarm. Our only hope was to get back to the lake and jump in before we got stung."

I laughed even harder. "You really have no idea?"

"No. But I have a feeling you are about to tell me."

"Danny and I followed you and Nora Jane. When we saw you kissing, Danny threw a stone and hit the hornet's nest. He did not see the nest. All he wanted was to scare you. When the hornets started swarming, we ran back to the lake and hid in the bushes. I thought you knew it was us."

"You were kissing. . . Nora Jane?" Mama asked. "Cole you should not." Speaking came difficult so she shook her head in disapproval.

"Actually, Mama, it seemed to me that Nora Jane was doing most of the kissing," I explained, coming to Cole's defense. "You should have seen her when she came out of the water. Nora Jane was always so immaculate with every hair in place. But when she came out of the lake, her stringy, wet hair stuck to her face, and reeds, grass and mud clung to her as nature's wardrobe. She looked like a drowned cat."

"And sounded like one too," Cole said. "I had to push her under the water because all her petticoats filled with air and she floated. So I put my hand on top of her head and pushed. She accused me of trying to drown her. I guess I was a little rough, but it was better than getting stung by hornets."

"She did not see it that way. You should not have tried picking the grass out of her hair," I said, laughing so hard I was crying.

"No. Never thought she would blame me. I saved her and she thanked me by pushing me back into the lake." After a minute, Cole's voice strained under the thought, he continued, "You and Danny spied on us, did you?"

"Sure, we did it all the time."

Cole's face turned a light shade of pink as he glanced at Mama. His brow creased. Slowly he shook his head.

I was sure other moments came flooding into his memory but he was too embarrassed to ask if we had been watching. Instead, he told of the time when he and Daddy found themselves in enemy territory cut off from our supply lines.

"We were living off the land, avoiding any contact with people. About the third day we came upon an old farm house. In the barn there was a nanny goat needing milking. The thought of fresh milk sounded good but we could not get close to that old goat. She did not like gray uniforms, I guess. Daddy saw an old apron and bonnet hanging on a hook by the door of the barn so he put them on. You should have seen him. He kept telling me not to laugh. I told him he had better hurry because if we got caught by a Yankee patrol he could have been shot as a spy. But the trick worked because the goat thought he was the farmer's wife and let Daddy milk her. That night we dined in fine style with milk and a fresh apple pie I took from the window sill of the farm house."

"You stole a pie?" Mama was shocked.

"War makes people do things they wouldn't normally

do."

More family stories were shared and laughed over as the afternoon whiled away. I felt a wonderful peace as I watched Mama's gentle smile brighten her face.

"Sarah . . . it's time to call Robert. He did not want . . . to sleep all afternoon." Mama's lungs wheezed like the wind blowing through the missing boards of an old barn. Dark circles under her eyes and the pale, almost gray, color of her skin told a story we did not want to hear. I hesitated, then reluctantly went to call Dr. Bardlow.

I was out of the room for only a short time, but when I returned with Dr. Bardlow I could feel something had changed. Something was different. Cole stood by the window looking out over the land. His left hand resting on the window sash and his right stuffed into his trouser pocket. The setting sun poked through the clouds to spread rays of golden light. Long shadows moved across the winter lawns and pastures. The western sky, bathed in a wash of red, orange and gold promised an end to the rain.

"Sarah, come here." Mama patted the bed. When I sat beside her, she took my hand in hers. "It will only be a matter of time. . . before the marshal comes to . . . move you off the land. You must go to. . . ."

"No!" My jaw muscles tightened as I clenched my teeth. I turned to look at Cole over my shoulder. He did not turn around. "I will not give up so easily."

"Unless you have all. . . the money by the first. . . there is nothing you can do. We are. . . people of honor."

Her words stung into my heart. I could not believe I would just walk away from Rosewood as the slaves did after the war, leave and never look back. There had to be another way. "Cole, did you say you would take me to California? Did you give your word?"

"Yes. We are out of choices. If we want to keep the horses, we need land. We will never get another piece of property here. In California the land is free for the taking.

We can build another Rosewood. You and I together."

Anger boiled within me but I did not want to upset Mama. "We will discuss this later," I said through clenched teeth.

"I am getting so very. . . tired, but stay with me until. . . I fall asleep. Cole tell me about . . . John." Her breath rattled in her chest. Words came slowly, as if each one formed through a great effort.

At first Cole hesitated then started relating the story in slow, sorrow-filled words. "When I finally found him on the battlefield, he said he knew I would come. 'Tell Ellie that I was always faithful to her.' Then he said something about Sarah having the gold, but I was not sure what he meant. He gave me his watch and ring. Shoved them into my hands and told me that I was the master of Rosewood now. The last words he said were, 'Take care of Mama and Sarah. Tell them I love them.'" Cole's voice broke and he took several deep breaths to keep from crying. His face shadowed in sorrow, he stood at the foot of the bed holding onto the bed post.

Mama motioned for Cole to come closer. She took his hand. "This ring has been in the . . . family for generations. The master. . . passes it down to his son. Now. . . it is yours. Be a wise master." Mama ran her fingers over the ring on Cole's right hand, a golden horseshoe with a reddish-brown sardonyx in the center, cut flat to let light pass through.

"Elizabeth, you must not strain yourself by talking. Please just rest," Dr. Bardlow pleaded.

"Robert, stop fussing. If you must do something, go and fetch. . . me some warm milk. That will help me sleep." After Dr. Bardlow left, Mama turned to Cole and me. "I want both of. . . you to know you are. . . loved far beyond words. . . can express. Carry my love with you. Never hate me. I did my best. . . . I do need to rest now. Cole do not forget your. . . promise." Her words were but a whisper. "Tell Robert I will not need the milk. Sarah, please turn out the lamp."

Cole left the room before I did and walked in front of me down the hall. I had to hurry to catch up with him before he got to his room. I grabbed his arm and pulled him around to face me. I felt my cheeks hot with anger.

"How can you give up? This is our home. The bank and those Yankee money lenders have no right to take it."

"We have a debt that must be paid. Since we have no money and the crop failed, we have no choice. I have tried to sell off portions of the plantation to raise the money, but no one will buy it. It seems that people are afraid of the banker and his power over their lives. Right or wrong, we have to abide by the law. At least we still have the horses. We're young. We will make a new start out West."

"You are happy about this. You are treating this tragic situation like a wonderful new adventure."

"No, Sarah. I am doing the best I can with a hopeless cause." Saying that, he turned and walked away.

Sometime during the night, Mama's angels came to take her into the presence of God.

Only seven people attended the graveside service. Thomas and Martha Tadwell, Robert Bardlow, Seth, Leah, Cole and I. Since Reverend Tadwell had announced Mama's passing during Sunday services, I had expected other landowners to attend. But no one else came.

"Times are bad. People are concerned with their own lives. They have no time to deal with the dead," Dr. Bardlow said, trying to justify the actions of people. "Attending a funeral is like confronting their own mortality. We have just survived a great war and people do not want to think about dying anymore."

All of his excuses did not ease the pain. Standing on the small hill overlooking our land, putting Mama's body into the ground, and covering it with dirt, I felt the loneliness of the ages wash over me. Inside I was empty. My black dress pressed tightly against my body as the cold wind wrapped around me. The wind sent leaves flying across the hilltop and down into the barren fields. I pulled my cloak around me. The warmth of Cole's hand on my arm did not give any comfort either. I did not hear the words Reverend Tadwell said. I am sure they were fine words, but my heart was too heavy to listen to promises of a bright future and a happy reunion in heaven.

The tall pine sentinels standing at the pedestrian gate moaned in the wind. Rain clouds gathered in the east. Another storm was on its way.

Cole had hired a man to dig the grave and cover it again. I did not know who he was but I appreciated his help. When the service ended, the Tadwells and Dr. Bardlow went to the manor where Leah had fixed dinner.

Cole and I stayed at the cemetery to watch the man fill in the grave and to pay him for his work. We walked up the hill to the oak tree at the very top where the other Sarah lay sleeping for the past twenty years.

"Cole I do not know if I can leave Rosewood. I am not like you. I have no desire for adventure. I want the security of a home, a warm fire, shelter from the rain. A trip all the way across this country to a place and a man that I do not know is too frightening for me to even think about."

"I will be with you. We will do it together."

I looked into his gray eyes. They were hard as flint. His face was set toward the West. I knew there was no changing his mind. We were going to California.

CHAPTER 15

The clatter of horses' hooves and the rattle of sabers told the story before the two soldiers and the marshal turned onto the brick drive. Cole and I stood on the verandah to meet them.

"Good afternoon, Marshal," Cole said, feet astride, arms folded over his chest.

The Yankee marshal, who had replaced Marshal Bayless, had no desire to be cordial. He came right to his point of business. "I have a notice of eviction for a Cole Brighton. Do you know where I can find him?" He held a folded paper in his hand.

"I am Mr. Brighton."

"Then, this is for you." The marshal did not dismount but nudged his brown horse forward to the steps and handed the paper to Cole. "I take it you can read."

Cole glared at him but ignored his statement and answered instead, "Do you have further business here?"

"No. Just serving you notice. That's all."

"Then consider your work finished. Good day."

"Before I leave, I have to make sure that you

understand what the notice says. Since you didn't meet the loan payment, the bank is foreclosing on Rosewood Plantation. You must be off the property by midnight on the first of February. Everything stays with the property. You can take nothing except your personal belongings. All furniture, livestock, including horses, stay with the plantation. Is that clear?"

"Perfectly."

"You cannot!" I shouted. Cole laid his hand on my arm and shook his head.

"That's right, Reb. Keep her quiet. You know your place," one of the soldiers said, moving his horse between us and the marshal as if we posed a threat.

The marshal backed his horse away from the verandah, "Remember, you have until midnight on the first. Then I'll be back." He turned and rode away, but he posted the two soldiers as guards to watch the house.

Inside the parlor I flew into a rage, wanting to hit something or someone. I pounded my fist into the settee cushions. "What are we going to do? We cannot take the horses. What is the matter with those men? The horses are ours. They were never part of the loan." I screamed trying to release my frustration. Seth and Leah came running.

"You all right?" Seth asked.

"No! I am not all right. Those. . . those Yankees!" I groped to find angry words to express my rage. But the worst word I could think of was "Yankees," which in my mind was tantamount to swearing.

Cole showed no emotions. His voice held strong as he announced, "The marshal gave us until midnight on the first of February to get off the plantation. We have known it was just a matter of time before the bank would foreclose. Leah, Dr. Bardlow would like you to come and cook for him. He will pay you for your work. Seth, the Tadwells said they would make a place for you in their home, if you want to live with them."

"I thought Dr. Bardlow might like my cookin' his meals. I'd be right proud to be doin' for the doctor," Leah said, trying not to cry. "At least them money baggers waited until Miss 'Lizabeth gone to her reward before they come swoopin' down on us."

Tears glistened in Seth's eyes. "Be hard leavin' this ol' plantation and my Rosie."

"It's going to be hard for everyone to leave. We have no choice." Cole put his hand on Seth's shoulder but he looked at me as if to reinforce his words into my mind.

"What are we going to do about the horses?" I challenged. "We cannot just leave them too."

"Let me take care of it when the time comes. Right now we have plenty of work to keep us busy."

The next few days filled themselves with preparations to leave. Leah and I divided the food into three portions: hers, Seth's and ours -- ours being doubled. We baked the last of the flour into breads, portioned out the hams, bacon, cheese, and beef jerky and divided the jars of fruits and vegetables. Cole spent his days writing letters and tending to the horses. He mended the landau and painted it maroon with gold stripes to look like new.

The day came when Cole hitched up the buggy and brought it to the back of the house. "Leah, load your things. It's time for you to leave. I want you to have the landau and horse. No one took inventory of our things and the carriage and horse weren't listed on the loan papers. Mr. Sharply will not miss them. All he's interested in are the Arabians. So these are yours. Go as if you were just on your way into town. The soldiers will not stop you."

Leah touched Cole's hand. "Thank you, Massah Cole."

Within a short time, Leah's things were in the buggy. I could not believe this was really happening. All my life Leah had been in the kitchen at Rosewood. Whenever I needed someone, I could go to Leah. Now, she was leaving me.

Cole and I walked through the rose garden to watch her drive down the bricks and turn onto the lane leading to the Old Mill Road. The guards did not seem to notice her, just another ex-slave about her business. Little did they know that she was not returning to the Plantation. But then, they were not interested in ex-slaves, they had orders to watch Cole. He made himself quite visible walking to the carriage house.

I ran upstairs and stood on the balcony of Mama's room to watch Leah as long as I could, until the willow trees in the distance hid her from my view. I remembered when Daddy and Cole left that day to join the Confederate Army. I watched from this same balcony. That day was filled with hope. This day was filled with sorrow. I knew I would never see her again. I had come to depend on her so much. What would I do without her?

That afternoon Dr. Bardlow and Reverend and Mrs. Tadwell came to say their goodbyes. Seth prepared to leave with the Tadwells. All of his belongings fit into an old carpetbag.

I gave Martha the silver candlesticks and told her to take anything she wanted. Cole gave Daddy's books to Dr. Bardlow and Reverend Tadwell and invited them to help themselves to the remainder of our belongings. "The more you take the less Billy Yank will get." Cole put his arm around Seth's shoulders. "The black carriage horse is yours. Payment for a job well done."

"No. Massah Cole, I can't take the horse."

"Another horse will be a big help to us, Seth," Reverend Tadwell said.

Seth smiled. "How you feed another horse?"

"God will provide."

Fear showed in Seth's eyes. "That marshal says all horses needs to stay on this here property."

"Seth, I know what the marshal said. That does not mean I have to agree with him. The horse is yours. I have written out a bill of sale and dated it months ago. You will not have any trouble with the law."

"I never thought I would ever leave Rosewood a free man. Now I don't wants to go. My Rosie is buried out behind the slave quarters. My whole life is here. What am I goin' to do?"

"You come with us, Seth," Mrs. Tadwell said. "We will give you a nice place to stay and you will not have to work anymore. And maybe, when the time comes, we can bury you beside Rosie. One more grave is not going to matter to the new owners."

"I guess it's time to go. Saying goodbye is always the hardest," Dr. Bardlow said.

The six of us slowly walked to the front door, out onto the verandah, and down the steps to the carriages. As always I looked to see if traces of blood still stained the bricks. Cole went to get the black horse for Seth.

When he returned, Dr. Bardlow said, "The two of you take care of yourselves and write when you get to your Uncle William's. I know life will be different out there, but it will probably be better." The doctor took me in his arms and whispered, "Sarah, your uncle has a secret to tell you."

"What?" I tried to pull away, but Dr. Bardlow would not let go. He did not want to look into my eyes or perhaps he did not want me to look into his.

"I cannot tell you, but William can. All your questions will be answered in California." He released me and quickly entered his carriage.

"Is this a ploy of Mama's to get me to California and you are acting as her agent?"

"Your mama made me promise that I would not tell you, but William is free to tell you the truth."

"Do you know this Uncle William?"

"I met him a long time ago."

I wanted to pursue the subject more but Mrs. Tadwell came bouncing up. "Goodbye Sarah, we will miss you.

Please write. Tell us all about the trip west and about California."

"i will." I hugged her. "Thank you for being my friend and for being such a good friend to Mama." I could not find words to pour out my heart, but I knew she understood.

"You will be in my prayers. You know that I always pray for you and Cole, now more than ever."

"Thank you. I shall be praying for all of you here at our sweet home." A lump swelled in my throat.

Cole helped Seth into the Tadwell's carriage and tied the horse on behind. "If anyone asks about us do not tell them where we have gone. Just say we have an aunt in Boston and might have gone to her." Everyone nodded in agreement.

Cole and I watched them leave. Cole held his arm around my shoulders as I waved goodbye.

"Sarah will write when we get to Uncle William's place," Cole called after them.

CHAPTER 16

Loneliness lay over Rosewood like a heavy, dark shroud. An indescribable emptiness welled up from deep within me. For a long while Cole and I sat on the settee in the parlor not saying a word. Shadows grew long as the sun dipped below the trees. A shaft of light spread across the floor and climbed up the wall.

Finally Cole said, "We need to think about leaving."

"Not yet. We still have a few days."

"Sarah, I want you to listen to what I have to say." He took both of my hands in his and held them firmly. Slowly and deliberately he picked his words. "We will be traveling through some very rough country. There are men out there who have no honor, no respect for women. If anything would happen to me you would be at their mercy."

"What are you trying to say? If you want to frighten me, you need go no farther. I am already afraid."

"No. I do not want to frighten you. I want to protect you. I believe you should travel disguised as a boy."

"A boy? How can I travel as a boy? Do you not have eyes in your head?" I tried to stand, but Cole held me and would not let go of my hands. "You are hurting me."

"Then sit still. I do have eyes. That is why I want you to pass as a boy. My life will not be worth a Confederate dollar if some of the riffraff out there take a mind that they want you. And your life will not be worth living if they get their hands on you. I have seen what some of those men are capable of doing. Animals act better than they do. Believe me, it was not just Yankees either. Some of our Southern gentlemen were equally as vicious. When we reach Independence and link up with a wagon train you can become a woman again. But until then you will pass as a boy."

"How can I do that? One look and everyone will see that I am a woman."

"You will need to wear boy's clothes. I am sure we can find something in the attic. Mama always kept some clothes of ours. Baggy pants, a loose vest, a jacket should cover some, but you will need to bind yourself up with strips of cloth. And. . . ."

"Bind myself up! You have to be joking."

"And you will have to cut your hair."

"No! Never! Not in a million years. That is totally out of the question. How could I ever go back to being a woman with short hair? You are out of your mind, asking me to do such a thing. Let go of my hands. I do not want to hear another word. I will never cut my hair." Cole let go and I bounded off the settee and ran from the room.

Two days passed. The miracle I waited for was not going to happen. Once again my prayers were as whispers in a raging wind. God did not listen. I busied myself setting things aside to take with me on the journey: the family Bible with it's family history, a family photograph, letters, Mama's wedding dress, Grandmother's wedding ring quilt, the few pieces of jewelry we had left, the dueling pistols with which Mama shot Mr. Molack, a chamber pot, more quilts and blankets, a pillow, mirror, brush, combs, sampler frame, dresses, shoes. The pile grew larger each day. Everything I saw I wanted to take. These were all I had left to remind me of Rosewood. Each item became precious to me - - my treasures.

"I found these old clothes in the attic. Try them on. They will probably fit," Cole said, coming into my room with his arms filled with boy's clothes which included a brown pair of britches, a blue shirt with ruffles down the front, a brown vest and jacket. He threw them on the bed.

I felt the coarse wool material. "I will not wear this wretched fabric."

"Put them on or I'll do it for you."

"You would not dare." He took two steps forward. "All right, I will do it. Turn around." Cole did as he was told. "You are certainly reverting back to that frontier man with your language and mannerisms." I took off my dress, put on the britches, tucked in the shirt and buttoned the vest. "Well, what do you think? Can I pass for a boy?" I put my arms out to the side and slowly turned around.

Cole looked me over shaking his head. "You need to bind yourself tighter. Take the shirt off." He pulled his knife out of the sheath on his belt and cut a strip of linen from the tablecloth. "This should work."

"My tablecloth. You ruined it!"

"You don't need it."

I held out my hand for the cloth. "I will do it."

"What on earth do you have on?" Cole stepped closer and pulled open the unbuttoned shirt.

"My undergarments."

"Lace and blue bows. Not today you don't. Put on these flannels." He held out a pair of white cotton flannel underwear. "This chest band goes on under the flannels, next to your skin."

"I am not going to wear flannels. Who is going to know? No one will see my underthings."

"You might want to wash them once in a while. We can't take a chance. Put this on." He threw the undergarment at me, the one piece kind with a flap in the back.

"Oh, no. I am not going to wear this. You cannot make me." I dropped them to the floor and stomped on them.

"I will not tell you again. This is not a game. Put it on and be quick about it."

"I hate you!"

"I don't care if you hate me or not. Just obey me." Turning to the table, he asked, "What's all this? I said to put the things you will need for the trip on the table. Not everything in the manor."

"I need all that."

"This?"

"It is a chamber pot."

"I know what it is." He held the pot by the round handle with one finger. "You don't need this on the trail. These dresses aren't going. You're a boy, remember. If anyone sees all these clothes how are you going to explain them? We are traveling on horseback, not by wagon. Lighten the load." He saw the pouch with the small amount of jewelry we had left. "I'll carry this."

"Why you?"

"Because no one will question my masculinity and should they, I can prove them wrong. Can you say the same?"

I felt my face flush with embarrassment.

"What are all these rags? Come on, Sarah, you don't need all this stuff."

"Yes. I need those rags."

"What for?"

"I may look like a boy and I may act like a boy, but once a month my body will remind me that I am still a woman. That is when I will need those rags."

My words took a minute to soak into Cole's mind. When he finally realized what I had said he turned a light shade of pink. "Take what you need but nothing more." He turned on his heel and left the room, calling back, "I'm going into town. I will be back in a few hours. You get things done around here."

One last time I wanted to dress up and be the mistress of Rosewood. Taking off the wretched boy's clothes and tossing them on the bed I retrieved my green velvet gown from the pile of dresses that had fallen to the floor. I pulled it over my head and wriggled around to button the buttons that climbed up the back. Each time I had to dress myself my temper raged over the difficult task of buttoning stubborn buttons, of lacing my corset, of hooking shoes hindered by a tight corset that did not allow me to bend over and a hoop skirt that prevented me from seeing my feet in the first place. I truly missed Lily.

Standing in front of the mirror I said aloud, "You look lovely, my dear," as if a suitor stood beside me saying the words. "May I have the honor of this dance?"

"Why, sir, you are so handsome. Of course, I would love to dance with you." I held my arms out, as if dancing with a tall mysterious lover that only I could see. The music played for my ears alone. We twirled around my room and out onto the balcony overlooking the foyer.

"You dance divinely," my imaginary lover whispered in my ear. "Shall we walk in the garden?"

"Yes. It's such a beautiful winter day." I giggled to myself. Descending the staircase, I ran my fingers over the polished wood and though, *My lover is not only in my dreams, now he comes to visit me while I am awake. People would surely think I am moonstruck if they were to see me talking to my shadow.* I opened the door onto the verandah pretending he did. "Thank you kind sir," I said as I curtseyed and squeezed my skirt together on both sides to fit through the door.

"You lead the way." He motioned with his hand toward the woods. We strolled past the carriage house, the sycamore tree and onto the path that led into the ravine, over the footbridge and to the cemetery beyond.

Rain drops glistened on the leaves of the ferns hidden in the shadows of the pines. Dogwood, hawthorn and other broadleaf trees quietly slept the winter away, while the daffodils, crocuses and lilies were slowly awakening to send new shoots through the muddy, leaf covered ground hoping to bloom by spring. The air felt crisp against my cheeks and the breezes carried the fragrance of pine and moist earth.

"One last time, to say goodbye," I told myself as I entered the cemetery through the little gate.

I knelt at Mama's grave. Elizabeth Kensington Brighton the inscription read. I traced the letters with my finger.

"I knew if I waited, you'd come to say your goodbyes," the gruff, raspy voice said.

At first I was not sure if my imagination had played tricks on me or if I had actually heard a voice. Then I saw the shadow tower over me, spreading across the grave and blocking out the light. I turned to look, but all I saw was a huge figure silhouetted against the sun. I shielded my eyes.

"Who are you?"

"I've come for my gold."

In an instant I knew him -- the man in the woods. Soberly realizing we were alone, fear slammed into my heart like a blacksmith's hammer. I jumped to my feet but caught the heel of my shoe in the hem of my dress and stumbled backward a few steps before I regained my balance. "I thought Cole paid you."

"Five dollars ain't what I call payment for a prize like you. I put myself out to bring you home. Now, I want what's ownin' to me."

"That was two years ago. If you had come with me to the house then, I would have paid you. Five dollars is all we agreed upon. I do not have any more. The Yankees took it all."

"That's too bad." He moved closer to me, licking his lips like a wild animal moving in for the kill.

191

Something hard hit the back of my head. I had not realized I had been steadily backing away from him until I could not move any farther. I had bumped into the old oak tree at the top of the hill. I turned to run but he grabbed me and flung me against the tree again. His body pressed against mine. The stench of stale tobacco and whiskey belched from his mouth. The memory of that day so long ago came rushing into my mind.

"You're always with someone, never alone. Almost gave up on ya. But here ya are come dancin' up the hill like a little rabbit I once caught in a trap. Its eyes were like yours, wild, full of fear. Its heart beat like yours, so fast, I could almost hear it." He forced my hand to my chest to feel the pounding of my heart. "Feel it?"

I yanked my hand away but his remained. His fingers curled around the fabric of my dress. *Scream. Fight. Get away.* Thoughts flew in my mind. "Help! Help!"

"You can scream all you want. No one's here to help this time. I seen your brother ride away and the slaves all gone. It's just me and you." He covered my mouth with his.

I turned my face to the side. His mouth moved to my throat, to my shoulder and to the nape of my neck as I struggled to free myself.

"Nice." Yellow teeth emerged through his wicked smile. "You're so white. Like fresh cream. All clean 'n soft. Not like those whores on Front Street in Wilmington." In one quick move, both of his hands grabbed at the bodice of my dress, ripping it apart.

As he stepped back to see his handiwork, I sprang from his hold. He caught the sleeve of my dress and ripped it from the shoulder. I didn't stop. Ten strides down the hill, he grabbed me again and flung me to the muddy ground. His bulk landed on top of me. Hysterical screams flooded out of my mouth. The more I fought, the greater his pleasure.

A shadow moved between us and the sun. A howl, resembling the lost souls in hell, thundered over our heads. The weight of the evil monster on top of me eased as he was lifted and hurled through the air, crashing down on the headstone of Sarah's grave. It broke at the base, leaning against the gnarled root of the oak tree. I scrambled to my feet, pulling the ripped material of my dress together. The sound of flesh smashing against flesh drowned out all other sounds. Groans of pain registered in my ears as I reached the bottom of the hill. I stopped at the little gate. Only then did I see who was my deliverer - - Cole.

Blood splattered Cole's clothes. Hands, the color of raw meat, smashed again and again into the face of my assailant. Using the headstone as a table to lay his victim against, Cole continued to beat him until exhaustion made him stop. The evil man's blood ran down the stone into the dirt.

"Get up!" Cole yelled. "I'll kill you with my bare hands."

"No more. I've had enough," the hoarse voice came barely audible. "Don't kill me. I'll do what you say. Just don't kill me."

"I should make you get down on your knees and apologize to my sister but she's seen enough of your ugly face. And killing you isn't worth all the trouble it would cause me." Cole yanked him up on his feet and shoved him toward the large gate where his horse waited. "If I ever see you again, I will kill you. Now get."

The man stumbled to his horse, mounted and rode away.

I ran to Cole, holding together the shreds of my dress. "You should have killed him. How do you know he will not come back and kill us?"

"He won't. He's a coward. He hid in the woods for five years so he wouldn't have to fight in the war. He skulked around waiting until you were alone before he made his move. He won't be back."

"Are you alright? He did not . . . ?" Cole asked, picking up his black overcoat he had pulled off to be able to have the freedom to fight. He put the coat around me. His eyes darkened with concern.

"No. Thanks to you he did not harm me. I was so scared." A shudder of fear shook my body.

Cole took me in his arms. "You are safe now."

I looked at the headstone. "It is broken. How sad."

"It isn't really broken, just toppled over. I'll fix it." He started to lift the stone but stopped. "Sarah, look here." He dropped to one knee and lifted a sack out of the hole where the headstone stood. As he opened the strings, Cole's face filled with surprise.

"What is it?"

"Gold! There must be thousands of dollars here."

"What? Where did it come from?"

"This is what Daddy was trying to tell me when he said, 'Sarah has the gold.' He meant the gold is buried under Sarah's headstone. All those business trips he made before the war. He must have been converting dollars into gold. Whichever side won, gold would still be good."

"Do you know what this means?" I clapped my hands and spun around with glee. "We are rich! This is the miracle we have been waiting for. We do not have to leave. We can rebuild Rosewood."

"Sarah, you forget the deadline for the loan payment has past. I was at the bank this morning trying to work something out. Mr. Sharply is not in charge anymore. It's a man from Boston. And he wants the land. He does not want the loan to be paid. We can offer more than what we owe but he will not take it."

My new found hope dashed to the ground.

"We need to get back to the house and finish packing," Cole said after he repositioned the stone. "I do not want to alarm you, but the Molack brothers are back in town asking questions. I want to be gone from this place tonight. Put miles between us and them by morning."

"Are you afraid of them?"

Cole looked at me in a strange way, but he did not answer. Instead he whistled for Zephyr. The big horse came running. "Help me put the gold into the saddlebags."

Cole led the horse and, with his arm around me, we hurried along the path through the ravine toward the house. The sun's last rays still crested the trees above Garland Hills but the manor lay in shadows.

"Will you be all right? I need to saddle your horse and bring the animals around back. While I pack Old Danger, you get yourself ready. Take only what you need." He turned aside to the stable, and I continued on to the manor. I assured him that I would be all right.

I entered the empty house, aware of my being alone. Every shadow held a monster. Behind every door or around each corner an unseen evil lurked. The pounding of my heart competed with the sounds of my footsteps echoing through the halls. Quickly climbing the stairs and running into my room, I slammed the door behind me. I leaned against the door for a long time, unable to move. Shadows deepened as the light faded.

Slowly I got up and lit the lamp and stood in front of the mirror. My beautiful dress was torn beyond repair. I felt violated, unclean. I could still see his face next to mine, hear his voice, smell the stench of his breath, and feel his hands touching me. I wanted to scrub my skin raw to get rid of the feel of his touch. I shook thinking about what might have happened if Cole had not rescued me.

"Cole was right," I said aloud. "I need to pass as a boy." I grabbed the scissors out of the sewing basket on the dresser. With shaking hands, I cut my curls. My hair fell to the floor as tears rolled down my face. Reluctantly, I put on the boys clothes.

The knock, accompanied by Cole's voice, told me it was time. "Come in," I said. He stood in the doorway wearing beautiful Confederate gray trousers, a pullover buckskin shirt with fringe, laces instead of buttons, black army boots calf high, a black hat pulled down over his face and saddlebags slung over his shoulder. "Are you ready to go? Everything is packed, except for your things."

"How do I look?" I turned away from the mirror, standing feet astride with my hands on my hips. The short hair sprang into soft curls falling into my eyes and over my ears, touching the collar of the brown jacket which hung down to my knees and covered the blue shirt, brown vest, and baggy trousers.

"Well, I guess it will have to do. You need a hat." He left the room and quickly returned with a brown felt hat which he set firmly on my head and fixed the brim to hide my eyes. From the grate in the hearth he took some soot on his finger and smeared it on my face.

"Cole! Stop that."

"Now you look like a boy. Stand round-shouldered and don't look anyone in the eye. Speak only when spoken to and then mostly grunt. We should be able to pull this off. Are you ready?"

"As ready as I will ever be. I am still so afraid of the outside world. Going into town was a great accomplishment, but now to leave Rosewood forever. Cole, I am not sure I can do it."

"You are stronger than you think. You can do this. I am right with you." Cole smiled. He took the quilts from the table. My personal things I had already put into my saddlebags. The family Bible with the family photograph taken the summer before the war, stayed on the table.

"No room for this," Cole said.

To his surprise, I did not argue. All the fight had gone out of me. I filled my eyes with the memories of the manor as we descended the stairs for the last time. Memories that would have to last me for a lifetime.

"What about the soldiers?" I asked.

"They've been taken care of. I tied them to the pine tree. It should take them until morning to get free. By then we will be long gone."

We mounted the horses at the kitchen door and rode around the rose garden to the brick drive. Cole rode Zephyr, not fully trusting Shadow Run yet. He led Shadow,

Black Dancer and Old Danger, our mule. I rode Misty Morn and led Midnight Star and Fire Storm.

The waning moon still hid behind the cottonwoods but its luster was bright enough to light our way.

I looked over my shoulder to carve the image of Rosewood into my memory. "I would much rather see it burned to the ground, than to think of those Yankee money lenders sitting in Mama's parlor with their muddy boots on her carpet."

"Whoa." Cole pulled up on the reins and looked at me. Then, without a word, we turned around and rode as fast as we could back up the drive.

"Hold the horses and wait here," Cole said, dismounting and running into the manor.

Presently, I heard the shattering of glass. On the third floor flames licked up the drapes. Then came another smashing sound. This time the fire flared up in Mama's room. Still another lamp broke somewhere in the house. Minutes later, flames danced in the windows of Daddy's office and in the parlor. Soon the whole house was engulfed. The roar of the fire and the groaning of the timber frightened the animals.

I waited. "Come on, Cole. Get out of there."

The roof gave way, collapsing through the attic and slave quarters into the second floor. White smoke belched through every opening.

"Where are you? Cole! Get out of there."

The horses pawed the ground. Nervously they moved away from the heat. I held tight to the reins. Old Danger brayed, kicking in the air. The clatter of the pots and pans on his back added to the sound of crashing lumber.

Suddenly, Cole came running through the front door.

"You had me worried," I yelled.

"I thought you might want to keep this." He handed a large bundle to me before swinging into the saddle. "Put it in your saddlebag and be careful with it."

I opened the cloth. "The Bible and the photograph! Oh, thank you."

"Let's hope no one reads the family history and finds out that Danny died and Sarah lived."

The manor groaned as the walls started to give way.

Nudging Zephyr forward, Cole said, "Let's ride. We have a long way to go."

PART TWO

THE JOURNEY WEST

CHAPTER 17

The hollow sound of our horses' hooves echoed through the lonely night as we came to the bridge on Mill Creek Road. To the left was the familiar way into town, to the right the road led toward Goldsboro, Raleigh, Winston-Salem and beyond to places I had only read about. We took the right fork into the unknown.

Willow oak trees grew on both sides of the road, intertwining their branches to form an archway through which we rode. Spanish moss hung from the old branches creating ghostly apparitions dancing in the night wind. With each bend in the road, I looked over my shoulder to see if I could catch a glimpse of the red glow from the fire. We traveled north, intending to bypass towns or settlements. I pulled the collar of my jacket up around my ears and huddled low in the saddle to get some protection from the cold.

We passed a farm with a lamp in the window. I remembered all those years I had lit a lamp for Cole in the parlor window, praying he would come home. I wondered who had lit the lamp in the house and for whom it was waiting. A wife, a mother, someone was waiting at this late hour. We rode on. In the distance a dog barked. Lonely came his cry. As lonely and empty as I felt. Still we rode on.

The damp air of the cloudless February night seeped through my jacket, chilling me to the bone. I could not remember a time when I felt as hungry, as cold, or as miserable as I felt now. Cole showed no signs of discomfort nor of stopping to rest. His eyes seemed to search the road ahead. Now and then he turned to survey the distance behind us but never slowed the pace. I shifted my weight in the saddle trying to stretch my legs.

A red glow could be seen in the eastern sky. Not that of the fire that consumed the manor but rather the red glow of dawn. "Cole, when are we going to stop? I am tired and hungry."

"Soon, when I find a good spot to set up camp."

I looked around, not a house nor an inn could I see. "What are you looking for?"

"You will see." The sky grew lighter and lighter. My stomach growled louder and louder. A large clump of oak and pine trees grew off to the left a short distance from the road. "This should serve us well," Cole said, leading the way down a slope and across the field between the road and the trees.

Wild blackberry bushes grew in the field and along the split rail fence that bordered the oaks running west along a small creek to mark the boundaries of someone's farm. The trees formed a winter canopy over our heads. The large, old branches of the oaks hung so low they lay on the ground.

"I'll start a fire," Cole said as he dismounted. "You get some water from the creek. Watch that you don't fall in."

"Why would I fall in?" I dismounted, took the coffee pot from Old Danger's pack and headed for the creek. My legs felt stiff and stretching did not alleviate the kinks.

"How long before we get to Independence?" I called.

"I can't say. Depends on the weather. I want to be

there by the end of March or beginning of April at the latest. The early trains start leaving about mid-April, and we have to get outfitted first. I have written a letter to a friend who will get a wagon for us and have it ready when we get there. It's always best to be in one of the first trains out. We will still find water, grass, and firewood along the way. Some of the last trains have a rough time of it. We can talk about the trip while we eat. Get the water so I can make coffee." Cole unpacked the animals and led them into the tall grass behind the trees, out of sight from the road.

Tall, slippery, dew soaked grass edged the creek concealing its banks. "Do not fall in," I said to myself. "Do not give Cole the satisfaction of the last word." I held onto a branch of a nearby bush and leaned over as far as I could. Fragrances of oak, pine, damp earth and wet grass gave way to the smell of a wood fire, ham and potatoes. Cole had started breakfast.

"How do you want your eggs?" Cole asked, as I entered the shelter of the trees. The skillet sat on a rock almost in the fire. Cole crouched beside it, watching the food cook.

"Not runny."

"Put the pot on the flat rock. Get the coffee and bread from the pack. We'll eat in style as long as the food lasts."

"I am so hungry I could eat my boot."

"We will save that for some other time. It is a long trip to California. Never know when cooked boot will come in handy," he teased with a twinkle in his eye just like Daddy.

Cole had spread out a bedroll next to the fire for me to sit on. We ate off tin plates and drank from tin cups. "This certainly is not what I would call etiquette or good manners," I said, enjoying every bite.

"We won't tell anyone."

"You are a good cook. You can do all the cooking on the trip."

"Oh, no. It doesn't work that way. We share in

everything. Many hands makes for light work. But since I cooked, you can clean up. I will get a bucket of water for you to wash the dishes." He got up and left the seclusion of the trees.

"Watch that you do not fall in," I called after him. *I will just lie here for a minute until he gets back with the water,* I thought, stretching out on my back, looking up into the branches of the trees. Not a speck of sky could be seen through the tangled canopy. *It is so warm and cozy . . . I could stay here . . . for a long . . . long . . . time.*

"Sarah. Sarah. It's time to go. Wake up." Cole knelt beside me gently shaking my arm.

"What? Where am I?"

"We're on our way to California."

"Oh. I thought that was a bad dream."

"No. It's getting late. We have to get on the road again."

I blinked my eyes, not quite remembering where I was. Sunlight filtering through the green pine trees surrounded me in a dreamlike world.

"Come on, Sarah, get up." Cole's voice held an urgency never heard before. "We have stayed here too long. We need to get moving. Troops might be after us already."

Then I remembered. I sprang up from the bedroll. Aching muscles recalled last night's ride. "I need to go to the. . . ." I looked around.

"Over there." Cole pointed his thumb to a bush.

"You are joking with me." My eyes widened in disbelief.

He shook his head. A smile spread across his face.

Walking to where he had pointed, I grumbled under my breath. "Who said I would not need a chamber pot?"

"What is taking you so long? Can't you hurry?" Cole called impatiently after only a few minutes. "The horses and mule are already saddled and packed." He paced back and forth kicking rocks and twigs out of his way.

"I am hurrying. Because of this one piece undergarment you made me wear, I have to take everything off. There has to be a better way to do this. Oh, no. I am caught on a bramble bush."

"Do you need help?"

"No! Stay where you are. I can manage." Finally, I emerged from the bushes.

Cole laughed. "I don't think you need to carry your own bush with you. I'm sure we can find plenty along the way." He pulled a branch from my trousers.

"I told you I was caught." I laughed along with Cole.

"It's good to hear you laugh again. Thought we may have left our happy Sarah back at Rosewood."

"No. I am here, hidden under all these boy's clothes. I guess I have not had too much to laugh about lately. I will try to do better in the future." We mounted the horses.

Cole set his face to the west and we rode all afternoon. The air changed from the moist, pungent, coastal air to a dryer, sweeter savor of grasslands. Woods and marshes were replaced with open meadows and rolling hills.

"We're on the Piedmont already. Can you feel the change in the air?" Cole asked, looking at me through eyes filled with concern. "From here we'll start climbing across the plateau and into the foothills."

I turned to look over my shoulder. If only I could see the two tall longleaf pines that stood guard at the small gate of the cemetery, maybe I could see the smoke from the house. I stretched tall in the saddle, craning my neck to no avail. Rosewood was gone forever.

"Are you all right?" Cole asked.

"Yes, I am doing fine." I tried to make my voice sound reassuring even though I did not feel fine. Lost and afraid were the words that came to mind.

"We'll stop in a few hours and take a short rest. But I want to keep pushing on into the night. We need to make the most of a clear sky and the moon's light. A few nights from now we won't be able to travel after dark because the moon is waning."

I noticed his eyes searched the countryside as if he were memorizing each tree, farm, or bend in the road.

"What are you looking for?" I asked, tugging on the horse's lead ropes.

"Just making sure we're on course. Do not want any surprises."

I pulled my hat down to shade my eyes as the sun lowered to eye level. "Every evening we will be blinded by the sun."

"At least we'll know we're going in the right direction. Sooner or later we'll have to hit California. When we get to the ocean we'll stop. We should be there by September, maybe in time for your birthday. Let me see, you will be twenty-one. Right?"

"Right. Twenty-one and an old spinster with no hopes of ever getting married," I said under my breath.

The rustling sounds of small unseen animals in the underbrush faded as the temperature dropped. I rummaged in my saddlebag for a pair of gloves and a muffler to put around my ears. Red and gold painted the sky and blurred into a blue black as twilight caressed the land.

"Starlight, star bright, first star I see tonight. I wish I may, I wish I might, have this wish I wish tonight." I closed my eyes and wished for a man to love me, a once-in-a-lifetime kind of love.

"That's the evening star." Cole pointed to the star I had just wished upon. "It's really not a star but the planet Venus. We'll follow it all the way to California. Every night it will be the first star out and it can be seen for about three hours after sunset."

"Just like the Wise Men who followed the star to

Bethlehem."

Cole smiled and urged Zephyr to quicken his pace. "It's going to get cold tonight. No clouds to hold in the warmth of the day. We'll need to find some cover in a few hours. Something like the trees we had this morning would be good."

This morning? Was it only hours ago? Was it only last night when we left Rosewood? This day seems to have dragged on forever. My thoughts turned back to the plantation. *What would I be doing if I were home? Supper would be over. I would be helping Leah clean the kitchen. Mama would be in her room. Mama, I miss you.* I took several deep breaths. *Do not cry, Sarah. Do not let Cole see you crying. Come on, what was it that Mama used to say? 'We women of the South are the backbone of the nation, forged in the fires of adversity. Strong as steel.' Now is not the time to crumble.* I shook my head, adjusted the horse's guide lines and nudged Misty to quicken her pace. "I have to be strong," I said aloud to reassure myself.

Shortly after the moon hit its zenith, Cole pointed to a grove of cottonwood trees off the road to the right. "We'll make camp over there."

Under the shelter of the trees darkness crowded in around us. I gathered sticks and dry leaves to make a small fire while Cole unpacked the animals and picketed them in the grass to graze. Except for the coffee, our meal was cold leftover ham, bread, cheese, and dried apples. I portioned the food onto two plates.

"I am almost too tired to eat," I said, plopping down on my bedroll. "Do you think the soldiers are after us?"

Cole did not look at me when I handed his plate to him. "Where did that thought come from?"

"You had mentioned it this morning and I watched you all afternoon looking over your shoulder."

"Yes, we are being followed. Don't know if it is the soldiers or the Molack brothers. But I plan to stay ahead of them. When we get to the mountains, we'll cut through the woods, stay off the main roads."

"What will they do to us if they catch us? The soldiers, I mean."

"As far as they are concerned these horses belong to the moneylenders. They hang horse thieves."

"They would not!"

"I'm not going to take the chance to find out."

After we finished eating, Cole took my plate and cup. He filled the cup with water and said, "You get some sleep. I will clean up, but first drink this warm water." He handed the cup back to me.

"Why? I had enough coffee. I am quite satisfied."

"Just drink the water."

I took the cup and drank. "There, are you happy?"

"Why does everything have to be a confrontation with you? Can't you do what you are told without an argument?"

"If you tell me why I am doing something, I will do it. That is, if I agree with you."

"That is just my point. Sometimes it is best you don't know. You need to learn to trust me."

"You are treating me like you treated Shadow Run. You wanted him to want to be ridden. He was happier the way he was, just running free. You want me to give you full control of my life, no questions asked. I cannot do that. It is difficult enough I have no say about going to California. But I still want some control. You just say do this or do that and I am supposed to jump. I cannot accept that. Tell me why you want something done and I will decide if I am going to do it."

"Hold on there," Cole said, holding up his hands as if to surrender. "The reason WHY is because you aren't drinking enough water. Don't want you getting sick on me.

You think if you don't drink you won't have to go behind the bushes. But if you don't get enough liquid into your body you will get sick.

"Besides that we need to get an early start. An extra cup of water will make you get up. The Indian women do it all the time."

True to his word, in a few hours I awoke needing to find a bush. "I hate this!" I complained, thinking of the next seven months. "It is not going to be much better on the wagon train. I wish we were at Uncle William's already."

"Time will pass quickly. One day we will look back on this as a great adventure."

"I never was the one who wanted an adventure. That was you, remember?"

Each day Cole and I rose before first light and rode until long after dark. Cole picked our path in the dark like a nocturnal animal. Rain and cold became our traveling companions. The days melted into each other while the landscape changed as we entered the foothills of the Blue Ridge and beyond to the Great Smoky Mountains. Trees grew denser. We saw red-cedar, black gum, dogwood, oak, pine, black willow, tamarack, ash, maple, and many others I could not identify. Woody fragrances surrounded us the deeper we rode into the forest. Not another person seemed to be in this part of the world, just Cole and I. We were no longer riding on a road, but cutting through the forest on animal trails or foot paths. I remembered the stories I had read about early pioneers such as Daniel Boone. He must have come this way.

"Do you hear that?" Cole asked. "Sounds like a waterfall up ahead."

We rode a little farther and then, rounding a bend in the trail, we saw it.

"Oh, my, I cannot believe the beauty of this place," I gasped, blinking my eyes. Looking up at the water tumbling over the rocks into a vapor-shrouded pool that nestled at the bottom of the cliff was almost spellbinding. The mist caught a fleeting ray of sunlight, creating a rainbow. Trees, shrubs and huge rocks hugged the contour of the pond.

"We're in luck. It's a hot spring. Think it's time for a bath," Cole said, dismounting Zephyr.

"Here? In the open?"

"Why not? Haven't seen anyone in days. Plenty of bushes for privacy. Couldn't ask for a better spot. We'll give the horses a rest too. They've been hard pressed." He took the packs off the animals and hobbled them in a small meadow along the banks of the stream that flowed from the pool.

I was not sure about bathing in deep water. I could not swim.

Cole sat on a rock and pulled off his boots. I did the same. He stripped off his jacket and hung it over a bush. I took my jacket off and shivered in the cool air. He unbuckled his gun belt and hung it on a branch where it was easy to reach. He slipped his buckskin shirt over his head. I watched him. He unbuckled his belt, unbuttoned his trousers and pulled them off without giving me a second glance. I fumbled with the buttons of my vest, not diverting my eyes from his muscular torso. His flannels hugged every curve of his body. A strange tingling feeling washed over me.

Cole stepped into the water and silently slipped beneath the crystal liquid. I watched his blurred form swim to the middle of the pool before he surfaced for air. The waterfall created a churning of white water near the cliff but mere ripples lapped the edge of this side of the pond. Crystal clear water reflected the colors of the fast moving pewter clouds, the trees, the rocks, and the dark depth at the center of the pond.

"Water's wonderful. Come on in."

"I cannot swim."

Cole swam to the edge and stood up in waist deep

water. "It's shallow here. I'll teach you how to swim. Don't be afraid." He held out his hand.

I finished taking off my britches and shirt, thankful for the breast band and the wretched underwear Cole insisted I wear and waded into the warm water. Large rocks lay at the water's edge, half submerged. I sat on one, dangling my feet in the soothing liquid.

"Don't be a sissy. Get wet." He splashed me.

I kicked at him. "It is too deep."

Cole picked me up in his arms. "You'll learn to swim one way or another."

"No! Let me down." I struggled to free myself.

"Don't squirm. I might drop you."

I wrapped my arms around his neck. "Cole, I am afraid. Take me back to the rock."

"I know you're afraid. Don't worry. I'm just teasing. I would never drop you." He walked deeper and deeper into the water. I felt my bottom getting wetter and wetter.

"Let go of my neck and lie flat out on the water. Feel my hand on the small of your back? I won't let you drown. Don't sag in the middle. Keep this up so you will float." He put his hand on my bottom. "Just relax and let the water carry you."

I did as I was told, stretching out on the water. I tried to relax. *This is not so difficult. I can do this,* I thought. Just then, air billowed in my flannels and I floated away from Cole's protective hand. "Help! Cole, help me." Panic surged through me and I forgot everything Cole had said. My first instinct was to put my feet down and touch bottom.

Cole started to laugh. "You're okay. Come back here." He pulled me back to him, splashing water over me. "You need to get all wet and that won't happen. It's just air."

"I believe I am finished for now."

"No. California's a long way off. We have many rivers to cross between here and there. You need to know how to swim or at least float. Let's try this again. Stretch out on the water and watch the clouds drifting in the sky. Don't think of anything else."

As the afternoon progressed, Cole gave me the confidence I needed to overcome my fear of deep water. Eventually he taught me how to swim. Of course, I would need plenty of practice.

"I think you've learned enough for one day. Why don't you get out and dry off," Cole said, as he swam into deeper water. "I'll stay here 'til you're dressed."

I shivered as the cold air penetrated my wet underwear. After gathering my clothes and boots from the rock and bush where I had hung them, I tiptoed gingerly across the bare, hard packed ground toward the saddlebags to get my blanket.

The ground reminded me of the old folk story of the Devil's Tramping Ground. I remembered Leah telling the story of how the Devil would come every night and walk around and around in a certain place in the North Carolina Mountains until the ground was worn so hard that not even a blade of grass could grow. An evil spirit drove away every twig and leaf from the land. 'And to this very day,' she would conclude, 'the Devil's footprints can still be seen.'

I shivered and searched the earth for strange footprints. "That was just a story to frighten children," I said aloud, slipping off my wet garments and quickly dressing. Without underwear my britches chafed against my skin. "The Devil does not walk about thinking of what mischief he can do to little children." I dismissed the thought and started getting the last of the food out of the packs.

While I busied myself with supper, Cole got out of the pool and dressed behind the bushes. "Once you got the hang of swimming, you did pretty good," he said, walking toward me. "Never can tell when it'll come in handy. We'll practice some more before we hook up with the wagon train." He picked up the edge of my blanket and dried his hair. "When we get to California, we'll swim in the ocean."

"When we get to California, I will be a lady again. I will not be swimming or wearing boy's clothes. But one thing I would like to learn is how to shoot a pistol."

His eyes widened in amazement. "I was just thinking that very thought. But are you sure?"

"Never can tell when it'll come in handy," I said, turning his words back on him. "If Mama had not learned how to shoot from her grandfather, I dread to think what would have happened to us." Anger and fear rattled my spine as the vision of that night passed before me.

"Yes, you're right." A thoughtful look deepened the color of Cole's gray eyes. "You may have to know how to use a gun before this trek is over. The Indians are on the warpath again since Sand Creek. Black Kettle, Chief of the Cheyenne, wanted peace but after his family, along with most of the families of his tribe, were massacred, all hell broke loose on the plains. They were still fighting hot and heavy when I left for home. And we're traveling by way of the Santa Fe and old Butterfield trails. Along that route, we could run into Comanche and Apache Indians, two of the most savage tribes. Learning to shoot would be a good idea. We'll start right after we eat.

"And speaking about eating, it's your turn to cook. I'll get a fire going and water for coffee." Cole left the shelter of the trees to look for wood and to check on the horses.

I had lost track of how many days we had been on the trail. We slept at odd hours and we rode long into the night. Time was mixed up But of all the hours we spent together, I liked meal times the best, especially the evening meal. That was when Cole seemed more relaxed, less demanding. When we sat around the fire eating, he talked about old memories, good things we both wanted to remember. In those brief snatches of time, I got to know my brother.

"I regret being away from home for so many years," he said softly, looking into the black coffee in his cup, swirling it around before drinking. "How old were you when I left? Eleven?"

"Yes. I just turned eleven."

"I missed all that time watching you grow up. Now look at you. You're a woman. A very beautiful woman." He fixed his eyes on me from across the small fire.

I returned his gaze without blinking and held it for some time. Desperately, I wanted to know the thoughts hidden behind those steel eyes.

"You grew up and I don't even know you." He shook his head slowly as if a great sorrow held him captive. "I thought Rosewood Plantation, Daddy and Mama would always be there. Like a rock, safe and strong. I could go away on my adventures, as you call them, but my security would still be there when I came home. I wasted so many years looking for a dream when I had it all the time. Now it's gone." His voice faded to a whisper.

I wanted to put my arms around him and hold him. He seemed so lonely. But he got up and went to get the animals in from the meadow. The window into his soul had opened for a moment, but it slammed shut again, leaving me outside.

I busied myself cleaning up, putting out the bedrolls and hanging our wet things over a rope I tied between two low branches. I found the small cake of rose scented soap in the bottom of my saddlebag where I had hidden it and washed my hands and face.

"You want to learn how to shoot? Get over here," Cole called from the edge of the pond.

I wrapped the soap in a small cloth, shoved it into my pocket and ran to meet Cole at the pool.

"Let's move closer to the waterfall, its roar will drown out the shot." Cole led the way through the shrubs and over rocks until we were almost beneath the falls. The wind blew the mist away from us. Cole handed me his empty Colt Dragoon Revolver and shouted, "I want you to get used to the weight and pull of the trigger before I load it."

"It is heavier than I remember."

"Hold it with both hands at arm's length. Lock your elbows. Squeeze the trigger. Don't jerk it." Cole stood behind me and wrapped his arms around me to hold my hands around the gun. He sniffed at my face. "Smells like roses?"

Click. I pulled the trigger.

"Good. Do it again. Only this time keep your eyes open."

Click.

"This is easy," I said.

"See that little stone on top of that large rock." He pointed to a stone the size of an apple sitting on a boulder. "Sight up on it."

Click.

"I think I am ready to shoot," I said, proud of myself and as eager as a child with a new toy.

Cole took the gun. A mischievous grin lit up his face as he filled one chamber and handed it back to me. "Don't shoot your foot off." He stood behind me and sighted over my shoulder.

I took aim on the stone and squeezed the trigger. The sound of the hammer striking the cap thundered in my ears as the gun recoiled, knocking me back into Cole's waiting arms.

He laughed. "It isn't as easy as it looks." He reloaded two chambers and put the revolver into his holster, walked away a few paces, turned, drew the gun, and fired. The little stone flew into the air. He fired again. The stone shattered into a thousand pieces. A twinkle of satisfaction gleamed in his eyes.

I stood with my mouth open. I had never seen Cole shoot before. Now, I observed him with a new respect.

He walked over and put another little stone where the first one had been. "Now, let's do it my way. Sight up on the stone and pull the trigger."

Click.

"Again."

Click.

Several more times I shot imaginary rounds at the stone. I pretended it flew into the air and I shot again, shattering it into pieces. Slowly the stone became a Yankee shooting at me from behind the rock. Then more Yankees came from behind trees and bushes. I shot them all. I was in a fight for my life, shooting at everything that moved.

Cole placed his hand on my shoulder, "I think you've shot . . . ."

I jumped and screamed. "Do not do that! I have told you before not to sneak up on me. You will cause me to have heart failure."

"I wasn't sneaking. You weren't paying attention to what was going on around you. A bear could have come and carried me off and you wouldn't have heard it. I was about to say you can use real bullets now."

Cole loaded the gun and moved the stone to the trunk of a fallen tree that stretched into the pool. "This is so you don't get hit by a ricochet."

I continued to practice shooting at the little stone. I never did hit it, but I came close several times.

"It's getting too dark to see the rock," Cole finally said. "We need to turn in so we can get an early start in the morning. We lost more than half a day, today."

"It was the best day I have had since we left the plantation." I put my arm around Cole's waist as we walked back to camp.

"You sure smell good. Nothing like a boy." He sniffed at my face again.

"It is my rose petal soap. I packed only one, small cake. Do not worry. No one will find it." I pulled the soap out of my pocket to show him.

"When you smell like this, one won't have to look very far. Sarah, Sarah, what am I going to do with you?"
Putting his arm around my shoulders, he mussed my hair.

"Just love me."

"I do. That's the trouble. I do."

CHAPTER 18

The aroma of coffee beckoned me out of a sound sleep. As I stretched, I felt every recoil of the gun from the night before. My arms and shoulders ached with the remembrance of shooting that heavy revolver.

"Good morning sleepyhead," Cole said. "It's about time you woke up. Breakfast is ready. We're having fish this morning."

My stomach turned over. "Who can think about food? I am not even awake yet. What time is it?"

"Time to get started. Get up."

"You caught fish? When did you sleep?"

"I had a few hours. I don't need much sleep."

"If I do not get enough, I will be cranky all morning."

"I've noticed."

"No, no, you are supposed to say, 'Why, Sarah, you have such a sweet disposition. You are never cranky.'"

"Why, Sarah, you have such a . . .a. . .. What was the rest of that line?"

"Sweet disposition. But if you are not going to say it with conviction, there is no need for you to say it at all." I pretended to be huffy as I crossed my arms and looked off in the other direction.

Cole laughed. "In that case, get up. You can sleep when we get to Independence. Right now, we need to get on the trail again. Your underthings are dry. Put them on. We can eat when you're dressed."

Reluctantly, I got up and headed for the bushes. I washed the sleep out of my eyes in the warm pond, wishing we could stay for a few more days. The water felt wonderful, but the air chilled my skin to goose flesh when I took off my clothes to put on the breast band and the flannels. "This is such a bother. I cannot wait until I can wear a dress again," I said aloud.

By the time I finished dressing, Cole had already put the packs on the animals. He had rolled up my bedroll but left it on the ground for me to sit on while eating.

I looked at him hunkered down at the fire. "You have shaved."

"Thought I would get rid of the stubble and trim the mustache." He rubbed his cheeks and raked his fingers through his hair, pushing the hair away from his forehead.

The light of the fire bathed him in a golden glow. *How old is he?* I thought, *Twenty-nine, maybe thirty? He would probably be married by now if it was not for the war. I wonder what he would look for in a wife.*

"Is something wrong? Do I have dirt on my face?" Cole asked.

"No. Why?" I plopped down on the bedroll.

"You were staring at me."

"It is just that you look so much like Daddy. I was wondering how old you are."

"I'll be thirty on July thirtieth. Do I seem old to you?"

"No. Not at all. I was just wondering, that's all."

Cole gave me a tin plate with two fish. "From here on in we'll be living off the land. Make the best of it."

"Why can we not go into a town and buy food?"

"Don't think that would be wise. We need to stay out of sight for a while longer. Give whoever is following us a chance to doubt the wisdom of their direction. Let them think that maybe we went the extreme southern route through Arkansas into Texas."

We finished breakfast and packed the remainder of the gear on the mule.

"Are you going to ride Shadow this morning? I thought you were uncertain of him."

"Shadow is not fighting me as much. He is actually a better ride than Zephyr, more even gait. I just did not want to struggle with his disobedience and willful stubbornness." Cole turned his head and looked directly into my eyes. "I knew he would come around to my way of thinking sooner or later. I just had to give him some time."

I pretended the point of Cole's message was lost between the giver and the receiver.

The almost light of predawn still clung to the land as we mounted and rode across the stream, leaving our marvelous pond behind. The leaves of countless autumns crunched beneath the horses' hooves. Bare branches moaned in the chilly wind. Away from the steam of the pond, the covering of the trees, and rocks that held in the thermal warmth, the world grew cold. Dawn was still an hour away.

We rode up and down ridges. Wound our way deep into smoky valleys and up onto mountain spines. The daylight came on crimson and revealed a threatening sky. Through thick wooded areas and in and out of open meadows, we traveled. Along streams, over rocks, and around tree snags, I struggled to keep up with Cole. The scent of rain grew ever stronger as it intertwined with the forest and loamy earth fragrances.

"Do you feel the stillness? Even the birds and animals have taken cover. I don't like the looks of those clouds. They're heavy with ice. We need to find a place to hole up for a day or two. Let the storm pass," Cole said.

"We should have stayed at the pond."

"No. We need a cave. I don't want to be out in the open. Let's head over toward that rock face." He pointed down the ridge to a cliff on the other side of the small glen.

"Do you think we can get over there before the storm breaks?"

"One way to find out. Follow me." He prodded the big horse forward.

Slipping and sliding, half running and half walking, we made our way to the bottom of the ridge. At the foot of the upland, we found a road.

"Might as well take it. Seems to be going toward the outcropping at the head of the valley." Cole pointed to the gap at the mouth of the valley where the two ridges almost met.

On the valley floor, the wind did not cut into my face as much as it had on the top of the ridge. Not that the air was any warmer, just less wind. When the clouds began to release a steady drizzle, I pulled my hat down over my eyebrows to keep the rain away from my face. Water dripped off the brim of the hat and ran down my back.

Cole shook his head and pulled the horses to a halt. "Here, put this on." He took his slicker out of his pack and handed it to me. "Wear it like a tent. It'll keep you dry."

"What will you wear?"

"I have my coat. I'm used to the rain. In the war, rain and mud were commonplace."

"Thank you. I appreciate this." I pulled the slicker over my hat and buttoned it under my chin, leaving one button open for the reins. I could tell Cole was laughing at me, but I did not care. I was dry.

Almost to the gap, we came around a turn in the road and stopped in our tracks. In the middle of the road sat a covered wagon with a broken axle. The back end of the wagon was propped against the wheel lying on the ground. Three towheaded boys were huddled by a small fire beneath a canvas tarpaulin.

"Well, hello there," Cole called.

The boys cowered away.

"We're not going to hurt you." Cole dismounted.

Moans came from inside the wagon. Fear jumped out of the boys' eyes.

Cole walked to the rear of the wagon and looked inside. "You better come over here," he called to me.

I climbed off Misty and looked into the wagon. My eyes widened in disbelief. A lamp hanging from the center rib of the wagon top illuminated a woman lying on a makeshift bed writhing in pain.

"Looks like she's birthing. Get in there and help her," Cole ordered.

"Me? Why not you? I have no knowledge about giving birth to a baby."

"You've watched horses give birth."

"That is quite different."

"You know as much as I do. The only difference is, this time you'll be able to understand what the mother is saying. Who do you think she would want in there at a time like this? A strange man who doesn't know anything, or a strange woman who doesn't know anything?"

Before I could answer, I felt myself being lifted by the seat of my britches and the collar of my jacket, over the tailgate and into the wagon.

The oldest of the boys came and stood beside Cole, followed close behind by his brothers. "Papa went for the doctor. He has been gone for a long time."

Cole smiled. "Don't worry. We'll help your mama. What's your name?"

"I am Karl. I am the oldest, eight years. My brother Juergen is six, and Paulie is the youngest. He is four only." All three boys wore short leather pants, long, white woolen stocking, heavy boots, leather vests over white shirts, leather jackets, and red knitted caps and gloves. Blue eyes looked at us from round faces with rosy red cheeks.

"I am very happy to meet you. I am Mr.. . .ah. . .Mr. Friend." Cole looked at me with a knotted brow, slowly shaking his head. He turned back to Karl and said, "We need hot water. Do you have a big kettle?"

Cole busied himself outside while I turned my attention to the woman on the bed. Wooden barrels marked china, crystal, clothes, and blankets supported wood planks over which a mattress had been placed. A flour barrel served as a table on which sat an empty pan, a cloth, and a basket with a baby blanket, scissors, string, a needle and thread, and a knife.

"Who are you? Vhat you do here?" she asked in a robust voice, thick with a German accent.

"I am here to help you." I hung the slicker over a crate and moved a box out of the way to get closer to the woman.

"Vhat can you do? You, a young boy."

I could hear the pain and disappointment in her voice. "I am sorry that I am not the doctor, but I can help you if you let me. I am not a boy. My name is Sarah."

"Vhy you dressed like boy?"

"My brother and I are traveling to Independence to hook up with a wagon train going to California. We thought I would be safer dressed as a boy."

"Then I am glad you are here. My man vent to get doctor. But I do not think I can vait for Herr Doctor. Something is wrong. My boys popped out like chicken eggs. No trouble. This one is not so. I am in such pain." She gritted her teeth, grabbed onto the bedding trying not to yell. A deep moan escaped her lips.

"Cole, do you have some cold water? She is soaked with sweat," I called.

Presently, Cole stood at the rear of the wagon with a bucket of water.

"Things do not look so good in here," I whispered. "I

wish her husband would get back with the doctor."

"Don't count on that. You do what needs to be done."

I shook my head and returned to the woman. "You know my name but I do not know yours." I poured the water into the pan on the barrel and took off my jacket, hung it over the crate with the slicker. An old shirt, probably belonging to the woman's husband, served well as an apron. I slipped it on backwards and rolled up the sleeves.

"I am Gretchen Delvick. Ve are German. Ve go to California too." She forced a smile while I applied the cool cloth to her feverish forehead. Thick, golden braids hung over her shoulders framing her round face. Just as the boys huddled at the fire, her blue eyes reflected fear.

"Gretchen is a lovely name. You already have three fine boys. Do you want a girl this time?"

"Yah, a little girl. It is always good to have the sons first to help in the field mit their papa but now I vant a girl for me."

"Do you have a name picked out for her?"

"Oh, yah. Ve go to a place called Anaheim. It means Ana's home. I vill call my little girl Anna." Once again a pain gripped her and she screamed.

"Push! Push hard." I moved the lamp from the rib overhead to the foot of the bed and placed it on a box with the word 'tools' written in red letters. *Now is no time to be modest,* I thought, spreading Gretchen's legs apart.

"I can see the baby's head. But she is caught. No, Gretchen. Stop pushing."

Through clenched teeth Gretchen said, "Knife is in the basket. You must cut."

"Cut! Cut what?"

"Just above the opening. You can see."

Yes, I could see to what Gretchen was referring. I reached for the basket and the knife, took a deep breath and made a small incision. Gretchen screamed. Blood spurted over the shirt I wore. I slipped my hands into the passage and took hold of the baby. Lowering the baby passed the pelvic bone and turning her, I could see two eyes, a little nose, then the mouth, and a shoulder.

"Here she comes." Excitement raised my voice. "One more push, Gretchen. You can do it."

Gretchen was exhausted but she gave one last push, blood gushed and the baby was in my arms. A gasp of air filled the little lungs and the baby began to cry.

"Hello, Anna. Your mama has been waiting for you. Gretchen, you have a little girl, just what you wanted."

"Is she all right?" Fingers und toes all there?"

"She's perfect." I stood up.

"You are not done yet. You must tie and cut the cord."

"I do not remember this part when birthing horses."

"And you must take the afterbirth and bury it deep. Do not let an animal smell it, or it will dig it up and the child will be cursed. Und you must sew up where you cut."

I put little Anna on Gretchen's stomach while I tied the cord and cut it. More blood. I wrapped the birthing membrane in a cloth.

Gretchen looked at each finger and toe. Tears of joy ran down the tired mother's cheeks. "Ve need to vash her and wrap her. Keep her varm, yah?"

Cole stood ready at the back of the wagon with a pan of warm water. "I'll trade you."

I gave Cole the bloody towel in which the membrane was wrapped. "Bury this deep." I took the pan and bathed little Anna, wrapped her in the blanket and placed her into her mother's arms. Then I stitched up the incision with the hem stitching Dr. Bardlow had taught me to do at Safe Harbor, and I cleaned up most of the blood.

"You sleep now. I will be back to check on you in a little while." I trimmed the lamp and hung it on the wagon rib again. A smile of peace and love lit Gretchen's face as she looked at her daughter.

I climbed out of the wagon just as a large, muscular man rode up on an old, tired, chestnut mare. The man wore a long, black rain slicker and a black felt hat pulled down over his eyebrows. He had the same big, blue eyes and round face as the three boys. Obviously, this was Mr. Delvick.

"Vhat you doing in my camp?" he shouted, reaching for his rifle.

"Hold on, Mister. We're just here to help," Cole said, holding his hands up in plain sight.

"Papa, they are our friends," Karl said, jumping between his father and Cole. "They helped Mama. Ve have a baby."

"Yes, you have a little girl. Her name is Anna," I said, climbing over the tailgate and running for cover under the tarpaulin. "Gretchen is doing fine too. They are sleeping. Both had quite a time of it."

Mr. Delvick's eyes widened when he saw the blood on his shirt that I wore. "I should have been here, but I vent for doctor."

"Why didn't he come back with you?" Cole asked.

Mr. Delvick dismounted and walked to warm himself at the fire. The rain was coming down hard but the tarpaulin kept the fire from going out. "I could not find anyone. Not a house or a farm or a town. I think I should come back before this storm gets vorse."

"We don't need the doctor anymore," Cole said. "What we do need is to get out of this canyon. I'll help you fix the axle and wheel on the wagon. Then we can move to higher ground. I found a cave up there, big enough for all the stock." Cole pointed to a rock outcropping about a half mile away. "I've already started cutting a tree for a lever to lift the wagon."

"Then ve do it."

I returned to the wagon to check on Gretchen and Anna and to retrieve my raincoat. Hanging the bloody shirt over a crate, I said softly to the sleeping mother, "I will wash it out later."

Once again under the tarpaulin, I asked, "Boys, where does your mother keep the food?"

Karl opened the large Emigrant Basket to reveal carrots, onions, potatoes and salted beef. "Is this vhat you vant?"

"This is perfect." I filled a kettle and tied it onto Old Danger's back. "Boys, come with me. We will go to the cave, get a fire started and cook this food. I am sure the men will be hungry by the time they get the wagon fixed. I know I am hungry now." I put the three boys on Zephyr's back, packed a bundle of wood on Fire Storm, and mounted Misty. Leading Old Danger and the horses, except for Shadow, we made our way to the opening in the cliff wall.

The cave was about ten feet up the face of the cliff with a gentle slope leading to a ledge outside the opening. As Cole had said, the cave was large, plenty of space for our animals and the Delvick's one horse, two oxen, and a milk cow. The mouth of the cave gaped eight feet high and about six feet wide. Inside, a rock shelf went back almost ten feet and then sloped down enlarging the cave into a big room. Soot from other fires scarred the ceiling by the entrance. Musty odors closed in around me as I held the lantern high to illuminate the cavern.

"Boys, help me start a fire on the shelf by the opening. I will unpack the animals. Karl, please set the kettle in the rain to collect water."

I felt a tug at my coat. "How is Papa going to get the vagon up here?" Juergen asked, his little face twisted in a frown.

"Cole and your papa will find a way. I do not think the wagon will fit inside the cave but it can sit on the ledge outside." I smiled to reassure him there was nothing to worry about.

By the time the covered wagon was brought up the hill, snow had begun to fall and the day was spent. Cole and Mr. Delvick positioned the conveyance at the entrance of the cave to serve as a windbreak. Inside the shelter we were safe and warm, while outside the storm picked up momentum.

"I was hoping we wouldn't run into a blizzard," Cole said as he helped Mr. Delvick get Gretchen out of the wagon and bring her to the fire.

"Yah, ve thought all the bad vether vould be more north. Ve left our farm in Virginia six veeks ago. Ve vanted to be in Independence by the time the baby vas born. But ve have had such bad luck so far. Und ve just started. Ve go to California."

"We're heading that way, too."

"Maybe, ve travel together. There is safety in numbers, yah? Ve can help each other out."

"Supper is ready," I said, getting the plates from the box Mr. Delvick had pulled inside the cave.

"Stew, Das richt gut," Gretchen said.

"Mama, ve must speak English. Mr. Friend and his sister do not know German," Karl said, pulling little Paulie away from the snow that had gathered at the mouth of the cave.

"Yah, Karl. You are right. I said the stew smells good."

"Thank you. We have coffee and bread, too. I am afraid all of this food is from your larder. We have used up our food. We started living off the land. Mr. Delvick, we will replace what we use," I said.

"That is not necessary. You have more than paid for vhat little food you eat. Und since ve are going to be traveling together, please call me Rudy."

I started filling each plate. Cole took his supper and sat with his back leaning against the wall of the cave where he could look out over the land. He placed his cup on a flat rock beside him.

"Since we are on a first name basis, you can call me Cole and this is my sister, Sarah. Our last name is

Brighton, not Friend." Cole ignored the surprised look on Rudy's face. "Why are you going to California?"

Rudy's blue eyes glazed over with a faraway look. He sat next to Gretchen by the fire. His words came painfully slow. "Ve left Germany because ve heard of the good land here in America. My oldest brother inherited my father's farm, und I, und my younger brother, vorked for him. Three years I vorked to get money for the passage. Months ve vere on the vater. Day und night, saw nothing but sky und ocean. Then, ve landed in Virginia. Such beautiful country. Good to grow crops. Our farm vas doing very good vhen the var started. Ve lost everything und have no more money to start over. So my younger brother, who vent to California to find gold a few years ago, said to come to Anaheim. He has a vineyard. Yah. He grows fine grapes und sends the vine to France. Und, vould you believe, France sends the vine back to America mit French vine labels. So ve go to Anaheim, California, to raise fine French vine."

Cole laughed. "I'll bet I've had some of your brother's wine."

"Yah, it is good vine. Und vhy do you go to California?"

"We have an uncle there. I promised our mother I would take Sarah to him. He is the only family we have left. We, too, lost everything in the war."

"Cole, I think you need to get some wood for the fire," I said, seeing that the supply I had brought up the hill was running low. My heart was heavy as Cole recited the ravages of the war.

After supper, Cole and Rudy took the axes and left the cave. Karl and I cleaned the dinner plates and washed them in melted snow. Juergen and Paulie snuggled by their mama as she told a story of three boys on a marvelous journey to a faraway land. On their great adventure they were brave and strong. Her voice sounded like music on a summer's evening. I found myself sitting by the fire listening to her story. Karl cozied up to me.

Later that evening, when the Delvick family was bedded down on the other side of the cave, Cole stretched out our bedrolls in the soft dirt beneath the entrance shelf. "I apologize for making you go through such an ordeal this afternoon. I didn't realize it would be so difficult birthing Anna."

"Cole, you should have seen it. I actually helped bring a life into this world. I do not have words to tell you how that felt. Do not apologize. I should be thanking you. I was there to help Gretchen and see the miracle of birth. What a wonderful experience."

"Sarah, you amaze me."

"Cole, I have a question to ask you."

"Ask."

"How can we travel with the Delvicks? If whoever is following us should catch up with us while we are with them, will not their lives be in danger too?"

"I have been thinking about that. We need to make sure their wagon can make the trip to Independence. It is not in very good condition. But it's probably all the Yankees left them. Rudy is lucky to have it. However, it won't take the rough journey ahead. Rudy has already done major repairs. They need our help. But you're right. Depending on who is following us, their lives may be in jeopardy."

"How do you know we are still being followed?"

"When I was out West, I seemed to have picked up a sixth sense about these things. I can feel we're being followed. Don't ask me how, I just know." He got up and placed another log on the fire. "That should last till morning." He returned to his bedroll. "If anything should happen to me, you would be safe with the Delvicks. They'll make sure you get to Uncle William."

"What do you mean if anything should happen to you?"

"One can never tell. This is a hard trip and any number of things could happen. If the Yankees are following us, I could be arrested. But let's not talk of that tonight. Everything will work out, don't worry. It's getting late. You should get some sleep. Good night, little sister." He leaned over and kissed me on the forehead, patting my hand. "Don't worry," he whispered.

I crawled deeper into my bedroll, pulling the blanket over my shoulders and turning my face away from the fire. Thoughts of my soft, feather bed and pillow danced around in my head. I recalled my wonderful bedroom. The fragrance of lilac soap would be filling the air. There, feelings of safety and security had surrounded my world. The memories of Mr. Molack intruded but briefly and were dismissed. I chose not to dwell on the evils of that man. I wanted only the good memories residing in my loneliness. I longed to be back at Rosewood where familiarity embraced me. In my mind's eye, I walked once again down the halls into rooms vibrating with love. *Homesickness must be the worst kind of sickness of all,* I thought. *Doctors do not have a cure and it eats away at the very fiber of a person.* Tears rolled down my cheeks as I peered into the darkness.

CHAPTER 19

Time became our enemy while we waited for the snow to melt and the roads to dry enough for the wagon to travel without getting bogged down in mud. Each day we stayed in the cave meant that we might not get to Independence before the first wagon trains would leave. Cole impatiently tended to our animals. He reinforced his bond with the horses by touching and gently petting each animal. He and Rudy discussed the journey and what we could expect. Cole mended leather harnesses and made sure our equipment was in good order. He carved flutes for the boys from thin tree branches, and taught them how to play a simple tune. Cole and Rudy went hunting. They dressed out venison and rabbit. I cooked the meals, baked breads, helped Gretchen take care of the children and slept.

At last the day came to leave the safety of our cave and venture on to Independence. With the aid of ropes and pulley, the oxen strained against the weight as the wagon complained with squeaks and groans down the incline to the road at the valley floor. Fresh air, saturated with the scent of pine and earth washed by nature, replaced the dusty, stagnant odor of the cave.

We were once again following the sun on its westward journey. The mountains gave way to a great valley. Rivers, flooded by the melting snow, proved to be difficult to cross. The gradual climb to the tabletop that Cole called the Cumberland Plateau and beyond to the Highland Rim Plateau seemed easier than traversing the ridges of the Unaka and Great Smoky Mountains. When the road fell away to the Central Basin, I believed the most arduous part of the journey to be over. I was wrong.

The trip took on a new dimension with the Delvick family traveling with us. Cole and I were never alone. I missed the closeness he and I had been developing. Mealtimes were the hardest. Cole and I used to discuss our wants and dreams for the future, remembering good times, and planning our odyssey together. Now, Cole talked with Rudy about the trip and equipment. I had to be satisfied to chat with Gretchen about the children and cooking.

I was learning to accept the good with the bad, missing my talks with Cole, but growing to love the children, the games they played after dinner and the songs they sang at bedtime. I loved Gretchen's soft manner and her easy acceptance of everything - - so much like Mama.

Even though ammunition was dear, Cole continued to teach me how to shoot. I began to hit the target.

When the food supply ran low we pooled our money and Rudy went into town to purchase what was needed. Cole and I stayed with Gretchen and the children out of sight.

Upon his return, Rudy brought back a wanted poster. It read: Cole and Sarah Brighton, brother and sister, wanted as horse thieves by the United States Government. Two hundred dollars reward.

A surprisingly good artist sketch of our likenesses centered the page.

Rudy handed the poster to Cole. "Vhat vill you do?"

"The question is, what will you do? Two hundred dollars is a lot of money."

"Does a man put a price on the lives of his vife und kinder? If you did not help us, ve vould have died in that blizzard. I do not believe you are a horse thief."

"Thank you. You're right. These are our horses. We just took what was ours. I had planned to tell you that we were on the run before we left the cave but the time never seemed right."

Once again my anger against those blue belly Yankees boiled and spewed out of my mouth. "We only took what was ours. They said we could not have our own horses. I hate Yankees, every one of them."

"Calm down. An attitude like that will only get you into trouble," Cole chided. "We need to keep a cool head and outsmart them at their own game. They aren't looking for a man and his brother traveling with a family."

"That means I have to be a boy all the way to California." My dreams of buying a pretty dress in Independence and getting back my own identity vanished.

"It does not have to be all the vay to California," Gretchen said. "I vill buy a dress for you und you can vear it vhen ve are out on the trail, yah? Once ve are mit the vagon train the people vill protect you."

"No." Cole handed the poster to Gretchen. "I do not want to trust anyone else. The more people who know, the more chances we'll be taking. Greed is a powerful motivation. We just fought a war because of it. It's not going to kill Sarah to dress as a boy until we get to Uncle William's place where she'll be safe. If someone recognizes me, I could be arrested. It won't be my first time in a Yankee prison. But I don't want to leave Sarah to fend for herself."

"Do not vorry. Ve vill help you." Rudy looked at his family. Everyone nodded in agreement.

I urged Cole to tell the rest of the story. The Delvick's needed to know before they were caught in the middle of a gunfight.

Cole chose his words carefully. "We think you should be aware of one more thing. We are being hunted by two men, brothers." Cole told the story of how Mama had shot Frank Molack and his brothers seeking vengeance for the death. "So you see that traveling with us may not be the best situation for your family."

Rudy thought for a moment before he said, "Friendships do not depend on maybe or vhat ifs. You are our friends. Ve travel together and face vhatever comes as partners."

Gretchen smiled in compliance. "This vay you need us as much as ve need you. Ve feel safe mit you. Rudy is a farmer, not an Indian fighter. I am so afraid to travel vest mit a vagon through Indian lands. But you can protect us."

Cole interrupted her, "I'm not an Indian fighter. I spent some time on the frontier, but I'm just a man like countless other men who travel through Indian lands. I would much rather trade than fight. When we get to Independence, I'm going to ask around for a wagonmaster who believes the same way I do. The last thing I want to do is fight my way to California."

"You see, this is vhy ve need you. You can find a good vagonmaster for both of us," Rudy said. "Ve trust you. Ve vill make a good trip together. Yah?"

Cole and I knew they were right. We needed them as much as they needed us.

Independence at long last became a reality as we entered the city from the south on Main Street. The deeply rutted road led us to Lexington, the southern boundary of the town square where, in years past, the wagon trains formed. The city hall, courthouse, the Nebraska House, the Merchants Hotel and clusters of other buildings lined the streets of Lexington, Kansas Avenue, Maple and Liberty. A rail fence in front of the courthouse kept the emigrant cattle from eating the grass. Blacksmith sheds, livery stables, stores and saloons mingled together. The sound of incessant hammering and banging came from the continuous building and the work in a dozen or more blacksmith's sheds throughout the city. The streets were congested with people, wagons, carriages, horses, and herds of cattle. I had never seen or heard such a commotion in all my life.

"All I want is a bath and a bed. Can we stay in one of the hotels tonight?" I asked as I took in the sights and smells of this big city.

Gretchen looked uneasy. She whispered something to Rudy. "Ve vill stay mit our vagon, not in a hotel," she said.

"The wagon trains leave from Westport," Cole said to Rudy. "They used to leave from here at the Liberty side of the square before the Independence landing silted over. Now the river boats go on down to Westport Landing or Kansas City Landing. Take the Westport Independence Road. You can't miss it. Sarah and I will stay the night in town and meet you in the morning. I'll ask around to see who's taking a train out this year."

We watched as the Delvick's wagon rambled down the street and turned the corner before we pulled the horses to a halt in front of the hotel. "Stay here and keep out of trouble. I'll go in and see if they have a room." Cole dismounted and tied the horses to the hitching rail.

I watched as Cole entered through two large oak doors with an oval glass window in each panel. The hotel stood quite impressively in its three story grandeur, with lace curtains and heavy red drapes displayed in each street front window. The pristine white building still smelled of fresh paint. I shifted my weight in the saddle, growing more impatient by the minute. From the saloon next door, loud music banged from a tinny piano. Shouting voices poured into the street. A man came flying through the swinging doors of the establishment and landed in the muddy road. The flying man cleared the boardwalk in front of the saloon without setting a foot on the wood. A tall, lean man with shoulder length blondish hair, wearing black pants, a white ruffled shirt, black vest, and a black hat followed the thrown man through the doors. A pair of Colt revolvers were strapped to the man's hip.

"I should kill you like a lying, cheating dog. But I won't this time. If I ever see your cheatin' hide again, I will. Now get."

The man on the ground scrambled to his feet, grabbed his hat and ran toward the stables.

"If there's one thing I can't stand, it's a cheatin' gambler," the tall man said to the men standing around him. Before returning to the bar, he noticed our horses. His golden tanned face harbored the bluest eyes I had ever seen.

"Mighty fine lookin' horses you have there, boy. They for sale?"

"No." I pulled my hat down over my forehead and looked away.

"Give you top dollar for 'em."

In my deepest voice, I said, "They're not for sale at any price."

He walked around the rear of Shadow, patting the horse on the rump. "I don't believe I've ever seen a horse as fine as this'en. What kind of breed is it?"

"Arabian."

"Never heard of it."

"You best watch out mister. That horse kicks."

Shadow laid his ears back and snorted, pawing the ground. The man took the hint and moved away.

"Smart move, mister. In another second you would have been flying through the air like that man you threw out of the saloon."

"I hate smart mouth kids," the man said under his breath, walking to the boardwalk. "If you decide to sell, I'll be here for another week or so. They call me Coyote. I'm the scout for the Dawson outfit. Ask anyone, they know me."

Cole came out of the hotel. The two men exchanged glances, but no words were spoken.

"What was that all about?" Cole asked as he mounted Shadow.

"He wanted to buy the horses. He's a scout for a man named Dawson."

"Dawson's taking a train out this year?"

"The scout said they would be leaving in a week. Why? Do you know him?"

"Only by reputation. He's a good man. We might see about hooking up with him. But for now, we need to take care of these animals. We'll head to Weston's Blacksmith's shed and talk to him about a wagon. He's the man I wrote to. After that, I'll buy you the best steak in town."

The stable was filled to busting its sideboards with animals. But seven more could always squeeze in somewhere, especially at two dollars a head.

Talking with Mr. Weston proved to be fruitful. "Of course, I have your wagon," said the huge man, sweat glistening on his body. "That's what I do, make wagons. I got your letter and made one of the finest wagons you'll ever see. Now, it all depends if you can pay. This good wagon and a team of oxen will cost you one hundred and fifty dollars, cash. I make wagons out of seasoned hardwood to withstand the long trip across country and the durn blasted temperatures out there."

"I have seen your work. There is no need to sell me on your craftsmanship. That's why I wrote to you."

"I have a prairie schooner out back. I'll show it to you." Weston put aside the wheel rim he was working on and led the way to the back of his shop. Four fine looking wagons stood in a row. A double thickness of waterproofed canvas covered each wagon. Tar and grease buckets hung from the sides. Extra parts, wheels, axles, tongues, spokes, and canvas were slung under the wagon beds. "This one is ready to go. In the corral over yonder are oxen. Pick out the ones you want. I'll have everything ready for you tomorrow."

Tomorrow. My insides started to quiver. Excitement and fear mingled together. I walked over to look inside the wagon. "It's so small. I'll have to live in this cramped space for the next three or four months?"

"It could be more like five or six months. But for us, a prairie schooner is better than a Conestoga. We don't have any furniture. All we need to carry is food. We'll have plenty of room." Cole walked with Weston back around to sign the papers and pay half down. He would pay the rest the day we took possession.

I tried to visualize myself living in a wagon for five or six months. The trip thus far was bad enough, but I never seemed to look beyond Independence. I did not really think about the Indians nor the hardships of the frontier. Independence was the last jumping off place, the last of civilization. Out there, only God knew what awaited us.

Cole and I still carried the mud from the road on our clothing when we entered the elegant dining room at the hotel. We had our saddlebags slung over our shoulders, and Cole carried his riffle in his hand. We were seated at a table in the rear of the room, almost in the kitchen.

"I wish I could have cleaned up a bit before dinner," I whispered, noticing all the ladies in their beautiful dresses. Independence might have been at the edge of the frontier, but fashion was still a way of life.

"The women of the wilderness insist on wearing the latest styles. It's their way of bringing civilization to the remotest places," Cole said as he saw my eyes survey the lovely clothing. "Don't be so sad. The time will pass quickly. You'll see, before we know it, we'll be at Uncle William's ranch." He reached across the table and squeezed my hand. His sympathetic smile and sparkling eyes gladdened my heart.

After dinner, Cole sent me to our room while he went to check on the horses one more time. The hotel, filled to overflowing, had only one room left. We had paid eight dollars each for a room and a bath. Shock rushed over me when I opened the door and found four men sleeping on the floor. Stale whisky and body odor accosted my nostrils. One small, empty bed awaited me in the middle of the room and in the far corner stood a copper tub with no curtain or screen for privacy.

"What are all you men doing in my room?" I shouted in disbelief.

"Shhh, keep it down. Can't you see folks is tryin' to sleep?" one man said, as he rolled over.

"You paid for the bed. We paid for the floor. So shut your trap, kid," another said.

"You what?" I could not believe my ears. They were actually going to share our room. "I will not sleep with all of you men in here. We will just see about this." I turned on my heel and headed down the stairs to the desk.

"See here, mister," I called to the clerk. "I want a private room for me and my brother. The one you gave us has four men sleeping on the floor. That will never do." I plunked the key down on the counter.

"Listen, kid, that's all I have. Take it or leave it, but the hotel policy is you don't get your money back." The clerk slid the key back to me and turned to sort papers into little cubbyholes.

"What seems to be the matter?" came a voice from behind me.

I turned to stare into the embroidered vest of the man I believed to be the owner of the hotel and saloon. My eyes climbed up the vest to a smooth shaved, weak-chinned man with a pencil line mustache and dark eyes hooded by heavy lids. He towered over me by almost a foot. The aroma of brandy and cigars clung to his gray suit. A leering smile seemed fixed on his face.

"This kid doesn't like the room, Boss. Too many people in it."

"Then give him another one."

"We don't have any. We're full."

"I'll tell you what I'm going to do. I have a set of rooms you can have for as long as you like. Take my key. It's the double door at the top of the stairs." He handed the key to me without changing his expression.

I did not know if I should take it or not. Does he know that I am a woman? Thoughts raced through my mind. I looked around for Cole. He was nowhere in sight. "This is much too generous," I said, taking the key. His hand closed around mine and held it tight a moment too long. I did not look at him, only at our hands clasped in conflict. I yanked away.

"You're a strong boy. How old are you?"

"Fourteen." I lowered my voice. My teeth clenched and a shiver gripped my spine.

"I'll show you to the room myself. It's right up here." He took my arm and squeezed it as he ushered me up the stairs.

I tried to break his hold but could not. Once again, I looked anxiously for Cole as the man shoved me into the room. The entire suite was done in red - - velvet drapes, carpet, settee, and bed swags. Gold fringe tassels skirted the bed.

"Aren't these rooms everything I said they were? Come over and sit on the bed. It's the softest mattress this side of Chicago." He bounced up and down on the thick, quilted coverlet sending gold fringe swinging with each bounce.

"I do not think I should be here," I said, backing away from him.

"Nonsense. You are my guest."

I turned the doorknob. It was locked. "Open it this minute!" I stamped my foot to accentuate my words.

"My, you're a sweet thing. Are you traveling alone?"

"No. I am with my older brother. And if you do not let me out of here he will kill you."

"Now, there's no need to get all riled up about this. I'm just being friendly. I thought you were a friendly person, too. I'm putting myself out to help you and this is the thanks I get for it? You'll have your brother kill me?"

"Well, I do thank you, but I think I should be going. We do not want to put you out." I turned the knob again in hopes that it would open. It didn't. "Let me go."

"That door is tricky. The knob sticks from time to time. I am not trying to keep you." A smile of satisfaction crossed his face.

"Kid, is that you?" came Cole's voice from the other side of the door.

"Yes. I am locked in."

"Stand back. I'll shoot the knob."

"No. Don't. I'll open it. Don't break the lock." Swearing, he got up and opened the door.

As soon as the mechanism clicked in the lock, Cole kicked it wide open. "Come on, Kid, let's get out of here." He grabbed my arm and pulled me down the stairs.

"He knows I am a woman," I whispered.

"Not necessarily. To a man like that, it doesn't matter if you're a boy or a girl, it's all the same."

I yanked my arm out of Cole's hand and stopped dead in my tracks. My eyes flew wide open and my mouth gaped in shock.

"Sarah, you've led a very sheltered life at Rosewood. People are not as good as you would want them to be. They don't live by the same rules as you or I were taught. Remember the man in the woods? You can't trust anyone. This was my fault. I never should have left you alone. I thought you were going up to our room."

"I did. But there were four men sleeping on the floor. I went down to get another room. All the other rooms were taken."

"So Mr. Nick offered his rooms to you."

"Mr. Nick?"

"That's what everyone calls him. The last time I saw him, he was cheating some poor farmer out of his outfit. One of these days, Nick will run up against someone who'll put a bullet through his heart, if he can find it."

Cole stopped at the front desk on the way out. He slammed his rifle on the desk. "I want my money back for the room," he demanded.

With trembling hands, the clerk handed over the money without a word of protest.

Cole turned to me, "Shall we go?" Cole opened the oval glass paneled door and led the way outside. I resented his not letting me go first, but then, I was supposed to be a boy.

"What are we going to do now?" I shivered against the cold night air.

Cole put his arm around my shoulders and we walked east along Maple, then north on Main Street toward a yellow house at the end. "This used to belong to a woman named Molly. I've stayed here a few times. We'll see if she still owns it and if she has a room. This isn't a hotel or a boarding house, so I don't want you to be shocked when you see the ladies."

"What kind of a house is it?"

"Well, it's . . . a. . . you might say. . . it's a . . .house of fallen angels."

"You mean a . . .? I cannot bring myself to say the word."

"It's not as bad as all that. Molly's a very nice woman."

"I cannot stay in a place like that. What will people think?"

"What people? Who cares what people think? You want a hot bath and a clean bed?"

"Not one that's been slept in by countless women doing God only knows what. How can you ask me to stay in such a place?"

"It's either that or the barn. And don't think the stable

is clean and sweet smelling like the Mary and Joseph and the baby Jesus story in the Bible. No barn in a crowded city is clean and sweet."

"How many times have you stayed there? Did you stay with this Molly? Or were there others? Cole, how could you?"

"Sarah, what I do is my business. I don't answer to you. Now as I see it, we have one of two choices. One, we could leave town and camp on the road to Westport. That means you will forego a soft bed and a hot bath. And just smell the air. We'll have rain before morning. Or two, you could swallow your pride and come with me to meet Molly."

My face felt the cold air filled with the promise of rain. My body longed for a hot bath and a soft bed. I thought of what Mama would say. *'We need to behave like the ladies of Rosewood. Your daddy would not want us to forget who we are.' But I am not Sarah anymore. She is buried somewhere under all this dirt and boy's clothes. Would Mama and Daddy be disappointed with me if I were to go into a house of prostitution? Mama did what needed to be done to survive. She killed a man. I suppose I have to do what I must in order to survive.* "You are right, Cole. I will swallow some of my pride." I took a deep breath. "Lead the way."

CHAPTER 20

The front door of the yellow, wood framed house was opened by a huge darkie dressed in a black suit, white shirt, and gloves. He escorted Cole and me into the parlor to the left of the long entry hall. It was a large room decorated with gilded mirrors, white woodwork trimmed in gold, a gold and crystal chandelier, and maroon velvet furniture. It held all the charm of a French salon. Two enormous reproductions hung on the walls. The first, The Bathers by Fragonard, displayed buxom, nude women frolicking in a pond. The other, Poussin's The Rape of the Sabine Women depicted women being carried away by powerful men. Both paintings aroused a sensual awareness of my own body hidden under the boyish disguise.

"Well, as I live and breathe, if it isn't my Johnny Reb come back to see me," the red haired woman said as she came through the gold drapes that swaged the door frame. Without hesitation, she ran and threw her arms around Cole's neck, planting a kiss firmly on his lips. Her pink feather boa trailed in her wake. "I thought I would never see you again. You said you were going home to the plantation."

"I did. Now I'm heading out again. This time I'm taking the kid, here, to our uncle." Cole broke her embrace when she turned to look at me. "This is Danny."

My mouth gaped and my eyes popped wide open as I surveyed this strangely clad woman. Her dress was a brilliant pink with pink feathers trimming a severely plunging neckline which hardly covered her ample bosom. I could feel my face growing hot. I could not take my eyes away from her. Her flaming red hair resembled a lion's mane and hung freely to her well-endowed buttocks.

Cole stepped close to me, put his right arm around my shoulders and closed my mouth with his left index finger. "Molly, I would like you to meet Danny. Danny, this is Molly." Cole seemed pleased with himself that he could tell such lies with a resonance of truth.

When I opened my mouth to speak, sounds refused to come. Never had I been at a loss for words until now. I just smiled.

"We've had a long trip and we're tired," Cole apologized. "We were wondering if you could put us up for the night. The hotels are filled and . . . ."

"Why, of course. I always have a room for you. The kid can stay in the little room in the attic. My sister stays there when she comes to visit. You, my dear man, can choose a room, any room you want. The girls will be happy to see you again. Follow me." She took a lamp from the table and led the way into the entry hall and up the stairs, past the second floor and up to a room on the third. In the room, Cole stood in the middle of the cubicle so he would not hit his head on the slanted ceiling.

I shuddered at the thought of being in an attic room. Only slaves and hired help stayed in such places. With a sigh, I entered into the charming, girlish surroundings. A single brass bed, white vanity, chest of drawers, wardrobe, and a rocking chair barely fit in the cramped space. White eyelet bed covers matched the curtains on the one small window. Wood floors were covered by a braided rag rug.

"I'll have Addie heat some water for your bath. You look like you could use one, both of you." Molly looked from Cole to me and back again. With a big smile, she said to Cole, "I'll help you with your bath." A long, creamy leg rubbed against him.

"We sure could use a bath. But this room doesn't seem large enough for a tub," Cole said, backing away from her advances and hitting his head on the ceiling. His face turned crimson as he saw my shocked expression.

Molly moved toward Cole again, like a cat moves to a dish of cream. "You're right. He'll need to go down into the kitchen. Don't worry. None of my girls will accost him. He's too small. We throw his size back. We like men, or haven't you noticed?" She walked her fingers up Cole's arm.

Cole cleared his throat. "Do you think you might have a nightshirt the kid could use? We've been on the road for months, sleeping in our clothes."

"I should have something that fits." Molly rubbed her hands over Cole's chest. "You don't need something to wear. I've never known you to wear a nightshirt."

Again, Cole's face flushed. He shook his head as he held Molly at arm's length. "Maybe this wasn't such a good idea to come here. You're giving the kid the wrong impression about me."

"Nonsense. If he doesn't understand these things by now, he soon will." She turned toward me and winked one of her big, brown, doe-like eyes. Lighting the lamp on the dresser, she said, "I'll be back in just a minute with a nightshirt."

"My word, she is certainly blatant in her desire for you," I said, once the door was closed behind Molly.

"She doesn't mean anything by it. She's that way with everyone."

"She must be good at what she does."

"She is," Cole said, with a grin of remembrance on his face. "You should be comfortable here. The bed seems soft." Cole felt the mattress.

"Yes. It is not as bad as I thought it would be. Just where are you going to sleep?"

"Don't worry about me. I'll make do." He could not keep the smile from dancing across his lips.

"I just bet you will."

Molly returned with an extra quilt and a nightshirt. "This is a little frilly, but it's the best I can do. No one will see you in it." She held up the nightshirt, which was more of a nightgown. It was white cotton with long sleeves and a low neckline. The sides were slit half way up to the hip. "Addie is heating the water. So when you're ready, just go down to the kitchen. It's at the rear of the house, beyond the entry hall. Put those dirty clothes on the back porch and Addie will wash them in the morning." She gave Cole a big smile and fluttered her long eyelashes. "Now, Johnny, it's your turn. Come with me." Taking his arm, Molly led the way through the door.

Watching the light from Molly's lamp fade down the stairs, the icy fingers of loneliness gripped my heart. I sat on the bed, pulled off my boots and put my hat on the vanity. I ruffled my fingers through my hair. *It's getting long,* I thought. *It should be cut again.* I got up and pulled the curtains back from the little window to survey the city. At the other end of the street, lights from saloons and hotels flooded onto the boardwalks. People and wagons still crowded the roadway. The continuous sounds of building, the hammering in the blacksmith's sheds as they got both animals and wagons ready for travel and the racket of an ever growing city only emphasized the homesick ache deep within me. In the distance cried the lonesome sound of a riverboat steam whistle.

Slowly I descended the stairs to the kitchen with the nightshirt in one hand and the lamp in the other. Giggles and muffled moans came from behind closed doors.

"You must be Master Johnny's brother? My name's Addie," the thin, black woman said. "I have your bath water hot and waitin' for you in da tub. There be soap and a towel on da stand. And I puts a towel over da chair to give you more privacy. A young boy like you needs his privacy. I goin' ta bed now. Jest puts your clothes on da porch when you is done. See you in da mornin'."

She did not give me a chance to respond. Taking her lamp, Addie went down the hall and disappeared through the third door on the right, under the stairs.

"Why does everyone call Cole, Johnny?" I mused aloud, as I closed the kitchen door and set my lamp on the drainboard at the far end of the room to conceal the tub in shadows. While stripping away my filthy clothes, I thought of the pond and the lovely day I had with Cole. Slipping into the tub, the water washed over me, and once again, I was feeling Cole's strong arms around me as he taught me to swim. Vigorously scrubbing my hair and body, I became aware of the faint fragrances of roses, Mama's favorite flower. She always smelled of roses. More memories crowded into my thoughts as I returned home to Rosewood Plantation, to walk the halls once again in my mind. Unable to hold back the tears, I allowed myself to cry. Deep sobs shook my body. I pulled my knees up and wrapped my arms around them, placing my forehead on my hands. Tears rolled freely down my face. I wished they could wash away all the heartache and make the loneliness go away, but they couldn't.

I do not know how long I was in the bath when I heard footsteps in the hall and men's voices close by. Panic jolted me back to reality. Springing from the tub, I grabbed the nightshirt and the towel and haphazardly dried my hair while wriggling into the shirt at the same time. The white cotton material clung to my wet body. Grabbing my dirty clothes, I jumped out the backdoor just as the men entered the kitchen. I shivered in the night air, waiting for them to leave.

"I don't care what yeah say, I saw that Cole fella at the smithy's."

I stood on tiptoes to look through the window. The smaller man held up one of the wanted posters.

"If'n we don't get him soon, someone else will."

The other man threw a handful of kindling and some paper into the stove and lit it. "Well, there's nothin' we can do 'bout it tonight. You can prowl 'round the blacksmith's shed and saloons if'n you want, but I'm gonna wash off some of this here trail dust and have me a good time upstairs." He pumped water into a big black kettle and set it on the stove to heat. "We knowed they'd be here. He probably hid the girl in a hotel somewhere. We'll need to find her, too. Mornin' will be soon enough to get our business done." He started taking off his clothes.

"Well, I'm not gonna stand around here and let this reward money slip through my fingers. We know that girl's the one the Hollinger's been lookin' for.

"They been lookin' for a long time. One more night ain't gonna matter. That sweet honey upstairs is awaitin' for me tonight. And I ain't gonna disappoint her." He stood totally naked, waiting for the water in the kettle to get warm.

I ducked away from the window when I saw he was naked. In the darkness of the porch, I leaned flat against the house trying to make myself blend into the woodwork. The thought that these two men are the Molack brothers, came screaming into my mind. *They are here to kill Cole. And who is this Hollinger that has been looking for me? Is that the Yankee Carpetbagger?*

I heard the younger brother say, "I'm gonna see if'n I can find her. I'll start at the Nebraska House and work my way 'round the square. Someone's seen her." The back door flew open and the smaller of the two bounded out onto the porch and down the steps.

"Shut the damn door. It's cold in here."

My heart raced as I watched the man stride into the darkness. I heard the gate slam. I knew he was gone. I stood motionless for a long time. When I heard the kitchen door close, I took a deep breath and looked through the window. The kitchen was empty. I waited a few more minutes before I slowly opened the door and went in. I took the lamp and crept down the hall and up the stairs.

The house was quiet except for a few giggles and the occasional squeaking of a bed. I made it safely to the little attic room and leaned against the door, thinking about what to do next.

"I have to warn Cole. Where is he? With Molly?" I started to leave but caught a glimpse of my reflection in the mirror. "I need to wear something other than this nightgown." Quickly I searched through the wardrobe, pulling one beautiful dress after another out and tossing it onto the bed. The traveling dresses were too much like the clothes I used to wear and if the Molack brothers saw me, they would recognize me immediately. The other dresses were those of the women of the house. Even though, I had a desire to see what I would look like in one of those, I feared being seen and mistaken for one of Molly's girls. I was about to make a choice when a knock sounded on the door.

"Kid. Let me in," came Cole's voice.

"Cole. I'm so glad you're here." I pulled him into the room and quickly shut the door. "I have something to tell you."

"I have something to say first. The Molack brothers are in town."

"That's what I was going to tell you. When did you see them?" I followed Cole's gaze toward the bed and all the dresses now sliding to the floor. Sheepishly, I started hanging them back up in the wardrobe. "I was looking for something to wear. I wanted to find you and warn you about the Molack brothers."

"I saw one of them at Weston's shed. I know he saw me but maybe he didn't recognize me."

"He did." I told Cole about what happened in the kitchen, leaving out the part about seeing one of them naked. "I wonder who this Hollinger is."

"I don't know. And I'm not sure I want to find out. At any rate, we'll be safe here for the night. You get some sleep."

"What are you going to do?"

Cole smiled. "Haven't decided yet."

"Remember, one of the brothers is here in the house. So you be careful."

CHAPTER 21

The sound of rain drumming on the roof and splashing against the window woke me. Cole was sleeping in the rocking chair wrapped in the extra quilt, his stocking feet braced on the window sill. I turned over onto my stomach, bunched the pillow into a ball under my chin, and watched Cole sleep. Seeing him brought strange pleasure to me. When he was awake, he oozed strength and confidence, at times almost to the point of arrogance. But now his defenses were down. He seemed tender, vulnerable. I wanted to touch him. Like Molly, I wanted to run my hands over his bare chest. I wanted. . . .

"What are you thinking about?" Cole asked, without opening his eyes.

"What? Nothing." My voice went up an octave. "I thought you were asleep."

"I was. But when you changed your breathing pattern, I woke up."

"My what?"

"Your breathing pattern. When you're asleep, you breathe deeper, more of a rhythm. When you're awake, you breathe shallower. It's different. I could hear the difference and it woke me. What were you thinking about?"

"I was thinking about last night, the Molack brothers, Molly, and just why does everyone call you Johnny?"

"Molly calls me Johnny because I'm from the South, Johnny Reb. I just didn't tell her my real name. Quite a few people know me as Johnny. Since the wanted poster has my real name on it, it seems prudent not to change it now. Wouldn't you say?"

"Why was Molly so glad to see you? Surely, she has many men who frequent her establishment. Why would you stand out in her memory so vividly? Especially after such a long time?"

"I'm a very memorable person."

"I do not buy that. Try again."

Cole smiled. "I helped her out of a financial difficulty just before the war. She said I would always have a bed if I came this way."

"And you have come this way often?"

"You won't let it rest until you know the whole story, will you?"

"No."

"After I was taken prisoner by the Yankees, they let me come out to the frontier to escort wagons across the wilderness. I was assigned to General Pope. He was relieved of his command after the second battle of Manassas and sent west to take over a fort in the northwest. He hated Rebels with a passion. My only salvation from his wrath was a man called Whittaker. He needed a scout and I was it. I had worked for Whittaker before the war. He taught me more than I could begin to tell you about the frontier, Indians, and people. I owe him my life. Each spring, we started from here and in late fall we came back here to winter. I got to know Molly quite well, but not the way you think. I'm sure she would like our relationship to be more than what it is, but to me she's just a friend."

"But after what you said last night, you have been with her."

"Gees! Sarah." Cole sat up and stared at me. "You do get to the point. You are my sister, not my wife. What I do is my business. Now no more questions."

"Just one more. What kind of financial problem did Molly have?"

"That's Molly's business. Ask her. If she wants you to know, she'll tell you. Now, if you don't have any more questions, I need to get going." Cole stood up and stretched. "I have to go to Westport and talk with Dawson about hooking up with his train. I don't think Addie washed your clothes because it's raining. So you have a choice. Come with me and wear your dirty clothes or stay here and I'll have your meals sent up. I'll stop at the store and buy some new clothes for you. It'll be good to have a change or two on the trail, anyway."

"I will stay here. Remember that the Molack brothers are looking for you. Do not get caught and leave me here at Molly's. This is not the kind of life I had planned for myself."

Cole laughed as he exited the room.

I whiled away the day by trying on the beautiful dresses I had found in the wardrobe. My meals were brought to the door and left with only a knock to indicate their arrival. The dreary day slowly passed in an array of color as I put on one dress after another. Some dresses shocked my modesty with low cut necklines and high slit hems. The velvets and brocades with high collars, long sleeves, and hems to the floor I could have worn to church on Sunday. These were the dresses that were familiar to me, the others were the dresses that enticed me.

My favorite of all the dresses lay on the bed daring me to put it on and to go downstairs. I pulled the strings of the corset even tighter than before. The red dress slid over my body like color on a flower. The plunging neckline slashed deep between my breasts, revealing creamy white skin and the edges of firm mounds. The material at the shoulders was gathered in gold clips to give a fullness to the bodice and leave the shoulders bare. The back plunged dangerously low and draped in layers of chiffon. Elbow length, red gloves and a long, chiffon scarf completed the ensemble.

By evening I heard the doorbell clang time and time again. Gentlemen came calling.

I sat at the vanity combing my hair and draping the scarf over my head, pulling one end over my face like the women in faraway, mysterious lands. I thought of dancing in the moonlight with my secret lover.

The door opened.

"Here I am, Kitty. Your servant to command," said the tall, blond haired man whom I remembered was called Coyote. He still wore the black trousers and white shirt, now unbuttoned to reveal a muscular, tanned chest. "You ain't Kitty. Must have taken the wrong turn. She said the first door at the top of the stairs."

I stood up and moved away from the light of the lamp. "She must have meant the top of the second floor."

He looked back down the stairs. Then turned and stared at me. "It don't matter. One whore's the same as the next." He moved closer to get a better look. I stepped deeper into the shadow. "Ain't never seen you here before."

"I ain't one of Molly's girls."

"You an angel?"

"That's right. I'm an angel in a house of fallen angels. You best be leaving. Kitty will be wondering where you are."

"I have seen you somewhere. I never forget a face, even if I can only see the eyes." He reached out his hand and pulled the scarf from my face. The scarf slid from my hair to my shoulders. Coyote continued to gather the chiffon as if gathering fragile flower petals. "You smell like roses. Roses in full bloom."

"You, sir, smell of whiskey. I must ask you to leave."

He started to sway slightly. "I gotta sit down. Suddenly, I'm not feelin' so good."

"I should not wonder. It must be the whiskey. You are quite inebriated."

He slumped to the bed. Grabbing my hand, he pulled me down to him. With his other hand, he cupped my head and gently positioned his mouth to meet mine. Soft were his lips. Strong was his body beneath me. His arms held me against him and I felt the strength of his manliness. Excitement and fear raced through me. I knew propriety demanded that I should struggle to free myself but . . . but . . . this titillating feeling made my breath come in gasps. I felt Coyote's hand slip down my throat. He pulled the dress off my shoulder and gently kissed the hollow of my throat. My breath came in gasps. Suddenly, his body went flaccid. He passed out.

I lay on top of him for just a minute wishing the encounter was not over. I knew in my heart this was for the best, but my lips still felt his touch and my body wanted more.

Cole stood in the doorway. "What's going on here?"

"This man got lost." I scrambled to my feet. "He should be in Kitty's bed, not mine. Being here in the brothel, I feel as if I went from under the lion's paw into its mouth."

Cole crossed over to the bed and lifted an eyelid of the unconscious man. "What do you expect, dressed like that?" The tone of Cole's voice was that of irritation, but the glint in his eyes and the smile on his face told another story.

"You were going to bring some clothes for me to wear. If Coyote had found me in the nightgown, what would he have thought?"

"Coyote? This is Coyote? You've done it now. Dressed like that, one doesn't need much of an imagination to think you work here. You better not let him know that it was you here in this room Maybe he won't remember all this in the morning. Here are some boy's clothes, put them on." Cole handed a package to me as he pulled Coyote off my bed and slung him over his shoulder.

I opened the bundle. A pair of awful overalls, a calico shirt, and a jacket were to be my wardrobe for the next five months. Surely no one would ever guess a woman was hidden underneath.

The next morning, I decided to go downstairs to eat breakfast in the dining room with Molly's girls. If I could pass the test of their scrutinizing eyes, I could fool anyone. Addie gave me the bundle of clothes she had washed. She introduced me to the girls as Johnny's kid brother. After a few polite hellos and glad to meet yous, the ladies ignored me as their conversation centered on the unbelievable escapades from the night before. I blushed to hear the frankness of their words. Suddenly, my attention was drawn to the voices coming down the stairwell.

"Kitty, I know what I saw."

"You had a little too much to drink. You know that you can't hold your liquor. Believe me, no one is in the room on the third floor. You were just up there, the room is empty. The only woman you were with last night was me."

I could not resist the temptation to look around the corner. Kitty and Coyote were standing by the front door. She held his hat in her hands while he finished buttoning his shirt.

"She had soft golden hair like an angel," Coyote persisted.

"Through your drunken haze, everyone must have looked golden. Johnny said he found you out by the privy and brought you to my room."

Looking in the mirror, Coyote took his hat and placed it on his head, running his hands along both sides to round the brim.

"My, but you're handsome, Mr. Coyote," Kitty said in a

throaty voice as she wrapped her arms around his neck. "When will I see you again?"

"In the fall. Two more wagons joined yesterday. That makes thirty. So we'll be pullin' out sooner than expected. Between now and then, I'll have plenty to keep me busy. Most of them people are green as grass. I'll have to season them up a bit before we get to Indian Territory. Now's when the work begins. So, Darlin', give me one more kiss to last all the way to California." Coyote tightened his hold on her, grabbing a handful of brown hair and bringing Kitty's open mouth to his. The embrace lingered. When he started to pull away, she did not let go. She opened her dressing gown and rubbed her eager body against his.

"Stay with me," she whispered.

"I wish I could, Darlin'." He pushed her away and closed her gown after taking one last look.

"Did your angel kiss like that?" Kitty's voice was filled with passion.

"No. Can't say she did. But I know now that you ain't her. There was somethin' different 'bout her. Don't know what, just different." He patted Kitty on her bottom. "See you when I get back. I'll bring you somethin' from California." With that he left.

Kitty came into the dining room, sadness clouding her brown eyes. She sank into the chair at the end of the table. "That Coyote, he thinks he was with an angel last night. He kept talking about a beautiful woman dressed in red. I spent the night listening about her. Then he passed out, again. This morning he tells me that he'll be pullin' out soon. He won't be over to see me 'til next fall."

"Well, Kitty, if'n you can't give the man any more pleasure than that, it looks like Coyote's up for grabs," one of the other women said in a catlike tone.

Kitty stood up, knocking the chair over. "You jest keep your hands off'n Coyote. He's mine." Kitty flew across the table at the other woman. Arms and legs flailed in the air as screams and screeches vibrated off the walls. Everyone stood back to give the fighting women room. Addie quickly removed the china to save it from getting broken.

"They've been itchin' for this here fight for a long time," one woman said to me, as she pulled me out of harm's way. "Ever since Coyote took a fancy for Kitty, Lilac has had her nose bent out of shape. It wouldn't be so bad if'n your brother would have given Lilac the time of day, but he doesn't."

"Why would that make a difference?" I asked in my best boy's voice.

"Oh, child, your brother is the catch of a lifetime. Haven't you noticed?" She looked at me. "No. I don't suppose you would. Take it from me, women almost melt into their shoes when he looks at them with those steely gray eyes. And his voice, that deep, wonderful voice, can send shivers up the spine of the most respectable woman. I tell you, it certainly does mine." She got lost in thought. Her hazel eyes glazed over as she entered the world of daydreams.

"Stop this at once!" came Molly's stern voice, as she and Cole entered the room. "What is the matter with you? We have guests in the house and you behave like alley cats."

Both women lay on the floor in a heap of bloody scratches, pulled hair, and torn clothes. Upon seeing Cole, they scrambled to their feet and tried to pull themselves together in a presentable fashion.

"We didn't know that Johnny was still in the house," Lilac said, running her fingers through her brown hair and letting the torn camisole fall freely away from her breast. She smiled when she saw Cole's gaze drift to her bosom. "If you see something you like, it can be yours."

My mouth dropped open, and I felt the heat rise in my cheeks. I knew my face must be turning crimson.

Cole crossed the room to Lilac and gently closed her

red, silk morning gown over the torn camisole. "That's a splendid offer. Maybe some other time. The kid and I were just about to leave."

"Yes, of course," Lilac whispered.

Cole took her arm and escorted her out of the room. In the doorway he stopped, lifted Lilac's chin, and kissed her for all to see. "It would have been my pleasure." Turning to me, he said, "Kid, are you ready? The horses and wagon are packed. It's time to go. Thank you, Molly, for your hospitality. It is always a pleasure to see you."

"Anytime, Johnny. You come back anytime." Sadness laced Molly's husky voice.

I gathered my saddlebags, hat, jacket, and the clothes Addie had washed, and followed Cole out onto the street. He took to a fast pace with his long strides causing me to almost run to keep up. "Slow down. I want to talk to you."

"Talk."

"I thought the wagons were not going to pull out for a few more days."

"They weren't, now they are. One train left yesterday. Mr. Dawson doesn't want to be too far behind. Another train will be ready by the end of the week and we don't want to be pushed by them. Monday seems like a good time to get started."

"Monday," I said to myself. I did not really hear the rest of what Cole was saying. My thoughts conjured up wild Indians killing women and children and setting wagons on fire. A shiver shook my body.

"Sarah?"

"Oh. What?"

"I said, do you have any other questions? But I don't think you heard the answer to your first question."

"Yes, I did. At least, I heard enough. I have just one more question. Why did you kiss Lilac?"

A smile lit Cole's face. "What harm did it do? I know she fancies she and I being together. She has made it very clear how she feels. Most of the other ladies have their special fella they can dream about. Kitty has Coyote. Molly has Mr. Fletcher at the bank. Rue has the young fella from Waller Ranch."

"But Lilac started the fight."

"Only because Kitty has been riding her like a cowboy on a buckjumper. Come next winter, Coyote will be back again. Lilac's dreams will never come true. Not with me, anyway, because I'll never see her again. By kissing her in front of all the other ladies, I gave her a memory to hold on to."

I thought about Lilac's dream of living with Cole all the way to Weston's blacksmith shed.

Misty Morn neighed a welcome as I rounded the corner of the stable. "I missed you, too," I said. "I brought you something." I fished around in my saddlebag for the carrot I had saved from last night's dinner.

The horses and Old Danger were tied to the back of the wagon. Hanging from the wagon's sides were two cages filled with hens and a big white rooster. A black and white milk cow and the extra oxen waited in the corral.

"Climb up. Throw your saddlebags in the back," Cole ordered. "I'll pay Weston and we'll be ready to pull out."

I put my foot on the wheel hub, grabbed hold of the seat and pulled myself up onto the wagon. Inside the wagon were all of our earthly possessions - - barrels of food, tools, canvasses, and a brass bed. My heart leaped with joy when I saw the bed. "At least I will not have to sleep on the ground anymore," I said aloud to myself.

The morning air felt cold on my cheeks. I pulled my jacket tight around me, folded my arms across my chest, propped my boots against the front of the wagon, pulled my hat down over my face and waited. The sounds of a waking town crowded into my thoughts, the rhythmic pounding of the blacksmith's hammer against metal, someone briskly sweeping the boardwalk, wagons rolling down the street, people talking, horses swishing their tails and snorting, and chickens clucking. I opened my eyes when I heard footsteps.

"Okay. We're all set. Do you think you can handle the wagon?" Cole asked as he untied Shadow Run.

"I think so. It's the same as a carriage, only bigger." I sat up, pulled on my gloves, took hold of the reins, and released the brake. Cole got the extra oxen and milk cow out of the corral, mounted Shadow and led the way onto Liberty Street. I gave the oxen a slap with the leather straps and the wagon started to roll. When we got to the corner, we turned west along Walnut, made a few more turns and finally we came to the Independence-Westport Road.

"The merchants got tired of having their wagons bogged down to the wheel hubs in mud, so a few years back they all pitched in to have this road paved. Makes traveling easier," Cole shouted as he came along side of the wagon. "How are you doing?"

"So far, so good."

Houses were scattered along the way. Some were large, grand houses, others were log cabins. I wondered about the dreams of the people who live behind the closed doors. *Did they plan to end up on this road in Independence, Missouri, the last outpost of civilization before the Indian Territory? Were these people happy? Or were their dreams shattered like Lilac's and they had settled for second best?* I thought of Cousin Amy Ann. She wanted to have the man she married love her, not just her fortune. I wondered if Aunt Maggie had arranged a marriage for her daughter in Boston. *Would Amy Ann be happy married to a Yankee? Or did she have to settle?* I remembered what Martha Tadwell had said to Mama so long ago about my having to settle for seconds because I was getting past marrying age. *Am I going to be as pathetic as Lilac hanging on to a dream that cannot be?* "Oh, God," I whispered. "Please let me find a man that I can love and one who will love me for myself."

I watched the wind blow some leaves into a whirlwind and carry them across an open field and they were gone. I felt like those leaves, having no choice of where I was going.

From the top of a rise, I lifted my eyes and saw the beginnings of Westport, a new town with an unsteady population, and the sea of canvas topped wagons. I stopped the wagon to take it all in.

"Do you see those hills?" Cole asked, pointing to a blue-green ridge way off in the distance. "That's the way we'll be heading. Most of these wagons will be going north to Oregon."

"North. That's the way you went when you were with Mr. Whittaker."

"Many times. I don't envy those people their trip. The Sioux are edging for war, and now that the War Between the States is over, many soldiers are being assigned to the West. The white man doesn't want to live in peace with the Indian, and with hotheads like Custer coming west to take command, who knows what's going to happen. But we'll have our hands full enough with the Cheyenne still on the warpath over Sand Creek. Chief Black Kettle won't listen to words of peace. He tried that before. And when we get to the Southwest Territory, there could be plenty of action. In sixty-four, Kit Carson moved the Navajo on what the Indians called The Long Walk. No one has forgotten the heartache that has caused. But like I said, the war is over, and more troops are stationed out West, so the way is becoming safer to travel. We have a good man leading us. Dawson doesn't want any trouble. So we should have a fair trip. That is, if you keep away from Coyote." Cole laughed his barrel laugh that caused me to join in with him.

I pulled my hat down over my forehead and we headed toward the town of Westport.

"Kid, ve are happy to see you," Gretchen said, as I guided our wagon alongside of the Delvick wagon. "You vill stay mit your vagon 'til ve leave, yah?"

"I think we will. Cole, uh, Johnny, that is, does not want to stay in town. He thinks we will be safer out here. The Molack brothers are in Independence. We saw them."

Gretchen's hand went to her mouth as she gasped, "Did they see you?"

I set the brake, secured the reigns and climbed down from the wagon. "It's a long story." I walked with Gretchen into her camp and told her what had happened, leaving out some of the more awkward parts, such as seeing the older Molack brother naked, and the part about Coyote in my room. "We have plenty to do to keep us busy until we pull out on Monday," I concluded.

"Yah. Now is the time that my stomach starts to quiver mit excitement. I have already met some nice people who vill travel mit us. Mr. Dawson is a fine man, und that Coyote, mench, vhat a handsome man."

"I have seen him. But he must not find out that I am a woman. Do you understand?"

"Yah, if that is the vay you vant." She shook her head in disappointment. I could tell she had planned to play matchmaker.

CHAPTER 22

"My name is Dawson. Folks call me Dawson. No mister, no boss, no captain, just plain Dawson," the burly man said as he stood on the tailgate of his wagon. All the people who had signed on to his train had been gathered for a camp meeting. Three lanterns placed on poles lit the area. I crowded behind Cole and peeked around him to be able to see without being seen. Dawson's stature only reached five feet, six inches but his burly chest, broad shoulders and commanding voice spanned the gap and made him a giant. His round face supported a white, walrus mustache, thick bushy eyebrows, and red vein clusters on his cheeks from too much sun. A tired, old, brown hat covered thinning, white hair. Smoke blue eyes, that had seen more than he could ever begin to tell, surveyed the crowd.

"For the next four or five months, I am the law. Whatever I say goes. If anyone doesn't like it, now is the time to get out." Dawson said the speech as a matter of routine. Each time he started a new trip across the wilderness the same words came out of his mouth. "My job is to get you to California in one piece. Coyote and I aim to do just that. Any questions?" He waited for a moment and then continued, "We travel from sunup to sunset, six days a week. I've found that resting on Sunday keeps the womenfolk off my back, and the stock works better with a day of rest. However, that day of rest is for the animals, not you folks. That is the day you men will mend your gear, slaughter and dress out a cow to be shared with the entire train, and make any repairs that might slow us down. You women will bake bread, do laundry and get things ready for the next week of travel. You have a list of supplies you can buy at Bridger's grocery. It's that there two story building. Jim Bridger just bought that grocery last February and he has mighty fair prices. Now you can go into Independence to get your goods, I don't care. Just get everything on the list. For those of you who can't read, I'll go over the list now so that you know you ain't being cheated.

"Each person, not wagon but person, needs two hundred pounds of flour, twenty pounds of sugar, ten pounds of salt, ten pounds of coffee, one hundred and fifty pounds of bacon, twenty-five pounds of rice, fifty pounds of dried beans, chipped beef, tea, dried fruit, vinegar, mustard, pickles, and tallow. Fresh vegetables such as potatoes, carrots, onions, or turnips can be packed in a sand barrel. This should run between three to six hundred dollars, depending on how much food you brought with you. Chickens in cages are always good for fresh eggs, and a milk cow for each wagon. Along with all that, you need two rifles and one thousand rounds of ammunition. I don't want to fight our way through Indian lands, but just to be on the safe side, I want to be prepared. At the bottom of the list, you'll see ten calico shirts and ten beef cattle. That's per wagon. Those are for trading with the Indians. Any questions?"

"How can you expect to trade with those savages?" one man called out from the back.

"I've been doing it for many years. Believe me, it works."

"I'm not an Injin lover. I'll shoot um first," another

angry voice was heard above the crowd.

"If that's the way you feel, best you find another train to hook up with. I'll tell you right now, if anyone of you shoots an Indian, except in self-defense, you'll answer to me. And most likely, I'll shoot you before I'll risk the lives of everyone on the train."

A gasp was heard throughout the crowd. *What have we gotten ourselves into?* I wondered. Cole said Dawson was a good man, but I did not like the way he was talking. "He's a dreadful man," I whispered to Cole. "We should look for another train."

"He's doing what needs to be done. We want someone who can get us to California. Dawson can."

"For you men who are outriders, you need to find a wagon to carry your provisions. In return, you will help drive the team or herd the cattle," Dawson continued. "Some of you people have room in your wagon to store some extra things, so help these fellas out. Since this is a family train, I'll not tolerate profanity or bad language of any kind around the women and children. Liquor is strictly prohibited. Each life depends on everyone working together. If someone is drunk, his judgment is off. If I find you drinking, I'll put you off the train. You have from now 'til Sunday night to drink your fill. Kelly's saloon over yonder will be happy to oblige. Kelly's is owned by A. G. Boone, old Daniel Boone's grandson. He serves a good drink for a fair price. But come Monday morning, you best be ready to pull out. And one more thing. A family's privacy is important when people are crowded together like we are on a wagon train. So you ask for permission before entering someone's camp. Now I want to introduce Coyote, our scout."

Coyote climbed onto the tailgate. "I have just a few words to say. Usually we travel the Santa Fe Trail across Kansas, Colorado, and into New Mexico territory where we'll pick up the Butterfield stage trail to California. However, since Chief Black Kettle is causing such a ruckus along the route, this year we'll be cutting down through Oklahoma, into Texas and on to California. It might take a few weeks longer but it'll be safer."

Once again, moans and groans rumbled through the crowd.

"How much longer?" came the voice from the back.

"Can't rightly say. But it's easier traveling, and we'll find plenty of water and grass for the animals. Any more questions?"

I watched Coyote look over the crowd. His black trousers and white shirt had been replaced with buckskins. His pullover shirt had a V neck opened to mid chest. A red, chiffon scarf was tied around his throat.

I gasped.

"What? What's wrong?" Cole asked.

"Where did he get that red scarf? That belongs to the dress I was wearing."

"He had it when I took him down to Kitty's room. I stuffed it into his pocket. He must not have found it until he changed clothes."

"That proves he was with another woman, not Kitty."

"Like I said, stay out of his way."

Coyote continued, "On this trip, we're lucky to have a former scout from the Whittaker party traveling with us. Johnny, step up here and let the folks get a look at you."

Cole hesitated. "That's okay. I'm just a traveler this time." Cole waved his hand and everyone turned to look at him.

"He's a Reb," shouted a mean voice from the crowd.

"We'll have none of that on this train," Dawson thundered. "The war is over. All of us lost someone, but we have to put that behind us. On this train there are no Yankees or Rebs, we're just people trying to get from Missouri to California. And I'm right proud to have Johnny goin' with us. He knows more about Indians than just about anybody. If we get into a scrape, you'll be mighty thankful he's on your side."

I had not thought that we would be traveling with Yankees. I hated them with my entire being, but I never dreamed that they would hate me, too. I never did anything to them. They were the ones who raped our land, killed our people, and destroyed our homes. It was our way of life that was totally changed, not theirs. Why should Yankees hate Southerners? But I could hear the anger in the voices around me and I knew the Northerners hated me as much as I hated them. How could we travel together with these feelings cutting us to the bone?

Dawson closed the meeting with one last statement. "Like I said before, I'm the law beyond this point. If any of you have second thoughts, now's the time to spit it out." He waited. "Good. We seem to be in agreement. From now 'til Monday morning you all have plenty to keep you busy. Get your wagons and animals ready. Once we pull out, there's no turning back."

"Come on, let's go back to our wagon," Cole said, putting his hand on my shoulder.

I wanted to hug him, but boys do not hug. "I'm afraid of those men," I whispered. "They really hate Southerners."

"They're just full of hot air. They won't do anything."

"How can you be sure?"

"Most of the people on this train are decent, respectable folks. They want to start over, the same as we do. The loud mouths who incite people to violence usually need a following before they get brave. Dawson will see to it that doesn't happen. Besides, look around you. A good share of these people are Southerners."

I looked at the people going to their wagons - - some men wore Confederate gray trousers like Cole, women wore black mourning dresses, and children were dressed in ragtag meager pickings. Yes, these were people who had survived the war. I began to feel more at ease.

The next few days filled themselves with last minute chores. Cole and I took on an outrider to help herd the cattle. Luke seemed like a good sort of man. He was in his mid-thirties, on his way to the gold fields. We loaded his supplies into our wagon and still had room for the things Cole had bought, two comfortable chairs, a table, and a commode, for which I would be forever thankful.

Rudy wanted to buy two more oxen, and Cole and I needed to buy the ten cattle for trading and about twenty head for our own use. Despite my uneasy feeling, we returned to Independence.

The cattle pens were behind Weston's blacksmith shed. The men talked to Weston and struck a deal for the animals, while I waited with the horses. Cole was about to move the cattle out of the corral when we heard a voice call out.

"Brighton! I've been looking for you. Did you think you could get away with killing my brother?"

Turning, we came face to face with George Molack who stood, feet astride, in the middle of the blacksmith work area. "I didn't kill anybody," Cole shouted, his hand eased to the butt of his gun.

Rudy went around his horses and pulled his Henry rifle from the scabbard of the saddle. He stood behind his horse, the rifle resting across the saddle and pointing at Molack, waiting to see what he would do next.

I looked for Elias, but he was not to be seen. "He's probably hiding in the shadows ready to shoot you," I whispered, seeing Cole's eyes searching for him, too. I dismounted. "I'll go around the shed and come up the other way."

"Stay out of this. You'll get hurt."

As usual, I did not listen. I slowly went around Misty and pulled my gun out of the saddlebag. People started taking notice of something happening and cleared the area. Rudy walked along the edge of the corral as I moved to the shed and into the shadows of the overhanging roof. George slowly closed the distance between Cole and himself.

Cole stood his ground.

"The last place anybody saw Frank was at Rosewood Plantation. Nobody seen him since. I'm sayin' you killed him," George bellowed.

"You can say whatever you like. The truth is, I was away fighting the war when your brother left Rosewood."

"He was killed on your land. That makes it your fault."

"You don't even know if he's dead."

"I'm done talking."

I ran down the side of the shed, onto Liberty Street, along the front of the building, and into the alley on the other side. My heart quickened when I saw Elias crouching beside a rain barrel. Rifle in hand, ready to shoot Cole, he whirled around and stood up when he heard me. I became as stone cemented to the ground. A bullet whizzed by my ear. Elias fell to the ground holding his side. A hand closed onto my shoulder and pulled me against the building. I stared into hazel eyes, crested by a frown.

"I thought it was you," he said, knocking my hat off and lifting my chin to the light of the afternoon sun.

He looked familiar, but I could not place him. My eyes fell onto the star pinned to his shirt. The word Marshal screamed out at me.

The shattering sound of gunfire thundered through the air. "Let me go! That's my brother." I twisted out of the marshal's grip and ran to the back of the shed. People had already gathered around the man lying in the dirt. I fought my way to the front of the crowd.

Cole knelt beside Molack. "He wouldn't listen to reason."

"It was self-defense, Marshal," one old man volunteered.

The tall marshal grabbed my arm and pulled me toward Cole. "Both of you come with me," he ordered. "Some of you get this man and the other one around the corner to Doc's. When they're patched up, bring them to me." The lawman pushed me toward his office.

Once inside the brick building, the marshal turned to me and said, "You don't remember me, do you?" His voice sounded disgusted with me.

"Should I? You look familiar, but I cannot quite place the face." My heart pounded. Here was a man, a marshal, who knew me. I looked at Cole. He slowly shook his head and shrugged his shoulders, indicating that he did not know the man either.

The marshal sat behind the big desk, pulled a wanted poster out of the drawer and shoved it across the desk top at us. "I take it this is you?"

I looked at the poster and then at Cole. Feeling the color drain from my face, the room began to spin. Cole grabbed my arm and eased me into a chair.

"What are you going to do about it?" Cole asked.

"What do you think I should do?"

"Since I took only what was mine, I think you should let us go."

A smile broadened the marshal's face. "Just like that. Let you go. The people entrusted me to uphold the law. I would be letting them down if I let horse thieves get off, free as a bird." The glint in his eyes suggested a cat playing with a mouse.

"We are not horse thieves. Did you not hear my brother? We took only what was ours," I said.

"What have you done to yourself? You look like an urchin that begs for food on the street corner. Did you have to cut your beautiful hair?" His eyes bore a cavity into my soul.

"Who are you? I know you from somewhere."

He laughed. "You saved my life. I'm Major Christopher Ward. I was one of many who came to Safe Harbor for help and found an angel of mercy. I told you then that I would never forget your kindness. That's why I'm letting you go. But you've got to be quick about leaving town before the U.S. Army forces me to arrest you."

"We're pulling out in the morning with the Dawson party," Cole said.

"That's good, because I've heard tell of a military detachment heading our way. They should be here in a day or two. I'll try to sidetrack them north. But if they catch up with you, you're on your own. Understand?"

"Yes, and thank you. What about the Molack brothers?" Cole asked.

"Is that their names? I've seen them skulking around but didn't know who they were. You shot in self-defense. Lots of witnesses said so. You're free to go. I'll keep the brothers in jail until their wounds heal. That will give me time to check through back posters and see if they're wanted somewhere. If not, I'll send them north, too.

"Thank you so much," I said, as I stood to leave.

"It's truly a shame to hide such beauty. I wish you well." He took my hand and kissed it. "If we could have met under better circumstances, first the war and now, well, I would have loved getting to know you."

"And I you, sir. Unfortunately we are not in control of our own lives at the moment. But I do thank you for your kindness."

Rudy waited for us on the bench outside the marshal's office. "Is everything all right?"

"Yes," I said, linking my arms through his and Cole's. "We are on our way to California."

CHAPTER 23

Above the curtain that covered the opening in the canvas at the front of the wagon, I watched Orion fade into the fire opal sky of predawn. The day we had been waiting for was creeping over the horizon -- the beginning of a new adventure.

"Everybody up," thundered Dawson, as he rode his big, black horse around the inside of the circled wagons. All the wagons of our party had been moved to the far southern end of the flat land last night. We camped together in a circle, practicing for the trip ahead. From now on, we would camp with our wagon tongue to the outside, rear wheel of the conveyance in front of us. The oxen, cattle, and horses were outside the circle.

I slowly crept out of bed. The cold morning air pinched my skin into gooseflesh as I pulled off the nightshirt I had taken from Molly's house. Baggy overalls, a calico shirt, jacket, boots and the old brown hat buried Sarah so deeply I was afraid no one would be able to find her again. My transformation into Danny, or the Kid, was complete. Dawson's voice came calling again, "Pullin' out in one hour."

"Kid, how's it going in there?" Cole asked, as he untied the back canvas and climbed into the wagon.

"I am ready."

"Good. Then out with you while I change. I milked the cow and got a fire started. You get breakfast going." Breakfast consisted of Johnny-cakes cooked on a board by the fire, beans and a slab of bacon cooked in the skillet, and coffee.

When Cole emerged from the wagon wearing his buckskins and gun, my breath was drawn away. Before me stood a man of the frontier, strong, confident, and rugged.

"Isn't this great?" Cole asked, rubbing his hands together to warm them. "I've always loved the first morning of a new trip. You can just feel the excitement in the air."

I could not help smiling at him. He had returned to his first love, the frontier.

"Where did you sleep last night?" I asked, forcing myself to turn away from him.

"Under the wagon. Why?"

"I did not hear you."

"What can I say? You sleep soundly. I guess that's the blessing of innocence."

"Oh, and you sleep lightly, so you are not so innocent? What dark deeds lurk in your past?"

"I'll never tell." Cole rummaged in the box where we stored all the cooking utensils and retrieved his cup. "Is the coffee ready?"

"Coffee, that sounds good," Luke said, coming around the wagon with a cup in his hand. Since we were transporting Luke's food and gear, he would be a part of our camp from now on.

"Help yourself," I said in my deepest voice. I wondered how long I could keep up the pretense, and what people would say when they discovered I was really a woman.

The sun's first rays had spilled over the bluff by the

time Coyote strolled into our area. "Mind if I enter your camp?"

"No. Come on in," Cole invited.

"I have the numbers for the position you'll be in. Draw one." Coyote held out a hat filled with numbers written on little pieces of paper.

Cole picked one. "Sixteen."

"That's where you'll start today. Tomorrow you'll move up one space, and the lead wagon will move to the back of the line. That way no one will ride drag all the time."

"Would you care for a cup of coffee?" I asked, handing Coyote my cup.

"Thanks, Kid." He pushed his hat back on his head. "Now, where have I seen you before?"

I looked from him to Cole and back again not knowing what to say. Surely he could not recognize me as the Angel in Red under these boys clothes.

Cole offered, "You took a liking to our horses out front of the saloon a few days back."

"That's right. You're the kid with the big gray. What kind of horse was that again?"

"Arabian," I answered through clenched teeth.

"Arabian. Wonder why I've never heard of that breed before? I didn't know those were your horses, Johnny."

"Yeah. My grandfather brought two from England and we've been trying to raise a stable of Arabians. George Washington favored the Arabian."

"The five horses are all we have left. The Yankees took the rest," I said, turning my face toward the fire.

"This is my kid brother, Danny," Cole said.

Coyote stroked the red scarf tied in a square knot around his neck. It hung over one shoulder, the ends moving in the cool air. Coyote's blue eyes studied me for a minute before he said, "It's almost time to get under way. Thanks for the coffee." He tossed the last of his coffee into the fire and handed the cup back to me. "Next time I'll bring my own cup." He turned and with long strides walked toward the Gilroy wagon.

I filled my plate and quickly ate while watching Gretchen put out her breakfast fire and load her things into their wagon. Karl helped his father hitch up the team and Juergen and Paulie helped their mother. Anna slept in the sling draped over Gretchen's shoulder and around her waist.

Behind us were Mr. and Mrs. Gilroy, newlyweds, on their way to make their fortune in the West. I had not met many people yet. Cole thought it would be best if we stayed mostly to ourselves. I hoped Rudy and Gretchen's position number was close to ours.

Cole finished eating and put his plate, fork, and cup in the bucket of warm water I had heated for the dishes. Luke did the same. Cole loaded the chairs and food barrels into our wagon. Luke went to get our team and hitch them up. I washed the dishes, gathered the eggs, put out the fire, and had the cooking box ready to load into the wagon. Standing on my bed, I hung the milk bucket, with its tight lid, over the middle rib of the canvas top to splash and churn all day. By the time we made camp tonight, I would have fresh butter and buttermilk to make the biscuits. The dust cover was fastened securely over the bed, but I pulled the extra canvas over everything in the wagon to keep things clean - - a hopeless task.

As everyone climbed into their wagons and waited for the order to move out, the air grew heavy with anticipation. My heart pounded. I double checked our campsite to make sure we had not left anything behind. Cole sat ready. His hands fastened around the leather reins.

"Did you tie the horses securely?" I asked.

"They're fine."

"Did you put the big box into the wagon?"

"Yes."

"Did you. . . ?"

"Yes, Sarah, I did everything. We're all set to go. Now

relax."

"Where's Luke?"

"He rode out to the herd. He'll be about a mile behind us."

People from some of the other wagon trains came to say goodbye. "Have a safe trip. God go with you," they called. "See you in California."

"We'll be hot on your heels," one man yelled to Dawson.

"I'll see you in the cantina on Oliveria Street in September. Last one there buys," Dawson returned.

The crack of the first whip broke the air. "Stretch 'um out!" Dawson shouted as his wagon started to roll toward Wornall Road.

Coyote led the way, mounted on his strawberry roan. The next wagon pulled into place and the next. The sounds of whips cracking, oxen lowing, people shouting, and the creaking and groaning of wagons slowly gave way to singing. The women took up the song, "Wait For The Wagon." Before long, everyone was singing as we moved farther and farther away from Westport.

"Where the river runs like silver, And the birds they sing so sweet. . .. hum . . . . Wait for the wagon, wait for the wagon, wait for the wagon, and we'll all take a ride." I sang long after everyone had stopped. The festive excitement lingered into the day.

Bouncing up and down, swaying this way and that as the wagon seemed to hit every rock or hole in the crudely paved road soon became wearisome. "Cole, I think I would like to walk for a while."

"Be careful when you jump. Don't get hooked up on the wheel."

"Jump? What do you mean jump? I want you to stop the team."

"Can't do that. Climb down off the seat. Put your feet on the wagon tongue and jump past the wheel. Be careful to clear it. I've seen people get caught up and get crushed. If you go out the back, you need to move fast out of the way of the next wagon. Like I said, be careful."

For a moment, I sat there wondering if he was teasing me. "You really are not going to stop?"

"Nope."

In a huff, I climbed over the front of the wagon and stood on the tongue wondering if this was a wise decision on my part. Finally I jumped, landing beyond the wheel. "That wasn't hard," I yelled back to Cole.

Many women and children were walking alongside their wagons. As I watched them, I realized they were gathering twigs and grasses, twisting them into bundles, and letting them dry in the warm sun. I ran up to Gretchen who walked at the rear of her wagon two positions in front of us.

"What are you doing?" I asked.

"I am gathering things to make a fire for tonight. Coyote told us it vould save time vhen ve make camp in the evening. He told us vomen many things to help make life easier on the trail. But you missed his talks because you stayed in town."

"He was in town, too."

"At night. But during the day he vas at Vestport, und he told us many things to do. Of course, you have Cole to help you. He knows all about traveling mit a vagon."

I started pulling clumps of grass, twisting them into bundles and putting the bundles on the tool box to dry in the sun. The morning sped by quickly. I lost myself in the task of gathering and singing. Noon came and went and I started wondering what we were going to do about eating. I was getting hungry. When I looked up, I saw Dawson riding down the line giving instructions.

"We'll take a short break at Dyke Branch up ahead. It'll give you time to eat and rest the team. No fires." He rode on to the next wagon.

We did not circle the wagons. We just stopped where

we were and sat in the shade of some trees. We ate bread, cheese, dried beef, and fruit and drank water. Everything tasted marvelous.

The next half hour, Cole watched me as I drove the team. "You're doing good. How does it feel?"

"Fine."

"Well, you can drive 'till we make camp. I'm going to ride up to the front of the line and talk with Coyote. Keep a taut lead." With that he climbed over the front of the wagon, jumped to the ground, untied Shadow and rode away.

"This is not hard." I braced my feet against the wagon and leaned back on the seat. Slowly the team plodded along mile after mile. I took off my jacket as the sun grew warmer by mid-afternoon. Unbuttoning one button of my shirt, I wiped the sweat from my throat. "It sure is hot today," I said to the air. Now and again, I felt myself starting to doze off, but a tug on the reins always brought me back to the task at hand. "I wish I had someone to talk to. It would make the time pass quicker," I told the back end of the oxen. I thought of what I would make for the evening meal. I thought of what I would be doing if I were at Rosewood. I conjured up the image of life in California and still the team plodded along.

By the time the sun dipped behind the trees, my arms and shoulders ached and my lower back burned like fire. Cole came to drive the team into position in the circle.

"I'll take it from here." He took the reins out of my hands. I gladly relinquished them to him. "By the time we get to California, you'll be an old hand at this."

"No. I'll just be old."

"If you're going to wear your shirt unbuttoned, tie a neckerchief around your neck. A boy your age would be getting an Adam's Apple."

I pulled the bandanna out of my pocket and tied it around my neck.

Cole made camp and I started a fire with the twisted

grass and twigs I had gathered along the way. I watched the children play tag in the circle of the encampment and wished I had as much energy as they had. But I was exhausted and planned to go to bed as soon as I finished with the dinner dishes.

Luke and Cole sat at the fire talking and hardly acknowledged my going to the wagon. I lit the lamp and started to undress when I heard Coyote's voice ask permission to enter our camp. I pulled off my overalls, shirt, and flannels and was unwinding the breast band when Cole's hand grabbed the lantern through the rear of the wagon.

"What are you doing?" I yelled, holding my nightshirt in front of me.

"With the lantern behind you, you're casting a shadow play on the canvas," Cole whispered. "I didn't realize it until I followed Coyote's gaze and saw you. I don't think he knows what he saw, yet. But one of these days he'll put it all together. From now on, dress in the dark."

I was sound asleep when I heard Cole's voice whisper, "Sarah, move over."

I opened my eyes to see him standing at the foot of the bed holding a board, beautifully painted with pink ribbons and bows carried by blue birds through the red outline of a heart. The top scallop resembled lace.

"What's that?" I asked, rubbing my eyes.

"Gretchen gave it to us. It's called a bundling board. I've seen you sleep. You take your half out of the middle. This will make sure you stay on your side of the bed. In Gretchen's family, it's used when guests come to visit and there aren't enough beds for everyone." He placed the board down the middle of the bed and fastened it securely to both the head and foot frame. It provided a wall of privacy.

I could hear Cole take off his boots, holster, and shirt. I felt his weight as he lay on the bed. I listened for a long while to the sounds of the night - - crickets, cows in the distance, an owl far away, babies crying, people talking low, a giggle from the newlywed's camp and the creaking noise of their bed as it rocked to and fro.

"Are you asleep?" Cole asked softly.

"Not yet."

"I want you to know I'm proud of you. You did a fine share of work today."

"Thank you." I felt satisfied.

Days passed uneventfully. When we came to the town of New Santa Fe, the beginning of the Santa Fe Trail, Dawson told us that this was the last place to buy anything before we leave the states and enter Indian Territory. But the prices were higher than a cat's back, as Mama often said, so very few people went into town. From there, we made good time and spirits were high. On the evening of the fourth day, Coyote came into our camp.

"Kid, how old are you?"

"Uh, fourteen."

"Thirteen," Cole quickly corrected.

No, Johnny, I'm fourteen. Why?"

"It's your turn to ride night guard. Every man fourteen and older has to take his turn. I'll have someone spell you at midnight."

"He's never ridden herd before," Cole offered, frowning at me.

"I didn't think so. I'll go out with him to show him the ropes," Coyote said in his easy going manner. "I'll be back after supper."

I watched him walk away. "Why didn't you tell me?" I admonished Cole.

"I tried to get you out of it. But you always have to have the last word."

"Tell me what I do out there. I do not want to make a fool of myself."

Cole's eyes sparkled as he began to talk. "I'm glad you're taking it so well. The Sarah of a few years ago would have refused to go."

"Well, the Danny of today has no choice."

"Night riding isn't hard. All you have to do is keep the cows calm and quiet. Don't make any sudden moves or talk loud. That'll spook them. Sing or whistle, they like that. If they should get spooked and start to stampede, which isn't very likely on a night like this, don't get in front of them. Let someone who knows what they're doing try to turn them. You just ride alongside and keep the cattle from spreading out too far. Take Zephyr. He's a better mount for this kind of work."

I had barely finished eating when Coyote came into our camp. "Ready to go?"

"Guess so." I mounted Zephyr and we rode off to the herd.

"Since we crossed the river today and the cattle drank their fill, they should be content," Coyote said as we came over a rise and saw the herd. "You know you aren't alone. Jake Adler and Frank Sims are out here, too. You'll be on the south side working up against the ridge. If anything happens, get out of the way. We don't want to lose you."

"Thanks."

"I'll be back 'bout midnight." He rode away. The night got lonely.

Singing softly, I rode slowly around the end of the herd. In the distance I could hear one of the other men doing the same. A coyote yapped—a real coyote. Velvet blackness covered the sky with pinholes of light shining through. The Big Dipper hung almost overhead. Slightly to the south, the Lion made its appearance and beyond that rose the Virgin following close on the Lion's heels. Since the beginning of time it has not changed. I felt like Cole was the lion and I the virgin, always following after him, chasing, but never catching.

I continued to sing as the two constellations moved

across the sky, and they were almost straight overhead before Coyote returned. "I thought you would never come back," I said. "No one told me how lonesome it would be out here."

"You didn't sound lonely. For a kid, you sure have a good voice."

"It hasn't changed yet." I lowered my voice.

Come along, I'll ride with you back to camp. One of the outriders is taking his turn in your place."

"How often will I have to do this?"

"Shouldn't be more than once a week. It depends on what the men are doing. Why?"

"Just wondering."

"You strike me as different from other kids your age."

"How so?"

"I can't put my finger on it just yet but somehow something doesn't sit right." He watched me as if he were trying to remember something but couldn't.

I just smiled.

The day came when we left the Santa Fe Trail and turned south toward Texas. The familiar ruts and markers of the trail gave way to flat land and the uncertainty of direction. We were totally dependent on the wisdom of Coyote and Dawson. People did not like that feeling and murmurings of discontent arose. Coyote was gone more than he was with the train.

Late one afternoon, Coyote came racing up to the wagons. His horse was in a lather. The train halted.

"I wonder what's happening?" I asked, looking around the wagon in front of us.

"Don't know, but here comes Coyote. He'll tell us."

"Johnny, saddle up and come with me," Coyote said, reining in his foaming horse. Worry lines were carved into the man's forehead.

"What's happening?" Cole asked as he climbed down and mounted Shadow. "Stay with the wagon," he called as he rode off with Coyote.

Everyone sat ready to defend the wagons against whatever was out there. Thoughts of Indians leaped into my mind. The stillness that hung on the air became unnerving. No one spoke. Oxen swished flies with their tails and stomped on the ground. The gentle wind blowing against the canvas and moving through the tall grass created an empty sound. I climbed off the wagon and walked to stand next to Rudy. He held his rifle in one hand and the yoke of his lead oxen in the other.

"What do you think is wrong?" I asked.

"Don't know, but look." He pointed to birds circling in the air toward the direction Coyote and Cole rode. "I think something is dead over there."

I shuddered. "It isn't just a small rabbit is it?"

"No, too many birds. It is not good." His voice trailed off as he choked down the lump in his throat.

We waited in silence.

A small cloud of dust rose just beyond the rise. The two men cleared the crest and were coming at a fast clip. Coyote stopped at Dawson's wagon, but Cole came straight back to me.

"It's a herd of buffalo, slaughtered. Left to rot in the sun."

"Oh, that's awful," I said.

"That isn't all of it. The buffalo hunters have been killed by Indians. We buried them."

"Do you think the Indians vill be after us, too?" Rudy asked, giving a searching scan of the horizon.

"It's hard telling, but Coyote thinks we should keep moving tonight. We'll have an almost full moon and the cattle need to get to water since they haven't had any for three days. We don't want to make camp here, so close to this slaughter, in case the Indians should return."

The wagons lumbered over the rise and into the valley of rotting buffalo meat and sun bleached bones picked clean by animals and vultures. The stench rose up to greet us like a slap in the face. I got sick to my stomach and lost my dinner over the side of the wagon. We passed the two freshly dug graves of the hunters, not even a cross to mark them, but I could not feel sorry for them. How could they have caused such carnage?

We moved on.

The evening meal consisted of cold beans, hard bread, dried apples and a slab of ham. We stopped only long enough to milk the cow and to make coffee. People's tempers were on a short fuse and quarreling broke out over the least little thing. The festive feeling of the first few days had faded when we left the Santa Fe Trail. Now the hardships of the journey became a reality.

By morning we entered a small valley filled with wildflowers and oak trees - - a lovely place in contrast to the site of the buffalo slaughter. I filled my eyes with all the beauty of this valley, hoping to rid myself of the sights and smells of the destruction which we left behind us. A quiet, blue-green stream meandered through the glade.

We stopped to fix breakfast and water the stock. Cole filled our water barrels while I packed a hamper of food to eat at noon. Luke came into camp for breakfast and to fill his water flask. I wrapped Luke's meal in a towel and handed it to him before he returned to the herd.

All day we traveled through the valley. Cole rode up front of the line with Dawson, I drove the wagon, and Coyote was scouting the land for Indians far ahead.

That night we made camp beside the stream. The animals had plenty of water and grass. I had just finished clearing the evening meal away when Coyote came into our camp.

"Kid, it's your turn for night guard," he said as he poured a cup of coffee.

My heart sank. I could hear my soft bed calling my name. All I wanted to do was sleep. "Are you sure? Can't they watch themselves?"

"I'm sure and no, they can't watch themselves. I'll go out with you."

Cole started to stand, but I put my hand on his shoulder. "That's alright. I'll do it. You need to get some sleep. You're driving tomorrow."

I saddled Zephyr, and Coyote and I rode off to the herd about a half mile downstream.

"I'll stay out here with you. I've seen Indian signs all day and don't want to take any chances."

"What kind of signs?" I asked.

"Just stuff - - pony tracks, broken grass and moccasin prints. I know they're out there."

"You sound like Co. . . uh. . . Johnny now. He knows when he's being followed without seeing the person."

"Johnny's a good man. You take the river side and I'll circle 'round back. Ira Olander, one of the outriders, is out here, too. If you see Sims, tell him you're taking his turn. He needs to get some supper."

"Will do. See you later." I urged Zephyr along the bank. Cattle were still at the stream drinking, which made maneuvering Zephyr around them difficult. Moonlight reflected in the blue black water. Softly I sang, "Dreams of the summer night, tell her, her lover keeps watch, while, in slumber light she sleeps, my lady sleeps. She sleeps, she sleeps, my lady sleeps."

I heard a noise. A branch snapped. Leaves rustled. I pulled my rifle out of the scabbard. My eyes could not penetrate the darkness under the trees. "Sims, is that you?" I called.

No answer.

I pulled back on the reins and made Zephyr back up. I did not want to go any farther into the oaks that grew along the water. In the daylight it didn't look as ominous as it did at night, and all the talk of Indians didn't help matters any. I heard a low whistle. Somewhat like a bird call. "Who's there?"

Again, no answer.

Whether it was the night air or fright that caused me to shiver I had no idea. All I knew was I wanted to get out of there. I turned Zephyr and prodded him to move, all the while remembering Cole's warning about sudden movements stampeding the cattle. But at that moment, I did not care. I wanted to put the herd between me and the oak grove.

"Hey, hey, slow down. What's your hurry?" Sims grabbed Zephyr's bridle.

"Where did you come from?" I asked in an obvious show of relief.

"I was over 'cross the stream. I heard somethin'."

"I did, too. But it came from that oak grove. I think we should move the cattle closer to the wagons."

"Sounds good to me."

At that moment, Coyote joined us. "You two hear somethin' strange?"

We told Coyote what each of us had heard. "The Kid here thinks we should move the herd closer to the wagons," Sims ended.

"Good idea. Anyone seen Ira?"

"No," I said.

"He ain't 'cross the stream. I was just over there," Sims added.

"Yeah. Me too," Coyote said, looking around.

By now I was scared, really scared. All I wanted to do was to get out of there. "Let's move the cattle. Once they start moving, Ira will catch up."

"Okay, take it slow and easy. Herd 'em, don't push 'em." Coyote started whistling and swinging his coat to get their attention. It worked. Slowly the cattle started moving towards the wagon camp.

"Kid, ride on ahead, get help. Tell Dawson to wake the camp. We could get attacked by morning."

CHAPTER 24

Cole anticipated trouble and had already brought our animals inside the enclosure of the wagons. He waited in Dawson's camp.

"Coyote is moving the herd up. We can't find Ira. I think Indians got him," I yelled, quickly dismounting as Zephyr slid to a halt. "They need help bringing the cattle in. Coyote said to wake the camp because we may be attacked before morning."

Cole took Zephyr's reins and swung into the saddle. "I'll bring in the cattle. You roust the camp. Don't tell anyone 'bout Ira. Don't want people going off halfcocked and shooting at everything that moves out there." He whirled Zephyr around and disappeared into the night.

I woke one side of the circle while Dawson woke the other. We met at our wagon. I didn't have to tell anyone about Ira being missing, fear has a way of muddling otherwise clear thinking. Confusion soon turned into chaos as everyone tried to get their animals into the circle and fortify their position against the danger hidden in the darkness. However, I did see Rudy and Luke ride out to help bring in the cattle.

Dawson, standing on a box, he had drug to the middle of the corral, shouted for all to hear. "Everyone come over here! Simmer down and listen." The people grew silent. "Now, we don't know if'n any Indians are out there or not. All we know is that Coyote thinks it's best to move the herd closer to the wagons. We've been seein' Indian signs all day. That doesn't mean they're the same Indians who killed the hunters. These Indians could be peaceful. Let me remind you, I'll shoot the first man who fires a shot and kills an Indian without cause."

"If'n there ain't trouble, why did ya wake us?" one man shouted.

"Like I said, we don't know. It's best to be on the safe side. What I want from you is to keep an eye out. If you see anything movin' out there, let me know. It's likely them Indians will wait 'til mornin' before we see them."

In the distance, the sound of a gunshot echoed in the night. Everyone stood like statues. The velvet blackness of the land that lay just beyond the wagon enclosure became like a great wall, impossible to penetrate.

My knees banged together, and I feared the tears that threatened to fill my eyes would betray me.

Dawson jumped off the box. "Now everyone get to your wagon and stay put. Keep your fires low and your heads down. Kid, you come with me 'til Johnny gets back."

Sitting by Dawson's fire, drinking coffee from Coyote's cup, I could not stop shaking. I thought of other times I had been afraid - - when Mr. Molack came after me and Mama shot him, the time in Bayard's cabin and again when he attacked me at the cemetery, and the gunfight in Independence. But none were as frightening as this. I looked at the gun on the box next to me. "I've become quite good at hitting rocks and twigs, but I wonder if I can really shoot a person," I said to the old man who traveled with Dawson and Coyote and worked as their cook and wagon driver.

"Well, sonny, yah do whatcha gotta do. Shootin' a

man that's tryin' to kill yah jest comes natural like." He spit a stream of brown tobacco juice into the fire. Steam rose with a sizzle. "No tellin' if'n we're gonna fight or trade. Dawson's a sly old fox when it comes to dealin' with Injuns. Been travelin' with him and Coyote for nigh on ten years now and ain't had more than a handful of scrapes with them red devils."

The old man squatted on his haunches, stirring last night's rabbit stew simmering in a black kettle. His tattered brown hat covered a thatch of gray hair hanging over the collar of his coat. Gray whiskers covered the lower part of his bony face. The glow from the fire softened his hatchet features as he squinted to see me.

I remembered what Reverend Tadwell had once said when his wife complained about gaining weight. *'Never trust a skinny cook.'* Watching the thin man at the fire, I wondered if he ate his own cooking.

Steadily closer came the sound of the cattle and the drovers whistling to move them along. I thought of Cole out there and prayed that he was safe. Time crawled toward morning.

"That coffee sure smells good," Cole said, coming up behind me.

Startled, I shrieked. Leaping off the crate, I grabbed my gun.

"Don't shoot. It's only me." Cole held up his hands in surrender.

My scream had aroused the camp and some men came running with guns drawn.

"It's okay. Go back to your wagons." Cole turned the men away.

"I didn't hear you coming into camp," I said, feeling the need to defend my actions. "I've told you before, don't sneak up on me."

Cole smiled his usual heart melting smile. His eyes twinkled with mischief. "What did you think you were going to do with the gun? If I were an Indian, I wouldn't have spoken. I would've just grabbed you like this." He put his arm around my throat and pulled me against his warm body. "Now, what would you do?"

Tugging at Cole's hand, twisting and turning, I tried to escape, but could not break his hold. With his other hand Cole tickled me. I have never liked being tickled and Cole knew it. "Don't! Don't, I'll scream," I threatened.

"No, you won't. You would rather be tickled than draw attention to yourself again."

Cole knew me better than I thought. I lifted the heel of my boot and brought it down hard on top of Cole's foot. He released his grip as he howled in pain.

"I told you not to tickle me."

Dawson and Coyote stepped into the light of the fire. Rudy brought Gretchen and the children into Dawson's camp. Luke joined us, but Mr. Simms went to his own wagon.

Cole limped over to a box and sat down. "I think my foot is broken. Teach me to mess with the kid." He glanced over his shoulder. "Come here where I can keep an eye on you. Don't want you sneaking up behind me."

I took my place on a crate between Cole and Coyote. I didn't feel afraid anymore. Was it because the men were safely in camp or because Cole had taken my mind off the Indians? His little tomfoolery seemed to have worked. I sat quietly and listened to the men talk of bringing the cattle closer to the wagons.

The conversation turned sober as Coyote began to speak. "We found Ira. He's dead. Buried him in the grove. Seems his horse threw him. Broke his neck."

"We heard a shot," I said.

"Had to put his horse down. He broke his leg stepping in a hole. When he fell, Ira must've gone over the horse's head. Didn't suffer none. Killed him outright. He was green as grass. Hardly knew how to ride. Come from Boston." As Coyote talked, he kept staring into the fire, poking at the burning wood with a stick.

"Did he have family?" Gretchen asked.

"Seems to have had a wife and a few youngins. Best write her a letter when we get to a town," Dawson said, straddling his chair with his massive arms resting across the back. "That's the trouble with greenhorns goin' west. They don't know enough to stay out of dark groves at night. Yet, they're goin' to brave the frontier for the dream of gold. Stupid, downright stupid."

"Most of us people are greenhorns. None of us have traveled vest before, except Johnny," Rudy protested.

"Yes, but a farmer knows how to ride and handle stock. Them city folks don't know nothin'. I hate travelin' with a wagon train of city folks." Dawson looked toward the east. "Looks like mornin's about an hour away."

"We better get back to our wagon," Cole said as he stood. This time he forgot to limp. The game was over.

Shimmering light crested the green hills, chasing the night away. Meadow larks twilled their song to greet the new day. Roosters crowed. Cows and horses milled around creating dust. We watched. No one dared speak above a whisper. Time passed. An hour slipped by. We waited.

Coyote entered our camp. "What do you make of it, Johnny? Do you think we spooked too easy?"

"Your guess is as good as mine. You saw the signs, heard the whistles, same as I did. I'd have bet the plantation we would have been under attack by first light."

"Dawson wants to take the chance on movin'. I agree. I took a look around and didn't see one feather. If'n they were here, they're gone now."

"Then let's do it. No use sittin' here." Cole turned to me. "Get it packed up. We're leaving."

"Are you sure they aren't hiding out there?" I protested. "Might be they're just waiting for us to open up the circle."

"No. They've cleared out. Maybe your singin' drove them off," Coyote teased.

I turned in a huff and started throwing the tin plates and cups into the chest, mumbling under my breath. "That's it, tease the kid. When we get attacked, I'll remind them that I didn't want to leave."

All morning we pushed the oxen hard to put distance between us, the stream, and hopefully the Indians. Cole rode Shadow at the front of the train with Coyote and Dawson. I drove our wagon. The blisters on my hands from working the team had turned into new calluses. My muscles were no longer sore. And the swaying and bumping of the wagon became second nature. I realized I wasn't a greenhorn anymore, but a seasoned pioneer. I had put the genteel speech of the plantation behind me and had taken on the dialect of the frontier.

With the threat of Indians far behind, my mind filled itself with daydreams to overcome the boredom. My imaginary friend took his place beside me. *"You're handling the team quite well,"* he said.

"Why, thank you, kind sir." My words were swallowed up by the cranking and groaning of the wagon. "Are you going to follow me all the way to California?"

"To the ends of the earth, if need be."

"Will you not miss your home in the South, your fine plantation?"

"With you by my side, I'll be happy living in a wagon. You are the only woman I will ever love."

I giggled to myself. "If only you were real."

Looking up, I saw the Pingal wagon in front of me slow to a stop. "Whoa," I called, pulling back on the reins. "I wonder what's happening."

"Why don't you get down and have a look?" my friend advised.

I waited. Since each day the wagons rotated position, today I was last in line. I didn't like not knowing what was happening up ahead. I climbed down and checked the ropes on the horses. They were firmly tied to the back of the wagon. Our milk cow didn't need a rope. She was so used to walking, she would follow anything that moved. We had to tie her up at night so she wouldn't wander away.

I saw Mrs. Pingal get down from her wagon. She held the small of her back when she walked. She was in her early forties and pregnant for the first time. Her belly was so large and she so petite, she looked as if she were carrying a pumpkin under her dress.

I stood by my wagon and waited. The afternoon sun traveled toward the horizon. Flies buzzed around my ears. Everything was still and quiet. Too quiet. I untied Misty and swung onto her back. "Come on, Girl, let's find Cole."

I rode past all the wagons. People gathered in small groups. Men held rifles ready to defend what was theirs. Some men were heading to the front of the line. When I reached Dawson's wagon, the cook stood by his team looking off across the open land toward a small rise.

"What's the matter?" I asked. "Why have we stopped?" Other people gathered around us.

"Injins." The cook pointed to the rise. Dust clouds drifted above the knoll.

"Where are Johnny and Coyote?"

The old man just pointed.

"They're out there with the Indians? What about Dawson? Where's he?"

"Same place." The old man turned and walked to the rear of his wagon. "No use wastin' this time. Best get supper started."

"How can you be so cavalier? Doesn't it matter to you that Indians are just beyond that hill?"

"They're just talkin'. If'n there's trouble, Dawson will let me know."

"How?"

"They'd a come high-tailin' it over the ridge by now.

No, this bunch jest wants to jaw a spell."

I dismounted Misty and stood watching the knoll. Slowly, without giving much thought to what I was doing, I started walking toward the rise. The sounds of the wagon train grew fainter and fainter as I concentrated on the hill. My strategy was to hide in the tall grass, keep low and watch. Touching the butt of my gun in its holster, courage surged through me.

The drama on the other side of the ridge mesmerized me. In the shade of a lone oak tree, five Indian men sat cross-legged in a circle with Cole, Coyote, and Dawson. The men talked more with their hands than with words. It seemed to me that the men were arguing. Dawson seemed to be holding his own as he held up five fingers. The old Indian showed ten, twice. Dawson shook his head, no.

Two young men came into the shade and sat behind the old Indian, outside of the circle. This action seemed to agitate Coyote. He no longer watched the old man, but his eyes scanned the landscape and his gaze concentrated on the knoll where I was hiding.

Suddenly, a large shadow moved over me and blocked out the sun. I rolled onto my back to see an Indian silhouetted against the sky. He reached down and picked me up by my shirt and the bib of the overalls and lifted me to my feet. A shocked expression spread across his bronze face as he quickly released me. I fell to the ground. Shock turned to curiosity. He dropped to one knee beside me and took hold of my shirt to yank it open.

I grabbed his hands. "Don't!" I growled in my deepest voice.

He tilted his head to one side. "You're a boy?"

I didn't know what to say. If I said yes, I was a boy, he would rip off my shirt for proof. But if I said no, and admitted to being a woman, would he take advantage of me? Again my thoughts flew back to Bayard and that day in the cemetery. Cole wasn't going to rescue me this time.

At that moment fear turned to anger and with anger came courage. "Get away." I shoved him back and scrambled to my feet.

He jumped to a standing position and grabbed my arm. With a swoop of his hand, he sent my hat flying. I saw the delight in his onyx eyes as he touched my hair.

"Yellow, like gold."

"Yes. Yes. Now let go. I'm going back to the wagons."

A smile warmed his stern features for just a moment. His golden red skin glistened with sweat. The smell of horse and the faint fragrance of grass clung to him. Black braids hung past his shoulders, tied with leather straps intertwined with beads. A beaded headband cut across his wide forehead. The planes of his face were chiseled sharply to a square jaw and a tapered nose with flared nostrils. He wore a vest beaded with a flower pattern of the Plains Indians, leather breeches and moccasins. His menacing stature towered above me.

"Come." He pulled me down the hill toward the men sitting under the oak.

I dug in my heels trying to resist. But against his savage strength, my struggling was futile. "Let me get my hat!"

The Indian stooped down, retrieved the hat, and plopped it on my head.

By the time we approached the circle, the bargaining had concluded and the men were standing. The Indian pushed me into the circle. "Who does this one belong to?"

Cole rolled his eyes and turned his face away.

The Indian stood over me, arms crossed, legs astride.

Coyote stepped forward. "Kid, what are you doing here?"

"I was watching from the hill when this Indian attacked me and forced me to come down here."

"Attacked you?" Cole turned around in defiance. "How did he attack you?"

Cole's temper was kindled -- his eyes aflame with anger. He moved to my side.

"Yellow Sky," the old Indian called. His raspy voice filled with authority.

I felt like a little dogwood standing in the middle of tall pines and I knew I had chosen the wrong word to describe what had happened. "Well, it wasn't as bad as it sounds. I'm not hurt. I was just curious to see an Indian. Now that I have, I want to go back to the wagon."

Dawson turned to the old Indian. "Chief, the foolishness of a child watching from the hill doesn't change anything. You have agreed to let us travel through your land safely."

"And you leave fifteen cattle for my people. White man kill buffalo. My people die when winter comes if buffalo are gone. You pay."

Dawson nodded. "Fifteen cattle, done." He went to get his horse.

The Chief and the Indians with him walked up the hill in the other direction.

Yellow Sky didn't move. His eyes fixed on Cole.

"I'll let you handle this," Coyote said as he followed Dawson.

"Come on, Kid. Let's get back to the wagons. You've done enough damage here for one day," Cole said.

As Cole reached out to take my arm, Yellow Sky stopped him. "This one belong to you?"

"Yes."

"Your woman?"

Cole's eyes widened in surprise. "Sister," he whispered. "They don't know she's a girl. Let's keep it that way, less trouble."

A smile of acknowledgement crossed Yellow Sky's face. "Are these white men blind?"

"No. They don't look on a boy with the eyes of a man."

Yellow Sky relaxed his stance and let us pass.

Shadow wouldn't let me ride him, even behind Cole. I didn't want to ride with Coyote, and Dawson didn't offer. I walked back to the wagons.

The next morning, fifteen head of cattle were cut from the herd and left behind as the wagons rambled over the knoll. I thought we had seen the last of those Indians, but I was wrong.

Chapter 25

Two days came and went. Storm clouds gathered on the horizon and a steady wind blew against us. Cole should have been riding at the front of the line with Dawson, since Coyote had been scouting up ahead and wasn't expected back for a few days. But Cole drove our wagon while I sat on the seat beside him. I combated the boredom by making pie dough and rolling it out on a cloth stretched on the seat between us. Dried apples had been soaking in a cinnamon, sugar and milk mixture since breakfast.

"Smells like we'll have apple pie for supper," Cole said, taking a deep breath. The fragrance of cinnamon and apples drifted up from inside the wagon.

"I have to do something to get back into your good graces."

Cole shook his head. "If you feel you need to get on someone's good side, you might think about making that pie for Dawson. He didn't say much, but he sure was angry. You could have messed up everything."

"How? You were already done talking."

"If the old Chief felt threatened in any way, he could

have called the bargain off. He has enough young braves to take the entire herd if he wanted. He didn't need to bargain for fifteen cattle."

"Then why did he do it?"

"Out of respect for Dawson. The Chief knows that Dawson is a man of his word, a good man. But with you watching from the hill, the Chief might have thought more men were out there watching, ready to shoot him and his people."

"But I'm supposed to be just a kid."

"An Indian is a man at fourteen."

"I'm sorry. I didn't mean any harm. It's just that my curiosity got the upper hand."

"Sarah, you need to think before you act. You jump into situations, and before you know it, you're in over your head."

"Not always."

"Well, let me think. Just since January, you got caught in the cemetery by that man from the cabin in the woods, you were in the hotel room alone with that Mr. Nick, you were in a very compromising position with Coyote at Miss Molly's, and now with Yellow Sky. I'd say you have had more than your share of mishaps. From now on, stay close to the wagon and try to stay out of trouble."

"None of that was my fault. You were the one who left me at the hotel and at Miss Molly's." I saw Cole wasn't listening. In a huff, I finished my pie in silence and planned to bake it when we stopped for supper.

All afternoon the wagons lumbered over the rolling terrain. Coyote had said that people were beginning to call this route the Chisholm Trail, named for an old trapper who traveled this way, bringing his goods up from Texas to the cities in the north. He said that some of the Texas ranchers might try driving their cattle this way to market. We were to keep an eye out for the herds, but I watched the thunder clouds form pictures in the sky.

"Look over there," I said, pointing to a pillar of fluffy

white. My anger was long forgotten. "Of what does that remind you?"

"An Indian, of course. He's got on a feather war bonnet and he's holding a blanket over his arm."

"I see a beautiful woman wearing a large hat, holding a basket filled with sweet biscuits and fresh breads that she is carrying to a sick friend."

"You sure have an imagination."

"Oh, I remember one time when you called me boring. You said you didn't think I had an imagination. Remember? The Christmas Eve before the war?"

"I do remember. That evening gave me the feeling of an almost magical time. I don't know if I can explain it to you, but. . . ."

"You don't need to explain. I felt it too. I have often thought about that night. It seems so long ago, but at times, like only yesterday. I wish we could go back. I wish the war had never happened. I wish. . . ."

"No need to wish," he interrupted. "The war has changed everything. We can't go back, only forward. People have changed, I have, you certainly have. I wonder if you would be happy going back to the life you lived before the war now that you have seen the world beyond the stone pillars."

"I'm not afraid of the world anymore. Not like I was. But I think I would have liked to have been mistress of Rosewood."

"Someday you'll have your own home, husband, and children. Everything you've dreamed about."

"I remember Cousin Amy Ann complained that she wanted someone to marry her for herself, not for what she has or for who she is. I suppose I'll not have to worry about such things. My chances of getting married are growing slimmer with each passing day. Just look at me. I'm almost as dark as a field slave. I have nothing to my name except Misty Morn and even my name isn't my own. I'm The Kid."

"I don't think you need to worry about getting married. Let Coyote know who you really are, and he'll wed you and bed you in a twinkling of an eye."

"Cole Brighton. You are incorrigible. All this talk that you've changed. You're still a scamp." I teasingly nudged his arm and we both laughed.

We were still laughing when the wagons came to a halt.

"Something's wrong. Here comes Dawson." Cole put his foot on the brake and pulled back on the reins.

"You two climb on down here," Dawson said, dismounting. He took his brown hat off and wiped the hat band, his face, and the back of his neck with a red bandanna. Before he began to speak, he replaced the hat on his head.

"I don't know what's goin' on here with the two of you, but I have that young buck, Yellow Sky, and a bunch of his friends up at the head of the train. He says he won't let us move until he talks to you. He's got himself ten of the finest ponies I've seen this side of the Mississippi and he says they're for you as a marriage price. Now I don't normally meddle with people on the train. What they do is their business. That is, until it interferes with my running the wagons. Then it becomes my business." He turned to me. His eyes narrowed. "I don't believe those ponies are to buy Johnny, here, so why don't you tell me what's goin' on."

Cole started to explain. "Actually, Dawson, the kid is my sister, not my brother."

"You don't say." Sarcasm filled his voice. "Go on. I'm listenin'."

"Her name's Sarah. We thought she would be safer traveling as a boy than as a girl. But so far, it hasn't seemed to have worked out that way."

"How does this young buck know and I don't? Even now, I can't see she's a girl. Short hair, baggy clothes, there's no sign of girl there. Maybe if I watched you walk,

I'd see somethin'."

"The Indian grabbed me. He felt I wasn't a boy." I blushed.

Dawson's eyes widened with surprise. "I'll be. You best not let Coyote know he's been fooled. He knows somethin's different 'bout you, but he can't quite put his finger on it. Knowin' Coyote, like I do, he'll worry on that bone 'til he comes up with the answer."

"The best part of the story is the 'Angel in Red' he's been talking about was really Sarah," Cole added.

Dawson's face lit up and he slapped his leg. "Now that's a good one. Everybody thinks he had too much to drink and he was just seein' things. But here you are right under his nose, so to speak." Remembering why he had come back to our wagon, Dawson's mood changed as quickly as a summer storm. "Well, that doesn't take care of matters at hand. You best go and talk to Yellow Sky. I don't care what you say just get him to let the wagons go."

"He must think you're special, with your yellow hair, to offer me ten ponies," Cole said. "Most marriage offers are with one pony, two at the most. But ten. I would be a rich man in his tribe."

"Ten of the finest I've ever seen," Dawson interjected. "Right nice marriage price."

"I might just take him up on it," Cole teased.

"Don't even joke about that," I said.

"Yellow Sky isn't a bad sort," Dawson said. "He'd be good to you."

Mounting Zephyr, Cole said, "You see, Sarah, you wanted to get married. God has provided a husband. And the best part is that you don't have to have a dowry. In the Indian culture, the man buys the woman. Yellow Sky wants you for yourself. Isn't that what you said?"

I caught the twinkle in Cole's eyes, and I knew he was only trying to set my temper flying. I refused to give him satisfaction. "Dawson, I made an apple pie. Do come after supper tonight for pie and coffee."

"You sure you'll be here?" Dawson grinned.

"He won't sell me. He is a man of his word and he gave his word to Mama to take me to California." I said it loud enough for Cole to hear.

Cole and Dawson rode up the line together.

Gretchen came running back to me. "Vhat is the matter?"

I told her about the events taking place at the front of the train. Her worry lines carved deeper into her forehead as the vision of me becoming the wife of an Indian formed in her mind.

I concluded, "Yellow Sky is quite serious. Cole has to be tactful in turning him down. Otherwise Yellow Sky will be embarrassed in front of his friends and that will never do." I paced back and forth, waiting for Cole to return. "How do I get myself into such situations?"

"Because you always vant to help. Your heart is good. You just do not think before you act," Gretchen consoled.

A half hour passed before Cole returned to the wagon. Anger flared his nostrils and pressed his lips together in a thin line cutting across his face. He threw his hat into the back of the wagon and stripped his shirt over his head.

"What happened? What are you doing?"

"He won't take no for an answer. He wants to fight. Winner takes all, you and the ponies."

"That's nonsense. I'll talk to him. I'll make him understand I can't possibly marry him."

Cole grabbed my arm. "You stay out of this. Yellow Sky has to maintain his position in his village. He can't be put aside by a white man or a woman. I'll handle it." Cole went to Rudy's wagon where Dawson joined them. Cole stood a head taller than the two men. His tanned body rippled with tension.

"I can't stand by helpless and watch Cole be killed. I have to do something."

"No, Sarah, you heard vhat Cole said. You must stay

out of this and let the men handle it," Gretchen protested.

"Gretchen, don't say anything. I'm going to settle this, or I'll be Yellow Sky's wife. I can't let Cole be killed."

I untied Misty, grabbed a handful of mane and swung onto her back, closing my knees tightly to her sides. She moved swiftly to the head of the train and beyond to where Yellow Sky waited with the ponies and his friends.

As I approached, Yellow Sky's face broke into a smile and he rode out to meet me. "You have come to me." His ebony hair hung loose to the middle of his back, held in place by a white beaded headband. The afternoon sun lent richness to his already reddish gold skin.

"No. I have come to talk." I dismounted, looking over my shoulder at the wagons. Cole, on Zephyr, was closing ground at a fast clip. Yellow Sky's friends moved between us and Cole, barring his interference.

Yellow Sky dismounted. He folded his arms over his bare chest in defiance.

In a voice loud enough for his friends to hear, I said, "Yellow Sky, you would make any woman proud to become yours. You have honored me with such a grand payment of ten ponies. Surely none of the women of your village have been so highly esteemed." I wondered how much of what I was saying he or his friends could really understand, but I continued, "If I were free to accept your offer, I would. But I have no choice. I must go to California."

Anger erased the smile from Yellow Sky's face as he shouted, "No! You stay with me."

I wondered if I hadn't made a horrible mistake. "Hear what I have to say before you get angry." I took a deep breath and continued, "My brother is an honorable man. His word is never broken. You, too, are such a man. He gave his word to our mother on her death bed that he would take me to our uncle in California. How can he break his word to his dead mother?"

"We will fight. When he is dead, his word is dead."

"Will killing my brother cause me to love you more? Do you want a woman who will hate you as long as she lives?"

"I will make you forget. I will be your shelter. No rain will touch you. You will no longer be hungry. I will give you food. Your loneliness will be swallowed up in my love."

"My, you do talk romantic." I fanned my face with my hat for a moment to think what to say next. "Who is there in your village to cry for you? Cole might win. Will your death make your sister love me? I think not. Yellow Sky, I don't want to go to California, but a bond has been made. Even death cannot change it. If I could stay with you, I would. But I cannot."

All my words were spoken. If they didn't work, Cole would have to fight him. Cole would never let me go without a fight. I knew that. I looked into Yellow Sky's dark eyes for any hint of softening. I waited.

A breeze lightly touched his hair as he stood with his feet apart and his arms still folded across his chest. The silence became deafening. At last Yellow Sky raised one hand over his head and motioned to his friends. Without a word he turned, walked to his pony, swung onto its back, and rode away. His friends followed.

I felt Cole at my side as I watched the Indians ride away, taking the marriage prize with them. "It's over. He's gone," I whispered.

"Yes, he won't be back. That was a stupid thing to do."

"I couldn't let you fight him. I just said what I thought he wanted to hear. He is a proud man. I had to let his friends know he wasn't foolish to ask."

"You can thank God that his father, the Chief, wants peace. A few years ago, Yellow Sky wouldn't have been put off by pretty words. He would have taken you."

"Yellow Sky is the son of the Chief?"

"You didn't know that?"

I shook my head.

"Let's get back to the wagons. We're burning daylight."

"Stretch 'em out. Still have couple hours of daylight," Dawson called.

"I guess everyone knows I'm a girl," I said to Gretchen as we walked behind her wagon.

"No. They do not know vhat vent on mit the Indians. You are still the Kid."

In the days that followed my encounter with Yellow Sky, I was happy to listen to the turning of the wagon wheels putting distance between us and the Indians even though each turning carried me closer to California and an uncertain future. We left Indian Territory behind and entered the state of Texas.

Dawson had said before we left Westport that Sundays would be special days and we wouldn't travel if he had a choice. Later in the year, when water would be scarce, we would have to keep moving, but until then Sunday was a day of rest and a day to socialize. The women wore their clean, white aprons that they saved for Sundays and special occasions. The day began an hour after sunrise, instead of an hour before sunrise, with everyone gathering in the center of the wagon enclosure. Dawson usually read Scriptures and led the group in a prayer. Mrs. Adler, a song leader in her church back home, led the singing of old favorite hymns before we went back to our own camps.

After breakfast I had time to make enough bread and rolls to last the week. If we were by a stream, I washed clothes. On this one day of the week we weren't in a rush to do anything. We didn't have to break camp and get on the road by first light. We didn't have to eat our noon meal on the fly. And at the end of day, when we were so tired we just wanted to drop, we didn't have to make another camp and cook by dwindling light. I loved Sundays.

Cole tended to the horses and our equipment. If

something needed mending, he fixed it before it broke entirely. Cole was a firm believer in the old adage, 'a stitch in time saves nine.' If meat was running low, a cow would be slaughtered and the meat distributed to everyone.

On this day more than any other, people visited from one camp to another. The women talked about children, cooking, and the family back home. Men discussed the trip, Indians, and the future. The children played within the corral of the wagons. But with all these groups, I found no place of my own. I didn't fit in anywhere.

Coyote became a frequent visitor in our camp. I always felt uneasy when he was near. He watched me with the eyes of a hunter. I felt he was waiting for me to make a mistake and to reveal my true identity. Also, I resented Coyote for taking so much of Cole's time away from me. Cole and Coyote enjoyed the same things. They were adventurers, thrill seekers, cut from the same courageous cloth.

"That bread sure smells good." Coyote shamelessly hinted for an invitation for supper.

"We'll be eating about three," Cole offered. "Come for dinner."

"Today?" I snapped, wrinkling my nose.

"Sounds good to me," Coyote said, misunderstanding my question for an invitation. "I'll be here." He got up from my chair, where he always liked to sit when he was in our camp, and strolled away.

I watched him and when he was well out of hearing range, I turned to Cole. "What are you thinking? The more that man is in our camp, the sooner he's going to figure out who I am."

Cole smiled. His eyes twinkled with mischief. "Don't you feel the excitement of the hunt? He knows you're different and he is drawn to you, but he doesn't know why."

"You're having fun at my expense. One of these days, I'll get even with you. You'll be on the other end of the stick and I'll be poking at you. We'll see how much fun it will be for you."

"Can't you see the humor in this?"

I hated to admit Cole was right. I thought of how bewildered Coyote will be when I finally tell him who I am. "I guess it is funny when I stop to think about it. But won't he be a little hurt, too?"

"I thought of that. You told Yellow Sky I was an honorable man. But since we left the plantation, my life is nothing but a lie. I'm on the run from the law. I'm telling everyone you're my brother. Even my name is false. That isn't very honorable. Now I'm developing a bond with Coyote, but I can't let him get too close."

"I'm living that same lie."

"I know. Does the end justify the means? That's an age-old question, and each man, or woman, has to answer it in his or her own heart. As for right now, it seems the best thing to do. It's not that these people don't matter, they do. But we won't be seeing them again once we get to California. At Uncle William's, you will be Sarah, I will be Cole, and we'll pray that the U.S. Army doesn't press charges against us for taking our own horses. I'm hoping that the Army will have bigger fish to fry than little ones like us."

Our conversation came to an abrupt halt with screams coming from the direction of the Pingal camp. Cole flung the harness aside and sprang to his feet. A crowd started gathering at Mrs. Pingal's tent. We rushed to join them.

"What's happening?" I asked as Mrs. Adler exited the tent.

"It's Mrs. Pingal's time. Mary Simms is with her. The rest of you can just go about your own business." Mrs. Adler shooed everyone away. "Johnny, why don't you take Mr. Pingal to your camp? There's nothing he can do here. He'd just be in the way."

"Is it going poorly?" Cole asked.

"It seems so," Mrs. Adler whispered. "She's almost

two months early. We'll probably lose the baby."

"What about Mrs. Pingal?"

"I don't know. Mary has nine youngin's of her own. If'n she can't help, no one can."

We took Mr. Pingal to our camp. I let him sit in my chair and drink coffee from my cup.

"We've wanted children for many years. She kept thinking God was punishing her by not giving her a child." Mr. Pingal spoke softly, almost to himself. "We didn't know she was expecting when we started the trip from Ohio. We've worked so hard to get the money. She didn't want to stay another year in Independence. What will I do if she dies? We've been together since we were sixteen. But I've always known her. We grew up in the same town. She's the only one I've ever loved." He put his face into his hands.

A pall hung over the camp as the afternoon aged. Scream after scream sent shivers through my body. People talked in hushed tones. June's summer heat offered no comfort. Cole attached a canvas to the wagon and stretched it out on two poles to provide shade.

I fixed dinner. Coyote and Luke joined us. But the joy of a Sunday dinner had left, and we found conversation difficult. At last, everyone ate in silence. The moon had already risen before Mr. Pingal insisted on returning to his wagon. Long into the night we could hear Mrs. Pingal moan. By morning silence told the story. She was too old for bearing children and the trip too arduous for her frail body. Both mother and child had died. Now a shroud of sorrow hung over the Pingal wagon as his bride of thirty years lay in a coffin made from the sideboards of their conveyance.

Cole went to lend words of comfort, as if words could help a grief-stricken man who had to say goodbye too soon to the one he loved.

I thought of the times death had come into my life - - Danny, Daddy, Mama. My memory returned to the cemetery on the hill. I remembered the two sentinels at the small gate and wondered if they still stood guard. I wondered if all the graves were cared for or if grass and weeds had overgrown the hill. I had told Yellow Sky that death didn't break a bond, but Daddy's word had been broken. We were not there to tend to Sarah's grave anymore. Homesickness washed over me like a great flood, and the tears I thought I had put behind me fell in a spillway down my face. I ran from the corral out onto the dry, sun baked land. Home lay in the direction of the rising sun, and that was the way I headed.

I didn't hear the big roan coming up behind me, but there he was blocking my way.

"Where do you think you're goin'?" Coyote asked, dismounting.

I wiped my face, trying to focus on the horizon through my tears. "I'm going home. I've had enough of this frontier. You and Johnny can have it."

"You're cryin'." He took out his bandanna and handed it to me.

"So what if I am," I snapped back.

"Don't let the others see you cry. They'll think you're a sissy."

"I don't care anymore! I'm tired of pretending I'm something I'm not. Mrs. Pingal is dead. We have to leave her out here in the middle of nowhere and move on. I can't do it. I . . . I . . . ."

I crossed my arms over my breast as Coyote pulled me close to him and wrapped his arms around me.

"Come on, Kid. I know it's hard. Johnny told me that you just lost your mama in January, but you can't give up. Hard times are what make us strong."

"I can't be strong anymore. I want to go home." I pushed on Coyote's arm to break his hold. But he didn't release me. My heart pounded like gunfire.

Surely he is going to realize I'm a girl, I thought. His clothes smelled of smoke from the breakfast fire and the aroma of shaving soap lingered on his face.

Suddenly fear took hold. My thoughts flew back to the man who had attacked me at the cemetery. I remembered his hands holding me tight. Then, as now, I couldn't break free. I struggled, flailing my arms at Coyote. My breath caught in my throat. I yelled, "Let go! Let go of me!"

"Kid, it's all right. I'll let go. Just calm down." Coyote held up his hands and stepped away from me.

"Leave me alone. I'll go back with you, but don't touch me. I don't like to be touched."

"You're a scrappy kid for your size. All you need is to get some muscle behind those arms."

"I didn't get enough to eat during the war," I lied. "That's why I'm small for my age."

"Stick with me, Kid. I'll teach you to be a man. When we get to the next town, I'll take you to the local sportin' house. The madam should be able to fix you up real good." He mounted his horse and held out a hand for me to swing up behind him.

"I'll walk." I wanted to put space between him and me. It didn't seem that he had noticed I was a woman yet.

"Don't be stupid. There are snakes out here. Remember Dawson said to walk in the traces of the wagon, not out in the open? Saturday night when we made camp, the men killed seven rattlers within our corral. Now give me your hand."

Looking around on the ground, I remembered the men killing the snakes. The warm weather had brought the creatures out in abundance. I hadn't thought about sidewinders when I left the camp. Grabbing hold of Coyote's hand, he lifted me up behind the saddle.

"Hold on tight. Sunny wants to run." He kicked the big horse and we lunged forward.

I wrapped my arms around Coyote's waist, as the strawberry roan's hooves raced across the north central plains of the Grand Prairies. "Don't tell Johnny," I said, as we entered the circle of wagons.

"Tell him what? That you and I took a ride. He doesn't need to know everything."

"Thanks."

Coyote pulled the horse to a halt beside our wagon. "Don't forget, we have an appointment in the next town."

Once again, the days melted into one another. I lost track of time. It really didn't matter if it was Monday or Thursday, it all seemed the same. Hill or river, grass or sand, it all needed to be crossed. Blue sky or rain clouds, hot sun or cold nights, each had to be endured. The songs of the first few days had been replaced long ago by grumbling and complaining which grew ever louder. Wagon after wagon broke down and needed fixing which caused unwanted delays. Where the land was as flat as a tabletop, the wagons traveled side by side, instead of in a line, to keep the dust out of people's faces. But that didn't help much. Dirt was in everything. The wind blew incessantly and rumors of wind driving women mad became the topic of conversation.

Cole spoke frequently of the wonders of California to keep my spirits lifted. I wished I could see the dream through his eyes. All I could envision were hardships, living in an unfamiliar land with an uncle we didn't know and who probably didn't want us.

"Here comes Coyote," I said. "Must be trouble up ahead."

Coyote rode beside our wagon for a few minutes before he said, "The town of Circleville lies just beyond those hills. It's a good place to make Sunday camp. The San Gabriel River runs past the town. It has a few stores, a blacksmith, a good flouring mill, and a church. Give the folks a chance to go to a real church for a change. We can stock up on supplies and get some of the wagons fixed." He smiled at me and winked an eye. "And the kid and I have an appointment to keep."

A lump tightened in my throat.

Cole frowned at me. "What kind of appointment?"

"I'll tell you later," I whispered

"We should reach the town 'bout sunset," Coyote continued. "I'll be back to get you after supper."

After Coyote and his roan had disappeared into the dust cloud, I explained to Cole what had happened and where Coyote planned to take me.

"You're joking." Cole's eyes twinkled with merriment, and a smile of realization spread across his face. "Don't kid yourself. He knows you're a girl. He wants to see you squirm. He wouldn't be taking just any kid into a whore house."

"In that case, I'll have to call his bluff." I smiled as a plan formed in my mind.

Coyote arrived in our camp as I finished cleaning away the dishes. Luke excused himself and headed into town.

"Thought I'd go with you two," Cole said, strapping on his holsters. "Never know what trouble you'll find with town folks."

What a lie, I thought. *He wants to be in on the kill. One way or another, someone will be left holding the short end of the stick and Cole doesn't want to miss out. He doesn't care who it is, Coyote or me, as long as he can watch.*

Darkness covered Circleville except for a few lights spilling from the windows of the saloon. A tinny piano plunked out *De Camp town Races* to cover the noise of a rowdy crowd. We tied the horses at the hitching rail and went inside.

Smoke hung like a fog and the smell of the place caused my stomach to churn. The wooden bar running along the back wall was held up by barrels. A few tables were scattered around the dingy room. My bravado waned.

Coyote boldly addressed the barkeep. "We want one of your girls for a few hours."

"All of yous?" The barkeep asked, his beady eyes resting on me.

"No. Just the kid, here, it's time he becomes a man." Coyote grinned. "Johnny and I'll take a whisky over at that table." He motioned with his thumb to a corner table away from the piano. "We'll wait for the kid."

"In that case, it'll be two bucks."

Coyote threw the coins on the bar.

Testing the coins with his teeth, the barkeep said, "Goldie's in the first room top of the stairs. Jest go on in."

Slowly I climbed the stairs. My heart became a drum pounding within my chest. I remembered the girls at Molly's. *Hope she's as nice as they were,* I thought. One more glance over my shoulder to see Coyote urging me to go in. Hearing him laugh set determination into my spirit. A deep breath, a turn of the knob, and I entered the small room.

On the four-poster bed in the middle of the dimly lit room laid a large woman wearing almost nothing. A flimsy black chiffon duster was draped loosely about her bare bosom. A black garter belt and silk stockings covered red panties. She raised herself up on one elbow and extinguished her cigarette. "Ain't you a little young?" She raked her long fingernails through her golden mane.

"Yes, I am. I need your help."

"Sure, sonny, jest come over here and sit yourself down next to me." She patted the bed, moving her large body over to make room for me. "I'll be as gentle as a . . ."

"No! You don't understand. Let me explain. I'm not a boy." I noticed her hand jerk to cover herself to no avail. The duster proved inadequate. "I'm here because I need to deceive a man downstairs." I related the story to her. "So I hope you'll help me."

"I'm not into charity. My time is worth money."

"You'll get paid. Coyote gave the barkeep two dollars."

"All you want is to talk? I can do that." She got up and

slipped a black silk robe over the chiffon and sat in the chair by the window. I sat on the bed.

"You needs to bounce up and down on the bed some, Deary," Goldie said. "Gots to make things sound natural like in here." She moaned and groaned.

We heard footsteps in the hall. They stopped at the door. Goldie moaned even louder. I feared it was Coyote and he would come in. She must have sensed my thoughts because she got up and placed a chair under the knob. Remembering the newlywed's wagon, I bounced faster. The bed springs squeaked to the rhythm of the bouncing. The footsteps retreated down the stairs. We waited another ten minutes before I emerged from the room.

Both Cole and Coyote had a grin spread across their faces when I joined them.

Goldie leaned over the railing, displaying all her wares. Above the din of the saloon, she called, "Come back again, Deary."

I waved at her. Turning to the men, I asked, "You two ready to leave?"

Cole pulled his hat down over his face as he led the way out to the horses. I could tell he wanted to laugh, but he didn't. I couldn't quite read Coyote's expression-- surprise, bewilderment, disappointment, perhaps a bit of all three.

"So tell me, Kid, how was it?" Coyote asked.

"About as I had expected."

CHAPTER 26

We said goodbye to Circleville and the sportin' house and headed toward Fort Concho where we would link up with the stage route. We also said goodbye to Mr. Pingal who had lost sight of his dream and who had found a saloon instead. The countryside stretched out before us in a blanket of wild flowers growing amidst coarse prairie grass and scattered mesquite. In the distance, mountains resembling sugar loaves marked our destination. Fish abounded in the crystal streams which zigzagged through the prairie. Once again, spirits were lifted and singing resounded throughout the wagons.

"It's amazing how a little shopping for the women and drinking for the men will revive the spirits of even the most cantankerous traveler," I remarked to Cole.

"We needed to break the routine of the wagon train. After Fort Concho the road will be getting very difficult. Coyote tells me we'll be coming into a small settlement in a few days, then Concho, and after that not much of anything until we're through those mountains." He pointed to the smoky-blue ridge still many days away.

I spied Gretchen walking with Anna on her hip and

holding Paulie's hand. "I think I'll walk with Gretchen for a while." I climbed over the seat onto the wagon tongue and jumped beyond the wheel.

Warm breezes blew out of the mountains and across the prairie. The unrelenting sun hammered its heat through my clothing, causing sweat to run down my back and between my breasts under the tightly bound band. My flannel undergarments clung to me. Dust from the wagons and animals rose to suffocate me. I moved away from the wagon into the grass. Fragrant flowers released their perfume, enticing me to pick them. After gathering a handful, I ran to catch up with Gretchen.

"Look, aren't these lovely?" I gave them to her.

"Sarah, boys don't pick flowers."

"Oh, I saw the Robert's boy picking some this morning."

"He gave them to Sallie Collins. He is sveet on her. But she has eyes for someone else."

"Who?" I always loved a good piece of gossip.

"Who, you ask. Vhy Cole, of course. Can you not see how she makes cow eyes at him?"

A twinge of jealousy spread over me. "She isn't his type."

"No, Sarah, you are not his type. She vould make a perfect vife for him. She is a hard vorker and loves children. She has good strong bones and can have many children for him."

"What do you mean, I'm not his type?"

"How do I tell you? I do not meddle in other people's business. But ve are friends. I see you two together. It is more than brother and sister."

My mouth flew open. "What are you saying?"

"No, no. I do not say you two are doing anything wrong. I know you do not. But I say you need to be careful of your feelings. Rudy varned me to say nothing. But I have eyes. I can see the vay you look at each other.

There, now I have said it."

"That's nonsense!" I protested.

"No, I think not. Vhat is more, Cole is a man of strong vill, but he is fighting a var mit himself. His honor vill not allow him to fail. It vould destroy him. I can see no answer for you. Both of you vill be hurt."

"I am his sister. We have a closeness most people do not have because we have gone through so much together, but you are making more of it than what's really there. Sure, we love each other, as brother and sister."

"All I say is for you to be careful. Do not be too close mit him. Brother or not, he is a man."

The small farming community of Shelby supported twelve sod or adobe houses, four stores, a cantina, a blacksmith shop, and a church. In the center of town grew a large oak tree. Beneath its boughs was a stone sweet water well that provided the town with water and refreshed many a weary traveler. Our wagons had been spotted several miles before we arrived in Shelby and a festive atmosphere had taken over the people of the town. Women had prepared food while the men of the town had set up tables in the square. Lanterns had been placed on poles to give light long after sunset. Instruments were dusted off and tuned up to play dance music.

As we drew closer, a delegation of townspeople rode out to greet us, entreating us to camp early and stay awhile. Dawson was happy to stop early and set up camp just outside of town near a pecan grove.

Pecans and wheat were the two crops sustaining this small town. Green shoots lifted their heads toward the sun causing the surrounding countryside to take on the appearance of green velvet.

"They should have a bountiful harvest this year," I remarked, viewing the land around us.

Cole climbed off the wagon. "It's a long time between planting and harvesting. Anything could happen. A farmer's life is never easy. They put in long hours and hard work for very little return. Most barely keep their own families fed."

"Weren't we farmers? We didn't have such a difficult time of it."

"Plantation farming, with hundreds of slaves doing the work, can't even begin to be compared to the life these people live."

I thought of the way things were before the war and the contrast after the slaves were freed. "I think you're right. Ranching is much easier. The cows take care of themselves."

"Not exactly, but in California we'll have a big ranch. Remember the view from your bedroom window? For as far as you could see, the land belonged to us. That's the way it'll be in California. And when you get married, we'll divide the ranch, half yours and half mine." Cole finished unharnessing the oxen.

"What if you marry before me? Will you build another house for you and your wife? Or will we all live together?"

Cole set the harness over the tongue of the wagon and turned to look at me. "Don't think I'll ever get married." A sadness I had never heard before filled his deep voice.

"Why? Surely you want to have a family of your own. Someone to love you."

He didn't answer. Leading the oxen to tall grass, he called over his shoulder, "You best get cleaned up for the party."

Cleaned up for the party, I thought. *Of course, there will be plenty of delicious food, but I won't be able to dance.* I remembered that Christmas before the war. Daddy let me join in the dancing. "But tonight only Gretchen will talk to me," I said aloud. *I need to remember to stay away from Sallie Collins's little sister who seems to have taken a liking to me. What's her name? Betsy. That's it, Betsy Collins. She must be all of about twelve. Of course, Sallie isn't more than fifteen. The nerve of her making eyes at Cole. I wonder if he knows she's sweet on him?*

I climbed into the wagon with a pail of water, stripped off my dusty clothes and washed. The cold liquid felt delicious after the long, sweaty ride. "I wish I could soak in a tub with lilac soap," I said to myself, as my thoughts flew back to the night Cole had come home from the war and caught me running from the bathhouse to the kitchen.

"Are you about finished in there?" came Cole's voice. "Most of the camp has already gone into town."

As usual I had lost track of time. "I'll be right there. Just have to put on my boots," I lied. I quickly wound the breast band around me and tucked in the ends. I threw on my clothes and pulled on my boots. "I'm ready."

When Cole loosened the canvas curtain, he saw my flannels on the bed. "You're not wearing those?"

"They're too hot."

Cole raised an eyebrow but didn't say another word. He led the way toward town.

The aroma of cooking meat greeted us before we entered the square. Sounds of music, people talking and laughing, the clanking of dishes, and the general commotion of folks gathering filled the air. A large pit had been dug in a grassy area beside the church. Flames licked at the roasting steer on the spit turned by a brawny man that I supposed to be the blacksmith. A heavyset woman dipped a mop in sauces and smeared it over the meat, determined to baste every morsel. Favorite family recipes were prepared and shared with pride. It was a feast the likes of which I hadn't seen since leaving home. I made it my duty to eat some of everything. Being a boy, I didn't have to worry about what people would say if I ate too much.

As the sun set in the haze of crimson and gold, and the lanterns were lit, the dance music began. *Turkey in the Straw* was followed by many other rousing dance tunes. I sat on a bench out of the way, tapping my toe to the rhythm of the fiddle. Cole danced with Sallie, Gretchen, the Simms girl, and several others from the train or the town.

"Why don't you get out there and dance?" Coyote asked, coming up behind me. He swung his leg over the bench, straddling it as he sat down.

"Why don't you?"

"I will if you will."

"I don't know how." I didn't look at him, but I could feel his blue eyes drilling holes through me. I scooted over as far as I could without falling off the bench. My anxiety mounted. I slouched my shoulders. I tried to ignore him, I couldn't. His presence unnerved me. He kept running his fingers over the red scarf tied around his neck. Finally, I turned to him and with great irritation in my voice asked, "What seems to be your problem?"

"You." Merriment danced in his eyes. "You aren't very friendly tonight. Thought a romp in the sportin' house would bring you out of your shell."

"What do you expect me to do?"

"I expect you to tell the truth."

"What truth do you mean?"

"The truth about you and about what happened in Goldie's room."

"I'm not the kind of person to kiss and tell."

"You're not the kind of person to kiss."

I sprang to my feet and quickly walked to the dessert table.

Coyote's laughter stung my ears.

Like an eagle coming in for a kill, Betsy Collins darted across the square. I looked for a place to hide but found none.

"Hello, Danny, I've been looking for you." She pulled herself to her full height of almost five feet. Smoothing the folds of her calico dress, she said, "Do you like my dress? Mama made it special for me before we started west. I was afraid I would outgrow it before I got a chance to wear it."

I cleared my throat. "It's nice." I felt sorry for her and thought how hurt she will be when she finds out I'm a girl. This quicksand of lies was pulling me down. One lie led to another and before I knew it people were getting hurt. I had never intended to hurt anyone.

Cole strolled to the table. "This cake sure is good. Have you had some Betsy?"

"No. I don't want any cake. I want to dance with Danny."

"Oh, Danny's a little shy. He doesn't dance." Cole took her arm and led her away. "We wouldn't want to embarrass the kid now, would we?"

"No."

"I knew you would see it my way. Why don't you ask one of the other boys to dance?"

Betsy slowly walked away looking over her shoulder only once before she smiled at one of the Simms boys who asked her to dance.

"Come with me," Cole said, leading the way beyond the light of the lanterns. He hurried my steps past the row of stores and homes, through a weed covered field, and into the seclusion of the pecan grove.

Music drifted on the mild night air. The aroma of the trees and a distant honeysuckle surrounded us. Cole took my arm to steady my step through the darkness of the orchard. I became very aware of his touch.

On the other side of the trees, Cole stopped. "Do you remember I once asked you to save a dance for me? I would like to collect it now."

"Here?"

"I saw the longing look in your eyes and your toe tapping to the tune of the fiddle. I couldn't dance with you in the square, but out here no one will see us." He pulled me to him. "Listen to the music." It was a waltz. With his hand lightly at my waist, we glided over the dirt as if it were the inlaid floor of our grand ballroom.

He held me close to him. I felt the warmth of his body against mine. My heart skipped beats. His hand cradled my head against his chest as he ran his fingers through my curls.

"I never noticed how soft your hair is. It was a shame we had to cut it."

"It's growing back." I whispered the words, not wanting to spoil the magic of the moment.

We twirled around and around long after the music stopped. Cole hummed his own melody to match the steps we were dancing. In my mind, I wore a beautiful blue gown and Cole the elegant clothes of a Southern gentleman. The years melted away, and we were back at the Christmas before the war. The moon became a chandelier, the crickets an orchestra, and we were the only two people left on earth.

He stopped. Slowly he tilted my face upward to greet his gray eyes. I felt his warm breath on my lips. Closer, closer he came. Then. . . then. . .nothing. He held me at arm's length, cleared his throat, and without a word hurried me back to our wagon.

"Good night, Sarah," Cole said, turning on his heel and walking away.

Bewildered, I stood with my mouth open, watching him leave. My thoughts reeled. *What have I done? Did I misread what almost happened out there? Did he almost kiss me?* I wanted his arms around me, his lips on mine. *Gretchen was right. It is more than just brother and sister love. He feels the same way about me. But now I have to stay away from him.* I had never wanted to let him know how I felt for fear he would be repulsed. Now he must be feeling the same disgust and shame with his own emotions. *We are honorable people. What will we do?*

Three days and nights Cole stayed to himself. He

didn't eat in our camp or sleep in our wagon. I put on an arrogant mask to conceal my hurt. Each morning Cole came into camp to hitch up the oxen and tend to our animals, but he rode away without talking to me. He rode point with Coyote. I drove the wagon.

"Why should I care?" I said, aloud. "If he thinks I need him he's got another think coming. I'll make a new life for myself without him. I'm strong. I can do it. I know we need to stay away from each other, but it hurts so much."

Fort Concho loomed before us as the citadel of the prairie. Twenty-five Union troops rode by us heading out on patrol. My heart turned to ice seeing their blue uniforms and realizing that all the troopers were Negroes except for the officer leading the column. Two years ago those men could have been slaves or on the run from bounty hunters, and now they are soldiers protecting white people heading west. The sound of their sabers rattling and the horses' hooves hitting the hard ground reminded me of troop movements on the River Road. A shiver shook my body as the last days of Rosewood flashed through my mind - - the end of the war, Cole's coming home, Mama's dying, and the marshal, along with the soldiers, coming to throw us off our land. My hatred for the Yankees blazed anew.

"Move over. I'll drive into the fort," Cole said, climbing onto the seat.

"I've managed these past three days without you. I can take the wagon into the post myself." Holding tightly to the reins, I cracked the whip. "Get up there."

"Suit yourself." Cole whistled for Shadow, jumped into the saddle and raced to the front of the line.

My heart sank. I wanted him to insist on driving, but he didn't. I wanted to talk with him, but instead I had sent him away. I just put another stone into the wall between us. *Are we ever going to be able to climb over the barrier we're building?*

Several homes were built close to the fort for protection from the Comanche. The fort itself housed only two companies of Negroes, or "Buffalo Soldiers" as they were called by the Indians, and four white officers. As far as I was concerned, the color of their skin didn't mean as much as the color of their uniforms - - blue, Yankee blue.

We made camp just outside the fort. I started unloading the wagon when Gretchen came running into our camp. "Do you know vhat they have here?" Excitement laced her German accent. "A bathhouse! Do you believe ve can take a hot bath tonight?"

"Oh, how wonderful. Do they have a tub and lilac soap?"

"Yah. They have everything. Now ve are on the main stage road and a voman has made it her business. For five cents a person, ve can take a hot bath. She has one side for vomen and one side for men."

I clapped my hands together with joy until a horrible realization washed over me. "Oh, Gretchen, I can't go into either side. What am I going to do? I want a bath. I want to soak in a hot tub. But I can't go into the men's side and they won't let me into the women's side." My joy dashed to the ground. I returned to the task of unloading the wagon. Gretchen retreated to her own camp.

Spying Cole entering the large gates of the fort, I ran to catch him. "Johnny. Johnny wait for me."

He stopped when he heard me call. "You don't run like a boy." A smile brightened his face.

"I've been told all my life not to run. Ladies don't run. Now you tell me I don't run like a boy. Who cares? What I need from you is help."

His face dropped into an earnest look of concern. "What's wrong?"

"I want a bath. Everyone on the train is going to have a hot bath in a tub. Everyone except me, that is. I can't go into the bathhouse."

"Oh, is that all." His concern faded. "Come with me. I'll see what I can do."

I had to step lively to keep up with his long strides as

he continued across the parade ground in the direction of the bathhouse at the far end of the field. Horses and wagons moved in and out of the fort, stirring up the dust which clung to my sweaty face and rested on my clothing.

Cole put his hand on the railing to mount the steps in front of the building as a young captain descended on the other side of the double steps. The captain glanced at Cole's hand and then grabbed his wrist.

"Well, Johnny Reb, I see you made it through the war. Not too many rings like that one, I'd venture to guess. I promised myself I'd never forget it or the man who wore it."

"You have made a mistake." Cole pulled loose from the captain's grip. "This was my father's ring."

The two men studied each other across the railing. They stood on the same step, one going up and the other coming down. The captain's stature equaled Cole's. "No. I'm not mistaken. It's you. I believe they called you Brighton."

I gasped. My heart quickened. The captain's gaze turned to me and then back to Cole. I searched his face to remember if he was one of the officers who had come to throw us off the plantation. Sandy brown hair escaped from beneath his hat. A well defined chin and a straight, slender nose hinted of noble ancestry. A thick mustache tried to conceal a slightly crooked smile and smile lines creased his tanned skin around his sparkling maple eyes. I saw no malice or fear in those eyes. Cole's face, on the other hand, remained clouded in worry, and resolve tensed his jaw. He, too, searched his memory to place this young officer.

"Do the boots fit?" the captain asked.

Cole tilted his head to one side as a smile of recollection spread across his face. "I see you made it."

"Thanks to you."

"You weren't a threat to me."

"You defied a direct order to shoot me."

My eyes grew larger as I listened to the exchange between the two men. Cole rarely spoke of the war. It lay in the dark recesses of his memory and he willed it to stay hidden.

The captain looked at me with a wondering glance.

I took a step behind Cole.

"My brother is shy. I didn't get your name."

"James Reed." The captain looked around Cole. "Did your brother ever tell you how he saved my life?"

I shook my head.

"I don't think the kid wants to hear about the war," Cole said.

"Yes. I do."

Captain Reed started to tell his story. A story he seemed to have told many times. "It happened a few days after Shiloh. My company was surprised by Rebels . . . uh. . . Confederate troops, I was cut down and left for dead. A few hours later, I heard men moving through the woods. By the time I realized they were more Rebels, it was too late. They moved around the dead picking pockets and shooting the men who were still alive. I lay as quiet as I could, trying not to breathe. I felt someone leaning over me and his hands going through my pockets. 'I know you're still alive, soldier,' he whispered. 'I guess this was your daddy's pocket watch. Don't want it to get stolen, do we? I'll put it under you. Your troops are hot on our heels. They should be here within the hour. Just lie quiet and you'll be home before planting time.' I opened my eyes to look into the face of a Confederate soldier. I'll never forget those gray eyes or the concern on his face. He smiled at me and then said, 'You won't be needing your boots anymore and mine are worn clean through. Yours look like they'll fit me fine.' His commanding officer yelled, 'Brighton, make sure he's dead.' Your brother pulled his gun and shot into the ground next to me. 'He's as dead as he's going to get,' he called back to the officer. That's when I saw the ring, a gold horseshoe with a brownish-red stone in the middle. 'Good luck, soldier,' he said as he walked away, taking my boots with him."

Cole had already mounted the steps and waited for the captain to finish his story. "No use killing a half dead Yankee."

"I have always known that hidden under your rough façade lurks a soft heart," I teased. "Tell the truth. You have no stomach for killing."

"Not needless killing."

"I'm glad he doesn't," Reed interrupted. "I owe you my life. If there is anything I can do for you, just ask."

Cole took off his hat and slapped it against his leg to beat the dust out of his britches. "Now that you've offered, there is one thing you may be able to help with. The kid needs a bath."

"The fort has a fine bathhouse just over there." The captain pointed to the building three doors down.

"Yes, we know about your bathhouse. I was on my way to take advantage of it. But you see the kid is a little shy. It's the way he was raised. Taking a bath with other men in the same room just doesn't set well."

"They have curtains separating each tub. It gives quite a bit of privacy."

Cole looked at me, took a deep breath, and tried to explain again. "No, what we need is a private place where the kid can be alone."

The captain's brow furrowed in thought for a minute. "The colonel has a tub in his quarters. I guess you can use it. He isn't expected back until tomorrow. I'll have the orderly fetch some hot water. If you'll follow me, I'll show you to the colonel's rooms."

I smiled at Cole as I stepped in behind the captain.

The colonel's quarters were rooms behind his office. We went through the sitting room and entered his bedroom. A bed, dressing table, wardrobe, wash stand, and two comfortable chairs furnished the small room. A large copper tub sat on a rag braided carpet almost in the center of the room. Two colored orderlies delivered four buckets of water, two hot and two cold. They poured them into the tub.

"Is the colonel back already?" one man asked.

Captain Reed ignored the question. "That will be all. You're dismissed." When the door closed behind the soldiers, Captain Reed said to me, "Soap is in the wash stand and towels are in the bottom drawer of the dresser."

Cole looked out the window and then turned back to me. "I'll take your clothes to get them washed. In this hot Texas air they will dry in no time. I'll wait in the next room. You can toss them out when you're ready."

"You have to get them back to me as fast as you can or go to the wagon and get my other clothes out of the trunk and bring them to me."

"You just soak in the hot tub. I'm going to get my bath first, then I'll bring your clothes back. By then you should be finished."

"I'll see to it that no one disturbs him," Captain Reed said. "The colonel is gone and no one will be coming in here."

"I guess this evens the score," Cole said.

"Not as I see it. One can hardly put a bath on the same scale as saving a life."

I listened as the two men argued. Finally, I cleared my throat. "If you two can finish arguing in the next room, I'll take my bath."

Sheepishly they retreated to the sitting room. I undressed and threw my clothes out the door to Cole.

"I'll be back in about forty-five minutes," he called through the closed door.

I heard the door to the office shut as I retrieved one bucket of water from the tub to rinse with after my bath. I found the towels where the captain had said and I found a small cake of lilac soap. Things couldn't get any better.

The liquid licked at my body as I melted beneath its caress. I scrubbed my hair and skin until I felt shining clean. Time slipped away in the illusive ticking of the clock on the wall as afternoon shadows crept silently across the floor unnoticed. When I heard the office door open, I knew it was Cole returning with my clothes. I stood and rinsed with the warm water from the bucket I had saved. The door to the bedroom flew open.

"Kid, you've got to get out! The colonel returned sooner than expected. He's coming across the parade ground right now . . . oh, my God, you're a girl." James Reed's eyes doubled in size and his mouth flew open.

"Get out!" I grabbed for the towel.

Captain Reed turned to leave, but stopped. "No. You're the one who has to get out. Didn't you hear me? The Colonel's back. If he catches you in his quarters, I'll get, well, I'm not sure what he'll do, but I don't want to find out. I'm due to get new orders any day now and I don't want anything happening to mess them up."

I held the towel in front of me and stepped out of the tub. "Did Johnny bring my clothes?"

"Your clothes? Damn, they're still at the laundry. Don't have time to get them now. You'll just have to make do with what we have."

"What we have?" I looked around the room. "What do you mean?"

Captain Reed opened the wardrobe. "The colonel's wife passed away a few months back. He hasn't brought himself to get rid of her things yet. This looks like it'll fit." He pulled out a blue gingham dress with white lace at the round neck and at the cuffs of the long sleeves.

"What about undergarments? I need a petticoat."

"Don't have time for all that. Put on the dress and be quick about it." He tossed the dress to me and started bailing the water out of the tub, throwing it out the open window.

Still holding the towel in front of me, I slipped the

dress over my head and wiggled around to help it fall over my wet body. The colonel's wife was somewhat larger in the bust than I and a bit taller. The towel dropped to the floor.

"Help me hook the back and tie the sash," I said, struggling.

Captain Reed's fingers quickly found each hook and eye. "Now I can see why you didn't want to go into the bathhouse. Why didn't you tell me you are a woman?"

"It's a long story. We don't have time to go into it now."

The creaking of the front door indicated the colonel had arrived.

The Yankee pulled at my arm and shoved me out the window. "Cover your hair with this." He handed a blue poke bonnet to me through the window. Picking up my boots and hat, he tossed them out after me. "I'll be in your camp later tonight. I want to hear your explanation."

My feet landed in the mud caused by the bath water the captain threw out the window. The skirt barely cleared the sill when I heard Captain Reed talking to the Colonel.

"Did you have a good trip, sir? I thought I would get your bath ready for you. I know how tired you must be."

I didn't wait to hear the Colonel's answer. I tiptoed out of the mud, covered my hair with the bonnet, tucked my boots and hat under my arm, lifted my skirt and ran for our wagon as fast as I could.

I cleared the tailgate and laced up the canvas, thinking I had made it safely home. Strangely enough, I realized I considered the wagon home. I threw myself on the bed being quite pleased with myself when I heard Coyote's voice outside the wagon.

"Johnny, you sly dog, keeping a woman in your wagon?"

"A woman? There's no woman in our wagon."

"I just saw her go in or at least I saw her skirt slip over the tailgate. Is she from town?"

I knew Cole. He would insist Coyote look in the wagon to satisfy his curiosity. "Johnny, I'm ready if you are," I called in a high pitched voice.

"What? Uh. . . well. . .I guess you caught me. I know I can trust you to keep this to yourself," Cole stammered.

"Sure. Is it that Collins girl? She's made it plain how she feels about you."

"No, she's too young. I'll talk to you later."

"Yeah, sure. Later." I heard Coyote walk away, chuckling.

Cole entered the wagon. "What the hell are you doing?"

"I got caught. The captain walked in on me. He knows I'm a woman."

CHAPTER 27

That evening Captain James Reed entered our camp. Hot embers shot skyward as Cole stoked the fire. Luke sat on a crate draining the last bit of coffee from his cup. When I saw the captain, I stepped into the night shadows.

"Good evening," Captain Reed said, strolling to the fire. His eyes searched the camp for me. "Is your brother here?"

"Yes, somewhere. I'd like to talk to you about what happened this afternoon." Cole's clenched teeth tightened his jaw. He didn't look up.

Luke wiped the inside of his cup with his shirt and tossed the cup into the dish crate. "Well, Johnny, I think I'll be headin' to the bathhouse. Get some of this trail dust off me. See yah in the mornin'."

"Johnny. Is that your name?" Captain Reed asked. "Johnny Brighton? All I knew was Brighton. Never thought I'd ever meet up with you again. Had an idea about traveling the South looking for you, but being stationed way out here all I could do was think about it."

"What took place between you and I happened a long time ago. It's done and over. What's important is here and now. My sister tells me you barged in on her this afternoon." The tone in Cole's voice was threatening, but he spoke quietly so no one in another camp could hear him.

I hid behind the wagon, peeking out to watch the two men. Cole was sitting in his chair poking a stick into the fire and the Yankee was standing on the other side of the flames.

"I assure you nothing happened. I didn't know she was a woman."

"But you certainly found out."

"The colonel came back sooner than expected. I had to get her out of his room. I thought she was a he. On my word as a gentleman, I didn't touch her."

"Keep your voice down. I don't want this getting around the camp."

"Do you mind my asking why she is dressed like a boy?"

Before Cole could answer, Dawson entered the circle of light. "Well, I see the two of you have already met. Good. That makes things easier. The captain tells me he'll be travelin' with us the rest of the way to California. He has new orders to the barracks at Wilmington. He and a company of buffalo soldiers will escort us through those mountains to the next post, and from there Captain Reed will be on his own. I thought you might let him store his gear in your wagon after he drops off the soldiers and their supply wagons at the next fort."

Cole groaned. His voice turned ice hard. "We already have Luke. I don't think there's any more room for the captain's stuff."

Dawson didn't expect that answer. He tensed. "With only the three of you, there's plenty of room."

"Let him move in on the newlyweds. They don't have anyone extra."

"That would cause more trouble than we want. Mr. Gilroy is a jealous man. When he has to ride night herd and leave his wife alone with the captain, it just wouldn't work."

"What about you? Coyote's gone more than he's here."

"No, Johnny, what's eatin' on you? I didn't expect this comin' from you. Some of the others, yeah. But not you."

"Don't want him around the kid."

The uneasiness became evident as Captain Reed fidgeted. "If it'll cause anyone a hardship, I'll pack my own things on a mule and be done with it. Hitching up with a train might take too long anyway. I need to be in California by mid-September. I'll just go it alone."

Cole threw the stick into the fire and sat back in his chair. Dryly his voice formed the words, "We'll be in California long before September. It's too dangerous for one man to travel alone through the desert. If the Indians don't get you, the lack of water will. Only a fool would venture such a task."

"Listen, Mr. Bri. . . ," Captain Reed started to say.

"That's okay, Dawson. We'll work this out. He can travel with us," Cole interrupted, before the captain could call Cole Mr. Brighton.

"Thanks, Johnny. I knew you were the man to ask." Dawson breathed a little easier. "Best be getting' back now. We'll be leavin' at the crack of dawn." Dawson turned to Captain Reed. "We'll be glad to have you with us. Never can tell when extra guns will come in handy. Good night." Dawson walked out of the light toward his own wagon.

Captain Reed turned to Cole. "Listen. If you don't want me in your camp I'll cook my own meals and sleep away from your wagon."

"No. It isn't you personally. It's what you think you know about me," Cole said. Taking a deep breath, he continued, "There's something I'm going to tell you. Listen hard. My name isn't Brighton, it's O'Shea. Johnny O'Shea. And that kid is Danny. Not a girl, but a fourteen year old boy. If you're going to travel with us, you'll treat her like a boy. Do you understand?"

"I'm not sure. Why is she dressed like that?"

"That's our business. All you need to know is she's passing as a boy and let it go at that. I didn't shoot you once, but if you lay a hand on her I won't hesitate to gun you down without a second thought."

"You won't have to worry about me. I owe you my life. I won't do anything to cause you grief." I could hear the awe in the Yankee's voice.

My heart pounded. I hated Yankees. I didn't want anything to do with them. Now, one is riding in our wagon, eating at our fire and sleeping in our camp. And this one I hated most of all. He knows our real name.

The sun hadn't crested the horizon when Dawson called, "Stretch 'um out." One after another, the wagons broke the circle as our journey continued west toward the mountains. Soldiers from Fort Concho divided their column into two parts, one half riding point and the other half bringing up drag. Rumors of Indians spread. Cole rode at the head of the line with Dawson because Coyote had left camp during the night to scout the way and leave markers indicating the trail was clear. Captain Reed rode in front of the first column. Luke was with the herd, a few miles back. I drove our wagon.

The first few days all went well. Even though we were steadily climbing, the going was easy. I felt safe with the soldiers escorting us. By the fourth day, storm clouds started forming over the mountains. The tops of the clouds were pristine white against the cornflower blue sky but the underbelly was indigo, so dark I couldn't tell where the clouds stopped and the mountains began. Back home, I loved summer storms which came up suddenly and cooled everything off for a few hours each day. They came and went quickly. Out here, storms caused flash floods, created mud bogs that trap wagons, and washed out trails. Thunder and lightning threatened to stampede cattle. Out here, summer storms were dangerous.

Without Cole sitting beside me, I had no one to talk with. The hours crawled by as slowly as the wagons moved. Again, boredom became my companion. I didn't share Cole's dream of a beautiful life in California and the memories of home were too difficult to relive. Even my imaginary lover didn't take his place on the seat beside me. I felt forsaken and alone. The beauty of the land was lost to my eyes, and the joy of a new beginning, which kept most of the other women going, didn't fill my heart.

By midafternoon on the fourth day, after leaving Fort Concho some forty miles back, we came upon Camp Concho, an old deserted post, now in a dilapidated condition. It rested on the banks of the Kiawah Creek. Coyote was waiting for us. We made camp early to give the stock a rest. They had been pushed to their limit the past few days. We pulled the wagons inside the fallen gates of the old post.

Even though Captain Reed camped with his men, Cole considered him a threat. Cole spent the nights at our wagon but he kept his distance from me. He talked with me only when others were present and then only about matters pertaining to the trip or the condition of the wagon. That night in the grove when he almost kissed me was weeks ago, but Cole was determined not to let it happen again.

I cooked the meals and washed the clothes but mostly kept to myself. I remembered Cousin Amy Ann's remark, I could never fall in love with someone from North Carolina. It's all too rural,' and wondered again if love was a matter of choice. I didn't want to feel the way I did about Cole. It shamed me to think I could be falling in love with my brother. I couldn't help myself when I saw him or heard his deep voice. I wanted to be with him, touch him. But I didn't. My life was a pretense - - my name, my sex, my age, and now even my feelings.

Gretchen came into our camp carrying a basket filled with luscious currants which grew near the creek. "These I vill take to the Robert's vagon. They are all down mit the cough and sore throat. The mister is only one still vell."

I covered the cast iron kettle with a lid to give the rice time to simmer. "I'm cooking catfish and rice. Luke caught six nice sized fish. One's probably five pounds. I can take some over to them. I'm sure Mrs. Roberts doesn't feel like cooking."

"That vill be good for the mister but the rest of the family needs soup. I have beef soup I vant to take over to them, too."

"You shouldn't be going to their wagon. You're nursing Anna. You can't afford to come down with the cough. I'll take the berries, soup, fish, and rice and tell them it's from both of us."

"Yah, that might be for the best. I go and get the soup and you can take it to their vagon."

I placed a large portion of catfish and rice on a tin plate along with two slices of buttered bread, wrapped it with a cloth and hurried to get the soup from Gretchen.

"Make sure I get the kettle back," Gretchen called as I swiftly walked across the circle.

Mr. Roberts sat alone by his fire. I could hear his wife and the children coughing in whooping spells from inside their tent. "You best stay back," he called.

"I've brought some supper for you and soup for the family. Mrs. Delvick picked some tasty currants she thought you might like. She would have carried them over herself but she has the little one."

"Thank her for me. Just put it down and leave. Don't want to be unsociable, but we got the whooping cough. Don't need to be spreadin' it all over the train."

"Mrs. Delvick made the soup and she wants her kettle back when it's empty." I backed away, relieved that I wasn't expected to stay.

The cold evening wind chilled my body, as I stood by our fire. *What a contrast between the weather of the mountains and that of the prairie floor,* I thought.

Cole came up softly behind me. "Put your jacket on. Don't want you to get sick like the Roberts family." He handed the brown jacket to me.

I took it and jabbed my arms through the sleeves. "What do you care?"

As soon as the poisoned words left my lips, I wished I could have pulled them back. Cole's eyes filled with pain. With a deep sigh he said, "If you don't know by now what you mean to me, more words will never bridge the chasm between us." He walked away.

I grabbed my basket and ran from the circle of wagons, through the fallen section of fence, and out toward the berry bushes. Standing by the creek in the fading evening light, I said aloud, "I didn't dig the chasm between us, he did. I don't understand what's happening. All my life I've waited for Cole to come home - - first from trips with Daddy, then from the frontier and last from the war. But this is the worst. He's here, but he's not. God, what am I going to do? Please make these feelings go away. I know it's wrong for me to love him. Stop the hurt in my heart. Just stop my heart from breaking." I slumped to the ground under a cottonwood tree and cried.

I don't know how long I lay there on the cold ground. When I looked up through tear-blurred eyes, darkness had closed in around me. But I could see the glow of the camp fires through the trees. I thought I would sit there for a while longer to give Cole a chance to worry about me, but the thought that he might not even know I was missing infuriated me. The sounds of small animals moving in the underbrush, coming to the stream to drink, frightened me and the howling of a coyote nearby set me on my feet and headed back toward the camp.

A figure moved in the shadows. "Well, Miss O'Shea, isn't it a little late for you to be wandering in the woods?" Captain Reed asked, stepping out from beneath the branches of a tree.

"I was picking currants by the stream. Didn't notice how late it was getting." I concealed my empty basket.

"And you, what are you doing out here in the dark?"

"Just taking a turn around the camp to make sure everything is secure before calling it a day. I'll walk with you back to the wagons." He stepped forward to take my arm.

No, thank you. I'll find my own way." I side stepped his advance.

"You don't like soldiers much, do you?"

"Not blue-belly Yankees."

"Well, at least you're honest."

"I'm always honest."

"I can see that. That's why you're dressed like a boy, carrying an empty basket."

Anger prickled my skin. I pushed by him and stomped away.

He called after me, "Remember, the war is over and we need to learn to live in peace. We aren't enemies anymore."

I turned back to face him. "Your kind can't be trusted. You come in and lie and steal. Take what isn't yours. Burn the rest. When we take what belongs to us you place a bounty. . . ."

"Go on. A bounty on your head. Is there a bounty posted on you and your brother? Or is he really your brother? Did you steal those horses? Is that why you've changed your name?"

"I don't know what you're talking about. My name is O'Shea, and Johnny is really my brother. We are going to California to live with an uncle." I hoped my voice sounded confident and not quivering as my insides were.

"If you say so. I just want you to know that I'm not your enemy. The Indians out there are, maybe wolves or mountain lions, and at times the land and the weather, but not me. I want to be your friend."

"My friends don't wear Yankee uniforms." With those cutting words, I turned toward camp leaving Captain Reed standing alone in the dark.

CHAPTER 28

Sometime before morning the dreaded cry woke the camp, "Stampede!"

I jumped out of bed and threw on my clothes, covering everything with an oversized slicker in case the storm clouds broke and released torrents of rain.

Cole smiled when he saw me climb out of the wagon. "You don't need to do this," he whispered. "You can stay in camp."

"I'll go." I pulled my hat down on my head with both hands, determined to make the best of a terrible situation.

"In that case, stay close to me."

I was saddling Misty when Captain Reed rode up. "What on earth are you doing?"

"I'm riding with the men." I pushed Zephyr away to give me room between him and Misty. The horses moved nervously about. I pulled the cinch tight.

"Here, let me do that for you." Captain Reed dismounted.

"I can manage. You just take care of your own things." I brought the stirrup down and mounted.

Cole, riding Shadow, came along side. "Ready?"

"Let's do it."

Captain Reed mounted his horse and moved between me and Cole. "I can't believe you're letting her go. She could get killed. It's dangerous for a man out there, yet alone a woman."

"She'll be fine. She rides as good as any man, and she's a whole lot smarter than most."

I couldn't believe my ears. Cole's voice resounded with pride. A warm feeling washed over me which made this entire ordeal worthwhile. Captain Reed didn't say another word.

The three of us rode out to catch up with Dawson and the other men. Even the soldiers turned out to hunt for the cattle. Once away from the wagons, blackness enveloped us. The thick rain clouds covered the moon and stars. A few men carried lanterns, but they proved inadequate for such a large group.

Shouting to make himself heard, Dawson yelled, "Divide into teams. One lantern with two or three riders. It's still about two hours before dawn, and all we want to do is keep up with the cattle so when they tire out we'll be within striking distance. So pair up and stay close."

I don't know how it happened but Cole and I got doubled up with Coyote and Captain Reed.

After about a half hour of hard riding, Dawson called to the captain, "I think the soldiers should go back to camp. Don't need them and we've left the wagons unprotected. Daylight's comin'. I'd feel better if the women weren't alone."

I thought the captain would go back with his men, but he didn't. He just ordered the sergeant to take over and lead the soldiers back to protect the camp.

"Aren't you going back?" I asked.

"No. The sergeant's a good man. He'll do what's right. Why, are you trying to get rid of me?"

"Yes."

"I should know better than to ask you a direct question. I'll get an answer I might not like."

I pulled the collar of my rain slicker up around my ears and I nudged Misty forward. "It's going to be daylight soon," I said aloud, but mostly to myself.

We moved slowly around the base of a cliff, picking up cattle that couldn't keep up with the main herd. The front riders had turned the herd and they were slowing down. We came to a bluff where we could see several lanterns below moving methodically over the land rounding up the cattle. The sudden feeling of "I've done this before" flashed through my mind. The recollection of the night when Mama fell into the river, when I stood on the bluff at Rosewood watching the lanterns in the pasture below, screamed at me. A shiver crawled up my spine and the nagging feeling of impending doom gripped my heart.

"Cole! Something's wrong!" I yelled.

"What's the matter? You okay?" Both of the other men looked at us through questioning eyes.

"I'm not sure. I have a bad feeling. I think we need to get back to the wagons."

"I've got the same feelin'," Coyote admitted. "It's been naggin' at me since the sky started turnin' light."

Without a word the four of us turned the horses and raced back to the wagons, hoping we were mistaken.

Peals of gunfire and the dreaded war cries of the Indians greeted us before we cleared the rise above the camp. My heart turned to ice.

Coyote held up his hand and we pulled the horses to a halt. The men drew their rifles from the saddles. We dismounted and crept to the crest of the ridge hiding behind rocks and brush. Below, bathed in the glow of first light breaking through the clouds, we saw the fort under siege. Two dozen or more Indians had taken up their positions in the rocks and trees across the wide clearing from the fort and along the creek.

"Thank God Dawson told the soldiers to return to the fort," I said. "If he hadn't, all the women would have been killed by now."

"The soldiers have their hands full," Coyote said. "Let's even the odds some. Spread out. We'll catch 'um in a cross fire."

Cole moved down the ridge to the left while Coyote and the captain went right. I stayed where I was behind a large rock. My insides quivered like cheese that hadn't set yet. When I had faced Elias Molack in the streets of Independence, I wondered if I could actually kill a man. I found out that I had no stomach for killing. But this was different. I couldn't think of Indians as men, but as savages trying to kill us. The image of Yellow Sky with his dreams of a wife and children and a home on the land clouded my mind. I wiped my eyes and waited for someone to shoot first. The shot came from the left followed by rifle fire on the right. I took careful aim and pulled the trigger of my revolver again and again.

A resounding cheer echoed from the people in the fort. Obviously they thought all the men had returned, not just four of us. The same idea must have struck the Indians as they retreated into the mountains they called home.

We received a hero's welcome of cheers as we rode through the fallen gates. Captain Reed dismounted first, running to his sergeant who had taken a bullet in the shoulder. "How bad is it?"

"Jest a flesh wound, sir. Can't say the same for some of the others. Lost three men. More's wounded, bad. They took us by surprise. Weren't in the gates, yet, when they come at us out of nowhere. How'd you know we was in trouble?"

"Woman's intuition." The captain's maple eyes locked on mine.

"How's that, sir?"

"Nothing. Let's get you bandaged up."

I ran for our medicine kit. "Bring him over to our wagon," I called, more or less taking charge. I remembered what Dr. Bardlow had taught me about applying bandages and which patients should be treated first. "Bring all the wounded over here. Johnny and Coyote, fetch the bandages from the army supply wagon. We'll need more than I have in my kit. Don't just stand there, move!"

"You've got it." A smile touched Coyote's face. "Never thought I'd be taking orders from a kid," he said under his breath as he ran by Captain Reed.

"You don't know the half of it," Reed returned. He came close to me and whispered, "Do you think it's fitting for a woman to be tending to wounded men? Black men at that."

"I ran a hospital during the war. If Northern women like Miss Alcott and Miss Barton can serve on the battlefield, can't I help with the men who saved our wagon train? Now, out of my way, I have work to do."

"Don't think it's a good idea to keep the wounded out in the open," Cole said. "It'll be raining by noon. That old building over there would make a good hospital." Cole pointed to a long, low building in better condition than most of the others. Some of the front wall had fallen in and all the windows were broken, but the roof had held through years of storms. The place would be dry and warmer than a tent.

"You're right. We'll set up the hospital over there."

Gretchen came running. "Vhat can I do? I vill help mit the vounded, yah?"

"Yes, Gretchen, we need your help," I said, pointing to the dilapidated structure. "Would you please tell Captain Reed to have all the wounded taken to that building. We're going to set up the hospital inside."

"And I vill get the vomen to clean the dirt out of the building." She hurried away to tend to her chores.

Some soldiers tore planks off other buildings and

placed them across barrels to make an operating table. I covered the boards with a canvas. Other planks were nailed over the window openings to keep out the wind.

One by one the wounded were brought into the hospital, starting with the most serious. Cole and I dug out arrowheads and bullets, bandaged each man, and had everyone carried to a bedroll on the floor away from any draft.

Shortly before noon, the accuracy of Cole's prediction came true. A cloudburst drenched us. "I'm glad you thought about using this building as a hospital," I said, looking out the opening where a door used to hang. "I wonder how the roundup is going?"

"The boys will be all right. They'll be back soon. We need to keep our mind on the task at hand." Cole tossed a bandage to me. "Tie it tight."

Cole lifted the soldier while I tied the bandage around the man's head. Even as I placed the white cloth over the wound, blood seeped through. *He's lost a lot of blood,* I thought. *I'll bet he wishes he had stayed on the plantation where he was taken care of and safe.*

When Cole removed his hand from the man's shoulder, it came away bloody. "He's been shot in the back, too. Help me get his shirt off."

I gasped when I saw the man's bare back and chest. Lash marks scarred his torso like a patchwork quilt. "Oh, my, maybe he wasn't so safe on the plantation," I said out loud.

"Safe? What makes you think he was safe? Most slaves weren't, especially the field workers. Daddy didn't believe in whipping, but not all slave owners felt the same. Something happens to a man when he has the power over the life or death of another human being. So often the evil lurking in the darkness of his mind comes to the surface when he knows he can't be punished. Rape, murder, out and out cruelty come bubbling to the surface. It's all there in every one of us. That's why we need laws to govern our actions. Unfortunately, the slaves fell outside the protection of the law, as do the Indians. So to the slave owner, they were fair game. Whatever happened to them was justified in the eyes of the master. Good Christian people treated slaves like animals, property to be bought and sold. Or if the Christian master thought of the slave as a person, they were quick to point out the curse of Canna where Noah said that his descendants would be slaves to his brothers. After all, we were just fulfilling prophecy. I don't know if the day will ever come when all people will live in peace with each other."

"This soldier is the last one," Captain Reed interrupted, as two men carried the wounded soldier to the table. "The burial detail finished just before the cloudburst."

Coyote entered, dripping water on the wood floor. "Sure is coming down. The riders are back. They're bringing the herd up the creek. Didn't lose a single head."

Wiping the blood off his hands, Cole said, sarcastically, "Well, that's the best news we've heard all day. Three men dead, ten wounded, women and children hysterical, whooping cough spreading throughout the camp, Indians waiting to attack, but not a single cow was lost."

Evening found the five of us, Cole, Coyote, Reed, Luke and me in our camp for supper. Coyote and Cole had hoisted a canopy and trenched the outer edges to allow the rain to run away from the camp. The fire was at the edge of the tarp to allow the smoke to escape but kept the heat in to keep us warm.

Coyote sat cross-legged on the dish crate. "You did a mighty fine piece of work, kid, tending to the wounded. Where'd you learn to do that?"

"During the war, we had a hospital at our plantation. Dr. Bardlow taught me how to care for the sick and wounded."

Cole's gray eyes narrowed as he slowly shook his head. Knowing I had already said more than I should, I tried to change the subject. "I hope the rain doesn't keep up all night."

Captain Reed leaned back in the chair he had found in one of the buildings. "Tell me, kid, what made you think there was trouble back at the wagons?"

"I can't explain. I just knew. Coyote had the same feeling. Ask him."

"I've been out on the frontier all of my life. I can sense when things aren't quite right." Coyote looked directly at me. A mischievous twinkle danced in his blue eyes.

"Years ago, on a night much like last night, except then it was raining, our mama had a terrible accident. I suppose the similarities put me on edge," I said, as I fidgeted with the buttons on my jacket.

Captain Reed poked a long stick into the fire. Red-orange flames sparked anew on a seemingly dead log. "When you called to Johnny, you called him Cole. What's that? Some sort of family name?"

Cole and I exchanged glances.

"It's nothing," Cole said. "Just what the kid called me when we were young."

Captain Reed continued to stoke the fire. Under his breath he said, "Cole Brighton. That sounds familiar."

I didn't want to show any signs of fear, but it seemed as if we had embraced a rattler. If Captain Reed could identify all the pieces of the puzzle, he would surely arrest Cole.

"I'm going to check on the wounded one more time and then turn in. It's been a long day," I said, stretching and yawning.

"I'm headed out to the herd. See if I'm needed out there," Luke said.

"I'll go with the kid." Captain Reed jumped to his feet.

We cleared the canopy and ran for the old building.

From more than a dozen tents we could hear the sounds of whooping coughs above the din of the rain.

"Don't think we'll be getting off in the morning by the sounds of all the sick," Captain Reed said, when we reached the shelter of the caving in porch.

"It surely does sound desperate, but we can't stay here. The Indians might return, and if we linger too long on the trail, we'll run out of food."

"I wouldn't worry about the Indians. They'll think twice before attacking us again." Captain Reed turned to look at me. I turned away. Gently he lifted my chin to lock his gaze onto my face. "I haven't had the chance to thank you personally for tending to my men. I know how difficult it must have been for you, saving the lives of Yankee soldiers, black ones especially."

I removed his hand from my chin and took a step back. "Black or white, they all bleed red. I hate Yankees, but I would never stand by and watch one die if I could do something to help. You must really think I'm a terrible person if you see me so callous."

"On the contrary, I think you are a wonderful woman. I would love to get to know you better. Possibly even become your friend." A moan came from inside the building.

"We have no common ground for a friendship. Please excuse me. My patients are waiting."

The rising of the sun brought the familiar call to "Stretch 'em out." Dawson had no time to delay for the sick or wounded. Muddy bogs, irritable cattle, wounded men, and people down with the cough made the traveling slow and difficult. At mid-morning we came to the top of a steep incline which switched its way back and forth to the valley floor.

"Each wagon will need to be taken down one at a time." Dawson called. "We'll take them straight down."

"Move over," Cole said to me, as he climbed onto the seat. "I'll take it downhill. The road's too dangerous for you to drive."

"I can do it. I've driven this far. I can drive downhill." I held on to the reins.

"Sarah, I'm not going to argue with you." He took the leather straps from me. "You're doing a fine job being a boy, but let's not be foolish about this. None of the women will be taking a wagon down. Those women whose men are too sick to drive will have Coyote or someone else drive their wagon. You can help get the wagons into position."

Ropes and pulleys were fastened around a large boulder securely embedded into the ground. Several teams of oxen were attached to one end of the ropes while a wagon and team were chained to the other end. Slowly the wagon rolled down the steep grade being held back by the oxen. Eight wagons made it down the hill with little or no trouble. At the bottom, each conveyance was unhitched and the oxen brought uphill to be attached to the next wagon.

"Keep it moving," Dawson ordered. "Bring Delvick's wagon into place."

The Conestoga rolled into position. "Gretchen, you und the children valk down the hill. It vill be safer for you," Rudy said. "Johnny, you look after my family, yah?"

"Sure, Rudy. Remember to take it slow and easy. Not too heavy on the brake. Don't want to burn it out. Let the oxen do the work."

Slowly the large wagon started to move, groaning and complaining with every turn of the wheels. Rocking and swaying it started to pick up speed -- faster and faster.

"Hold it back!" Coyote yelled from the bottom of the grade, kicking his roan to head up the hill to lend assistance.

"Hold the oxen!" came another cry.

The rope around the rock slipped. Gretchen screamed when the wagon lunged forward. Everyone could clearly see Rudy was in trouble. Cole mounted Zephyr and raced down the hill as quickly as the sure-footed horse could go. By now the oxen topside were sliding in the mud, unable to regain their footing. A rope snapped.

"Cut 'em loose before we lose the teams," Dawson barked.

"No!" Gretchen shrieked. "It vill kill my Rudy."

I stood by her side watching in horror, helpless. Little Karl's hand slipped into mine. His blue eyes filled with terror.

Cole swung a wide loop when the wagon started to tip. The lasso looped the lead ox. Coyote did the same on the other side. The horses skidded to a halt causing the ropes to draw taut. Rudy managed to stay seated while the wagon swayed the other way. Slowly the men gained control as the oxen on the ridge got a footing in the slippery mud. The conveyance came to a halt. Rudy, though badly shaken, waved to Gretchen that he was all right.

"Danke Gott," Gretchen whispered, clasping her hands in prayer.

When the wagon reached the bottom, everyone let out a cheer. The Conestoga was pulled aside, but the oxen weren't unharnessed. Both Cole and Coyote rode up to the top.

Cole spoke first. "Eight wagons are too many for the teams. We need to rotate the animals more often. Bring up fresh animals for the next six wagons."

After seeing the danger, I decided to let Cole drive our wagon. A rope line had been stretched over the hill to help the women and children walk the slope. Gretchen, carrying Anna, and the boys started down the embankment. I untied Misty and rode down the hill leading the other horses. Old Danger and Beulah, our milk cow, tagged along behind. Once I had our animals downhill, I rode back up to help where I was needed.

Our wagon came next, followed by the Gilroy's. I drove each wagon into position at the top of the hill and gladly relinquished the job of driving the wagon to one of the men. Hours of tedious work brought all the wagons to the valley floor. But as night approached, the cattle still needed to be herded down the incline. Every available man, though bone weary, rode back up the steep grade to do his part in moving the cattle.

I mounted Misty, ready to ride up the hill when I heard Dawson call to me, "Kid, you stay with the wagons. Don't need you this time."

"Are you sure?" I asked, relief filled my voice.

"Sure. You've worked hard today. Get some rest."

Men sick with the fever and cough, some too ill to sit a horse, set up camp. They pitched tents and gathered wood for fires.

"Sarah," Gretchen whispered. "Some of the vomen are too sick to cook. Vhen their men get back, they vill vant a hot meal. Vhat do you think about cooking for everyone? Ve can set up a common kitchen und feed everyone. I'm sure Mrs. Adler vill help, too."

"That's a splendid idea. I'll go around and tell the others. Each family will have to bring their own plates, but we can cook everything and have a feeding line like in the army. What will the menu be?"

"Beans, vhat else? I have beef ve can roast over the fire."

"I'll build the fire in the middle of the circle. And I have some beef, too. Maybe some of the other women have something they can contribute."

I went to each wagon telling the women not to cook and what our plans were. To my surprise many of the healthy women came to help. By the time the men returned to camp, we had a spread that dazzled the eyes and delighted the palate. The sick and wounded were fed at their wagons, but the rest of the group gathered around the fire, ate their fill, sang songs and enjoyed each other's fellowship. Double guards were posted, but the terror of the Indians and the hardships of the day were soon forgotten.

Reluctantly, I pulled myself away from the group to check on my charges. Most of the wounded soldiers were able to ride, but the ones who weren't, rode in the army wagon. After being jostled around all day, some of the wounds had started bleeding anew. I had put on clean bandages before supper, but I felt the need to check them again. Sick folk on the cold, damp ground wasn't the best, but the ground was all that was available to us. Canvas had been placed under each bedroll to keep out the moisture.

"Did all of you get enough to eat?" I asked. "Is there anything I can get you?"

"No. Doin' fine," one soldier said.

"Then I'll turn in. See you in the morning." I strolled to our wagon and rested in the shadows, listening to the singing.

"It's nice, isn't it?" Coyote asked, coming up behind me.

I sucked in my breath with surprise. "You walk as quietly as Johnny. Scare the life out of a body."

"Didn't mean to do that."

"Yeah, that's what Johnny always says, too. Well, it's been a long day. I'll be turnin' in. Good night." I started to untie the canvas over the tailgate.

"Good night, Miss Brighton."

I gasped. "What! What did you call me?"

"Miss Brighton. That is your name, isn't it?" A smile of satisfaction escaped his lips and spread across his entire face.

"I don't know what you're talking about."

"No, lady, you ain't gonna get away so easy this time. I've been watching you. Oh, you have the walk and the talk down. But it's the little things that give you away. Like your hands."

He reached out and took my right hand in his. "This

isn't the hand of a fourteen year old boy startin' manhood. No, even with all the calluses, it's still a woman's hand. I'll admit, you had me fooled for a while. Especially after the whore house incident. But I've watched you with the wounded. No boy would do what you did. You have the gentle, caring spirit of a woman. That you can't hide. The women tell me it was your idea to organize the meal tonight. Believe me, it was sure appreciated."

"It wasn't my idea. Gretchen thought of it. I just asked everyone to help."

"That's another thing, you and Gretchen. The two of you came in together. That's why she talks to you. Most of the other women wouldn't give a boy the time of day. But she knows you're a woman. Oh, it's hidden under all the dirt, but I'm sure if I'd take you down to the river and strip away all those baggy clothes and scrub off all that dirt, I'd find quite a woman in there."

"You wouldn't dare. Johnny would kill you." I started backing away.

"Don't worry. I'm not gonna touch you. Just how many of these people know you're a woman?"

"It seems one too many," came Cole's deep voice. He had been leaning against the wagon, arms folded across his chest.

"I told you he walks as quietly as you." I moved next to Cole.

From the shadows, he stepped forward. "We didn't think it was anyone's business except ours how she was dressed."

"I've said it before. If something doesn't seem right, I can feel it. The kid just didn't set right. I had to get to the bottom of it."

"Well, now you know. So keep your distance. You're welcome in our camp to talk and drink coffee just like before, but stay away from the kid. Is that clear?"

"That's gonna be hard to do."

"Then I'll make it easier for you. I catch you touching

her, I'll kill you." Cole's muscles tightened with tension.

Coyote just grinned. "Well, it's getting' late. Think I'll turn in. Since you insist on bein' treated like a boy, it's your turn to ride night herd. Jake will spell you at two." He tipped his hat and strolled into the darkness.

The singing came to an end as everyone went to his own camp for the night. Cole went to check on our horses. I gritted my teeth while I saddled Misty and strapped on my gun. I didn't know why I was so angry. Maybe because Coyote got the best of me or maybe because I was so tired and wanted to go to bed. Riding herd for four hours didn't fit into my plans. But I would do it. I wouldn't give Coyote the satisfaction. And the other men were just as tired as I was. Someone had to do it.

I rode out as the half-moon crested the ridge, spreading a silver light over the stillness of the land. Because of the threat of Indians, we had doubled the guard. Munching on sparse grass and mesquite, the cattle remained quiet and docile.

"It's quite a contrast from the hectic day we had," Luke said, riding from the other direction. "The tranquility, I mean. It seems like another world, peaceful and still." He rolled a cigarette and lit it. "You smoke?" He offered the fixings to me.

"No, thanks. Never got the hang of it." I pulled my hat down and my collar up. "I'll ride between here and that tree yonder. See you later."

"Yah, keep a sharp eye out. Indians you know. Porter is over on the other side." He rode off in the direction he had come, whistling a haunting tune.

I hummed softly to myself, watching the rocks and brush more than the cattle. In every shadow I could see an Indian lurking, ready to jump out and knife me. The stories of white women being carried off to be made Indian slaves ran through my mind. I arrived at the tree, but beneath its branches the shadows lay thick. A twig snapped. I thought of Yellow Sky and his peaceful solution of bartering for a wife. My heart beat faster. If I made a sudden move, it might frighten the cattle into stampeding again. As I backed Misty away, my hand rested on the butt of my revolver.

"Who's there?" I called in a mean, low tone.

"Don't get scared. It's only me." Cole's familiar voice rang in my ears. He prodded Shadow Run forward and came into the moonlight.

"What are you doing out here?"

"I know you want to do things on your own, but it's risky for you to be out here by yourself. I thought I would scout things out a bit. And . . .you caught me."

"Well, if you think I'm going to be mad at you, think again. I'm so happy you're here. I didn't know I would be so frightened. Luke's just over there and Mr. Porter should be on that side, but I'm jumpy as a cricket. Did you see any Indians?"

"No. None have been around since the rain. But I'll stay with you if you want."

"Yes, I would like that. But you need to get some sleep."

"I couldn't sleep, anyway, knowing you're out here."

"Cole, I don't know what's happened to us these last weeks. We were so close when we started this trip. But now all we do is snap at each other."

"I know what you mean. Guess it's mostly my fault." He shifted his weight in the saddle but kept looking straight ahead.

Not wanting to look at him either, I focused my gaze on the distant ridge, silver in the moonlight. "I need you to be my brother for a little while longer. When we get to California and when I feel safe again, you can go your own way. I won't be a burden to you anymore. Until then, please don't leave me alone in this wilderness."

"Sarah, it's just that I have a lot on my mind. You've never been a burden. I can't excuse my actions or even explain them. But I never meant to hurt you. Believe me, little sister, when I tell you I love you. You're all I have left of my family."

"And? Go on."

"There isn't anymore."

"What about the part that you'll never leave. We'll always be together?"

"I can't see into tomorrow. Things change. Someday you'll get married and you won't want me around to tell your husband how to act."

"Oh, yes. I can just see the man who will want me as a wife. He would have to be quite desperate. My hands are calloused and hard as old boot leather and I smell like the animals. I've been walking like a boy for so long, I've forgotten how to glide gracefully into a room."

"Don't worry about the little things. Right now, I know of two men who would fight for your attentions. When the time comes, you won't have any trouble finding a husband."

"Speaking about the two men, how did Coyote know our name is Brighton? It's no surprise he discovered I am a girl. We both thought he would, but to call me by name shocked me."

"It caught me off guard, too. He must have heard Reed say my name the other night."

"We need to be careful of that Yankee. I'm afraid I said more than I should have when I got angry with him and blurted out something about a bounty. He asked me if we had stolen the horses and if the army had placed a bounty on us. Of course, I said 'no', but I don't think he believed me."

"We'll act the same as always. Reed may not do anything until we get to California. He needs us to help get him and his belongings there. Up until now it's been rather easy, but from here on in it's going to get rough."

I looked at him in disbelief. "It's going to get rough from here? What have we been going through? Three men are buried on that mountain, killed by Indians. Ten more are wounded. We almost lost Rudy and his wagon coming down the hill, and half of the camp is down with the cough. How much worse can it get?"

CHAPTER 29

I shouldn't have asked. The next day we traveled ten miles to a place called Mustang Pond, the last water until the Pecos River some sixty miles away.

"We'll be rationing water from here on out," Dawson informed us. "This here section is called the Stake Plains and nothing grows out there. 'Till we get to the river, we'll be on the wing day and night stopping only short intervals to eat. Tomorrow we'll fix the wagons that got out of kilter coming over the mountains and the women can wash and bake. Give the sick and wounded a chance to mend and the stock some rest. Day after that, we'll move out early before sunup. Get a jump on the heat. Any questions?"

The vastness of the land stretched out before us until one couldn't distinguish between the land and the sky. Somewhere out there was a fort where we would say goodbye to our colored troops and Captain Reed would move into our camp. I shuddered to think of it.

"How many days do you expect it'll take to cross?" Mr. Sims yelled.

"Maybe five, if we're lucky, more if we're not. The water needs to be saved for people and working stock only. That's why we'll travel day and night."

The reality of the desperate situation started to soak in. No water for the cattle or horses. No water for my Misty. We had put our lives on the line for the Arabians, and now they may die for lack of water.

While my breads were rising and cakes and meat were baking, I mixed up a remedy for whooping cough which Dr. Bardlow had mentioned so long ago. I hoped I had remembered it correctly - - a scruple of salt of tartar mixed in a quarter of a pint of water with eight drops of laudanum and a spoon of sugar. A teaspoon of this potion had to be given four times daily. I also distributed a rubbing compound of heated oils and herbs that had to be rubbed onto the throats and chests of the ill and kept warm with a cloth. I taught each family how to use the potions and left the care of the ill to the well member of each family. The people of the train jokingly started referring to me as Doc.

On the morning of June 27, before the sky started to turn light, Dawson sounded the signal to "Stretch 'em out." The sounds of the oxen straining at the harnesses, creaking of wood and the snapping of whips broke the stillness of the early morn. A covey of quail flew from their nests, startling some of the animals. The smell of dry sage filled the cool air. I felt the same excitement as I had on that very first morning when we left Westport. A new adventure awaited me.

We were still following the old Santa Fe stage line but the road became impossible to distinguish because many Texas cattle herds had been driven to market over this trail and had obliterated the ruts and markings of the road. Coyote and Cole had left camp many hours ago to mark the way for us.

Over flat land, ravines, and gullies the wagons rambled on. Unbearable hot days followed cold, moonlit nights. Every available man had been detailed to keep the cattle and horses moving. The women drove the wagons. By day we traveled side by side to alleviate the suffocating dust, but at night we lined up to follow one another so we wouldn't lose a wagon in the darkness.

At the break of dawn on the third day we said farewell to our colored troops as they turned aside to go to Middle Station. Captain Reed went with them but within two hours he returned.

"I'm glad I didn't get orders to that place," he said, riding alongside my wagon.

"I know what you mean," I answered. "Can't imagine living out here for any length of time. Why are the Indians fighting to keep such an awful place?"

"It's all they have. They've already been pushed off the good land and now they're losing this, too."

"How can they live out here? They can't grow anything, no water."

"There are pockets of water if you know where to look." He took off his hat and wiped the band. "Sure is getting hot already. Between here and California, I'm not attached with the Army, so I thought I would climb into your wagon and change out of this uniform. Don't want to be any more of a target than I have to be should we come against some Indians. And you won't have to call me Captain Reed anymore. Jim will do."

"I would be happy to see you out of that Yankee uniform, Mr. Reed."

"You would? A fine Southern belle, prim and proper, like yourself. Why, Miss O'Shea, I didn't think you cared." A smile intending to embarrass me took hold of his face.

I could feel the color rising in my cheeks. "I mean you can change into some other clothing. Stop smirking. You know good and well what I meant."

"Then I have your permission to enter your wagon and change? I'll draw the curtains so you won't be tempted to peek."

I sucked in my breath at the mere suggestion that I would be interested enough to peek. "Just be quick about it. And don't fancy yourself such an attraction to women."

He slowed his horse enough to let the wagon pass him. He grabbed the last rib of the canvas and swung over the tailgate. I could hear him rummaging through his things. "I've known a few women who would envy your position."

"They must have been quite desperate."

"On the contrary, they were the pick of Washington."

"Oh, that explains it. Yankee women. They have no taste."

He opened the canvas, climbed out over the seat, and sat next to me, still buttoning his tan shirt. "Well, what do you think? Do I look civilian enough?"

A pair of brown leather chaps covered worn, work trousers and a button-down, front-panel shirt clung to a well-defined torso. A black hat replaced the military blue. Only his boots and guns remained as a reminder of his true identity - - Yankee.

"You'll pass from a distance."

"In that case I best be getting out to help with the stock. May I expect to be taking my meals in your camp or will I need to make other arrangements?"

"I'll cook for you. But you keep your place, you hear?"

He whistled for his horse and mounted from the wagon. "It's going to be hard to do. Maybe if you put a little more dirt on your face, I'll forget my recollection of you in the tub." He tipped his hat and rode away.

At about six o'clock on the evening of the fourth day, we pulled into a place called China Pond, a misleading name since the land consisted of sand hills and not water. Coyote and Cole were waiting for us at this desolate place. A few out riders kept the cattle moving. Most of the men stayed with the wagons to eat and to get a few hours rest. A cold meal of beans, bread, and jerky washed down with a cup of water had to last until morning.

Cole looked burnt to the socket. He had had very little sleep since we left Camp Concho. The men ate in silence, too tired to talk. As I was packing the dishes, I saw Coyote taking Dawson aside.

"Bad goin' up ahead," Coyote said. "Have to pass poisonous alkaline ponds before we get to sweet water. It'll take every man who can sit a horse to keep the cattle away from the ponds."

"We'll do what needs to be done. Right now, get some rest. We'll pull out in two hours." Dawson turned and when he saw me, he came over.

"Did you hear what Coyote said?"

"Yes."

"How are you doing? Think you can drive your wagon through the alkaline flats?"

"Sure."

"The river isn't far. Another day or so."

"That's good. We have only a little bit of water at the bottom of the last barrel." Our conversation was interrupted by a commotion coming from the other side of our wagon. Dawson and I ran to see what was happening.

"Settle down, Zephyr. What's wrong with you? You're acting like a jughead," Cole admonished, trying to pull the big horse out of the sand dune.

Zephyr insisted on pawing the ground a short distance away.

"He's gone mad," Rudy offered. "You must shoot him."

"Johnny, what's happening?" I asked.

"Don't know. Stay back. Coyote bring a lantern over here."

Coyote held the lantern high. "Looks like the sand's wet. Must be water down there. Everyone get shovels and start digging."

Soon water came bubbling through the sand. "Everyone stand back. I'll taste it first. Make sure it's sweet water. Don't want it laced with alkali." Coyote scooped a handful and tasted the cold water. "Didn't think it would be bad. But can't take a chance out here. It's sweet."

We moved our wagon away from the ever growing

pool to allow everyone a chance to get water.

Dawson yelled, "There's enough for everyone to fill a barrel and to water the working stock."

At midnight we started moving again. "You didn't get enough rest," I said to Cole, who seated himself on the bench next to me.

"Had enough. I'll drive when we get to Castle Mountain Gap. The road's treacherously narrow."

In the pale moonlight, I could see the change of terrain and vegetation as we climbed toward the mountains. A variety of cactus, several kinds of cedar, along with Spanish dagger trees and ground covering flowers filled the countryside. Cool refreshing breezes blew out of the mountains. But the ever present threat of Indians overshadowed the loveliness of the land.

"We're on a stage route. Why don't we see any stage coaches?" I asked.

"They stopped running because of the war. I'm sure they will start up again soon."

"Oh."

"Don't worry. Coyote and I didn't see any Indians," Cole said as if he could read my thoughts.

"I don't want to be afraid, but I can't help it. I don't like the openness of the flats, and I fear the closed in feeling of the mountains. I wish we were in California already."

Cole sighed. "I don't."

"What?"

"I've been thinking. When we get to Uncle William's, if he's willing to take you in, I just might continue on with Coyote and Dawson. Go back to Independence and take another train across."

"And leave me there with a stranger? What if he doesn't want me?"

"I'll make sure you're welcome before I go. Won't just drop you off. I'll probably stay through the winter or at least 'till February. Isn't that what you said? Once you feel safe again, I'm free to leave. It isn't as if we won't see each other ever again. I'll come to see you at the end of each trip. Stay a month or two."

"Sure, if that's what you want. But what about the horse ranch? Wasn't that your dream? Isn't that why we stole our horses and became fugitives? My God! I'm dressed like a boy, going through all this hell, for what? So you can run off and play scout on a wagon train?" My temper boiled. Words spilled out of my mouth without first passing through my brain. "Going to California wasn't my dream. I told you not to promise Mama. But no! You couldn't listen to me. I told you not to meddle in my life. But you are a man of honor. Once you gave your word, wild horses couldn't stop you. Now I'm the one who will pay for it. You'll be off doing what pleases you and I'll be stuck with some old man who probably doesn't want me. I could have stayed with Dr. Bardlow or Reverend and Mrs. Tadwell instead of being drug across this God forsaken wilderness to. . . ."

"Stop it! Just stop it! Don't you see, I can't stay; I can't be around you. I'm your brother but. . . ."

"But what?"

His voice dropped to a whisper, barely audible above the noise of the wagon. "But what I feel for you isn't the way a brother should feel toward his sister. You said I am an honorable man. That is why I'm leaving before I do something we'll both regret." He looked off into the distance and fidgeted with his hands, trying desperately to do something so he wouldn't have to look at me. At last he grabbed the reins and slapped the leather straps against the oxen. "Yah! Get up there."

My heartbeat quickened. My breath caught in my throat. I had no words to tell of my feelings for him. They were best unspoken. We traveled in silence. I knew he wanted to get on Shadow and ride away from me, but he needed to drive through the gap, so he stayed.

My thoughts spun in my head as his words translated into 'I love you.' A pain rose in my chest as the truth of the situation took hold. I loved him too. All these months I had tried to fight the feeling, pretending it was just because I needed him that I wanted to be with him all the time. I depended on his being strong to keep me from stepping over that invisible line of morality. Not thinking of the future or the consequences of my dreams, I plunged headlong into the unsuspected snare of my own imaginary world. In my world it seemed perfectly all right to cultivate an unnatural love for my brother. No one would ever know. No one would be hurt. When we reached California, I wouldn't need him and the closeness of living together in a small wagon would change. My love would fade as I became involved in a new life and Cole would return to being just my brother. But sin is always a liar and a deceiver. What seems to be good and harmless turns out to destroy and ruin lives. I turned my face away so Cole wouldn't see the tears running down my cheeks. He was all I had. Everything I knew and loved was gone - - my parents, my home, friends, everything. Emptiness was all that remained. How am I going to live the rest of my life without Cole?

Castle Mountain loomed above us. Just before we entered the pass, Dawson signaled for a halt. "Everyone trim a lantern and hang it on the tailgate to light the trail for the next wagon to follow. Now we're going to take it slow and easy. Stay next to the wall and keep a short rope on the horses. Lead 'em out, Coyote."

The pass narrowed quickly as the cliffs towered high above the train on one side and the mountain fell into a deep chasm on the other. If Indians attacked while we were in the gap, all would be lost. We inched our way in the darkness past the steep walls, following the light from the Delvick's wagon and keeping as far away from the edge as possible.

Rocks on the narrow trail shook under the weight of the conveyances. I feared the road would give way, crashing the wagons down into the chasm. The moonlight didn't descend into the depths of the cavity, but we could see where several cattle had lost their footing and had gone over the edge. Dawson, determined that none of the wagons would be lost, kept a steady pace. Fear quivered my insides. The vibration from the heavy wagons knocked small stones from the cliff overhead, causing them to fall on us.

"Get inside the wagon," Cole ordered. "Don't want you to get hurt."

I did what I was told without an argument. In the wagon, I could cry freely. Cole wouldn't see my tears. "Oh, God, what am I going to do with the rest of my life? I don't want Cole to go away. My life will be empty without him." I lay on the bed, rocking and swaying, listening to the scree pelting the canvas.

As we emerged from the pass, Cole pulled our wagon to a halt. "I have to help with the cattle. Keep the oxen away from the alkali ponds. Just keep moving. The river's about fifteen miles. See you at the crossing." He climbed down, untied Shadow and rode away without a backward glance.

I wiped my face with the sleeve of my shirt and climbed over the bench to take my position as driver again. I could smell a change in the air. The stock could smell it too. They picked up their pace and strained at their harnesses. The whiff of grass and water drifted on the breeze. But the pungent odor of death accompanied it, as well. Overhead, vultures circled in the early morning sky.

An hour later we knew why the vultures had gathered. A thousand or more head of cattle lay dead, rotting in the hot sun. "They must have drunk from a poisoned pond," I said to myself. I pulled my bandanna over my nose to block out the stench.

Dawson rode up and down the line telling everyone to stop and water the stock. "Let 'em drink as much as they want. That'll keep them from wanting to get into the alkaline ponds. We'll be at the river by sundown."

I filled the bucket and gave it to the animals. Beulah,

the poor cow, needed good grass and plenty of water to keep her milk flowing. While the horses drank their fill, I brushed them.

"Firestorm, I do believe you're going to have a foal. How wonderful. The first of our new stable." Joy quickly dissolved into sadness as the remembrance of Cole's words flooded over me. The dream of a horse ranch evaporated as quickly as the hot sun evaporates dew. Cole was leaving with Coyote and Dawson.

"Dawson," I called when I saw him riding by. "Are those dead cattle ours?"

He rested his massive arms across the pommel of his saddle. Looking down from his big buckskin, he said, "No. They must be from a Texas herd being driven to market in Santa Fe. Looks like the rancher lost 'em all, poor soul. Take care your horses don't get into those ponds. Be a shame to lose such fine animals."

"Oh, I'm giving them plenty of water. I just felt Firestorm and it seems she is going to have a foal. I'm not sure when."

"Let me have a look-see." He dismounted and gently put his hand on the horse's belly. "Sure enough, I'd say sometime around late September or early October. Hope the father's Shadow or that black one and not that Appaloosa." He laughed at the thought of such a fine mare being ruined by a scrub stallion like Zephyr.

"I'm sure Shadow Run is the sire. She wouldn't let Zephyr near her."

"Horses ain't like people. They have no laws or prejudices to stop them from doing what comes natural like. All she knew was that she was ready and a stud was available, if indeed Zephyr is the sire."

My face felt hot under Dawson's gleeful gaze.

"Sorry if I embarrassed you. Keep forgetting you're a girl under all those dirty clothes."

"Sometimes I forget too. I can't wait until we get to California and I can put all this behind me."

"Still a long way off. How are things goin' between you and Coyote? Does he know yet?"

"Yes. He could see through my disguise. But I don't think he knows I was the one he kissed at Molly's that night."

Dawson laughed. "I wouldn't count on that. He didn't get the name Coyote for nothin'. He's a clever one. You take care, now. I'm going to ride up and see how the men are doing with the cattle. You help keep the wagons movin'." He mounted and rode up the line telling the women to keep the wagons heading west.

Sundown found us camped by the Pecos River at Horse Head Crossing. Before the wagons arrived, the cattle, not having had water for five days, smelled the river, broke loose and ran ahead of the riders. The men had a time of it keeping the cattle out of the deadly ponds but they managed. By the time the wagons got to the Pecos, the cattle had drunk their fill and were munching on tall grass. Cole unharnessed the oxen for the first time in five days and led them to water. He placed a picket line by the river in the grass. The animals would be happy tonight.

I set up camp and started a fire. Tonight's supper would be a slab of beef and the last of the potatoes. Captain Reed helped get supper together. He found some miner's lettuce by the river and picked it for a salad.

"With a little vinegar and oil, sugar, chopped onion, salt, pepper, this should taste good," he said, pleased with his find.

I had little interest in what he was saying. "You can fix it if you want."

"What's wrong? You should be happy."

"I'm just tired."

"You sit and I'll cook." He put his hands on my shoulders and ushered me to my chair.

I watched him chopping the onions and lettuce. He moved about the camp with the energy of a ground squirrel gathering acorns for the winter. "Are you always this . . . this . . . ?" I couldn't think of a word so I just waved my hand in the air and shook my head.

"Happy? Why shouldn't I be? I get satisfaction out of a job well done and we certainly did that today."

His infectious smile caused me to smile too. However, I didn't want to feel any joy. I wanted to wallow in self-pity and cultivate the loneliness gripping my soul. Cole entered our camp and just seeing him made my heart leap.

"Come with me," Cole said, pulling me out of the chair and leading the way past the wagons to the river's edge. He continued away from the commotion of the camp to a quiet place up river.

God's paintbrush had colored the azure sky vermilion and gold with streaks of lavender as twilight descended upon the earth. The quick running river splashed against rocks and gurgled over rapids as animals came to the edge to drink. The trees rustled in the warm evening breezes.

"Sit." Cole hit an old log twice with his hat to knock off any ants or spiders. "Sarah, I've been thinking all day about my decision to leave. Actually I've been thinking about it ever since that night in Shelby when we danced in the pecan grove. I felt something between us that I pretended didn't exist. I know you felt it too. Thought just staying away from you would be enough, but it isn't. I think about you day and night. It's driving me out of my mind."

He walked a short distance away to stand in the shadows of an old black willow which, in the fading light, made it impossible for me to see him. But his voice came clear and melodious to my ears.

"When I was captured by the Yankees and put in prison, I thought I would die. Not because my life was threatened, but because I had no choice over my own destiny. I'm in the same quandary today. What I want to do, I can't because of laws and morality. What I don't want to do, is what I must do for the same reasons."

"I don't understand."

"I want you to know that I'm leaving, not because I want to, but because I have to. I don't want you to hate me."

"Strange, that's what Mama asked of me, that I would never hate her. How can I hate the people I love?" I gazed out over the water reflecting the colors of the twilight. "You're right, I do feel a strong attraction for you. I always have." My soul opened and words I never dreamed of saying aloud spilled out. Since he stood in the shadows, it was more like talking to the wind or to myself than to him. "I remember, as a little girl, just wanting to be in the same room with you. I thought then that it was only because you were home so rarely. I was awestruck by you . . . such a handsome, worldly man. You were living life as a great adventure. I, on the other hand, was afraid to leave our property. Look at me now. Who would have ever thought I'd be out here in the middle of nowhere going to California. And, yes, I'm still in awe of you. You can do everything. When you're near, I feel safe and . . . wonderful. If you want to hear the words, then I'll say them, I love you. I love you with more than the love of a sister for her brother. I don't know what I'm going to do when you leave, but I know you must." Once again tears flooded my eyes and ran down my face.

"Thank you," he said, softly.

"Just let me stay here for a while. You go back."

"No, it's too dangerous out here alone. We've seen fresh moccasin tracks in the mud." He stood over me and lifted me to my feet. His touch sent ecstasy careening through my body. I wanted to melt in the feeling, savor it, enjoy it, but I rebuked it, turning my thoughts to matters at hand.

"Indians? Are we in danger?"

"We've posted guards. I'll stay in camp tonight. You'll be safe." His words were like warm cotton wrapping around me.

Quickly we walked back to the wagons. Once again I surveyed every bush and rock, looking for Indians. Weary as I was, I kept pace with Cole's long strides, half running to stay abreast. I realized my depression would pass. Cole was right. He had to leave.

CHAPTER 30

My heart ached the next morning as we traveled up river to a shallower crossing. Cole tried to drive our wagon but the pain of being close to me proved impossible to bear. It was tantamount to being slashed to pieces by the silence between us. Our wounds lay open with no ointment to soothe them. At last Cole asked Captain Reed to drive.

With his usual enthusiasm, James Reed gladly climbed onto the wagon and took the reins. He sat on the seat next to me whistling his little ditties and commenting on the scenery or anything else that popped into his head. When he saw he was getting little, if any, response from me, he finally said, "Don't be so solemn. I don't bite and Yankee isn't catching."

"I didn't think it was." I smiled. "I've been exposed to Yankee many times and haven't come down with it yet."

"In that case, you must have another problem. Care to share it with me? And don't say you're just tired. You slept the entire night."

"No. I'm not tired. The plans and dreams Johnny and I had made don't seem to be working out. I think I'm starting to feel sorry for myself. Don't worry. It'll pass."

"You have every right to feel sorry and alone. Through no fault of your own, you've lost everything. And now you're traveling to a strange place to start over. It must be a little frightening. I don't believe any of the women want to come west. This is a man's adventure, his dream. The women come because they have no choice."

I looked at him with my mouth open in amazement. "I can't believe you actually understand how I feel."

"In the short time I lived at Fort Concho, I saw it many times. If given a choice, the women would have returned to the security of their homes in the east. But the men never asked them their opinion. A man just sees free land, a new adventure, and he's off to conquer the world. The women and children tag along because they don't know what else to do."

"I could have stayed with friends, but Johnny promised Mama he would take me to our uncle in California. Once he gives his word on something, nothing can change his mind."

"If a man doesn't have his word and his honor, he's nothing."

"Yes, that's what Johnny always says."

"It must pain him to be living such a lie now."

"He did that for me, so I would be protected. If anything would have happened to him on the way to California, he believed I could survive better if everyone thought I was a boy. When we started this deception, we didn't dream it would turn out the way it has."

"Is that what's eating away at him?"

"Partially."

"And the rest?"

"I don't know. You'll have to ask Johnny." I turned away so he wouldn't see I was lying.

Two days of traveling up river brought us to Pepes Crossing where Dawson decided to take a chance to ford.

Rain in the mountains at the headwaters caused the river to be higher and swifter than usual for this time of year. We halted the wagons some distance from the banks to prepare for the crossing.

My eyes widened in disbelief when Coyote handed me a tar bucket. "You still insist on being treated like a boy?" He didn't wait for an answer. "Then the wagon needs to be sealed before you enter the river if you don't want everything to get wet."

I took the bucket and started painting, trying not to get the hot tar on me. Only once before had we needed to tar the wagon and that time Cole did it.

"No. No. You have to get into the cracks of the wood." Coyote took my hand in his and moved it in long strokes, sealing the edges of the boards. He reached around me to dip the brush into the bucket. I felt his strong body against mine, his arms enfolded me and his breath touched my cheek. The redolence of sweet grass replaced the pungent odor of hot tar. A tingling sensation danced up my spine as I became aware of his lingering touch.

"Humum." James cleared his throat. "Coyote, Dawson wants you down at the river. Seems that the cattle are reluctant to enter the water. I'll help the kid with the tarring."

I took the brush out of Coyote's hand. "That won't be necessary. I can manage quite well, thank you. You men go and help with the cattle. When I've finished sealing the wagon, I'll move it into position."

"All right, but don't try to drive it across by yourself," Coyote cautioned. "I'll be back to help." He tipped his hat, scowled at Reed, mounted his roan and rode to the water's edge where most of the men were coaxing the stubborn cattle over the steep bank into the fast-moving, cold water.

James placed another tar bucket on the fire. "When this is hot, I'll paint the other side."

"Aren't you needed with the stock?"

"They have plenty of men helping drive the cattle and horses. We need to get the wagons sealed and floated across before dark. Don't want to split the train, half on this side of the river and half over there."

I hadn't thought much about Indians these past two days, but James was right. We couldn't split the men up on two sides of the river. We worked fast and in no time the wagon was tarred on all sides and the bottom.

"I'll help Gretchen with her wagon. You can drive ours into line." I took my brush and bucket and walked to the Delvick's wagon.

Gretchen, Karl, and Juergen were busy painting tar. Little Paulie played a short distance away and Anna lay sleeping in her cradle under a tree.

"This is sure awful stuff," Gretchen said, as I came up on her. "Be careful, Juergen, not to burn your hands."

"Since Rudy is helping with the herd, I'll tar the bottom of your wagon," I said, crawling under the large conveyance. Karl had already painted one end of the underside and I started at the other. Long, cooled tar drips hung like strings waiting to tangle in my hair and wisp across my face like spider webs. I wished I had never volunteered to help, but *'once begun, a task must be done,'* I heard Leah's voice echoing in my mind as my memory flew back to the days after the war when she was determined to teach me how to do simple chores around the manor. *She surely wouldn't believe her eyes if she should see me now,* I thought, as a cooled tar drip splashed on my forehead.

"Kid, you need more tar?" Karl called. "My bucket is still some in. I put it on the fire for you."

"I have enough, thank you. I'm almost finished." The tar was cooling faster than I could work, but I painted thick layers onto the bottom boards and crawled out from under the wagon, confident that water wouldn't dare soak through.

Gretchen loaded the children into the wagon and

drove it into line. Two hours had come and gone since Coyote had handed me the tar bucket. It was just about noon, but the men couldn't stop to eat. The nervous cattle were still being prodded and coaxed into the water, rescued from drowning and boosted over the steep bank on the other side. The sounds thundering from the bawling cattle and the whistling and yelling men caused a din I almost believed could deafen the ears of God.

By the time the first wagon entered the river, most of the men had been swimming their horses for at least three hours, some longer. Tempers were flying. Four men escorted each wagon across, two at the front and two at the rear, with ropes tied on to steady the wagon. Each man drove his own conveyance across with his family tucked safely inside. The water rose past the hubs of the wheels until the wagon was floating and the oxen or mules were swimming. Never had we crossed such a high river. I held my breath and whispered a prayer as I watched wagon after wagon enter the water and come out safely on the other side.

"You're next," Dawson called, pointing to me.

I looked around for Coyote. Instead, Cole climbed onto the seat. "If we're going to go down, we'll do it together." He smiled and squeezed my hand. "Ready?"

"Ready." I hung on tightly as the wagon rolled down the steep bank, rocking and lunging with the unsteady steps of our team.

Cole whistled and yelled at the lead oxen, coaxing them deeper into the river. The water splashed around us and over the sides of the wagon.

"I'm getting wet," I yelled, trying not to let the sound of fear creep into my voice.

"Just hold on."

James and Coyote served as two of our escorts. The wagon lunged to the left. I lost my grip on the seat.

"Cole, help!" I yelled, as I fell into the water.

"Swim, Sarah! Swim!" Cole hollered, wrestling with the

oxen to keep the wagon from overturning.

The fast moving river quickly swept me away from Cole's reach. I remembered watching Cole swim at the hot springs. I kicked my legs and flailed my arms against the water.

"I'll get her!" Coyote yelled, as he slid off his horse into the river.

I felt his arm around my throat, lifting my chin. "Don't struggle. Just relax," he said. "I have you."

I grabbed his arm. "You're choking me. Let me swim."

"You can't! Let go before we both drown."

I started to protest, but I got a mouth full of water and started coughing.

Coyote flipped me onto my back and grabbed my collar. Gradually we came to shore some distance downstream. He dragged me up the bank, plopped me on my stomach and pushed between my shoulder blades.

"Come on, breathe."

"Don't! That hurts. I am breathing."

"Thought I lost you for a minute."

"Not yet. Thank you for coming to my rescue."

Cole finished driving our schooner to the other side and raced down the river bank to where we were. "Kid, you all right?" He took me in his arms and held me tight.

"Yes. But next time I'll ride Misty, if you don't mind."

Captain Reed, Dawson, Rudy, and some of the others were fast on Cole's heels. Everyone wanted to know how I was.

"The kid's fine," Dawson said. "Go back to your wagons. Let him have some breathing room."

"Thanks again, Coyote," I said, as we walked back to the wagons.

The sun had painted the sky in hues of reds and violets before the Adler wagon crawled up the bank. We left the Santa Fe Trail on the other side of the Pecos as it continued north. From now on we would be following the Butterfield Route into California.

After dinner I walked to the river to fetch a bucket of water.

"I wouldn't get too close if I were you. Might fall in," Coyote said, coming up behind me.

"I'll watch my step. Just need some water to wash off this tar. I thought I was being so careful not to get it all over me, but I was wrong. It's in my hair and everywhere."

"I thought you had enough of the river this afternoon. Water ain't gonna get that stuff off. What you need is coal oil. Come with me." He took my wrist and pulled me along toward his camp. I ran to keep up.

When we reached his camp, it was deserted. Their cook had already turned in for the night and Dawson was nowhere to be seen.

"In you go." Coyote pushed me into the tent and came in after me.

"I don't think I should be in your tent."

He ignored my words as he lifted a jug of coal oil out of a chest. "Sit on the bed. It's Dawson's but he won't mind." He lit a candle and placed it on a box. "Turn your face to the light." He dipped a rag in the oil and rubbed my forehead, my nose, and chin.

"Ow! That hurts. Don't rub so hard."

"You want the stuff off, don't you?"

"Yes, but not my skin with it. I didn't think I got that much tar on me."

"You're splattered like tiny freckles all over your face and in your hair. But I'll stop if you want. Sooner or later it'll wear off on its own."

"No. Go ahead, continue. But not so rough." I closed my eyes to brace against his vigorous assault.

I waited. When he didn't start rubbing again, I opened one eye. He sat on a box in front of me just smiling at me.

"Well?" I asked.

"I'm trying to decide if I should treat you like a boy and scrub the hell out of you, or if I should treat you like a woman and kiss you."

Both my eyes flew open as I leaned back away from him. "Perhaps you should act like a gentleman and escort me back to my wagon."

"I've never pretended to be a gentleman."

My heartbeat quickened, not because of fear of this man, but rather the excitement of the chase. A game of fox and hound as it were, though I was uncertain of which role I was playing.

"A gentleman doesn't need to pretend. He just is. You certainly display all the qualities of being a gentleman, honorable, loyal, dependable. Do I really need to fear for my virtue?"

The candlelight flickered in his pale blue eyes as the look of mischief toyed with his face. His voice flowed softly, and elegant words belied his frontier exterior. "Your virtue? Can a scarlet angel living in the attic of a brothel still maintain virtue?"

"Only if the angel was a guest and not a resident." *He does know,* I thought, trying not to smile.

"With one whose kiss is as warm as an evening breeze and as sweet as wild honey, how can I believe she was just a guest?"

"Could it not have been a kiss of innocence instead of experience?"

"If the kiss of innocence can burn into a man's soul and still bring to him the embers of delight on lonely nights, months later, then he has been wasting his time looking for an experienced woman, well educated in the art of love."

"I know very little about these matters. Mr. Jolette, my tutor, never approached a subject such as this. My heavens, Mama would have had him flogged. But I would think a man would prefer to teach rather than to be taught."

"Only if the student is willing to learn. I have found in my limited dealings with virtuous women that they are cold and prize their aloofness above their desire. Or perhaps they have no desire for such things."

"Oh, I assure you, even chaste women have desires."

"And you, Miss O'Shea, do you have desires?" He leaned closer.

"I do believe I must be getting back to my own camp. They'll be worried about me."

"Spoken like a true spinster. If a man gets too close, turn and run. Make sure to keep that smoldering fire in check. Don't let it burn to the surface or you might surprise yourself. Continue to dress like a boy. It's safe. No one will ever know there's a woman inside." He poked his index finger into the middle of my chest. "Come on, I'll take you back." He stood up.

Fury seized me as I sprang to my feet. "I am a woman in every sense of the word. It matters little what I wear, and I don't have to be bedded by the likes of you to prove it. When I decide to give myself to a man, he will know the pleasure of this smoldering fire raging to the surface. Until then, I'll keep my desires to myself."

Coyote's laughter sang a mocking melody. "You're a tempest when you're angry, never noticed it before but your blue eyes flash like lightning." He slipped the red chiffon scarf from around his neck and looped it over my head pulling me closer to him. "If you're going to be mad at me, might as well give you something to be mad about."

I struggled, but his strength held me close to him. He lifted my chin and brought his lips to mine with a caressing gentleness I'd never felt before. A flood of warmth washed over me as I melted into his arms and found myself returning his kiss.

When he finally released me, he whispered, "It's even sweeter than I remember. When we get to California, may I have your permission to call on you at your uncle's home?"

As quickly as my temper had risen, it dissipated. He had completely disarmed me. "If you wish," I said softly, in a husky voice swelled with emotion.

"I wish."

CHAPTER 31

Time held no meaning as we traveled with the sun. Each day presented the same chore as the day before: cover the distance of eight or ten miles. No matter how difficult the terrain or what hardships and hazards that came upon us, we pushed steadily west.

By the end of July, we entered the Sierra Blanca Mountains, the land of the Mescalero Apache. Snow still lay in the sheltered crevasses of the rocky crags. Cedar, juniper, spruce, pine and fir trees forested the range. Nestled between the mountains, beautiful valleys spread out in an abundance of fertile land.

One such delightful valley was Tularosa, with a population of about one hundred Mexicans. We found the Mexican people hard workers, but poorer than any people I had ever seen. *Our slaves lived better than they.*

"But they are free," James said, as he watched me wince at their living conditions.

"Can you read my thoughts?"

"You have a habit of comparing everything to the way your life used to be. I would venture to guess you were thinking your slaves were better off than these people."

"As a matter of fact, I was."

He smiled at me with a self-confident look. "Not all slaves were well cared for. Freedom comes at a high price. Take these people, for instance. They are probably in danger from the Apache, but they would rather live here than in their own country under a corrupt government."

"Maybe this was their land and their father's land before them, before the Yankee government stole the land away from Mexico?"

"If that is the case, they are now citizens . . . ."

Gunfire cracked the air over the noise of the wagons and animals. Our conversation came to an end. Someone had sounded the alarm.

"Get the cattle out of the corn field," Mr. Adler yelled.

I looked toward our herd and saw them in the Mexican's field, eating a healthy share of the still forming ears of corn. The wagons halted in their tracks as the men quickly rode to get the cattle out of the crop. Angry Mexicans came running with sticks and rocks to beat the animals. Who could blame them for being cross? Words I couldn't understand flew like weapons against Dawson. At last Cole stepped up, and in sign language, negotiated a deal: three head of cattle for safe passage out of their peaceful valley. All of a sudden, the valley didn't seem so peaceful anymore.

Cole took his turn driving the wagon as I rode Misty a short distance away. The little spirited horse, that had always been eager to run, now contented herself by just keeping up with the wagons. I indulged in my favorite pastime, dreaming of a mysterious lover coming to make me his own. *He will wear a black claw-hammer coat, white shirt with a vest, and black trousers. I will entice him in my green velvet cottage cloak covering a white silk dress, with a low cut neckline and gigot sleeves. We will dance in the moonlight. When the hour is late, he will carry me up to his room and he will make love to me. I'll give myself to him completely and . . . and....*

My face grew hot as I realized I had no idea what would come next. *Was Coyote right for wanting an experienced woman? He had asked for permission to come calling, but would he be happy with a woman as naïve as I? Could I hold on to a man such as Coyote, or would the call to adventure entice him away when he grew tired of me? What of James Reed? Could I live at a fort surrounded by Yankees? Would the memory of the war always be between us?* I looked over my shoulder at Cole. His thoughts seemed to be off in the distance as he absentmindedly let the team drive themselves. *Will I ever find someone to love as much as I love him?*

The monotony of each day being the same as the last, ground heavily on our nerves. Unbelievably hot, dry weather, lack of water and fresh food, broken wagons, dead stock, and dust that lay thick on everything eroded people's resolve. Indian signal fires at night and the beating of drums in the distance by day made everyone edgy. Fights broke out among us. People talked of turning back. Others threatened to go on alone, saying we were taking too long. When the Adler wagon broke an axle, the train came to a halt. The men had to cut a smoke tree for a new axle and mount it on the wagon. We all knew this task would take several hours and it would be dark before the work was finished.

Mr. Potter demanded we go on without the Adler's. "We'll lose a day of travel if we stop," he shouted.

"I'm not going to leave one family out here alone. This area is crawling with Indians. We've seen more than a dozen farms burned out or abandoned. No telling what would happen to the Adler's if they were attacked. More than likely, Mr. Adler and the boys would be killed and the women would be taken as slaves. The Adler's have four daughters. You want to leave them out here to the mercy of the Apache?" Dawson's neck turned redder the madder he got.

"We're not going to sit out here like ducks on a frozen pond waiting for those redskins to come down on us. We're moving on. Anyone who wants to come with me and my family get ready to pull out. I'll be leavin' for the gold fields as soon as I can cut my cattle out of the herd."

Dawson made a bold stand, but in the end five wagons left the train. With them went the Collins family. The Roberts boy wanted to go with them, however, loyalty to his own family and his commitment to help his father with the new farm prevented him from going. I knew he loved Sally Collins and his heart was aching.

"Vhat do you think, Johnny? Should ve go mit them?" Rudy asked.

"No. I'm in no hurry to get to California. We have strength in numbers. One week more or less won't matter. Those people are fools." Cole took the ax out of our tool box as Coyote rode up on his roan.

"Sorry to see 'em go. They have no idea what they're headin' into. I'll be ridin' out in the mornin'. Want to come along?"

Cole glanced in my direction. "Sure."

I shielded my eyes against the blinding sun as I watched the five wagons ramble over the desert. "God go with you," I whispered.

PART THREE

CALIFORNIA: SECRETS REVEALED

CHAPTER 32

I didn't see much of Cole those days as New Mexico faded into Arizona and at long last Arizona territory would give way to California. Cole rode with Coyote at point, leaving me to drive our wagon. Luke and James became my constant companions, taking turns driving and doing the heavy work. Cole came into camp only to sleep, but he was gone the next morning before I emerged from the wagon. He took most of his meals in Dawson's camp.

Gretchen replaced Cole as my confidant. Each evening I ventured into their camp to listen to her bedtime stories or to just sit and talk. She helped me with my sewing and mending. Tears of loneliness no longer filled my eyes. I fell into a hardness of getting the task done. California became my focal point.

We finally came to Fort Yuma. Standing at Roman's Ferry, looking across the Colorado River into the promised land, I felt sick. For some reason, all these months I had dreamed of green grass and trees. Now all I could see was more of the same sagebrush, cactus, and dirt we had been traveling through for more weeks than I could remember. The rugged hills resembled sleeping dragons.

Brown dirt sloped up to the jagged rock outcroppings that ran along the top like the spine of the sleeping creature.

"Don't worry, Kid," Jim said, putting his hand on my shoulder. "It'll get better."

"It has to. I can't imagine living out there. I could have stayed in Tucson if I wanted to live in the desert."

"Don't know if it'll be as green as your home, but it'll be better than this desert."

I thought of the green fields and trees, the refreshing rain, and the wonderful fragrances the land gave off after a shower. I remembered home. *The war had not only destroyed my home and family, but no one else could remember it the way I did - - no one except Cole. Could I share my family with anyone other than a Southerner? How could a Yankee understand what it was like growing up before the war and the difficulty of the adjustment the rebellion had put upon me? No, only someone from the South would understand.*

The Butterfield Trail led us across the Colorado River and down into Old Mexico. On the morning of the third day, the sun rose red as blood. Birds had taken flight, and animals had gone to ground. Coyote came into our camp. I didn't know what was happening, but I knew we were heading into trouble.

Cole came over to me. "I'm going to drive the wagon. You take Misty and the rest of the horses to that rock face. Coyote says there's a cave." He pointed to a rugged outcropping some distance away.

"What's going on?"

"Sandstorm. Don't want to be caught out in it. Help Gretchen and the kids. They can ride Zephyr. Leave Shadow with me in case I have to abandon the wagon."

The taste of metal flooded my mouth as I started saddling the horses. Fear was once again taking control.

Jim grabbed the harnesses out of the back of the wagon. "I'll get the other horses ready. You get the Delvick boys. Hurry! We don't have much time." Captain Reed took command as if he were back at his post.

I obeyed without question. The morning air held a stillness I had never felt before. Not a bird or a cricket could be heard. Our animals twitched nervously.

Gretchen came running, Anna tucked under her right arm and Paulie hanging onto her left hand, his feet barely touching the ground. Karl and Juergen raced ahead and reached our camp before she did.

"Come on, boys, you're going to ride Zephyr. Let Captain Reed help you up."

Jim lifted each boy onto the back of the sturdy horse. Karl first, then Paulie, and last Juergen. "Hold on tight." He helped Gretchen mount Misty and handed little Anna up to her. "You should have a safe ride on this horse. Head over to that rock outcropping. The kid and I'll catch up with you." He gave Misty a slap on the rump and they were off running.

"What have you done?" I yelled. "I was going to ride Misty."

"Guess you'll just have to ride with me." Jim mounted his big sorrel and held his hand out for me. "You can hold the lead ropes better if you don't have to guide a horse too."

I stood looking at him for a minute, trying to decide if I wanted to ride behind him or ride one of the other horses bareback.

"Kid, don't waste time. Get going," Cole commanded, as he slapped the reins against the oxen and hollered, "Get up there!"

The wagon started rolling, picking up speed with each slap against the oxen's back. The other wagons were moving out too. None were staying in line. Each was on its own. It could be likened to a great stampede. Dust billowed in giant clouds as the ground trembled beneath my feet.

Firestorm, nervous with fear, bucked, kicking Black

Dancer in the side. The lead rope slipped through my hands as Firestorm broke free and ran away.

"I'll catch her," Jim yelled, as he whirled his horse around in fast pursuit. But Firestorm outdistanced him and was gone in a swirl of dust.

"Had to let her go. We have to get to that cave before the wind hits us and before we get lost too," Jim said, returning to me without Firestorm.

"I can't! She's going to have a foal. We have to find her."

"Nothing we can do 'til the dust storm is over. Give me your hand."

I knew he was right. Reluctantly, I held up my hand and he swung me up behind him.

"Hold on." Jim kicked his horse and we lunged forward. I wrapped my arms around his waist and held on tightly, trying desperately to keep control of the three ropes to Midnight Star, Black Dancer, and Old Danger.

We had delayed too long. The wind caught us. Sand and pebbles pelted us as dust closed out the world. Jim pulled his neckerchief over his nose and mouth. I did the same and buried my face into his back.

"We can't go on like this! It's too dangerous for the animals. They might step in a hole and break a leg. We have to find cover and hold up 'til this blows over." He swung his leg over the horse's head and dismounted. The hot desert wind showed no mercy. Jim pulled off his outer shirt and tied it around his horse's eyes and let it hang to cover the animal's dust filled nostrils, all the while reassuring the frightened sorrel that he wouldn't let anything happen to her.

"You're all right, Sweetheart. We'll find a place to get out of this wind." He kept patting the horse on the neck and rubbing her face.

I slid off the back of the horse and walked beside Jim as we searched for cover. A narrow wash provided just what we needed. It ran north and south, sloping gently enough for the animals to walk down and was deep enough to keep us out of the wind. Jim unsaddled Sweetheart while I hobbled the others. Then we settled back against the east wall, huddled under Jim's tarpaulin to wait out the storm.

"How far away do you think the wagons are?" I asked.

"I have no idea. Don't know if they made it to the cave before the wind hit or if they're holed up like we are in a wash some place. Hope Mrs. Delvick and the boys made it to the cave. Hate to think she might be out there alone without her man to protect her."

"Don't trouble yourself about Gretchen. She's quite capable of fending for herself. I've never seen a woman as strong as she. I don't mean physically, although she is quite strong, but inwardly she's like granite."

"Have you looked into a mirror lately?"

I wiped my face with the back of my right hand. "I must look a mess. I'm covered with dirt."

"No. That isn't what I meant. You said that you've never seen a woman as strong as Mrs. Delvick. If you looked into a mirror you would have seen one."

"Me? No. I'm like a green willow bending in the wind. Almost everything frightens me."

"Sure can't tell it by your actions. Don't know of any genteel southern ladies, bred to the finer way of life, who have managed as well as you have. I regret that I'm a hated Yankee in your eyes. Wish there was something I could do to make you see me as a man and not a soldier."

"I do, too. I am trying. It's just that the wounds are still so fresh, the hurt too deep."

"Did the Union Army destroy your plantation or confiscate the lands?"

Wide-eyed, I glared at him, wondering if he was trying to pry information from me.

"You still don't trust me," he said, with a sigh.

"You're still the enemy."

"Your brother saved my life. I would never do anything to bring harm to him or you. If you don't know by now how I feel about you, I'll make it quite clear." He pulled his bandanna down and leaned over to me, slipping my neckerchief gently away from my face.

I felt like a woman from one of those Eastern countries that Mr. Jolette had talked about. To uncover a woman's face in the presence of a man was tantamount to giving in to him. My body tingled as he cradled my head in his hands, and gently touched my lips with his.

"I love you." His words were a whisper.

My heart banged against my chest almost loud enough for him to hear. Blood surged through my body. I wasn't sure what to do. Mama's warning echoed again in my ears, *'A young lady never allows herself to be alone with a man.'* I pulled away. The horrible memory of that wretched man from the woods and the ordeal at the cemetery the day we left Rosewood came flooding into my mind. Panic crested the ridge of sensibility. I wanted to scream, but instead I choked on a breath of dust filled air and started coughing.

"I've never had a reaction like that to one of my kisses." Jim patted me on the back. "Here, drink some water." He handed the canteen to me. "Not too much. Don't know how long we'll be here."

I took the water gladly. "I must tell you that I've never reacted like this to a man kissing me." The fear dissolved as I started laughing.

"Then I'm not the first?"

"Would you be disappointed if you weren't?"

"Not disappointed, just surprised. I always thought Southern Belles were well chaperoned."

"The war changed many things."

He raised an eyebrow. "Then perhaps you have good reason to hate Yankees."

"Most Southerners have good reason."

We sat under the tarpaulin listening to the wind howl and the pebbles hitting against the canvas. As the sun journeyed across the sky, the shade of the east wall disappeared. We baked under our shelter. Sweat formed rivulets down my face, around my throat, and between my breasts. Jim removed his long-sleeved undershirt and wiped his sweaty body. Light brown hair covered his chest. He had a scar from a bullet wound just below his ribs on the left side. My hand involuntarily moved to the scar.

"Is this from the war?" My fingers traced the circle.

"It's one of 'em. The other I can only show my wife, when I get one, that is."

I blushed. "I hope for her sake it hasn't impaired you in any way."

"Why, Miss. . . Miss Sarah, you never cease to surprise me."

"Nor you me. How do you know my name is Sarah?"

"Is it such a secret? I heard Johnny, or should I say Cole, call you by that name when you fell into the river. Sarah, it's a beautiful name. It means princess and you certainly are."

"My father used to call me his treasure . . . his golden treasure. But Johnny calls me Stormy when I get angry. He says I have a stormy disposition, calm one minute and raging the next."

Jim laughed. "Mother always called me Scrapper because I was the youngest of six brothers and I had to fight for what I got. Finally, after eight years, my sister was born. I thought I would have someone I could pick on but since she was a girl, I ended up protecting her more than picking on her."

"Are you and your sister still close?"

"We were. But the war changed that. By the time I returned home, she had already grown up and didn't need me anymore. She's married now and her first child will be born in October. Wish I could be home to see the little one, but life seldom turns out the way I plan."

"I know what you mean. Do you have someone, a girl, back home?"

His tawny eyes clouded over with a faraway look. "She didn't want to marry a soldier. All she knew was the military. Both our fathers were in the army. She grew tired of moving from post to post, never having a permanent home. She wanted to marry a farmer. Believe me, working in the dirt isn't what I wanted to do with my life. I can hardly stand all this dust of the wagon train. I wouldn't be a good farmer. So we stopped seeing each other."

"You didn't love her enough."

"No. I don't believe I did."

"You come from a military family?"

"Yeah, as far back as before the Revolutionary War. Of course, we were British then. All my brothers went to West Point, but I didn't get a chance. Father took ill and Mother needed me at home."

"Johnny was always away from home. He escorted wagons across to Oregon. All I ever wanted was to live at Rosewood and have a family of my own. I never wanted a great adventure. That was Johnny's dream. It's strange how dreams have a way of getting changed."

"Sometimes for the better. My Uncle Ulysses went from a failing shopkeeper to a general."

"Uncle Ulysses? You don't mean Ulysses S. Grant?"

"Yeah. He isn't really my uncle. He's a close friend of my father, so we kids called him uncle. He always brought gifts at Christmas and birthdays. Even if we were on the frontier, living in a small shack, Mother always made holidays and birthdays special."

"We had grand times at special occasions too. Life on the plantation was wonderful."

"I wish I could have known you when you were growing up. I would have come to call and sit in your parlor, sipping tea out of your mother's good china."

"Yes, and I would have received you. In the afternoon we could have walked through the rose garden. We had the most wonderful garden. Mama loved roses. I wish you could have seen our plantation. It was marvelous. We had the finest horses in all the Carolinas. People came from as far away as New York and Boston to buy our stock. Daddy took such pride in our animals. But now it's all gone. Only these five horses are all we have left. And Firestorm has run off and we may not find her. Here I sit in the dirt under a canvas alone with a man. Mama would have the vapors if she could see me now. One thing Southerners fear most is giving the wrong impression. I know I'm safe with you, but what will the others think when we get back to the train?"

"They won't care. They think you're a boy. I'm not concerned with anyone except your brother. I hope you explain things to him before he comes looking for me. I know I'm fast with a gun, but I sure don't want to test my hand against Johnny."

"He's very understanding. I'll explain what happened."

"Johnny is many things, but where you are concerned he's anything but understanding."

In time the wind blew itself out and we emerged from under the tarp. After giving the horses some water and rubbing the dust off their backs and out of their noses and mouths, we untied them and rode out to find the others. Cattle wandered over the desert waiting to be rounded up. In the distance, I saw riders coming. I recognized Shadow Run. Cole was leading the way at full chisel. I felt the muscles in Jim's back tighten.

"Here comes trouble," he said, urging the sorrel to quicken her pace.

"Are you two okay?" Cole shouted, closing ground fast.

"We're fine," I replied. "Are Gretchen and the boys at the cave?"

Cole brought Shadow to a halt beside the sorrel.

"Everyone made it to the cave, except you. We were worried."

Jim explained, "Firestorm ran away and I went after her but couldn't catch her. We got caught in the wind and had to hole up in a wash till it blew over. But we're fine."

"In that case, we'll start roundin' up the cattle before dark," Dawson said. "You two head on up to the cave and get yourselves somethin' to eat."

Cole glared at Jim and moved Shadow around to face the same direction as the sorrel. "I'll take you back to the cave, Kid. Give me your hand."

"I'm doing okay where I am. We'll be back down to help with the cattle when we've eaten."

Cole grabbed my arm. "I said I'll take you back." Fire ignited in his grey eyes.

"You better do what he says," Jim urged.

Swinging my leg onto Shadow's back, Cole pulled me the rest of the way over. I wrapped my arms around his waist. Without a word, Cole kicked the steed into action.

"Slow down!" I yelled. "The other horses are having trouble keeping up. They're tired."

"Are you sure that's the reason you want me to slow down?"

"Yes. Why else?"

"So your lover can catch up."

"Don't be silly."

"I'm not the only one who thinks something went on out there. Did you see the looks on Dawson's and Coyote's faces? They know you're a woman. And they know that Captain Reed knows you're a woman. Tell me what really happened out there."

"He was a perfect gentleman."

"Gentleman or not, he's still a man. He didn't try to kiss you or anything?"

"Well . . . it's not what you think."

Shadow came to a jolting halt. Cole turned in the saddle to lock his burning eyes onto my face. "What do you mean it's not what I think? We find the two of you alone. He's not wearing a shirt and you look like an unmade bed, and you tell me it's not what I think. He kissed you, didn't he? What else did he do?"

"Nothing! We sat under a tarpaulin and talked until the wind stopped. Nothing happened. What do you expect me to look like? I just came through a windstorm."

"I don't expect your shirt to be half unbuttoned and hanging out flapping in the breeze."

"It was hot under the canvas."

"So you took off your shirt?"

"No! I didn't take my shirt off. I just unbuttoned it a little. I didn't do anything wrong. Jim was afraid you wouldn't listen to reason."

"Jim, is it? What happened to Captain Reed?"

"I've been calling him Jim for some time. If you were ever in camp you would know."

"So this has been going on for some time already."

"What? Nothing has been going on, only what you imagine in your evil mind. Let me down. I'll walk." I slid off Shadow, threw the lead ropes at Cole and stomped off across the desert toward the cave.

Cole rode alongside. "There're rattlers out here. Come on, Stormy, don't be foolish. Give me your hand."

"I'd rather be bit by a snake than listen to anymore of your poison."

"Suit yourself." He quickened Shadow's pace and rode up ahead a short distance.

As soon as he rode away, I knew I had made a mistake. I walked faster, being as cautious as the dwindling light would allow. It was almost early candle-lighting time when Cole returned. Without a word he held out his hand and I took it. We rode to the cave in silence.

"Stay here. I'll get Firestorm. I'm sure she didn't go

far." Cole rode away without waiting for my answer.

"Cole and I have had disagreements many times, but this time he is really angry with me," I confessed to Gretchen the next morning. "It wasn't my fault that we got caught in the storm and had to hole up until it was over. I didn't do anything wrong. Why is he so angry?"

"I think he is more hurt than angry. He vas not there vhen you needed him. He promised your mama he vould see you safe to your uncle. He thought he had failed. You should have seen him vhen you did not come to the cave. Dawson, Coyote, and my Rudy had to hold him back from going out to look for you. He valked around like a vild animal. Ve could not see beyond the end of our noses and yet he vanted to go out in that terrible storm to find you. Believe me vhen I tell you he vas afraid for you."

"If he was so afraid for me he should be happy I'm all right. I don't understand why he's treating me the way he is. He isn't talking to me and he's so hateful."

Gretchen's eyes took on the look of hurt. "If he did not love you the vay a man loves a voman, this vould not be such a huge argument and you vould not be so hurt. You both know vhat you feel for each other is wrong. Yet, you do nothing to stop it."

"Oh, but we are. Cole will be leaving as soon as we get to Uncle William's ranch. We may not be able to change our feelings, but we can stay away from each other."

"Yah, that is good. He is jealous of Captain Reed. He vill be jealous of every man you like."

"But I don't like Jim. Not in that way."

"I know. But Johnny sees vhat isn't there. His eyes are clouded from the truth by the vay he feels for you."

"What can I do about it?"

"I vish I had an answer for you. I used to tell young people to follow vhat their heart says. But to you I cannot say that. For you and Johnny there is no answer, only pain. He is dealing mit it the best vay he can, that is by being angry mit you, and causing you to hate him."

"I wish we were at Uncle William's already. Everything will change when we get there."

"Soon, very soon, now. Then ve vill see."

CHAPTER 33

The day after the windstorm, all the cattle were rounded up and Firestorm was found sound of limb and spirit. We moved on. The going was slow. We turned north and started climbing into the mountains again.

At evening three riders came into our wagon circle. They were jolly fellows on their way to the silver mines at a place called Calico. They brought word of the Potter and the Collins families who settled in San Diego. Everyone made the trip safely. That was good news for all of us to hear. But the good was mingled with sadness. We said goodbye to Luke and a few of the outriders. They packed what stores they could carry in their saddlebags and headed off with the strangers for the dream of riches in the silver mines.

Cole still didn't talk to me, but he stayed in our camp. He brooded in his anger. Since Luke was gone, I think Cole wanted to keep an eye on Captain Reed. At first I was angry, but when I thought about the situation, I could see the humor of a jealous brother protecting his vulnerable sister. Jim must have felt uneasy, too, because he didn't talk to me either and stayed mostly to himself.

The second evening after Luke left, Coyote came into our camp.

"This is a fine evening for a walk," Coyote said to me. "Would you care to join me?"

I didn't wait for Cole to object. "I would love to walk with you." I followed Coyote out of the circle of wagons.

"Didn't know if I would get another chance to talk with you before you and the Delvicks break off toward the coast. It's just another few days, if all goes well. Tomorrow we'll be traveling through the Wagner Ranch and beyond that into the Temescal Valley. The road's good. I'll need to ride on ahead to make arrangements for a place to stay in Los Angeles, so I'll be leavin' in a day or two."

"Oh, we will miss you."

"Do you speak for the entire wagon train?"

"No, just for myself."

"In that case, I'm glad because I'll miss you too." We came to some large boulders that crested the brow of a meadow. We climbed up the rocks and sat on a flat stone at the edge of the overhang. The evening sky was slowly turning to lavender-blue with streaks of cadmium orange washing across the horizon. "This is where the Indian women used to come to grind acorns and corn. Look here where the rock is ground away in round holes. These are called Matati holes. The women used to watch their men practice with their bow and arrows in the meadow." He swept his hand toward the tall grass meadow below.

I didn't say anything. I knew he didn't bring me out here to give me a history lesson on Indian culture. He was groping for the right moment. Slowly he found his words.

"That night in Dawson's tent when I tried to scrub the tar from your face was about as close as I've ever come to askin' a woman to marry me."

My eyes widened and my mouth fell open for just a moment before I regained my composure. "No, Coyote. We don't know each other well enough to even think of marriage."

"Oh, I think about it all the time. I think about how nice it would be to wake up in the mornin' next to you. I could make you happy. I would teach you the fine points of making love. Now that I know you really weren't one of Molly's girls."

"Did you think I was?"

"For a few months, yeah."

I started to protest.

"Don't say anything. I know I was wrong. And I know this isn't the right time to talk to you about what my heart feels for you. Why, I don't even know what to call you. Been callin' you Kid all these months."

"Sarah. My name is Sarah."

"I know. But do you want me to call you Sarah?"

"Not while we're on the wagon train. Too many people still think I'm a boy."

"Then may I come to visit you at your uncle's ranch?"

"Yes. And what should I call you? Surely your parents didn't name you Coyote."

"Don't rightly know my real name. I was one of those white kids taken by the Sioux. Never knew my real parents. Dawson traded with the Indians. That's how I came to know him. He asked if I wanted to scout for him. I guess I was about fourteen at the time. The Indians treated me like one of their own. At the age of fourteen I was considered a man. I could make my own choices. So I did."

"How dreadful."

"What? That I became a scout? I'm not such a bad scout."

"No. That you never knew your parents."

"I had a good family. The Indians care for their children just like people living in fine mansions on big plantations. My mother was Little Bird. She was a soft-spoken woman whose husband and son were killed in a battle with the whites. I became her son. She loved me.

Didn't know I was different from all the other Indian boys. I was Little Bird's son. That's how I was treated."

"Why did you want to leave if it was so good there?"

"Little Bird died."

"Oh, I'm sorry." I sat quietly for just a moment and then continued, "You seemed to have taken to the white man's ways rather well."

"I've had many years to practice. I won't ever go back to the Indian ways, but there are things that I still miss. Most of it has to do with a family- - the feeling of belonging. Being a part of someone's life. Scouting for a wagon train doesn't lend itself to setting down roots. That brings me back to my original reason for wanting to come out here alone with you."

"Coyote, please don't speak of such things. Come to visit me at Uncle William's home. Let us move slowly concerning matters such as . . . what should I say . . . ."

"Love! I would call it love. But I won't press you now. However, I will give you fair warning, I will come to court you at your uncle's ranch." He stood and lifted me to my feet. He held me longer than proper and released me only when he heard someone coming. "We should be getting back to the wagons." As we returned to camp, we passed the Roberts boy talking with the oldest Adler girl.

The train continued toward Los Angeles, the city of angels. The stage route had brought us up from Old Mexico, across the mountains and the Wagner Ranch, along the base of the Santa Ana mountain range and through the Temescal Valley. Here the Indians were friendly and we traded for fresh vegetables. At the north end of the valley Rudy, Gretchen, the children, Captain James Reed, Cole and I turned west toward the coast. We took the road through the canyon that was formed by the Santa Ana River.

We stopped our wagons and watched the others ramble over the terrain. We waved and yelled goodbye until we couldn't see them anymore, before we turned and headed into the canyon. The emptiness of saying farewell to friends I had made, knowing I would never see them again, mingled with excitement quivering in the pit of my stomach over my new adventure – the last leg of the journey. Echoes of the horses' hooves, the lowing of the few head of cattle we had left, and the squeaks of the wagons bounced off the canyon walls that towered above us. California oak trees, tall grass, and cattails grew along the dry river bed. As the road twisted its way through the pass, the air changed. No longer the stale, dusty inland air, but a fresh salty sea air greeted us. We followed a well rutted road to the crest of a hill. There stretched out before us lay the coastal valley. My eyes scanned to the horizon where the Pacific Ocean blended into the sky. We had traveled from coast to coast across the wide expanse of our wounded nation. At the base of the hill, a sign pointed to the right. It read: Anaheim, 7 miles.

"We'll camp here one more night," Cole said. "In the morning, Rudy, you and your family will take that road into Anaheim. We'll continue straight ahead to the coast."

"Yah, one more night mit our friends," Rudy said, as if he was reluctant to say goodbye. "Come, Mutter. Ve set up camp under those trees."

As Rudy drove his wagon off the road to a stand of eucalyptus trees, Jim said, "I'll get my uniform out of the wagon and be headin' on. Let you know where you can send the rest of my things." He tipped his hat. "Want to thank you for letting me travel with you. Know it wasn't easy for you, Johnny. I assure you, I didn't take advantage of the situation."

"I know you didn't. Don't go. Stay the night with us."

"I was hoping you'd ask." Delight spread across Jim's face. "Didn't take to the idea of camping alone."

We settled our wagon at an angle to Rudy's and built a fire in the middle of the triangle. Gretchen and I cooked a large piece of beef. We turned it on a spit over the open fire. I made quick biscuits with flour, water, sugar, and baking soda. I didn't have any eggs or milk since my chickens had died in the hot desert, and Beulah had dried up from the lack of water and grass. We left her at Fort Yuma. I placed the fresh corn we bought in the Temescal Valley and the last of the potatoes under the firewood to roast. Soon the aroma of coffee and the cooking meal mingled with the fragrance of eucalyptus. The old trees cast long shadows in the evening sun as overhead sea gulls winged their way back to the ocean.

A feeling of peace washed over me. It was over. We had made it. This California wasn't what I had expected, but the hills resembled soft, amber velvet caressed by the warm summer sun. Sweet songs the birds sang drifted on the warm evening air. Golden rays danced across the sunbathed openness of the land. Oak, pepper, and eucalyptus trees grew along the roads, and in the distance here and there, houses and orchards could be seen. I couldn't see them, but beyond the river vineyards awaited Gretchen and her family. *Her new home,* I thought.

I watched Cole brushing the horses. Rudy mending his harness one last time, the boys playing around the trees, Gretchen putting a kettle of water on to boil, and Jim, dear Jim, tending to the sorrel he had so lovingly named Sweetheart. *What did the future hold for all of us?* I mused as I absentmindedly turned the spit.

"I think it is done," Gretchen said, bringing me back from daydreams. "Ve vill rake the coals to find the potatoes und corn, yah? Und ve must dunk them in the hot vater to get them clean before ve husk the corn or cut the potatoes. Of course, not all the charcoal vill come off but a little von't hurt. Mit all the dirt and dust ve have been eating these past months, ve vill hardly notice a little charcoal."

The meal was delicious. If anyone had tasted charcoal, no one said a word. We lingered over coffee, talking about the trip, laughing over things that didn't seem so funny at the time, and remembering absent friends we would always treasure. The sky turned black velvet with a million flickering lights. Another log blazed on the fire. Each of us felt reluctant to end the evening. Another story was told, then another, memories became engraved on our hearts. At last the time came to call it a night.

"Just one more story," Karl pleaded, almost asleep in his father's lap.

"No more. It's time for bed." Rudy carried the boy to the tent. "You vill not get up in the morning if you do not go to sleep now."

Gretchen helped the other two boys into the tent and went in after them. "Good night, see you in the morning."

"That goes for me, too," Jim said, stretching. Good night, everyone." His sparkling eyes locked on mine as a soft smile spread across his face. "Sleep well." He walked over to the trees and shook out his bedroll. Placing his saddle as a pillow, he turned in for the night.

Cole put out the fire as he had done so many times these past months. "Well, Sarah, are you anxious to meet Uncle William?"

"I'm a little concerned. What if he isn't there anymore. Maybe he moved on or died or something? What if he doesn't want me or what if. . . . "

"Whoa, hold on there. That's too many what ifs'. He'll be there. Don't worry. And he'll love you. I've been telling you from the beginning everything will work out just fine. Trust me."

Sleep refused to embrace me and morning seemed as if it would never come. Visions danced before my eyes of an old man, mean and unyielding or of me being left alone while Cole rode off into another great adventure. I tossed and turned until, while it was still dark, I arose and dressed.

Out of the crate in which we kept our clothes, I pulled the blue dress Jim had lent to me at Fort Concho. I had never returned it but then the woman was dead and didn't have need of it. But I did. Night after night Gretchen had helped me take in the seams and shorten it, until now it fit as if it were made for me. We had made undergarments out of the dust covers used to keep the bedding clean. I had decided weeks ago that it was more important to be dressed as a lady of quality when meeting Uncle William than to have a dust free bed, which was impossible anyway. I couldn't do anything about my short, unruly hair or about the awful golden color the sun had turned my skin, but I refused to meet Uncle William dressed as boy.

Before the light crested the ridge, I smelled smoke coming from our cook fire and heard the clanking of pans. Looking out, I saw Cole crouched by the fire. Gretchen was emerging from her tent.

"Good morning. You are up early," Gretchen said, moving to the fire.

"Couldn't sleep," Cole answered.

"Yah, I don't think any of us slept vell. Ve are too anxious about vhat today vill bring. Johnny, I know it is none of my business but I must speak to you about the Kid, Sarah. All these months I have vatched you. I know you love her. . . ."

"Gretchen, please. I don't want to talk about it."

"I know. You men never vant to talk about vhat matters most. But you must! You cannot just leave her mit your uncle and ride avay. You must see that she is provided for. That Captain Reed is a fine man and vill make a good husband. Let Sarah go mit him. Do not stop her."

"Go with him? Does she want to go with him?"

"I think if you give her permission, she vill."

"Well, I'll think on it. Don't worry. I'll see she's settled before I leave."

I knew Gretchen meant well but I wished she would mind her own business. I didn't love Jim. She knows that. "I'm not going to get angry with Gretchen," I told myself. "I don't want to spoil our last day together. Now smile as if you didn't hear what she said."

By the time I finished dressing and emerged from the

wagon, everyone was gathered around the fire drinking coffee. Cole was the first to find his voice.

"I had almost forgotten how beautiful you are." He came to take my hand and lead me to the fire. "I have the honor of presenting my sister to you. This is Sarah."

I blushed and curtsied.

"Papa, she is beautiful," Karl said, moving forward to get a better look.

"Why, thank you, Karl. That is indeed a fine compliment." I held out my hand to him.

"Come, sit mit me." Karl's eyes twinkled with the delight of his first crush.

"Sorry, Karl, she's going to sit with me." Jim stepped between Karl and me.

"I'll sit with both of you. How would that be?" I smiled at Karl and took his hand. "May I have your arm, sir?" I said to Jim. "Or don't gentlemen in the north give a lady their arm to escort her to a chair?"

"Oh, absolutely," Jim stammered as he crooked his elbow.

I drank in everyone's compliments as parched land welcomed autumn rain.

Cole fixed breakfast, giving me a chance to enjoy being a lady again. The meal was simple - - bacon, beans, bread, and coffee. Time passed almost unnoticed. The sky turned lighter and lighter and still we talked. No one wanted to think about breaking camp because that would mean we had to say goodbye. But at last Rudy and Cole packed the wagons. Jim saddled Sweetheart, while Gretchen and I lingered over our coffee. I held Anna and kissed the boys. My eyes started to sting as tears filled them.

"I'm going to miss you," I told the boys. "You come and see me sometime."

"Can ve Mutter? Please?" Paulie begged.

"Ve vill see. Right now, ve must say auf viedersehn."

"Already? I don't vant to say goodbye." Paulie put his little arms around my neck and held on tight.

"It isn't goodbye forever. We'll see each other soon. And I'll write each month. Your mama gave me your uncle's address. I'll tell you all about the ranch and you can write and tell me all about the vineyard and your new home."

"Come, boys, time to get into the vagon." Rudy called.

"I will write. Come and see us at Christmas. We'll have a big party just like we always had at the plantation." I hugged Gretchen. "Let me know how the boys and little Anna are doing." Tears flooded over my eyes and down my cheeks.

"Don't cry. You get puffy eyes. I vill miss you." Gretchen handed me a handkerchief. "Let us know vhen you get married. The captain vill make a good husband. Mark my vords, you vill be happy mit him."

A bittersweet smile touched my lips as the words of Mrs. Tadwell echoed in my ears, '*She isn't getting any younger. She'll have to settle for second best if she wants to get married.*' "I don't love him," I whispered.

"Love vill come mit time. You vill grow to love such a fine man as he. He can give you healthy children." She talked like an old slave auctioneer trying to sell his goods to a reluctant buyer when the price was too high.

I looked around for Jim and saw him emerge from the back of our wagon wearing his Yankee uniform. My breath caught in my throat and my heart burned in my chest. *Yes, the price is too high,* I thought.

"Come, Mutter, is time. Say your goodbyes. Ve must get started. Today vill be an exciting day for all of us," Rudy called from the wagon, tying three head of cattle and one horse to the tailgate.

"Yah, yah, he is anxious to see his brother. Und you have still a long vay to go before you meet your uncle."

We hugged one last time before each of us climbed onto the seat of our own wagon.

"Goodbye, take care. Don't forget to write," I called after them as they took the road to the right.

I kept looking back over my shoulder hoping to catch glimpses of their wagon, but didn't. They were gone. Once again I felt the loneliness of saying goodbye.

CHAPTER 34

By mid-morning we reached El Camino Real, the King's Highway. This was the main road between the missions. A road sign indicated that we had to turn south toward San Juan Capistrano.

"Here's where I leave you," Jim said. "Before I go I want you to have something." He pulled a folded piece of paper out of his shirt pocket and handed it to Cole.

Cole opened it. His expression turned to stone.

"What is it?" I asked.

Cole handed the paper to me and said in a dry voice, "A wanted poster."

In disbelief I looked from the poster to Jim and back again. I saw Cole's hand drop to his pistol. My heart pounded like cannon fire. Jim truly is the enemy, a rattler waiting to strike.

"How long have you known?" Cole asked.

"From the beginning, when I discovered that the kid was a woman. I had the poster at Fort Concho but I didn't want to believe the man who saved my life could do all the things you're accused of. So I got special orders to come west with the train, to keep an eye on you, so to speak."

"So now what, you turn me in or do we shoot it out?"

"Neither. I sent a wire to Uncle Ulysses and I got this reply at Fort Yuma." He handed the paper to Cole.

Cole read it aloud. "Because one good turn deserves another, all charges against Cole and Sarah Brighton are dropped. Sincerely, Ulysses S. Grant."

"I told you my uncle favored me," Jim beamed. "I didn't want you looking over your shoulder the rest of your life. I know California is a long way from North Carolina, but civilization is drawing this country together. Someday, when the railroad is built, we'll be able to cross from coast to coast in a matter of weeks instead of months."

Cole's body relaxed and he moved his hand back to hold the reins. "Guess the score's even. You just saved my life. You'll never know what it's like to be a wanted man. Honor is one value a man needs in order to look himself in the mirror each morning. I don't believe I did anything wrong by taking my own horses. They were never part of the deal. Yet to be accused of a crime by the government of the land, it's pretty hard to reconcile with my own values."

"Now you don't have to worry." He paused for a minute, looked down the road he was about to take, and then continued, "Since you know you can trust me, might I have a few minutes alone with your sister?"

Cole nodded approval.

I climbed down from the wagon. This time Jim helped steady my step. *How strange,* I thought. *For months I've been climbing up and down over the seat, standing on the wagon tongue and jumping beyond the wheel and no one offered to help. Now, I'm dressed like a woman and Jim is quick to lend a hand. Wearing a dress does have its advantages.*

He took my hand and we walked a short distance. His sparkling sienna eyes searched my face as his words sounded softly in my ears. "I'll never get used to saying goodbye to people I love. Getting to know you these past few months is an experience I'll cherish forever. You truly are a golden treasure." His hand reached out and touched a curl escaping from beneath my bonnet. "I know you'll never be able to return my love."

"I'm sorry," I whispered.

"Don't be. Someday the one you can love will come into your life. Until then, think fondly of me." He took my hand and kissed it.

"Will I ever see you again?"

"I have some work that needs to be done first but by Christmas it should be completed. I overheard you telling Gretchen you might have a Christmas party."

"Yes, if all goes as I expect and Uncle William does receive us into his home. And yes, you are invited."

"Then, I'll be there." He held my arm as he took me back to the wagon. "All I want for you is that you're happy."

"Thank you, James. You'll be my friend forever." I brushed a kiss against his cheek and climbed up onto the wagon. I wrote Uncle William's address on the back of the wanted poster and handed it to him. "See you at Christmas."

He mounted Sweetheart. "I'll let you know where to send my things. God go with you." He turned and rode north to the barracks in Long Beach.

"Sure you don't want to go with him?" Cole asked.

"No. I never loved him. He's a fine man, but he's a Yankee. That blue uniform would always be between us. If I forced him to give up the army, he would grow to hate me. I'm sure when he bleeds, he bleeds Yankee blue."

"I assure you, it is red. I saw enough of it."

"Was he really badly hurt?"

"He was gut shot. Didn't think he'd make it. Guess he had an angel looking after him."

"A Yankee angel and a good hearted rebel. Well,

brother, it's just you and me now. All these months, a country span away from where we started and it's still just you and me."

"Don't forget the six horses, soon to be seven, one old mule, four oxen and a few skinny cows. In some circles, we would be considered wealthy."

"And the gold. Don't forget about the gold."

"After outfitting us with the wagon, food, and cattle, and after paying for water and tolls along the way, we still have a goodly sum. That should do us for a while, wouldn't you say?" A smile of satisfaction lit Cole's face as he slapped the reins against the oxen to get them moving again.

I enjoyed the easy traveling on the well-worn dirt road. Meadowlarks sang out from the unplowed fields that lay beyond the row of trees lining the highway. Gentle breezes touched my cheeks with the fragrance of salt air, even though the ocean was hidden beyond the range of golden hills. All day we traveled, not stopping to eat, thinking that around each turn we would see the mission. By evening we heard the bells in the distance calling the workers from the fields.

"Won't be long now," Cole said, halting the team at the top of a small rise. Below us lay a fertile valley filled with orchards, vineyards, corn fields, and pasture land. In the midst of it all stood the mission and a small adobe settlement.

Amazement washed over me as we pulled onto the church property. "I didn't expect the mission to be in such disrepair. Coyote called this the Jewel of the Missions. I don't understand why." Pointing out the crumbled two-story building to the east, I continued, "Did the war get this far west? Just look at that building. It's in total ruin. It looks as if it was once a church."

Cole seemed disappointed too, as his eyes scanned the unkempt grounds. "I'll ask inside if someone knows where Uncle William lives. Wait here." He climbed off the wagon and entered the mission through an arched covered walkway.

"Ask about that building," I called after him as he disappeared through a doorway.

I waited.

The sun was sinking fast beyond the hills as a golden glow bathed the thick adobe walls and red tile roof of the mission. Arched column corridors supported by massive adobe pillars fell into the shadows beneath the large overhanging eaves of the low buildings. The lime stucco plaster, painted over the adobe to protect it from the weather, reminded me of the white alkaline plains of Texas. Pigeons flew home to roost in the trees beyond the first row of structures. Swallows darted in and out of mud nests attached to the walls of the buildings. Our oxen munched on weeds growing at the base of the four-bell Campanili wall. I remembered that I hadn't eaten since breakfast.

Finally Cole emerged from the mission and ran to the wagon. "The padre said William O'Shea lives just down that road toward the ocean."

"Is he still there?"

"The priest seems to know William, so I assume he's still living there. Nice fella, that priest."

"Did you ask about the ruined church? What knocked it down?"

"An earthquake."

"An earthquake! They have earthquakes out here?"

"Think nothing of it. Happened a long time ago. 1812, I believe the man said."

My thoughts went reeling. *This is indeed a strange new land, hot, dry, little water, and yet fertile. Now I hear this land has earthquakes. I hope I'm going to like living here.*

The information Cole received was correct. About a half hour later we turned off the road under an arch which read: *O'Shea's Hacienda*, and followed the drive another half mile. The house resembled the mission with its adobe walls and tile roof. Wide arches held up the overhanging eaves that shielded the windows like heavy eyelids. Light spilled through the windows onto the stone porch.

Cole stopped the wagon in front of the house. "Wait here." He got down off the wagon and stood for a moment in front of the steps. He looked at me over his shoulder, took a deep breath, and slowly climbed the stone steps, crossed the porch, and knocked on the heavy oak door.

"If that's Peter, tell him he's late, started without him." A loud voice boomed, as a middle-aged, round faced, Mexican woman opened the door.

"Si, what do you want?"

"My name is Cole Brighton. I was wondering if William O'Shea lives here."

Surprise gripped the woman's otherwise friendly expression as she spun on her heels calling, "Señor!" The door slammed in Cole's face.

My heart sank. All this way to have a door slammed on us. Cole would never have stood for this treatment back home. The name of Brighton opened doors not closed them. I knew I was right all the time. We weren't welcome in California.

Cole retraced his steps before the massive door opened again. This time a huge man stood silhouetted in the opening. As he lifted the lantern, the light revealed a round face that time had looked upon kindly. His mustache and beard were tipped with white and his thick, black hair was sprinkled with silver.

"Don't go. Please forgive my housekeeper. So excited she was, she forgot to let you in. We've been waitin' for you. Come in, come in." He turned to his housekeeper and said, "Set two more places and then fetch Jose to tend to the animals and have their things taken to their rooms."

Cole took my hand, helped me down from the wagon

and escorted me up the walk. "I'm Cole Brighton and this is my sister, Sarah. Are you William O'Shea?"

"Yes, yes, come into the light where I can rest me old eyes on you. I see your father in you, my lad. Aye, it's like John himself standin' before me. And you, child, I thought I would never be settin' eyes on you again. You have turned into such a pretty lass. You are so like. . . ."

"Do not stand out there in the dark. Come inside. Supper is getting cold," the housekeeper interrupted.

"She's right. Have you eaten? Socorro will be disappointed if you don't eat something."

"We haven't had a bite all day. That food smells delicious." I followed Uncle William into the house.

The red brick entrance spilled into two large rooms; a parlor was to the left and the dining room was to the right. Straight ahead the brick exited through double glass doors into a garden courtyard. We entered the dining room.

A massive black walnut table with eight black, ladder-backed chairs dominated the room. Two place settings were already on the table and Socorro was setting two more as we entered.

"We were expecting you weeks ago. I was beginning to fear something might have happened. Let me take a good look at you." Uncle William placed his hands on my shoulders and stood an arm's length away. His blue eyes filled with delight as he looked into my face. "Just look at you. So much like your poor departed mother, may God rest her soul."

I shot a questioning look at Cole and back to Uncle William. "But I don't look anything like Mama," I protested, but my words were lost as Socorro interrupted again.

"We have pollo con arroz."

"That's chicken and rice for you who can't speak Spanish." Uncle William winked at me. "You may not be used to our food. It's more Mexican and Indian than white man's food. These are tortillas. We eat them like bread. And Socorro can't set a table without frijoles, beans. You'll get used to the taste."

I smiled at Socorro as Uncle William pulled out the chair for me. "Everything looks wonderful. It's a treat just to sit at a table and eat off china plates."

"You must be hungry and tired. We'll be eating first and savin' the talkin' for later. Socorro will have the tubs in your rooms filled with hot water. I'm sure you would like a bath before you go to bed."

"Hot food and a bath, too. I thought this was California, not heaven," I teased.

Uncle William had a robust laugh. "'Tis a joy to have young people in the house again."

Cole remained strangely silent as he pondered the situation. Something seemed wrong. Even I could feel the discord beneath Uncle William's friendly greeting.

"That sorry I was to hear of your poor parents untimely passin' and the loss of the plantation. But now you are out here and I have need of a strong young man like yourself in my business. Would you be interested, Cole?"

"How did you know our mother had died and that we lost the plantation?" Cole asked.

"Elizabeth wrote many times in the years after John's death. She wrote of her plan to send Sarah to me. When the letters stopped coming I assumed that she had passed. A few months back I got a letter from my good friend Dr. Bardlow who wrote of the loss of the plantation, he told of how your mother had died, and that you were on your way."

"Your good friend?" I echoed.

"Aye, I have been writing to Robert for years. But enough about that. What do you say, Cole? Would you like to join me in my business?"

"What kind of business do you have?"

"Haulin' freight. I have me four wagons and haul cargo to the ships that anchor off Dana Point. The cargo comes from the mission and the small settlements here about. I want to expand to haul into some of the towns to the north. Things haven't been goin' so well this last year. The Catholic Church recently regained the mission from a family who bought it some years back. President Lincoln returned the mission to the Church and Father Moot is tryin' his best to restore the mission to its original productivity. But the day of the mission is gone, I fear. Now I need to look to the future, or get left behind. Some of the towns to the north are thriving, Anaheim, for instance, with its grapes and wine. There's a great profit to be made hauling to the ships at Emigrant Landing. But if I want to be a part of it, I need someone I can trust at the other end. I've been dreamin' about this ever since your mama wrote and told me you might be bringin' Sarah out."

"Don't know anything about the freighting business," Cole said slowly, as if he were turning every word over in his mind.

"I'll teach you. What I don't know, it isn't necessary to have in one's mind." Uncle William's voice rose with enthusiasm.

"I'll need to think on it before I make a decision."

"Of course, take all the time you want. After drivin' cross country, the idea of climbin' back on a wagon might not sit well with you."

Throughout the meal, Uncle William kept looking at me and smiling. He said many times how glad he was that we were there. The other guest, Peter, never arrived. Uncle William didn't seem to mind. "He comes and goes as he pleases," he said.

As the clock struck nine, I smothered a yawn with my hand. "Please forgive me, but I was wondering if I might go to my room? The day has been longer than most."

"Certainly. Socorro will show you the way. Do have a good night's sleep and don't rise too early in the morning. Tomorrow will be a day of rest for the both of you."

"Before I turn in, I would like to make sure the horses are settled for the night," Cole said, standing to stretch his legs.

"I would like to take a closer look at those fine animals, myself. I remember your father's stables. Such wonderful horses. What a shame it's all gone. Come, we'll walk together."

They left through the front door, while Socorro took me through the glass doors into the courtyard. A covered walkway joined each room as the doors opened onto the rectangular, enclosed garden. Roses still bloomed, and wisteria lent its fragrance to the night air.

Socorro opened the fifth door. "This is your room, señorita. I have laid out a dress for you to wear tomorrow. I see you do not have many clothes."

"I dressed like a boy coming across country."

Her pleasant face twisted in disapproval. "Now you will wear the dress I give you."

"Thank you."

"You have hot water, soap, towels, and a clean nightgown. I will see you in the morning." She lit the lamp on the table next to the bed. She then turned and walked back down the corridor toward the kitchen. Her black hair tied in a knot atop her head made her look taller than she really was.

The small room was dominated by a large bed made of smooth oak logs and lashed together with rawhide straps. A thick feather mattress lay atop a tanned skin stretched out and tied to the bed frame. The fragrance of sea air clung to the bedding. On an oval rag rug in the corner of the room sat a large copper tub steaming with hot water. An adobe fireplace was set into the corner of the room behind the tub. My eyes didn't look any farther. I undressed and slipped into the wonderful liquid. The elixir sent its soothing spell deep into every muscle of my body as swirls of steam drifted to the ceiling. I could have stayed there forever, but reluctantly, I washed and got out.

The nightgown was a bit large, falling off one shoulder or the other and revealing most of my breast. It was hardly worth wearing. However, for the first time in months, I didn't have to worry about anyone discovering that I was a woman. I breathed a sigh of relief as I climbed into bed and blew out the lamp. Briefly, I thought of the last few months as I snuggled into the soft bed that didn't move with each gust of wind. I was asleep before I finished my prayers.

Darkness still enveloped the room when a loud knock came at the door. "Sarah, wake up. It's Cole. May I come in?"

At first I didn't know where I was. But I responded to Cole's voice, "Yes. Come in." I sat up.

Holding a lit candle in his hand, he opened the door. "Firestorm had her foal. I thought you might want to come and see it." He walked to the table to light my lamp. When he turned around his eyes fell on my bare shoulder and beyond. A surprised expression swept across his face.

I grabbed the bed covers and quickly pulled them to my chin.

"Don't get embarrassed. It isn't as if it's the first time."

"You don't have to remind me about the night you came home from the war. You said you would forget about that."

"No. I said I would not tease you about seeing you naked."

"I was not naked!"

"Close enough. Now, get dressed. I'll wait outside." Cole left the room.

He always has the upper hand, I thought as I slipped on my blue dress. *But one of these days I will turn the tables on him. I will be the one who embarrasses him. One of these days. . . .*

Uncle William and two other men were in the barn when we arrived. Firestorm nervously paced back and forth in her stall. Hiding behind the mare was a gray foal with the lines of an Arabian. No appaloosa spots.

"Thank God! Shadow Run is the sire," I exclaimed with joy.

"We have our first colt." Cole's voice was laced with pride. "This is the beginning of our new stables." He hugged me and lifted me off the ground swinging me around and laughing. "We will name him Dream Chaser. He is the beginning of all our dreams come true."

"That sounds good to me. Dream Chaser it is," I confirmed, hugging Cole. Forgetting myself in the joy of the moment, I kissed him. It was just a little kiss, but it stopped Cole instantly. He gently put me down and returned to the stall to watch the horses. He did not look my way again.

The weeks flew by in a flurry of shopping and meeting Uncle William's friends. Everyone spoke highly of him. Uncle William proved to be a dear man. He laughed easily and he enjoyed having us with him, although, at times he seemed to be a bit confused about Mama. He would remark on how much I looked like her, or that she would be happy we were together again. These statements puzzled me. Cole reserved his approval. There was something that lay deep below the surface. Cole could not quite put his finger on it, nor could he forget the nagging feeling this uneasiness presented.

Almost every afternoon I wore my boy clothes and rode Misty along the ocean or over the golden hills. One Friday Uncle William rode with me.

"Out there is where the ships anchor in the spring." Uncle William swept his hand toward the ocean. "All the hides that the Indians and Mexicans tanned during the winter are thrown off those cliffs and they fly like kites onto the beach. The crew from the ships come ashore and pick up the hides. Of course, the captain comes ashore to pay the priest for the hides, and pick up the olive oil, and anything else that the mission produces. In the spring these hills are yellow with wild mustard. A long time ago, the mustard was brought from Spain and planted on the coast near the missions. That way the captain of the ships could see the yellow when still out at sea. But with the wind and the birds scattering the seeds up and down the coast, now one can't tell where the missions are anymore." We dismounted and walked the horses along the sand at the water's edge. Sandpipers ran in and out of each wave.

"Cole tells me that he can't stay. He has to be moving on," Uncle William said after a long while.

"It is not because of you. I think he would like to help run your business. But he cannot."

"I don't understand. Why not?"

I blushed. "It is a long story and I do not believe you would approve. Perhaps you should ask Cole."

"Strangely enough, Cole said that I should ask you. It sounds like the two of you are harboring some dark secret."

"No. It is nothing as mysterious as all that. We are just having a difficult time forgetting the past and starting fresh. Cole thought he would like to have a ranch out here. But now he wants to continue his adventure with the wagon train. He wants to return to Independence in the spring and take another train west." My voice broke with a sob as I took a deep breath to fight back the tears.

"There, there, child. Don't be crying." Uncle William enfolded me in his arms. "You will always have a home with me."

"Thank you. I thought Cole would take your offer of running the freight line but it seems he's going to be leaving soon. He's anxious to begin another adventure."

"I know how he feels. When I was his age, nothing could hold me in one place. I was off chasing the wind, so to speak. Trying to catch a dream. Just like Cole named that little colt, Dream Chaser. That was me."

"What made you settle down?"

"What else? A woman, aye, and what a woman. She was the most beautiful dark-eyed, black-haired woman I had ever seen. I loved her so much it broke my heart at the thought of being without her. Giving up my wanderin' ways was easy in comparison."

"What happened to her?"

His voice became soft. "She sleeps on the hill beyond the oak trees. She died in childbirth just like my sister. But this time the child died too. That is one of the reasons I am so glad to have you and Cole here with me. My house has been lonely all these years. I haven't the heart to move away and leave her alone on the hill. All the adventure has gone out of me."

"That's such a sad story. Back home we have a family cemetery where all the Brightons are buried. I loved going up there and placing flowers on the graves."

"Aye, I remember that cemetery well. That's where my sister. . . ."

"Señor William, señorita Sarah, I been told to get you. A visitor comes, señor Coyote from Los Angeles," Jose called from the bluff, waving his arms above his head.

"Coyote! Oh dear, I want to look my very best when I see him again. He knew I was a girl, but he never saw me dressed like one. Well, except once at the brothel."

Uncle William raised an eyebrow. "A brothel?"

"It's not what you think."

"I am sure it is not. I will sneak you in the back way, but you have to promise to tell me the story someday."

"I promise."

We rode up the winding road to the top of the bluffs and across the rolling hills to the hacienda. Dismounting at the rear of the house, Uncle William led the way through an iron gate into a small patio off his room.

"You need to go through here to get into the courtyard." He opened the door to his bedroom.

The chamber was darkened by heavy red velvet drapes over the windows. A canopy bed stood paramount in the large room. Filled bookshelves lined one wall, and a stone fireplace centered another. On the east wall hung a large painting of a beautiful woman wearing a red dress. A mantilla covered her black hair. It was unmistakably Uncle William's wife. Next to that painting was a rendering of a woman with blonde, curly hair, and blue eyes. She wore a blue dress and an ermine cape. She looked like me!

"Why do you have my portrait hanging on your wall? And how did you get it? I have never had a dress or cape like that." I stood in front of the two paintings gazing at them. "That isn't me. Is it?"

"No. It isn't."

"Then who?"

"We haven't the time right now. I will be tellin' you someday. But now, you need to be changin' your clothes to meet this Coyote." He pulled me toward the door.

"Stop! I need to know who she is. These past weeks you seemed somewhat confused as to what Mama really looked like. You say that I look so much like her. I don't look anything like Elizabeth Brighton. Now I see a portrait of me on your wall, but it isn't me. I want to know what's going on."

"You are right. It is true. Everything you have said is true. But when I tell you what you want to hear, I want to be tellin' both you and Cole at the same time. Until then, please trust me. Now your young feller is waiting."

Reluctantly I submitted and left the room. But the subject wasn't closed.

A half an hour later I peered at myself in the mirror and liked what I saw. My hair had grown long enough to style atop my head in soft curls, held in place by two inlaid abalone shell combs. Wispy curls escaped, falling gently along my cheeks, framing my face in a soft golden glow. The white blouse with its square neckline, a small standup collar, and long, puffy sleeves gave an elegance to the vivid Mexican skirt woven in swirls of red, green, yellow, black, and blue. I twirled around the room in my leather strapped sandals feeling the skirt spin in a full circle. I felt beautiful.

As I entered the living room, Cole, Coyote and Uncle William were deep in conversation about the wagon train, but Coyote stopped in mid-sentence when he saw me. His eyes flashed his approval.

"This can't be the kid?" he said, walking forward to take my hand.

I curtsied slightly. "Please, call me Sarah." I took his arm and let him escort me to the settee.

He sat beside me. "Can't believe such a goddess was hidden under those boy's clothes. I can't take my eyes off you. You're a vision, an angel."

"Yes. Yes, and she's still my sister. So if you don't mind, Coyote, remove your hands from her and sit over there." Cole's voice was stern and unyielding.

Uncle William's jolly expression turned to shock before it changed back into a smile. "Would anyone care for another whiskey?" He stood at the sidebar filling his glass.

"Yeah, pour me another," Coyote said, getting up but not taking his eyes off me.

Cole leaned against the mantel of the round, stone fireplace. His expression filled with anger. "I've had enough."

Coyote took the glass and downed the whiskey in one gulp. He turned to face Cole. "Your job is done. She's here, safe at Uncle William's ranch. You can relax your guard."

"Do you think an innocent lamb like Sarah could be safe with someone who answers to the name of Coyote?"

"I believe you have a coyote confused with a wolf," Uncle William corrected.

"Coyote, wolf, what difference does it make? They're all dogs to me."

"I don't believe it. You're jealous. She's your sister," Coyote said.

Cole's eyes turned almost black with anger as his fists

clenched into white knuckles. A fire burned in Cole's eyes, and it kindled to a rage as he tried to focus on my face.

Suddenly, all Cole's poise and restraint erupted in one quick jab to Coyote's jaw that sent him to the floor. Cole stepped over him and stormed out of the room.

I jumped from the settee to kneel next to Coyote. "Are you all right? I don't know what's gotten into him. I have never seen him like this before." With my handkerchief I dabbed the blood on Coyote's lip.

"Like I said, he's jealous." Coyote took my hands in his. "You have such a gentle touch. Am I bleeding bad?"

"No. Just a little bit. I'm sure you'll live."

"He caught me off guard. He could have never knocked me flat if I saw it comin'."

"So you say. Whatever did you mean by jealous? He can't be jealous. I'm his sister."

"No. You're not." Uncle William lifted me from my knees.

CHAPTER 35

I became rooted in stunned silence. The clock ticked countless seconds while an involuntary heat washed over my body. My tongue cleaved to the roof of my mouth and I could only whisper, "What?"

"You heard me. You're not his sister. That painting you saw hanging in my room is a portrait of my sister, your real mother."

"I do not understand. I am Sarah Elizabeth Brighton, the daughter of John and Elizabeth Brighton."

"No. No, you are not. I know 'tis hard to understand. Let me be tryin' to explain. Elizabeth wrote to me and told me that if you come to California, I have her permission to be tellin' you the truth. I wanted to choose a better time than this. And I wanted both you and Cole to hear it together. But the situation is out of my hands now. The time has come for you to be knowin' the truth. Come, sit next to me." We sat on the settee. Coyote sat in the chair next to the fireplace, still holding my handkerchief against his lip and eagerly listening to Uncle William's words.

"It all started a few years before you were born. My sister, Sarah, fell in love with a fine man from a family of means. Charles and Sarah were married and went to live in Boston with his family. One day I received a letter from Sarah telling me that Charles was dead and that his family was trying to have her declared insane so they could have the baby she was carrying. I went to her and stole her away. Charles's family paid a man to follow us and bring her back. For three months we hid out like opossums, moving only at night and leaving a winding trail for the bounty hunters to follow. That dreadful night was the worst rain storm I had ever seen. The horses were spooked by lightning and the carriage overturned. I ran for help to a big house across the field. The man and some of his slaves helped me free Sarah from the wreckage. We carried her upstairs in the house and placed her on a bed. The man's wife was in the throes of birthin' and the doctor was already sent for."

"You are describing the night I was born."

"Aye, that I am. But Elizabeth gave birth to only one child that night, a boy they named Daniel. My sister gave birth to the other child before she died."

"Me?"

"Aye, my dear. That distressed I was over the death of my beloved Sarah. I didn't know what to be doin' with you. I had no means to be taking care of a wee babe. You would have died. So I gave you to John and Elizabeth Brighton to be raised as their own. We buried Sarah in the family cemetery. John said her grave would always be cared for."

"And it was, until we left there. I took flowers to her each spring and summer. But why didn't Mama tell me who I really was?"

"Both John and Elizabeth were afraid you would not love them as much if you found out they were not your real parents. They also feared what others would say. Elizabeth wanted you to marry into the best family the name Brighton could achieve. If people wondered about your, shall we say, bloodlines, your prospects would become less desirable. 'Tis not just horse breeders who like to keep the bloodlines pure."

"You say my father's family is from Boston? Then I am a Yankee?" The words stuck in my throat.

"Aye, but you are a Southerner in your heart. The fact of the matter is that no one knew about the switch and we decided to leave it that way to protect you. The doctor gave his word not to tell and the slaves in attendance were given their freedom for their silence."

"So that's what Mama and Doctor Bardlow were arguing about. Mama was afraid that I would not love her. She asked me not to hate her. Now everything seems so clear."

"All went as planned. Elizabeth wrote letters regularly telling me of your well- being. I watched you grow up through her letters and I loved you like my own. When Cole hired Frank Molack to be the overseer, I thought for sure Elizabeth would tell you. But she didn't."

"What did Mr. Molack have to do with my knowing who I was?"

"He knew. He, or at least his father, was hired by Charles's family to bring you back to Boston. Cole didn't know who Molack was when he brought him to Rosewood. As a matter of fact, Elizabeth didn't remember, either. By the time she realized who he was, he had a foothold already. Both she and John were afraid to let him go. If he didn't know when he came to the plantation, he might figure it out if he were fired without cause. Elizabeth wrote many times how frightened she was of him."

"Now everything makes sense."

"By keeping the secret of your real lineage, I am afraid we have harmed you more than by telling you the truth."

"Harmed me?"

"I have seen the way you look at Cole and the way he gazes at you when he thinks no one is watching him. Your heart is telling you something your head cannot accept."

"That's why he is leaving. Down at the beach this afternoon you asked me why he did not want to stay. Now you know. We are afraid to be together."

"I believe John and Elizabeth saw it coming. They knew the two of you had a special bond with each other. That's why they did not mind that Cole was away from home as much as he was. They had hoped both of you would have found love with someone else. But I can see you never will. Watching the both of you these weeks, 'tis quite evident you need to be together."

"Oh, Uncle William, I'm so confused. In a matter of minutes, my whole life has changed. Everything I thought was sure is not anymore, and the one thing I did not hold out hope for, can now be real. I do not know who I am or where I belong."

"You are Sarah Elizabeth, and you belong with the man you love."

"Oh, thank you." I threw my arms around Uncle William's neck and kissed him. "I will go and tell Cole." Jumping up from the settee, I remembered Coyote sitting in the chair. "Coyote. Please excuse me. I. . . ."

"You have to tell Cole. I know."

"Please, don't be disappointed."

"I am disappointed for me, but happy for you. Run and catch up with Cole. I'll be all right."

I bounded out of the living room, calling, "Cole, Cole. Where are you? I have something to tell you." I ran to his room, but he wasn't there. "Socorro, have you seen Cole?" I asked, seeing her tending to the flowers in the courtyard.

"Si, señorita, he is gone. He rode out on his big gray horse. He said to tell you and señor O'Shea he could not stay here any longer."

"Socorro, have José saddle Misty. I'm going after Cole," I ordered as I ran to my room to put on my boots.

Socorro followed me into the dimly lit chamber. "But, señorita, it is getting late. Soon it will be dark. Let señor O'Shea bring señor Cole back."

"Don't argue with me. Do as I say. And have Uncle William send for the priest. We will need him to perform a wedding ceremony when Cole and I get back. Now hurry!"

Socorro was right. Evening was overtaking the land. By the time Misty and I reached the main road, the mission bells were calling the workers from the fields. An almost full October moon crested Saddleback Mountain. But the sun hadn't quite dipped into the ocean. Santa Ana winds summoned warm night air.

"North, Misty. He must have gone north." I pulled the reins to the left and kicked gently into the mare's ribs, urging her to run.

Misty Morn responded quickly. Soon we were flying down the well-traveled highway, passing ox carts, wagons and people coming in from the day's labor.

"Have you seen a man on a gray horse?" I asked one woman walking with a child, carrying a basket of corn on her head. *"El hombre en el caballo gris?"* I hoped my Spanish was good enough for her to understand.

"Sí, vi a un hombre montado en un caballo gris. Fue por allá." She pointed up the road.

"Gracias," I called, prompting Misty onward.

Sunset painted the sky crimson with wisps of gold and orange. Purple and indigo accompanied twilight in the east.

Fewer and fewer people were on the road as each person returned to the safety of his own home and the evening meal. I pictured families gathered around the table, eating and laughing, talking over the events of the day.

I remembered our family on the plantation, the slaves serving from the side-board. Daddy sitting at the head of the table carving the meat. Mama or Mr. Jolette making sure proper manners were being used. Most of the time, across the table from me sat an empty chair. Cole's place. He seemed always to have been gone to one location or another. Now I know why. He could not be near me and stay a gentleman.

I thought of Danny and me nudging each other under the table when something we didn't like was being served. Danny. Thinking of him brought tears to my eyes. *All these years and I still miss him.* Now to find out that he wasn't really my twin is to lose him all over again. I wanted to stop and cry, take time to mourn, cry for all the things lost, all the heartache of the past years. But there was no time. Cole would be gone forever if I could not find him tonight.

The road forked. One way went inland, fast and straight. The other way went down by the ocean through little fishing villages.

"Which direction would Cole take, Misty? We cannot afford to make a mistake." I dried my tears with the hem of my skirt and took a moment to think clearly. "If I were Cole, would I want to get away fast? Maybe go visit Rudy and Gretchen before I left the area? Or would I want to see the picturesque fishing villages? Perhaps think about sailing to faraway places across the sea?"

Misty pawed the ground and pulled to the left.

"Yes, girl, I do believe you are right. He would go by way of the ocean. I know you are tired, but you have to do this for me. I would not ask you to keep going if it was not so important. My life depends on your speed. Come on, girl. Let's catch up with Cole and Shadow Run." I patted Misty's neck and she responded with a canter.

The road became empty. Only the sounds of Misty's hoof beats on the road, the waves breaking in the surf, and an occasional night bird screeching over its kill broke the stillness of the balmy night. To the left, the ocean sparkled in the moonlight. To the right, coastal sage, thistles, wild mustard, and weeds grew along the rolling hills. Here and there clusters of California oak trees shadowed the narrow roadway. We topped a rise.

"Look, Misty. Down there. A rider. Is it Cole?" My heart pounded. "Yes, yes. It is him! Go, Misty. Go!"

The wind brushed against my cheeks and twisted my curls. Misty broke into a lather giving me the speed I demanded from her.

"Cole! Cole!" My words were lost in the sounds of the surf.

"Please, God, make him stop. Make him turn around. Come on Misty, just a little more."

An owl swooped down on an unsuspecting prey. Its white underbelly shone like a ghost in the night sky. My mind flew back to the night Mama killed Mr. Molack and the owl had flown over our heads. The slaves said it was an evil omen. It seemed as if evil had been following me ever since. But tonight I was going to break the poisonous spell forever.

I called once more, "Cole! Stop!"

This time he heard me. He pulled Shadow to a halt and looked over his shoulder.

I waved my arm above my head.

He turned his horse and started back toward me.

I slowed Misty. She was spent. "Thank God, you heard me," I called, when Cole drew near.

"Heard you? I didn't. I had a feeling I was being followed. I turned to look and saw you waving. I didn't know it was you until I got closer. What are you doing out here by yourself? Don't you know it is dangerous traveling these roads alone at night?"

"I had to find you. Come back to the hacienda."

"No. I can't go back. You have known all along I would leave. It is hard enough. Why did you have to make it more difficult by coming after me?"

"I cannot let you go. I want to be with you." I saw the astonished look on his face and I almost started to laugh. I decided this was my turn to pay Cole back for all the times he had embarrassed me. I dismounted and walked to some large rocks by the water's edge. I planned to make him uncomfortable before telling him the truth.

He dismounted and followed. Shadow and Misty wandered to the side of the road to munch on autumn grass growing under an oak tree.

"You can't stay with me," Cole chided. "You have to go back. I brought you to Uncle William. My part of the promise is fulfilled."

"But I do not want to live with Uncle William. I want to live with you. Look at me. I am not a little girl anymore." I started unbuttoning my blouse.

"What the hell do you think you are doing?" He stepped closer and buttoned the buttons I was undoing.

"I want to show you that I am not a boy."

"You think I do not know that? Why do you think I had you dress like a boy on the trip?"

"To keep me safe from unscrupulous men."

"No! To keep you safe from me. I could have taken care of everyone else. It's me, my desire for you that I can't control. Gretchen saw it. She was afraid enough that I would step over the bounds of decency. It was a constant struggle. But, as you have taken pleasure in pointing out many times, I am an honorable man. I would never do anything to disgrace you or myself in such a way."

"But you knew I was a woman."

"Yes. But I did not have to be reminded of it every day. You did not smell of sweet honeysuckle and your voice did not hold the soft ring of laughter. I was hoping the old adage 'out of sight, out of mind' would work."

"Did it?"

"No. That is why I had to stay away from you. Put distance between us. I am doing that again. I cannot be around you. One of these days you will catch me at a weak moment and we will both regret it."

Once again, I started unbuttoning my blouse. This time Cole did not stop me. "Let this be your weak moment. I want to be yours." I laced my arms around his neck and drew Cole's body to mine. "I am not a boy. I am a woman with desires too long forbidden."

Cole stammered for words. "Sarah, you . . . you do not know what you are doing." He loosened my arms and stepped away. His eyes surveyed my unbuttoned blouse before he chided himself and turned to look into the surging surf.

"It is not as if it is the first time you have seen me in my undergarments or much less, I might add. You were not embarrassed that night when Dream Chaser was born and you came into my bedroom or the night when you came home from the war and caught me running from the bathhouse to the kitchen in my thin nightgown. You took pleasure in reminding me about it over and over again."

"That was different. Those times happened by accident. Tonight you are playing the harlot. What has gotten into you?"

I reached forward and started unbuttoning his shirt. "I want you to remember the night of the worst summer storm you had ever seen. Mama was about to give birth and a slave was sent to fetch Dr. Bardlow. There was a knock at the front door."

Cole's forehead knotted in a frown as he held my hands in place, preventing me from undoing more buttons. "What has that to do with the way you are acting?"

"Think of the man at the door. Can you see his face? Who was that?"

Cole's eyes brightened with surprise when he realized who he was. "Uncle William! Yes, that is where I have seen him before. He was the man in black."

"And the woman was his sister. Take a good look at me. Do I resemble anyone in the Brighton line or the Kensington family? No. As I was saying, I am not a little girl anymore, and I am not a boy, and guess what? I am not your sister."

"What?"

"That is right. The woman in the carriage, Uncle

William's sister, she was my mother. Her name was Sarah too. That is why I am named Sarah, after her. That was her grave in the family cemetery. And I guess she really was family. Uncle William could not care for me, so he gave me to the Brightons to raise as their own. They never told anyone because the family of my real father wanted to find me. You inadvertently hired Frank Molack to be our overseer, but he was already hired by my father's family. Molack said some strange things that I never understood at the time. But now it all makes sense. Anyway, everything boils down to the fact that we are not brother and sister. We are not related in any way."

Cole took a minute to let my words soak in. "Not related?"

"No."

"I have been struggling against my feelings for you, but it isn't wrong?"

"Yes."

"I don't have to go away?"

"No."

"We are free to . . . ?"

"Love."

A smile spread across Cole's face and sparkled in his gray eyes. "Are you sure?" He pulled me into his arms.

"That is what Uncle William told me, and he should know."

"I have waited a lifetime to do this." He gently lifted my chin and softly kissed me. Not the kiss of a brother kissing his sister but that of a man kissing the woman he loved.

I knew at that moment, God really does answer whispers in the storm.

The End
Romans 8:28

ABOUT THE AUTHOR

Ruth Frey was born in Southern California. She graduated from Anaheim High School. She has an AA degree from Rancho Santiago Community College and a BFA degree from California State University at Fullerton. She was a wife for forty-five years. She is a, mother and grandmother. She has had many careers, a jeweler, a photographer, a social worker, and now she is trying her hand at being an author.

14572333R00268

Made in the USA
San Bernardino, CA
30 August 2014